Eduardo laughed

His laugh wasn't loud or overbearing but a genuine expression of amusement. His eyes, so rich with warmth, smiled, too. For a moment, she lost herself gazing into them, even after his laughter subsided. She cleared her throat and stepped toward the table, where she pretended to busy herself with collecting the folders and handouts. "So, did you have a question?" She kept her gaze on the papers in front of her.

"Question?"

She stole a glance at him and nearly gasped. With his eyebrows pressed together and his glasses dipping to the edge of his nose, she knew where she had seen his face before. Michelangelo's *David*. His eyes, his nose, and his mouth were all strikingly similar to the image she'd studied in college. And she'd studied the *David* closely: the toned biceps, the chiseled abdomen, and the intricately carved genitals…

A deep blush rushed her face, and she shifted her gaze to the desk. Why was she so embarrassed? She wasn't undressing him with her eyes. Even if she *had* paid attention to the wide shoulders and narrow hips that now caught her eye, she needn't be ashamed.

How long had passed since she had felt the warmth of desire for a man? Sarah swallowed hard and fanned her face. Apparently, long enough that even an innocent attraction burned her cheeks bright.

He relaxed his brows. "Are you all right?"

Sarah froze her fanning hand in mid-flap. "Oh… yes. I'm still getting used to the temperature here."

Praise for Wendi Dass

"Ms. Dass has written a fast-moving romance filled with colorful characters that keep readers engrossed from the first page. As the main character explores her new surroundings, she takes the reader along on all her adventures. Every scene is written in intricate detail. Through Sarah's eyes, I visited the Coliseum, the Pantheon, and so many other places. I could taste the mouth-watering gelato and Choctella she so loved. *BELLA CIGNA* is a satisfying novel with a happy ending. The only problem the reader will face is a deep desire to escape their world and purchase a one-way ticket to Italy."

~Mona Sedrak, author of Gravity *and* Six Months

~*~

"A beautiful story…this is definitely not a cheesy romance novel but a story around subjects many women will have experienced and can relate to."

~L. Jones

~*~

"Romance touched with a little bit of comedy, *BELLA CIGNA* captures the reader right from the get-go. A story of losing and finding yourself again, *BELLA CIGNA* is highly recommended to lovers of art and contemporary fiction."

~R. Salazar

Bella Cigna

by

Wendi Dass

Foreign Endearments, Book 1

Bella Cigna

Cover Art by *Jennifer Greeff*

The Wild Rose Press, Inc.
PO Box 708
Adams Basin, NY 14410-0708
Visit us at www.thewildrosepress.com

Publishing History
First Sweetheart Rose Edition, 2020
Trade Paperback ISBN 978-1-5092-3259-8
Digital ISBN 978-1-5092-3260-4

Foreign Endearments, Book 1
Published in the United States of America

Dedication

For Louisa

Chapter 1

A time comes when every woman must learn what to do with life's lemons. Some make lemonade. Some clean their garbage disposals. And some make a proper cup of tea.

Sarah Flynn always chose tea.

She dumped the water from her *Keep Calm and Carry On* mug into the electric kettle on her desk. The mug, the kettle, and the Vermeer print pinned to the privacy panel behind her dual monitors were the only personal effects that distinguished her gray cubicle from all the others in the D.C. federal office building. As the water heated, she reached into her lunchbox for the quartered lemon she'd packed that morning. She held a wedge in her fingers, preparing to squeeze it into her mug.

An obnoxious ding interrupted her classical music, and an instant message popped up on her screen.

—*Did you clock out for your break?*—

She jerked and squirted the lemon into her face. "Damn it," she muttered as she blinked the sting from her eyes. She typed a return message to her supervisor.

—*Yes, sir*—

She imagined her boss, Mr. Rosen, punching at his keyboard with two index fingers in his managerial office—a work area about four times the size of her box, with glass walls and a window. The glass walls were a luxury, except when someone caught him with his finger shoved up his nose—as Sarah had often done.

She squeezed the rest of the juice from the wedge into her mug. As the scent of citrus permeated her cubicle, she scrunched her nose. Why had life delivered her such a strong lemon as Mr. Rosen? Leaving her job at Central Elementary was bad enough—a job she'd loved, with children so charming she almost didn't mind their hovering parents. The job at Central had been with colleagues who'd supported her efforts to bring the arts into her third-grade classroom.

The kettle whistled, and Sarah blinked away tears. So much for that dream.

"Mrs. Flynn."

Mr. Rosen's voice jostled her from her thoughts. She jumped, her left knee banging against the desk. "Yes, Mr. Rosen?" She rubbed her knee. Why didn't companies make furniture to accommodate tall people?

He plopped down a stack of papers. "Here's another listing. I need it ASAP."

The stack looked thicker than a Tolstoy novel. He enunciated each letter as if he were delivering orders to an international organization designed to combat terror—though he was more than likely only delivering misclassified purchases for ballpoint pens and toilet paper. She checked the clock on her monitor: three-thirty. Even with the caffeine of three pots of tea, she couldn't get the listing done by five. "Sir, remember I told you I'm not working overtime anymore."

"You are today." He walked away.

The stench of his Chinese takeout breath lingered in the air, and Sarah scrunched her nose, but she couldn't summon the energy to protest. Her legs were too heavy to chase him through the maze-like arrangement of fifth-floor cubicles to remind him she didn't need the extra money. Hell, the way things had turned out, she hadn't needed to leave her beloved teaching job at Central to become a peon in the federal bureaucracy of government spending. The pay increase meant nothing now.

She poured water over a bag of English Breakfast tea, and the steam burned her cheeks. Without waiting for it to steep, she lifted the mug to her lips, but the aroma did nothing for her mood. If she had to spend one extra second in the office today, she might start pelting Mr. Rosen with the rest of her lemons.

This day couldn't get any worse. My life couldn't either.

The phone rang, and Sarah spilled hot tea down the front of her shirt. "Ow!" She pulled the blouse from her skin, slammed the mug on her desk, and picked up the receiver. "Mr. Rosen," she began, in as firm a voice as she could muster, "I can't possibly get this listing done today." A few beats of silence ensued.

"I'm sorry, I was trying to reach Mrs. Flynn." A woman's voice came through.

"Oh." Sarah tucked her long bangs, in need of trim, behind her ears. She softened her voice. "This is Mrs. Flynn."

"Very good. I'm calling from the Georgetown Fertility Clinic."

Sarah's breath caught in her throat. The Georgetown Fertility Clinic. She'd been on the waiting list so long she thought she'd be in menopause before they called. What woman struggling to conceive could pass up their guarantee? *Pregnancy in six months or your money back*, their brochure read.

"We've had a cancellation tomorrow, and you're next on the waiting list. Could you by chance make a ten-thirty?"

"Of course." The words came out of her mouth faster than Mr. Rosen could shout directives.

"Wonderful. We'll discuss payment options with you beforehand."

With a quivering hand, Sarah replaced the receiver. Suddenly, the stack of papers on her desk held renewed purpose. Perhaps Mr. Rosen's offer of overtime wasn't untimely after all.

She pulled her jar of sugar cubes from her bottom desk drawer and dropped three cubes into her cup. So what if she splurged? She was sure to gain a pound just by looking at the jar, anyway. With a smile, she brought the mug to her lips and took a large gulp instead of her usual dainty sips. The sweet, warm liquid washed over her like a bright afternoon sun, soothing the bitterness she'd built up over two fruitless years of pregnancy attempts, of hypodermic needles filled with hormones, and of the uncomfortable prodding of obstetricians with metal instruments and ultrasound wands.

The office bustle faded into a fog. Sarah lowered her cup and stood. In a daze, she floated through the office until she found herself in Mr. Rosen's office. The room was empty. She went to the window, overlooking the blossoming spring of downtown D.C. The white and pink buds of the cherry blossoms lined the street like giant, hovering snowflakes. Inhaling deeply, Sarah imagined the faint, sweet aroma of the ornamental trees instead of the stale odor of Mr. Rosen's sesame chicken. Had winter come and gone so soon? Had three

4

months of Philip's mandated break from fertility treatments been long enough?

Three months would have to be long enough. This time would be different.

"Mrs. Flynn?"

Sarah spun. Mr. Rosen had half a donut in one hand and a disposable cup in the other. She leaned back, the coolness of the glass pressing through her shirt.

"Is everything all right?"

"All right?"

He nodded. "Donuts in the break room." He shoved the piece in his mouth.

Mr. Rosen was taking her office intrusion quite well. Philip was always more agreeable after eating. Sarah took a step forward. "I can't stay late tonight. I've got to get home to my husband."

He licked his fingers. His brows met.

"But I promise I'll work overtime for the next two—no, nine—months. Promise." She started for the door. If she hurried, she'd have just enough time to hit Philip's favorite take-out restaurant.

Tonight will be perfect. It has to be.

****

When Sarah arrived home, the evening chill rushed into the entry. Philip wouldn't be home for another hour, which gave her plenty of time to dress the table with their finest china and put a bottle of wine on ice. She transferred the lobster mac and cheese to her ceramic bakeware and threw the Key lime cheesecake into the fridge.

As she folded her best linen napkins, she heard a loose floorboard from above squeak. Was Philip home before her? Maybe he had an event tonight and came home to change? She checked the calendar hanging by the back door, but April twelfth was blank. Her stomach dropped. If he had some swanky dinner with a senator whose vote he needed, why hadn't he penciled in the event?

The thud of a dresser drawer echoed down the stairs, and she rounded her shoulders. She threw the napkins over the back of a chair and marched to the staircase. "Phil?" She climbed the stairs to the master bedroom and found her lanky, blond husband bent over the bed. "Phil?"

He jumped and turned to face her. "Jesus Christ, Sarah. You scared the crap out of me." A suitcase lay open on the bed behind him, and he held a pile of clothes in his arms. "I didn't expect you home so soon."

Packing? How had he not written *a trip* on the calendar? She frowned. "I stopped working overtime two months ago." He wore his work clothes—a pair of khaki pants with a light blue, button-up shirt and a tie loosened at the neck. Business trip, for sure. Would they still have time for dinner? "I didn't realize you were traveling this week. You didn't write it on the calendar."

"Sarah," he started then stopped and took a deep breath.

"When's your flight?"

"Flight?" He exhaled then shook his head. "Sarah, I'm not traveling. I'm…"

His voice trailed off, and for a split second a hint of sorrow grazed his eyes. Then he replaced it with the calm gaze he used whenever he wanted something. Sarah straightened her spine. What did he want now?

6

Couldn't they have a quiet evening at home together for once?

"I'm leaving, Sarah. I'm leaving you."

His words tumbled off her. She must have misheard. "What?"

"I said I'm moving out." He resumed shoving things into his bag.

Sarah shook her head, and her hands trembled. "But…" The words died in her parched mouth. The room swayed left and right, left and right. She reached for the arm of the chair. Dropping into the seat, she buried her head between her knees.

The geometric pattern on the carpet swirled. The air around her thickened, and the rip of zippers, rustle of clothes, and shuffle of Philip's shoes echoed around her. He was really leaving…but why? Sarah raised her head.

Philip added more items to the bag.

His favorite ball cap. A bottle of cologne. The black silk boxers she'd given him for Valentine's Day. Wait—the ones she'd bought didn't have little white hearts. An iron vise wrapped around her chest, squeezing the air from her lungs. "Is there someone else?" Sarah could barely force out the words with the burning sensation in her throat.

Nodding, he zipped the suitcase and put it on the floor.

His affirmation hit her like a slap on the cheek. She searched her mind for an expletive, but her lips refused to move. They were numb, just like her hands and feet.

Philip exhaled. "I'm sorry, Sarah, but we both know this relationship isn't working anymore."

He spoke in a singsong voice that was sure to win

him an election one day. Tears burned her eyes as she translated that vague statement in her mind. *She* wasn't working anymore. She wasn't on his arm at political functions, looking graceful hanging on his every word. She wasn't preparing gourmet appetizers to entertain the conservative Midwest senator whose name she couldn't recall. And above all, she wasn't giving him children.

Casting her glance upward, she watched him through the distorted view of tear-sodden eyes.

He pulled up the retractable handle on his suitcase and stepped toward the door. He stopped in front of her and patted her cheek with his hand. "I knew you'd understand."

He spoke to her as if she were a child. Then he was gone. Sarah listened to the tread of his feet on the stairs and the front door opening and closing. Her head still spinning, she rushed to the window overlooking the front door and yanked it open. "Jerk!" The word, almost unrecognizable, tore from her throat.

Philip jumped and turned back.

With his head cocked to the side, and fern-green eyes flickering, Sarah wasn't sure if he was surprised or amused. Either way, neither response was an apology. She narrowed her eyes and reached for something— anything—breakable atop the dresser. She grasped a cool, hard object and hurled it out the window. The glass box, a trinket Philip had given her when they were dating, shattered at his feet.

Philip looked from the shards to her. His lips formed a hard, straight line, and he shook his head.

Sarah slammed the window so hard the remaining objects on the dresser rattled. A floor lamp teetered and fell to the side. She tightened her grip on the window frame, partly to release the tension that had built in her arms, and partly to keep herself from collapsing.

Philip tossed the suitcase into the backseat. Two boxes sat beside it, and a pile of clothes rested in the passenger seat.

A knot formed in her stomach. Sarah released her hold on the window frame and stumbled back. *This ordeal can't be happening.*

The car engine growled. Tires squealed.

Tears streamed down Sarah's cheeks as she staggered out of the bedroom and climbed the stairs to the third floor. By the time she reached the olive-green nursery, she could barely breathe with the heaving in her chest and the uncontrolled sobs. *This nightmare isn't happening.*

She scanned the nursery. Outlines of animals were sketched on the walls. An old desk sat where the crib would have gone. All were reminders that she was losing more than a husband. She was being stripped of a chance at a family. Dropping to her knees, she buried her face in her hands and rocked back and forth. Rocking, like the child she was meant to rock.

A soft hum interrupted her grieving, and she jerked her phone from her pocket, not bothering to check the caller ID. Maybe Philip leaving was a mistake? Maybe he had changed his mind? "Hello." Her voice gargled with phlegm.

"Sarah Miller," a digitalized voice replied. "I'm calling to confirm your appointment with Dr. Willis."

Sarah swallowed, her pulse reverberating in her ears.

"Please press one to confirm or two to cancel."

Sarah held out the phone, her fingers floundering on the touch screen as she pressed the number two. She didn't need the appointment now; she probably never would.

Chapter 2

Sarah opened her eyes, and darkness had settled around her, the only light from dim figures dancing on the wall. She uncurled, her body stiff from the twin bed that was too small for her frame. Her head throbbed. With a hand to her head, she tossed back the thick blanket and swung her legs to the floor. The scruffy carpet tickled her toes.

Carpet? Her bedroom didn't have carpet. Sarah peered through the dimness at the figures on the walls. Ballerinas spun across the wall. She turned her head to encompass the entire space. This space *was* her bedroom. Not her sprawling master suite, but her *childhood* bedroom. The light shone from her ballerina nightlight.

She stood, her hands finding the lamp on the nightstand. As her eyes adjusted to the light, she flitted her gaze around the room. Teddy bears sat on dusty shelves. Awards decorated the walls. Fifteen years had passed, and Mom hadn't changed a thing. Sarah dropped her gaze. A stain still remained on her shirt from the spilled tea.

Shaking her head, she fumbled with the buttons as she hastily removed her shirt and threw it into the corner. The coolness of the room fell on her bare arms, and she shivered.

She shifted her gaze from the crumpled shirt to a

picture hung above it on the wall—an acrylic self-portrait she painted in high school. Pulling a blanket over her shoulders, she strode closer. The dirty-blonde hair of her teenage counterpart skimmed her shoulders, just as her own hair did now. The girl's blue eyes smiled. Her thin lips curled upward.

Sarah stepped back. Could she ever smile like that again?

She pushed away the question and extended a hand to trace the bumpy outline of her nose. How noses had given her such trouble on canvas. She traced the lips then the eyes. The portrait displayed novice techniques she'd since mastered: the shadows under cheekbones, the unsymmetrical nostrils under the bridge, and the fuzzy outline of lips.

When was the last time she had picked up a brush? *The nursery. Acrylics.* She withdrew her hand.

"Sarah?" Mom called.

The door creaked open, and Sarah bit her lip to keep it from quivering.

"I thought I heard you." Mom entered the room.

A tightness grabbed. Sooner or later, she'd have to tell her mom about Philip leaving. She turned to her mom and caught her embrace. As Mom's petite frame pressed against Sarah's tank top, the disparity in their heights reminded Sarah just how different the two women were—in many more ways than just appearance. She clung to Mom in a tight embrace, the medicinal scent of Mom's anti-dandruff shampoo filling her nose. "How long have I been here?" Sarah pulled away from the embrace.

"Three days."

"Three days?" Sarah stiffened and dropped the

blanket from her shoulders. "Three days." Her voice came out shrilly. "What about Philip? What about work? What about the lobster mac and cheese?"

At the last question, Sarah's mother pursed her lips.

Okay, no one else cared about the lobster mac and cheese.

"Philip hasn't called." Mom picked up the blanket and returned it to Sarah's shoulders. "Only Meredith."

A blurred memory filled Sarah's mind. Meredith. She'd called her friend after Philip left. Sarah cried into her shoulder. Meredith told her everything would be okay.

Bastard, Meredith said. *What a bastard.*

"I told your boss you'd be out a few days." Mom furrowed her brows. "That you're sick."

Sarah flopped onto the bed. Thank God. At least Mom hadn't told Mr. Rosen the truth—that her husband had left her for another woman. Heaviness weighed down her shoulders. Definitely a bastard.

Her mom sat beside her and rested a palm on Sarah's knee. "This breakup isn't your fault."

Fault. Philip used that word—three months ago, sitting in their bedroom. Sarah could still see the goose-down comforter on the edge of the bed and could feel the bright winter sun streaming through her bedroom window. "Nothing implanted," she'd said in a flat tone.

Philip rubbed her knee. "It's not your fault, honey. These things take time."

Sarah swatted the tears from her cheeks but didn't respond. Of course, this failure was her fault. The doctors had been clear enough in their diagnosis. "We have to start again." She found her voice. "Have to harvest more eggs. I'll work overtime to pay for it."

Philip sighed and stood, running his fingers through his hair. "I think we should take a break."

"What do you mean, a break?"

He had walked toward the entry to the hall, the light from the sun casting a long shadow in front of him. "A break from the doctors. A break from trying."

The memory faded. Obviously, his idea of a break had also included a break from monogamy. She smacked her thigh. "Stupid jerk," she muttered.

"Excuse me?" Mom shifted her weight, the bed squeaking.

"Sorry. I mean, I should have seen this betrayal coming."

Mom frowned. "You had a lot on your mind."

Sarah ignored the comment. If she had to deal with any more empathetic comments about her failure to conceive, she might just burn down the house herself. "What am I going to do?"

"You can stay here. Keep me company while you figure out things." Sarah narrowed her eyes. No way in hell she was moving back home.

Mom stood. "Just temporarily. While you get settled."

Sarah softened her gaze. Mom always meant well, but did she have to be so damned mommy-like?

"Eventually, you'll meet someone else. Someone with the same goals as you."

And so damned optimistic? Sarah clenched her fists and dug her nails into her palms. If her father were still here, he'd know what to say. He wouldn't treat her like a twelve-year-old. She bolted to her feet and held Mom's gaze in her glare. "Who would that be, Mom?

What man who wants a family seeks a wife who can't give him children?"

"Oh, Sarah." Mom's finely lined lips fell into a frown.

But the response confirmed the truth. She would not have her dream. Not now. Not ever.

****

The next day, Sarah dragged her feet over the wide-planked floor of the National Gallery of Art. She hadn't bothered to pick up a map in the marbled column rotunda—she knew the way. In a small gallery in the west wing, the caramel wood paneling offered the perfect backdrop to the renowned Dutch collection. Landscapes and still lifes in vivid colors decorated the walls.

Sarah shuffled past them to the one she always visited. Vermeer's *Woman Holding a Balance*. The room was empty, as Sarah often found it, and she assumed her usual position—an arm's length in front of the piece that was no bigger than a standard computer screen. Air conditioning rushed past Sarah's bare ankles. She reached for her jacket to pull it closer around her shoulders but found only her cotton blouse. She snickered. Of course, she wasn't wearing a jacket—no one in D.C. wore a jacket in the thick of summer.

The woman holding a balance always wore a jacket. Her cheeks were always smiling. Her scales were always in balance.

Sarah stared at the painting. Soft light cast a shadow over the blue fur jacket and highlighted the swell in her belly. Tears filled Sarah's eyes, and she turned her back on the painting, finding her familiar cushion in the gray sofa in the center of the room.

She pressed a palm to her stomach. Her womb definitely didn't hold a child. Hell, her stomach had scarcely any pudge left to even hint at the fact. Her weight loss was the upside to having a cheating spouse—best diet ever. And balance? She glanced back at the thick-framed painting and scuffed a penny loafer against the floor. Her scales were as off-kilter as they'd ever been.

Clearly, hanging the print in her cubicle hadn't helped. Having it pinned to her bulletin board at Central Elementary hadn't helped, either. Maybe the print had helped back in college—that was when she'd bought it. At least then she could balance her art with her studies.

"How did I know I'd find you at the Vermeer?" A voice echoed off the high ceilings.

"Meredith." Sarah found her best friend standing above her. Dressed in yoga pants with bleach spatters and a sweatshirt with purple juice stains, Meredith looked like she'd been through a kiddy battlefield.

"Your mom told me you were here."

"Of course, she did," Sarah snapped. She stood to embrace her friend, and warmth seeped into her chest.

"How are you?"

Sarah shrugged and fought back tears.

Meredith motioned for her to sit again then joined her on the couch. "That you are here is funny." She reclined, stretching out her legs and crossing her ankles. "Appropriate given the news I have."

"News?" Sarah sat as straight as she could in the soft cushions. Did Meredith know something about Philip? About Amanda? Her stomach soured at the name of Philip's mistress.

"Well, an idea." Meredith scanned the room. "You know, you've been coming here as long as I've known you."

Recalling their college escapades, Sarah smiled. Dragging Meredith to the gallery had been almost as fun as sneaking into the opera. Well, almost.

"Do you remember when we had that grand idea to backpack through Europe?" Meredith asked.

Sarah laughed. "Yeah, after graduation. But then you abandoned our plans in lieu of marriage"

"Don't remind me." Meredith groaned.

Sarah frowned. "At least yours is still going strong."

Meredith rolled her eyes and pulled a flyer from her purse that read, *International Teaching Posts*.

"They're probably already staffed for next year." Sarah gave a dismissive wave. "It's mid-June."

"Come on. When did you turn down a dare?" She parked a hand on her hip and whisked the paper in Sarah's direction.

Sarah cocked an eyebrow. She could think of a few—skinny dipping in the college fountain and toilet papering their Geology professor's office came to mind.

"Okay, maybe that was me. But it's worth a call, isn't it?"

Taking the paper from Meredith, Sarah held it up. She stared at the words. *International. Teaching.* Escaping D.C.—hell, the country—couldn't be a better idea. And teaching? Sarah couldn't recall a day she didn't miss being in the classroom. She relaxed her hand around the cool sheet, and the paper warmed in her grasp. A tingling rushed her fingers, and a smile crept to her lips. "Yes," Sarah whispered. "I suppose it is." Perhaps a bit of Vermeer's light had pierced the darkness inside her after all.

****

"O-K-L-A-H-O-M-A, Oklahoma!"

Sprawled on her leather couch, Sarah shoveled microwave popcorn into her mouth. How did Meredith stand these cheesy show tunes? Catchy melodies or not, if Sarah had to watch one more overly choreographed dance, she might toss Meredith's prized Rodgers and Hammerstein collection out the window. Besides, the box of old DVDs did nothing for the realtor's recommendation of "staging to sell."

Sarah reached for the remote, but a sound at the front door stopped her. She jumped to her feet, held the remote in dagger position, and tiptoed to the foyer. Before she reached the door, it flew open.

Philip stepped into the foyer.

Sarah froze, and her heart pounded. When was the last time she'd seen him? Hell, spoken to him? Was the conversation about the listing price of the house or about who would keep the vacuum? Of course, he hadn't come for casual conversation, or, God forbid, to reconcile.

"Sarah, I didn't think you were home. The house is dark." He narrowed his eyes on her raised hand.

She gave a strained smile and lowered the remote. "I was watching a movie."

Tilting his head to the side, he smiled.

Her heart rate quickened, and she combed fingers through her hair. The motion dislodged a piece of buttery popcorn, and it fell to the floor.

His smile broadened.

What an impeccable smile. Sarah couldn't help but

return it with one so wide and so tense, her right cheek twitched. Why hadn't he called first—given her time to clean herself up?

Philip bent down and picked up the popcorn. "I was on my way to a ball game." He stood. "Just stopped by for my jerseys. Guess the movers forgot them."

The muscles in Sarah's face relaxed, and she cast her gaze over Philip's shoulder. In the driveway, his car idled. Amanda—the floozy—sat in the passenger seat, applying a coat of mascara. He'd brought *her* along? He should have left her home to glue on her false lashes and touch up her tacky highlights. Sarah swallowed a growl. "Let me get them for you," she said through gritted teeth.

Not waiting for his response, she started up the stairs. If he wasn't here to talk, then she didn't want him careening through the house, scrutinizing her untidiness, and leaving his alluring scent of balsam and cinnamon in the bedroom.

"I heard you're leaving town," he called up the stairs.

Sarah reached the closet. His side was bare, except the collection of sports jerseys hanging in the far corner. "A couple weeks." She didn't elaborate. She shoved the jerseys into a duffel bag, placing the red one on top, and headed toward the stairs.

"Isn't a showing scheduled for tomorrow? You might want to tidy up the place."

Sarah paused, hanging her foot in mid-air above the top step. *Tidy up? You leave me for some bimbo and expect me to slave away every time a showing happens?* She gripped the straps of the bag tighter, crept back to the bedroom, and tiptoed into the master bath. Under the sink, she found a bottle of toilet bowl cleaner with the words "NOW WITH BLEACH" emblazoned on the front.

"The game starts in twenty," he shouted.

If the bottle were Philip's head, Sarah would have bashed it against the mirror. She did the next best thing, opening the duffel bag and squirting the cleaner inside. She smiled—an earnest, ear-to-ear smile. Whoever said revenge was overrated? That person didn't know a thing about cheating husbands. She closed the bag and trotted down the stairs. "Enjoy the game!"

"Thanks." Philip took the bag.

Sarah whirled and headed back to her movie, humming "Oh, What a Beautiful Mornin'" until the gentle thud announced the closing door.

Maybe her future would be beautiful after all— especially if that future included Philip despairing over the ruin of his favorite sports jersey.

Chapter 3

Sunday afternoon tea at Meredith's had been a staple in Sarah's schedule for the better part of a decade. Meredith provided the tea—a strong black blend with a carafe of half-and-half on the side—and Sarah brought a treat for them to enjoy. The treat was often freshly baked, but since her kitchenware was now packed in boxes in Mom's basement, today she'd splurged on confections from a popular Georgetown bakery.

She opened the pink box containing four gourmet cupcakes: one for herself, one for Meredith, and one for each of Meredith's two children. For Amber, her friend's five-year-old daughter, she selected chocolate cake with strawberry icing, and for Steven, her three-year-old younger brother, she'd chosen vanilla on vanilla with rainbow sprinkles. Sarah smiled, cut Steven's into quarters, and placed them into a small plastic bowl. Amber would only lick off the frosting, so she handed the cupcake to her in its paper wrapper.

The children ran off with their sweets to the den, adjacent to the kitchen.

"No crumbs!" Meredith called after them. She topped her tea with cream before taking a seat next to Sarah at the counter. "They'll miss you."

Cupping the warm drink in her hands, Sarah leaned forward on her elbows. She tried to recall when she had gone more than a week without seeing her friend's young children, but she could only think of her extended vacation with Philip, just after Steven was born. The relaxing cruise to the Caribbean was the last trip they'd taken together. They'd walked on the beach hand-in-hand and wasted away mornings snuggling in bed. The two weeks had been a stark contrast to the struggles they'd encountered afterward with the in vitro attempts for a family like Meredith had, and Sarah didn't.

Sarah pushed away the thought and looked across to Steven and Amber. That today would be the last time she would see them made her chest ache. "I'll miss them, too." Her voice cracked, the bittersweet memories cinching her throat.

Meredith nudged Sarah's side. "Don't look so drab. You're off for a year to explore Italy. You're going for adventure…to find yourself."

Her friend's dreamy gaze meant she probably fantasized about some romantic nonsense. Sarah took a sip of her tea. "I *will* be working, you know. My visit's not like I'm on an all-expenses-paid vacation or something."

"Would you stop grumbling? It's going to be great. I'm jealous."

Sarah winced.

Meredith pulled back her hair in a ponytail, exposing gray hairs around her hairline.

Another reminder to Sarah that time was passing her by.

"Aunt Sarah!" Amber called from the den. "Come have a tea party with us!"

She forced a smile, grabbed the cream cheese-frosted carrot cupcake and her cup of tea, and raised an eyebrow toward Meredith. "My playmates await." Sarah headed for the den.

Meredith rolled her eyes. "I swear, sometimes I think these visits are more for the kids than us."

Sarah sat cross-legged at the spot on the carpet where the kids had already set up plastic teacups and saucers. She dined alternately on her dreamed-up scone and the actual calorie-laden miniature delicacy then she passed around a pink pot filled with make-believe sugar. Why couldn't she pause this moment in time—encapsulate the memory of Steven counting the sprinkles on his cupcake and Amber asking if she could trade her cake for his frosting? Talking to them on the phone, video or otherwise, wouldn't be the same as being here with them.

When she'd finished both her real and fictitious tea and cake, Sarah returned to the kitchen, where Meredith was busy chopping vegetables for what appeared to be a stew. Sarah sipped her tea, washing away the buttery frosting and sweet vanilla cake. "Are you sure it's okay to leave now?" she asked. "I mean, with things so up in the air?" She picked up a knife and a bunch of celery.

"Oh, stop worrying. The house is under contract, and the two of you are in agreement. What could go wrong?"

The contract could fall through, or the separation papers could get lost in the mound of documents on her lawyer's desk. Sarah hacked at a stalk of celery. "I don't know. I haven't signed anything yet."

"Would you relax? Everything will be fine." Meredith put onions in a pot and smiled. "Now, let's get on to the more important details. Pictures." She waved her knife at Sarah. "You're to send me pictures of every place you go."

Meredith taunted her with the knife, and Sarah leaned away. "Yes, Mother." She added her diced celery to the pot and returned to enjoying her freshly poured tea.

Meredith slammed the knife on the cutting board. "I assure you I am not keeping you on a short leash. I'm encouraging you to go out and have fun." She lowered her voice and leaned across the counter. "To have more nights like *you know what* with *you know who*."

Uh-uh. She did not just bring up that incident. Sarah put down her cup of tea with a heavy hand, the china clinking on the saucer. "Meredith! I thought we agreed never to bring that up."

"Come on, Sarah." Meredith snorted. "At least fifteen years have passed. Don't you find it the least bit humorous?"

Sarah pursed her lips. How was a one-night-stand with the infamous Ben Carter funny? "No," she grumbled.

"Ugh. Well, I would have taken your place. He was by far the cutest guy on campus. I still daydream about him sometimes."

"Meredith, would you stop?" She caught Amber spying from the den and lowered her voice to a whisper. "I told you a thousand times, I don't remember what happened."

Meredith cocked an eyebrow. "Oh, we all know what happened. He wasn't shy about telling everyone how he laid the beautiful, goody-two-shoes Sarah Miller."

"And that, my friend, is why tea is now my drink

of choice." Sarah sighed, picked up her teacup, and raised it in a toasting jest. She brought the cup to her lips and paused. Would tea still be her drink of choice in Italy? She shrugged. She'd find out in a few days.

****

A week later, the sun streamed through the arched glass entrance of Dulles International Airport. Amber and vermilion hues reflected off the metal *International Departures* sign. Suitcase wheels whirred, and the heels of business-women clacked. A tingling rushed through Sarah's fingers—was the rush excitement or trepidation?

The rolling suitcase in front of her inched forward, and the line of passengers followed like a row of dominoes. But Sarah's sneakers felt more like steel-toed boots. Perhaps the ten-minute cab ride hadn't been long enough to say good-bye.

"Next!"

Sarah lifted her bags onto the conveyer belt and handed the agent her passport. She glanced over her shoulder, catching the last of the sun's rays before the orange disk melted into the horizon. She stared through the wide, sweeping glass wall. The sky of the city—a city that held so many memories she wanted to forget—was a mixture of colors as alive as Vermeer's painting. Her eyes dampened with tears, but Sarah squeezed them away. She faced the counter and looked at the clerk.

"Do you have any questions?" The woman behind the counter handed her a boarding pass.

Questions? Sarah slumped her shoulders, and she struggled to see through the welling tears. She had too many questions. Was she making the right decision leaving D.C.? Would she ever forget Philip? Again, she tipped her head in the direction of the sunset—the brush-stroked sky. And would she ever attain Vermeer's idealized balances?

Sarah turned back to the attendant. "No questions." She forced a smile, kept her back toward the sunset, and strode forward into her future—whatever that might be.

Chapter 4

Half a day later, Sarah disembarked in Rome, her legs stiff. The gangway from the plane was no different than any Sarah had experienced—creaky floorboards and scuffed walls. The bathroom, where Sarah took note of her grimy clothes and filmy teeth, was alike those in the States, too. But the allure of a new city and a fresh beginning beckoned.

After a quick swish of mouthwash and a wipe-down with wet paper towels in the ladies' room, she tucked her purse under her elbow and made a beeline for immigration.

From behind a glass enclosure, a handsome young immigration officer spoke in a thick Italian accent, calling her forward.

As he flipped through her documents, Sarah scanned the room. The soaring ceilings, constructed of exposed metal, swallowed the sounds of the travelers corralled by ropes. The floors, ceilings, and walls were all white. The only bursts of color beamed from the hanging directional signs in shades of green and red—the colors of the Italian flag.

Even the people were different. The young immigration officer, the policeman at border control, and the attendant directing passengers were all tanned with dark hair. Their features were so dissimilar from Sarah's pale skin and fair hair, and they all gestured flamboyantly as they spoke in Italian.

Wondering if she should pinch herself, Sarah smiled. She was in Rome, Italy!

"Long stay." He looked up.

The immigration officer gave a gentle flip of his 'l.' Grinning, she nodded. Yes, her year-long trip was longer than a week-long stay of tourists passing through the city. Her trip was long enough to see all the city's architectural feats, explore all the art museums, and— she eyed the man in front of her—enjoy the handsome Italian men who looked nothing like Philip.

"I'll need documentation." He furrowed his thick brows.

Sarah stared at the hard line of his brow. Her work VISA wasn't enough documentation? Well, maybe she wouldn't enjoy *this* man. She extended a slip of paper through the opening in the glass. "Of course. I have a job as an English grammar teacher at the Saint Theresa School in Balduina."

His gaze stayed on the paper.

"If a problem exits," she added, "I have a contact number here." She offered him another sheet.

"*Un momento.*" He reached for the nearby phone.

His tone was curt. His movement was swift. Sarah inched her shoulders closer to her ears and tapped her fingers against the glass. Who was he calling? The US Embassy? The deportation office? She should have paid closer attention when the placement agency filled out the visa application. Maybe they'd forgotten the "h" at the end of her name. And the little card the airline attendant asked them to complete—would they ding her for writing one line in lower case?

As the man grumbled on the phone, he shot a glare

at Sarah, flicking his gaze to her fingers on the glass.

Sarah flushed and pulled back her hands. She turned her back toward him and busied herself with her cell phone. She had no signal, but the home screen image of Amber giving Steven a noogie drew her back to her last visit. Meredith said nothing could go wrong. A loud smack sounded behind her. Sarah jumped and turned.

"All clear." The officer lifted a metal stamping device from her passport and handed it through the glass. "Enjoy your stay."

Sarah relaxed her pinched shoulders, placed her phone in her purse, and smoothed her palms against her legs. She took her passport, reveling at the first stamp in her book. Meredith was right. She had nothing to worry about.

An hour later, scanning the arrival hall, Sarah couldn't help but admit she had a *lot* to worry about. For starters, her luggage was lost. Okay, her bags weren't really "lost"—the airline knew where they were. Somehow, knowing her stuff landed in Dubai didn't exactly make her feel any better. What if she never received her fuzzy, teddy-bear slippers or her volumizing shampoo? And her jeans! Her favorite jeans, special ordered in a size eight tall.

A man brushed past, knocking her purse strap off her shoulder. She gripped the strap—the contents of her purse were now the only belongings she had—and took a deep breath. She still had her passport, her money, and her toothbrush. She would get by.

Stepping into a room crowded with hired drivers holding little white signs, Sarah searched for her name. She didn't find it. She made a second pass around and this time spotted a petite girl in a short skirt and a midriff top who was engrossed in her cell phone. Hanging at an awkward angle, shoved under the girl's bare arm, was a sign reading "Ms. Miller."

Ms. Miller. How could she have forgotten she'd applied in her maiden name? Sarah made her way through the crowd. The girl sported a boyish hairdo. Unfeminine spikes plastered her hair all over her head. If not for the skirt, Sarah might have passed her for a boy. She extended a hand to the girl, who chomped on gum. "I'm Sarah Miller."

The girl stared for a hanging second, her agape mouth revealing a bright-pink piece of gum.

"Oh, um…" The girl must speak Italian. Why couldn't she remember how to introduce herself? *Mi cimo?* Was that it? Apparently devoting her flight to studying basic Italian phrases had proved futile.

"Sorry." The girl crammed her phone into her bra, and then squeezed Sarah's hand. "You caught me off guard. I was expecting someone…well…" She released her hand and blew a bubble. "I'm Anna."

Sarah opened her mouth to speak.

"Most girls"—Anna snapped her gum—"take these kinds of jobs right after college, you know. Veronica and I, we both came last year 'round this time. Only three months after our graduations."

As Sarah fought the numbness in her lips, she struggled to form a reply.

"Veronica's a nice girl." Anna adjusted her bra, tugging at the strap to secure the phone tucked inside. "Up and eloped with a German guy she met on holiday. Happened about two months ago. But I guess you figured something like that, for the post to open up last minute and all."

Sarah nodded. The taffy-jammed gears in her brain slowly processed Anna's comment.

"So, where's your stuff?" Anna asked.

"Huh?" Was thirty-three considered old these days?

"Your stuff." Anna pointed at the empty space beside Sarah.

Sarah shifted her purse to the crossover position. They'd have to come back to the discussion of how old she actually looked. "A mix-up with my luggage occurred."

"I get you." Anna smirked. "Happened to a friend of mine who traveled to Amsterdam last year. They confiscated her stuff at immigration after the dogs got a—"

"No." Sarah stiffened her shoulders. "That's not what happened. My luggage was lost. They said I should have it in two days."

"Don't worry." Anna winked. "I won't tell Sister Maria."

She could protest but the beginnings of jetlag took hold, and if she didn't find a bed soon, she might fall asleep standing. "Fine," she said through a deep exhale. "Can we go now?"

"Oh, right."

Anna scurried toward the exit almost as quickly as she spoke. The outside air was thick like a hot, steamy shower, and the sun burned bright in the sky. Fanning herself, Sarah took a seat in the back of a white, four-door minivan.

Seated beside her, Anna poked her head between the driver and passenger headrests as she spoke in

Italian.

Sarah only caught the words "*Balduina*" and "*grazie*."

Leaning back in her seat, Anna picked up her cell phone and grinned as she used her thumbs to type. She turned to Sarah, her thumbs still tapping, but kept her gaze on Sarah. "Sorry I'm so jittery. Had three espressos before I came. I'm not used to getting up so early."

Sarah checked her watch. Seven thirty p.m. Either Anna was a serious night owl or an honest-to-god vampire. Considering she thought Sarah was old, vampire was off the table. Sarah studied her new co-worker. Anna was like a young Meredith on steroids—or on three espressos. Sarah couldn't recall Meredith ever taking three shots, but if she ever did, her behavior wouldn't be pretty.

The taxi merged onto a highway ramp, and Sarah stared out the window. Buildings towered in the distance. Would they pass any sights along the way? The Coliseum? The Spanish Steps?

"So, you'll be teaching grammar in the lower school?" Anna asked.

"Yes. You?" Sarah kept her gaze on the approaching buildings.

"I teach maths, as they call it here, in the upper school. You know, trig, calculus, and the like."

The taxi hit a bump, and Sarah banged her head against the minivan's roof. Rubbing her head, she reconsidered Anna. Maybe this tomboyish free spirit had more to her than Sarah had thought. "What brought you to the school?"

"Well, you know. I wanted an adventure after I

finished at MIT." Anna popped her gum. "I was bored."

Bored? MIT? Sarah snapped up her dangling jaw. "Tell me, Anna. Did you know Italian before you came?"

Anna typed on her phone and shook her head.

Seeing Anna's thumbs fly across the screen, Sarah could only imagine how fast the neurons were firing in her brain. "And how long did you take to learn the language?"

"Three weeks. Well, four if you count written fluency."

Sarah opened her eyes so wide her lashes tickled her eyelids. Anna was no different from those quirky, disruptive kids in her classes—the ones who completed their worksheets faster than she could pass them out. Sarah marched those students straight to the gifted classroom. She narrowed her eyes at the spritely character across from her. "And did you find adventure here?" She silently estimated Anna's IQ.

"Yup." Anna looked up from her phone. "I've been all over. Not just Italy. Switzerland. Germany. Have my sights set on England this year."

Excitement brewed in Anna's black eyes, and a tingle rushed Sarah's spine. Anna was exactly who she needed—a translator, a navigator, and most likely a walking encyclopedia of Italian history. "How do you find the time?"

"We're done at school by four, and Thursday the school closes at one. We're supposed to use the free time for planning, but I always take off." She paused, snuck a peek at her phone, and grinned. "Just watch out for Sister Maria. She's a real stickler for rules."

During their brief telephone interview, Sarah

hadn't given much thought to the temperament of the nun and head of the school. As soon as she'd heard the words "Rome" and "living quarters provided," she'd been sold. Sister Maria could have pronounced herself the satanic nun from a horror flick, and Sarah still would have accepted.

"Like the two nights a week you're *on duty*," Anna continued.

Sarah pressed her eyebrows together. "Duty?"

"You know…monitoring the dorms. Just make sure none of the girls get in trouble. Oh, and lights out at ten, eleven for us."

"Wait." Sarah held out a hand. "We have a curfew?"

Anna nodded. "Sister Maria says we should set a good example for the girls. But"—she grinned—"just because your light is out doesn't mean you have to be in your bed." She pulled a key from her pocket and dangled it in front of Sarah. "Teachers have a master key, and I make use of mine."

Sarah slumped back into her seat and heaved a heavy breath. So much for catching an opera premier or stargazing from a quiet piazza. Anna's phone rang to a hipster song Sarah didn't recognize.

"Excuse me." She answered her phone and started chatting away in half Italian, half English.

Leaving Anna to her strange gibberish of mixed languages, Sarah surveyed her surroundings. Meredith wouldn't believe this. Hell, any American who hadn't traveled out of the good, ole, barely two-hundred-year-old USA would. The city was a juxtaposition of old and new. Ruins—authentic, millennia-old, crumbling stone structures—stood next to modern, glass skyscrapers.

Even the graffiti artists didn't distinguish between the two. Spray-painted words, all indecipherable to Sarah, blemished new and old structures alike.

The cab made a sharp right and ascended a steep street. The graffiti drifted into the background, and a green road sign indicated they were approaching Balduina, a suburb northwest of Central Rome. Sarah shifted in her seat to see out the rear window. Rome's skyline at last appeared. Domed roofs, bell towers, and steeples melted into the setting sun. Which dome was St. Peter's Basilica? Which was the Pantheon? Her heart raced. Did it matter? Soon enough, she would explore them all.

At *Via Massimi*, the cab turned. A mix of residential and commercial buildings, as well as vast, green, hilly areas, obscured her view of the city. They were getting close. Sarah made a mental note of the local *farmacia* and *supermacato.* Seeing as she had no toiletries, she would need to visit soon.

The cab stopped in front of a grassy courtyard enclosed by a stone wall. Three buildings flanked the corner lot, one of which bore a wooden sign etched with the words *"Scuola Della Santo Theresa."*

Anna spoke again with the driver in Italian. As she shoved her cell phone in her back pocket, she passed him some Euros. "Come on," she said to Sarah. "I'll show you your room."

They entered a stone building resembling an old church, with double wooden doors so large, Sarah's father wouldn't even have to bend his six-foot-eight frame to enter. She gazed up at a spiral staircase that ascended three stories to a large dome plastered in white stucco. At each landing, two wings spanned to the left and right.

"One teacher is assigned to each floor." Anna jutted her chin. "Veronica, the girl you're replacing, had a room on the first floor."

They walked through the foyer, turned right, and stopped at the first door on the right.

Anna used her key to unlock the door, and then removed a key from her pocket and handed it to Sarah. "Make sure you don't lose this, okay? Sister Maria would have my head!"

Sarah clutched the key. What would the room serving as her only private quarters be like? Closing her eyes and holding her breath, she pushed open the door. Darkness obscured the room and its contents.

Anna bent her arm around the threshold and flicked on the light switch.

Inside, a twin bed, a dresser, and a desk sparsely furnished a room about the size of her former master bathroom. Only a thin cotton bedspread and two pillows outfitted the bed. The desk was so small it might have even been for a child. Beige walls, which smelled recently painted, stood bare except for a cross above the bed. Without a doubt, this accommodation was Sarah's most pathetic since her college dorm room.

Sarah didn't cross the threshold. Stale air burned her lungs, and a knot formed in her throat. She squeezed her eyes shut, silently willing that when she reopened them the room would change. But when she did, everything was the same. Sarah just kept staring.

"You must be tired," Anna said.

Sarah nodded.

"My room is just above yours, so shout if you need anything."

Shout? Sarah scanned the room. No phone. No jacks visible. She drooped her shoulders. Nope—this room was way worse than the college dorm. Sarah turned her back on the room. "Would you happen to have a change of clothes?"

Anna looked Sarah up and down. "Umm, I have a shirt you could sleep in. Be right back."

The slap of Anna's flip-flops echoed through the hall. Sarah hovered for a minute before creeping over the threshold, one foot, and then the other. Inch by inch, the lump in her throat swelling with each step, she waded into the room.

Swallowing hard, she dropped her purse on the desk, eased onto the edge of the bed, and did a rough estimation of the length. Was it her imagination or had twin-sized beds shrunk? Her feet would hang off for sure. She fingered the thin coverlet. Would the blanket even cover her?

She stood, the springs squeaking, and took the few steps to the bathroom. Lime green tiles screamed 1970s. A pedestal sink and bare walls gave no indication of any storage space. The windowsill would have to serve double duty.

Beads of sweat dampened her brow, and Sarah was suddenly aware of the stifling heat. She opened the window, which screeched as she nudged it up. But the air outside wasn't any better. She stepped back into the bedroom and scanned the walls. The room contained no fan, no window AC, and no thermostat. Only a radiator sat below the window. Was she really expected to live in such antiquated conditions?

Above her, floorboards creaked. *Anna.*

"I told you I'll be by later," Anna said.

Her voice sounded through the ceiling as clearly as if she were in the same room.

"I'm just finishing things up here," Anna continued.

Sarah sighed. She could cross privacy off the list of amenities, too. The noise of Anna's footsteps and voice above ceased. A few moments later, Anna appeared in the doorway.

"Here you go." Anna held out a *fútbol* jersey and a bar of soap. Tomorrow, I'll take you to the local shops, and you can pick up whatever else you might need."

"Thanks." Sarah took the items and clutched them to her chest.

"I'll see you in the morning then." Anna turned to leave but then stopped. "This place isn't so bad. Once you start exploring the city, you won't mind the shabby room." She smiled. "Good night."

"Good night." Sarah closed the door. She washed her underwear and bra in the sink with the bar of soap and hung them to dry on the shower bar. Then she put on Anna's shirt and slid into bed. The size XL jersey hung on her shoulders like her dad's old flannel shirts and reeked of men's aftershave, the bed's metal coils poked her back, and her feet most definitely hung off the end. But she had a place to sleep, a nightshirt to wear, and a city, just steps away, that demanded to be explored. Wrapping her arms around her waist, she smiled. Tomorrow would be the beginning of a new Sarah.

****

9:00 a.m.—St. Peter's Basilica
11:00 a.m.—Castel Sant'Angelo
12:30 p.m.—Piazza Navona

Sarah added the word "lunch" before Piazza Navona and picked up the guidebook from her desk. Now for her afternoon plans. Head east to the Pantheon or south to the *Campo d' Fiori*? What did the travel guide recommend? She flipped through the book's write-up on the *Campo d' Fiori*.

Unease over her new surroundings had faded, not only because she'd almost mapped out a day of touring, but also because her suitcase had been delivered while she was out gathering necessities with Anna. She was now the proud owner of a pair of palazzo pants that fit her more like Bermuda shorts—she shoved those in the bottom of her dresser—an international cell phone, and even a quasi-acceptable tin of tea.

Anna had been quite tight-lipped throughout the morning shopping trip; perhaps she was hung over. But her disposition was a relief, as it meant she made no age comments or smarty-pants rebukes. She didn't even snap her gum when Sarah fumbled to count out change. Who knew Italians didn't use one-euro bills? Only coins.

Seated in her desk chair, Sarah dove into the guidebook, a smile tickling her lips. "The market at *Campo d' Fieri* closes in the early afternoon." *The Pantheon it is!* She added the landmark to her list. Four architectural feats in one day. If this excursion wasn't enough to make up for the lack of AC, she didn't know what would.

A floorboard squeaked above. Sarah looked upward. Cracks etched the stucco ceiling and plaster clung by a lifeline. What a miracle pieces of the dilapidation didn't crumble under Anna's footsteps. Anna was dainty—she also knew the city as well as a local. Should she invite Anna to tag along? No—the spunky brainiac would have to get up before lunch, and based on her zombie-like demeanor at half-past nine today, that awakening time seemed unlikely. So much for using her for travel assistance. But the tram couldn't be too hard to figure out, could it?

She thumbed to the transportation section in the guidebook. Ticket types galore: standard tickets, twenty-four-hour tickets, even weekly. They seemed easy to get ahold of, too. She'd just need to stop by the newsstand on the corner or find a machine in the metro station—

On the desk, Sarah's new smartphone jingled to let her know the battery was fully charged. Time to give the app Anna recommended for learning Italian a whirl. She dog-eared her page, swiped the phone's screen, and scanned the home screen for the app. She hesitated opening it. Should she call Mom? She picked up the phone, rotating it in her hand. Want and should were totally different things, but if she put off calling Mom for another day, her mom might just board a plane and hunt her down.

She started to punch numbers. After a few tries, she figured out how to tap in the international number correctly. Apparently +39 was to dial *into* Italy, not out. But, at last, the phone rang—an unfamiliar, muffled, machine-gun fire of beeps. Sarah pulled the phone from her ear, crossed to the bed, and fished her slippers from underneath. The beeps stopped.

"Sarah! I was so worried."

Mom's tone was one of typical exasperation. "I'm fine, Mom. Long couple of days, but fine." Sarah slipped on her fuzzy slippers and leaned back on the bed. But her feet still felt cold, and the bed was somehow even more uncomfortable than before.

"Well, you sound exhausted. I told you this trip wasn't a good idea."

"Mom." Sarah shut her eyes and prepared herself for Mom's haranguing, the constant, albeit well-intentioned, reminder of Sarah's state of affairs.

"I mean to just up and leave in the middle of a divorce is absolutely unheard of."

"Mother, please." Sarah's pulse quickened, and she tightened her hands around the thin coverlet's edge. "Everything's settled. We just have to sign the papers."

Her mother's snort crackled the receiver. "Settled? You should have taken that skirt-chaser to court."

Stiffness bounded her jaw. She clenched her teeth. *Just a few more minutes. I can get through this conversation.* Sarah focused on the coverlet, grasping a loose thread and unraveling the hem. Destructive, yes, but at least the motion kept her from clicking off. Or worse, hurling the phone across the room.

"You deserve more than just an even split, honey."

Sarah wound the thread around her fingers.

"You can still come home."

Tighter.

"Take him to court."

Tighter still.

"That Casanova deserves—"

And snap. "Enough!" Sarah's voice echoed off the plaster walls. Her fingers throbbed. The hem of the blanket was unraveled.

Silence reverberated through the receiver.

Sarah rolled her lower lip under her teeth. She needed to change the subject—fast—before she further damaged their already strained relationship. Standing, she returned to the desk, and picked up the guidebook. "Why don't you come and visit? You said yourself you always wanted to tour Italy." Sarah spoke in a steady tone.

"I don't know, Sarah. I haven't traveled since your father passed."

"I know, I know. But maybe now's the time to start again."

A sigh rushed the line. "Well, maybe."

They chatted a few more minutes, the conversation sticking to non-confrontational topics: the weather in D.C., Amber and Steven, and the great deal Mom scored on a sundress from the department store. The usual stuff.

When at last Sarah clicked off, she was relieved the talk hadn't veered back to Philip, or worse, Amanda. She returned to her tour planning. School started in a week, and if she had any hope of squeezing in sightseeing before she threw herself into preparations, tomorrow would have to be it. Hopefully, she'd find the tram stop. And, even more of a hope, she wouldn't miss her stop—or worse, find herself lost amongst a throng of non-English speaking locals.

****

The gravity of Sarah's offer didn't hit until the next morning.

I asked Mom to visit? She choked on her tea, inciting a coughing fit, and clutched the edge of the counter in the kitchen she would share with the residential students and teachers. What had she done? If she could maintain a civil conversation with her mother, perhaps she wouldn't have to resort to rash measures. But polite discourse was much easier when her past wasn't constantly thrown in her face.

Sarah released her grip on the counter and sipped her Earl Grey. *Things would be fine—Mom probably won't come, anyway.* The tickle in her throat subsiding, she took a seat at the empty table, and stared at her breakfast—high-fiber bread smothered in Choctella and purchases she'd made with Anna the previous day. She picked up the toast, sinking her teeth into the chocolate gooiness. Wow! No wonder they didn't sell peanut butter in Italian grocery stores. Who would want that after tasting—mmm, she took another bite—Choctella?

She licked her fingers, restraining herself from gobbling the rest in one bite. She examined the nutritional contents of the jar instead. The language read as gibberish. Probably better she didn't know. Undoubtedly, the spread had more sugar than the American standby, but the splurge was worth it, and she wasn't about to search for an international foods store.

International foods. She smirked. Who would have thought she'd ever live somewhere where American food was sold in an international store? As she retrieved her carefully crafted list from her pocket, she resisted the urge to tap her feet. She checked the clock on the wall. Eight thirty. Just enough time to catch the tram to Vatican City.

"*Buongiorno,*" a voice chimed.

Sarah jumped, dropping the list on the floor. A petite, middle-aged woman in a habit stood in the doorway. "*Buongiorno,*" Sarah replied in her best Italian accent, which was total crap.

"I'm Sister Angelica," the woman continued in English. "I hope I'm not disturbing you."

"No." Sarah bent and retrieved her list. "I was just finishing breakfast." Sister Angelica gave a small smile, the white of her bandeau a stark contrast to her olive skin.

"Sister Maria sent me to get you."

"Oh." Sarah shoved the list back into her pocket. "Of course."

With a bob in her step, Sister Angelica led Sarah out of the dormitory, across the courtyard, and into the main school. They weaved through the halls of the building, not so different from any other school Sarah ever taught in. White linoleum floors, offensive fluorescent lighting, and uniformly placed wooden doors decorated the building. At least this part wouldn't be an adjustment.

A few turns later, they reached a door with a large metal plate that read, "*Preside della Scuola.*" *President of the school? Principal?* Sarah would have to search the Internet later.

Sister Angelica gave a perfunctory knock on the door, poked her head inside, and spoke in Italian to the *preside*.

But instead of Sister Maria appearing, a man well over six feet tall emerged from the office. His gaze hung on Sarah for a moment, before he turned his attention to Sister Angelica. He spoke in rapid-fire Italian, but Sarah made no effort to decipher his words. She was too busy studying his face: his tan skin, his narrow Greek nose, and his curly black hair, sprinkled with gray.

"*Buongiorno, Signore Rossini,*" Sister Angelica said.

He nodded to the nun, and then shifted his gaze to

Sarah. "*Buongiorno.*"

The warmth in his voice matched that of his eyes. Sarah struggled to find her voice, and she was pretty sure her silence had nothing to do with her inferior Italian. "*Buongiorno,*" she croaked.

The man—Mr. Rossini—smiled back before striding down the hall.

His broad smile lifted his glasses right off his nose. His long legs moved in a steady gait. Something about him was oddly familiar.

Sister Angelica cleared her throat.

Sarah snapped her attention back.

"When you're finished, please come to my office, and I'll show you to your classroom." She pointed to a door across from Sister Maria's then gestured for Sarah to enter.

Sarah fought against the lump in her throat, swallowing hard. *Please let Sister Maria be more tolerable than Mr. Rosen. Please.*

Chapter 5

As Sarah took a step inside, the odd feeling that she'd seen Mr. Rossini before was replaced by an uneasiness in her gut. Maybe Choctella wasn't best before noon? She smoothed her shirt. Were simple khaki pants and a yellow knit T-shirt acceptable in a Catholic school? If Sister Maria provided advance warning, she would have worn her "work clothes"—a solid-colored, A-line skirt and a button-up, cotton blouse. Better yet, she could have dressed in all black—then she'd at least have blended in.

The office was large, about twice the size of Sarah's new living quarters. Floor-to-ceiling windows overlooked the courtyard and the dormitory beyond. File cabinets, a plain wooden desk, and chairs filled the space. Sister Maria sat at the desk under a five-foot-tall cross. Her outfit was a bit different from Sister Angelica's—a longer veil, with a rope belted at the waist. If Sarah had been raised Catholic, she would have understood the significance in the variation. Add that to the list for Internet searches.

Sister Maria lifted a hand and spoke in Italian.

A blur of muted t's and flipped r's spilled from the nun's mouth. *Sedia,* chair. *Phew.* At least she'd caught one word. Sarah took a seat in the armchair on the right. "May we speak in English?"

"Very well." With pursed lips, Sister Maria picked

up the top file from the stack on her desk and opened it. "I see you come to us highly recommended. Perhaps this reference will make up for your shortcomings in our native language."

Sarah bit her lip and nodded. She really needed to spend more time with that language app.

Sister Maria flipped through the file. "You have considerable experience in the classroom, and much more familiarity than most of our American teachers." She looked up. "May I ask what prompted you to leave your post in the States?"

With the nun's steely gaze on her, Sarah shifted in her seat. She might have been ignorant of many Roman Catholic practices, but everyone knew the church frowned upon divorce. Yet, how could she answer the question without bringing it up? "Some problems arose…" She chose her words. "Some issues in my personal affairs."

"I see."

Sister Maria cast her gray eyes over Sarah, and the silence in the room enveloped the two women. Sarah held the sister's gaze and strained to keep her lips curved upward, but the nervous energy pulsing inside made her lower lip quiver.

"Would these *issues* have anything to do with your husband not being with you?"

The words lodged in Sarah's throat, and she flushed. "Yes, ma'am. I mean, Sister."

Sister Maria stayed quiet, and her gaze bored into Sarah.

"My husband. He asked for a divorce." Sarah dangled her hands like awkward appendages. She scrunched her fingers then released, but the nervousness remained. She scratched the fabric on her thighs but still found no relief. Finally, she felt for her list in her pocket, removed it, and wriggled the paper as she waited for Sister Maria's response.

Sister Maria bowed her head in prayer.

She muttered a language Sarah didn't understand. Latin? Italian? Sarah wasn't sure. Was she praying for Sarah? For her marriage? A knot formed in her throat, and she wrung the paper.

Rosary clutched in her hand, Sister Maria crossed herself, and then raised her head. "Should you require any counsel, my door is always open."

"Thank you." The tightness in her throat eased, and she loosened her choke-hold on the paper. "I appreciate your kindness."

"Yes, well, I like to keep my staff under my care." Sister Maria rose. "Now, if only I could keep that young Anna from prowling around in the night like a thief, then my conscience would be clear."

Sarah couldn't contain her smile. She stood as well and was surprised to find Sister Maria at eye level. Taciturn and tall. Perhaps Sarah would get on Sister Maria's good side yet.

"My assistant, Sister Angelica, will help you get set up in your classroom." Sister Maria opened the door.

Sarah nodded and walked out into the hall. Sister Maria closed the door behind her. Well, that meeting could have been worse. She found Sister Angelica across the hall. Her office was smaller than Sister Maria's but otherwise similarly decorated—including a giant cross on the wall.

Without a word, Sister Angelica stood and guided

Sarah through the quiet halls to a first-floor classroom at the front of the building. "The supply closet is next to my office." Sister Angelica unlocked the door but didn't open it. She smiled and started down the hall.

Reaching for the knob, she hesitated. She stiffened her fingers around the list in her hand. Today was supposed to be a free day—a whirlwind tour of Rome's top sites—not a knee-deep-in-lesson-plans day. The rest of the week was reserved for work.

She sighed. A small peek at the room wouldn't set her back more than a few minutes. She turned the knob.

The door swung open with little effort, and a musty scent drifted out. Sarah stepped inside and slid her hand up a cool wall until she found a light switch. The same bright fluorescent lights that outfitted the hallways illuminated the room. A large plain space, the room had a chalkboard on the front wall, bulletin boards on the others, and student desks arranged in neat rows. Two windows overlooking the residential building supplied natural light, but…

Sighing, she swiped a hand over a student desk, dust puffed up, tickling her nose. What exactly had the prior teacher—what was her name again? Vivian? Veronica?—considered a lively classroom? With no posters on the wall, no alphabet tape on the student desks, and no mobiles hanging from the ceiling, this room was about as lively as Sister Maria's office minus the cross.

As she stared at the crumpled list in her hand, Sarah slumped her shoulders. She'd have to work non-stop to have this room ready for the start of school. And even then, achieving a cheerful classroom would be a small miracle.

She looked at her list, up at the classroom, and back at her list. The decision bobbed back and forth in her mind like a ping-pong ball. Each choice, prepare for the children or traipse around Rome, tugged at her heart. But only one had dozens of tiny minds at stake.

With a drawn-out sigh, Sarah wadded up the paper, tossed it in a trash bin by the door, and raced down the hall. "Sister Angelica." She spied swooshing robes ahead. "Could you show me that closet?"

****

Sarah stapled the letter 'E' onto her bulletin board and took a step back to make sure the word LITERATURE was straight. The navy letters offset the bright yellow and red paper she'd chosen for the background. The board looked good. But she hadn't gotten as far as she would have hoped in the last two days. With only one of the three boards finished, she had a to-do list longer than her bed. And she hadn't ventured outside of Balduina.

"*Charlotte's Web*. I love that book."

Sarah jumped, dropping the stapler on the floor. She turned to find Anna beside her.

"*The Boxcar Children. The Phantom Tollbooth*." Anna pointed to the book jackets pinned on display. "The kids'll love these."

"Thanks." Sarah bent and swept the scattered staples into a cupped hand.

Anna sat on the edge of one of the student desks. "So, you seem pretty settled in."

With staples in one hand and the stapler in the other, Sarah stood, and shrugged.

"Sorry we haven't hung out. Guess we're on opposite schedules."

Still clutching the office supplies, Sarah grinned. They had passed each other in the evenings—Sarah on her way to bed and Anna headed out. Maybe nocturnal mathematicians were the latest millennial trend. "How will you manage when school starts?"

Anna yawned. "I'll mostly go out on weekends then."

"That works."

With her hands, Anna spiked her hair. "I'm on the hunt for some *gelato*. Wanna come?"

Sarah perked up. "Around here?"

"Nah. In the city."

A tingling coursed through Sarah, like someone dumped the glitter she applied to the decorations in her veins. The city—Rome. Sarah surveyed her classroom. The desks were clean, each with an alphabet taped to the top. One bulletin board was complete, and everything was cut and ready to be applied to the others. But if she would stay on schedule, she needed to get through another week of lesson plans and start another bulletin board today.

Anna nudged her elbow. "Come on. Have you even gone into the city yet?"

Sarah chewed her lower lip. Visiting Rome was the point of taking this job, right? She was here to enjoy Roman culture, to experience the art she'd only seen in photos, and to take a break from reality. They were talking about grabbing a gelato, after all—not a whole-day, sightseeing adventure.

"Well?" Anna prodded. "You gonna hide out in here all day or what?"

Releasing her lip from beneath her teeth, Sarah slapped the stapler on the desk. "No. I'm not." She tossed the staples in the bin and grabbed her purse. "Well, are we going?" Anna gave her a mischievous grin.

"We're going all right." She drew a pair of sunglasses from her belt loop and slid them on.

Anna headed for the door at her typical warp-speed pace. Sarah paused at the threshold, her teeth grasping her lip again. Should she really be going out? And with this whippersnapper, no less?

"Bus isn't gonna wait, ya know," Anna yelled over her shoulder.

As Anna charged ahead, Sarah gave her classroom one last glance. She'd work later—finish another board and do another week of lesson plans, too. Gelato in the city—how could she pass up that offer? She flicked off the light and raced down the hall, hurrying to keep up. Hopefully Anna wasn't taking her on a wild goose chase.

****

The public bus bumped through narrow streets crowded with parked cars. Mint-green trams bypassed them, their pantograph rollers hissing against catenary wires. Helmetless passengers on mopeds whizzed past, ignoring all traffic signals and crosswalks. Sarah clutched the plastic handle of the bus. These people trusted their rosaries too much.

In the distance, St. Peter's Basilica dominated the skyline, its dome reminiscent of D.C.'s Capitol. Well, if the rosaries failed, at least the papacy watched over them.

A few stops later, Sarah followed Anna off the bus. She stayed by Anna's side through streets lined with tall buildings, many with laundry hanging over balcony railings. Farther into the city, the buildings stood taller, blocking the sun like a covered archway. Sarah was about to ask Anna if they were lost, but her friend turned a corner, and the cramped street opened into an expansive square—the *Piazza Navona*.

The sun beat down on the city's largest square, which was at least the size of a football field, and Sarah pulled out her sunglasses to take in the view. She strained against her bulging eyes as warmth tingled her fingertips.

Awning-covered storefronts lined the cobbled stone piazza. Rows of vendors selling trinkets, clothes, and prints abounded, and tourists flocked to them in droves. Fountains were scattered all around.

Anna headed toward the largest fountain.

At the center of the square, life-size carvings of cherubs and horses spouting water protected Neptune, the fountain's centerpiece. The splash of water faded against the buzz of conversations amongst those seated around the fountain's edge.

As Anna approached, she waved to a young man dangling his feet in the water. They instantly struck up a conversation in Italian.

With Anna busy, Sarah turned her attention to the street performers. A juggler tossed pins from head to hands and back. A man clad in bright silver spray paint stood as still as a statue, only moving when his audience was distracted. If Amber and Steven had been there, they would have insisted on dropping a coin in the performer's upturned hat. Sarah removed three coins from her purse and added them to the shimmering pile—one for Amber, one for Steven, and one for herself.

The man switched positions, lifting his hand to blow a kiss, and froze mid-motion.

Sarah beamed and added another coin to his lot. Had she been wearing a skirt, she would have twirled, taking in the endless sights.

But Anna had finished her conversation and plunged ahead.

If Sarah didn't hurry, she'd lose Anna in the crowd. She gave a brisk wave to the performer, tightened the laces on her sneakers, and scampered to keep up.

At the northern edge of the *piazza*, Anna veered onto Via Agonale. "Here." She pointed to a door and pushed it open.

The large wooden door looked more like a garage entrance than the door to a shop. Anna heaved her petite body just to budge it. Sarah followed her inside.

The *gelateria* featured a glass display similar to those back home, except the *gelato* was in oblong metal trays, as opposed to cardboard tubs. The containers held a variety of exotic, brightly colored flavors, like passion fruit and mango. "What's that?" Sarah pointed to a label she couldn't pronounce.

"*Stracciatella*," Anna said. "It's the Italian equivalent of chocolate chip. The best."

Sarah decided on the olive-green pistachio, handed the man behind the counter a two-euro coin, and accepted the spoon and striped plastic cup.

"Good choice," Anna said. "You should try it with chocolate sometime." She paid for her *stracciatella.*

Sarah licked her spoon. The smooth, cold treat melted on Sarah's tongue—no chewing required. A mild sweetness and saltiness lingered in her mouth as she swallowed. My God, how did Italians live here and not weigh a thousand pounds? She tugged on the waist of her jeans. Still loose. Not as loose as when she had arrived, but what did she expect? Choctella-slathered bread for breakfast did have its drawbacks.

They exited the shop and strolled the pedestrian-filled streets as they ate.

"My boyfriend, Francisco, is almost as irresistible as gelato," she said.

Smiling, Sarah scooped up drips of melted gelato on her tiny spoon. "Is that whose shirt you let me borrow?"

"Of course not. Francisco hates *fútbol*!"

Sarah discreetly licked the inside of her cup—as discreetly as one can, that is—then stifled a laugh.

They arrived at another square, much smaller than the *Piazza Navona*.

"I want to show you something." Anna gestured toward a building.

Sarah gave a little gasp and nearly dropped her cup. The building contained an expansive rotunda with columns lining the front. "The Pantheon," she squealed. She'd read about it in her tour guide about a gazillion times.

"Yep." Anna entered. "One of the earliest domes built."

Sarah hurried inside. Tourists filled the building. Some circled the perimeter, while others planted their feet in the center, necks craned to stare at the hole in the dome's arch. Light streamed through like a spotlight.

"Do you know how much math was needed to build this thing?" Anna swept her hand toward the dome.

Shaking her head, she worried Anna might provide

a complete lecture on the subject. But who cared about math? Sarah arched her back for a better view of the oculus. "Tell me about that feature."

Anna looked up. "The oculus and the door we came through are the only sources of light in the building. Also helps keep the place cool." She scraped the rest of her ice cream from the side of the cup with her finger then licked it off. "Mmm." She pulled out her finger with a loud pop and looked up again. "When it rains—which is quite awesome to see, I might add—the oculus ventilates the place."

"What happens to all the water?" She scanned the building.

"Aqueducts." Anna tapped a foot on the stone floor. "Drainage system built right in."

"Huh."

"Yep. And check this." Anna pointed to the spot on the wall where the light from the oculus shone. "You can use the position of the light to determine the time. Like a sundial."

"That's ingenious." Anna's explanation was much easier to decipher than the guidebook's three-page thesis. Sarah might have to ask Anna for more tutorials. Like how many people were needed to build such a feat? Or worse, how many had died trying?

"You didn't think I chose Rome for no good reason, did you?" Anna smirked.

A pang jabbed Sarah's chest. What if Anna asked her reason for choosing Rome? What if she had to explain that she hadn't *chosen* Rome at all—rather she had taken whatever post was available so she could leave the US.

Relax. They were discussing Roman architecture,

not the meaning of life. The twinge in her back eased, and she ticked a brow. "I thought you chose it for the night life."

"Well, the clubs, too." Anna smiled. "But I *have* been thinking about going back to school."

"Really? For what?"

"Math, of course."

"Really? Whe—" Sarah stopped mid-sentence.

The boy from the fountain stood a few feet away. He locked his gaze on Sarah and tapped Anna's shoulder.

Anna spun.

The boy's Italian words drifted over Anna's shoulder. Sarah sighed. As usual, the words were indecipherable.

Anna turned and grinned. "My friend wants to meet you."

"What?" Sarah's voice came out in a squeak. She stole a quick glance. The boy was about her height, with long, dark hair pulled back in a ponytail. He buried his hands in the pockets of his shorts, and he darted his brown-eyed gaze between her and Anna.

He pulled out a hand from his pocket and waved. "Marco."

His thick Italian accent sent a jolt through Sarah's stomach. She lifted an arm to wave back but ended up giving him an awkward salute. Straining to wiggle her fingers, she creaked out a reply. "Sarah."

"So-o—o, I'm meeting Francisco for dinner. You two wanna come along?"

"*Sì.*" Marco smiled.

"I don't think so," Sarah said simultaneously.

Anna glared then pulled her to the side. "What's

wrong with you?" she whispered.

"Nothing, he's just..." Sarah's iron posture morphed into the jitters. She wrestled a stray hair behind her ear to keep her fingers occupied. "How old is he?"

"Who cares? He likes you."

Warmth flushed Sarah's cheeks. No one had hit on her for years, let alone someone who was most likely a decade younger.

"Come on," Anna nudged her elbow. "It'll be fun."

Fun? To Anna, yes. Meredith perhaps, too. But an impromptu date with someone she hardly knew, someone she couldn't even converse with, did not sound like fun. Besides, didn't she have lesson plans to write? Bulletin boards to decorate? Sarah cleared her throat and kept her gaze fixed on Anna, even though she'd rather have looked back at Marco. "I can't," she said in a hush. "I'm sorry. I just can't."

She walked back to Marco and put a hand on his bony, broad shoulder. "I'm sorry, but I can't join you this evening."

Marco slumped his shoulders and cast his gaze to the floor. He didn't respond.

A lump swelled in Sarah's throat. "I can't go because..." Her brain felt like melting gelato about to seep out of her ears. "Because I'm married." The excuse popped out—or rather, it gushed out harder than the water from Neptune's fountain.

Marco opened his eyes wide, his long lashes licking his lids.

Stepping back, Anna replaced her scowl with wrinkled brows.

Without waiting for either of them to respond,

Sarah stormed out of the Pantheon, glancing over her shoulder, "Gotta run!" She traced her way back through winding streets, making full use of her sneakers' capabilities. As she ran, the scene from the Pantheon played over and over in her mind. Married? What had she been thinking? Any other excuse would have been better. *I don't speak Italian. I have other plans. I have a boyfriend.* But married? She stomped her feet harder against the pavement, heart racing and sweat moistening her forehead. Reaching the bus stop, she checked her phone and discovered a flood of texts from Anna.

—Married?—

—Where's your husband?—

—You could have told me—

Sarah's breath caught, and her heart thudded harder. She shoved her phone back in her pocket and took an empty seat in the air-conditioned bus. She positioned herself so the air blew directly on her face. It cooled her cheeks and dried her sweaty hair on her brow. Leaning back, she watched the *basilica* disappear in the distance.

As her pulse returned to normal, Sarah considered a response. Anna had been nothing but nice to her; she even shared information about her boyfriend and dreams of grad school. Sarah, on the other hand, had been less forthcoming. Biting her lower lip, she pulled out her phone and texted back.

—Getting a divorce. That's why I took job—

The bus stopped, and a group of young Italians boarded.

Her gaze on the group, Sarah studied them as they made their way to their seats. With tanned skin, shiny brown hair, and leather-strapped sandals, they could have easily blended in with Marco. Except not one was nearly as attractive as him. Sarah returned her attention to the phone and typed,

—*Sorry about Marco. Not ready to date yet*—

As the group took their seats, the bus lurched into gear.

Sarah's phone buzzed in her hand, and she picked it up. Anna. Another text.

—*Sorry :(But not as sorry as Marco*—

Sarah leaned back in her seat. Could she still draw the gaze of handsome, young men? If she ran into Marco again, she might find out.

****

Maybe the city allured her. Maybe the possibility of a chance encounter with Marco tempted her. Sarah wasn't sure. But for whatever reason, she ventured into the city early the next day. She toured Rome until midday, when the sun shined at its brightest and many shops closed for siesta. Then she returned to the school and worked until evening, when she went out once more—this time for a stroll along the Tiber.

As the sun set, Sarah stopped along a bridge connecting the city center with the *Castel Sant'Angelo*. Golden rays of light glistened on the rolling water. The water rippled and splashed against the embankment. Shadows of flags danced on the fortress walls.

Most tourists knew the castle as a stronghold during Rome's many sieges, but Sarah didn't think of the fortress in that way. Neither would Meredith. Holding her phone at arm's distance, Sarah snapped a selfie with the castle in the background. She added the label "*Tosca*" and clicked send. Meredith would be ecstatic. She'd taken her first official selfie—not one of the Rome Opera House, but close enough.

Sarah leaned on her elbows and enjoyed the cool breeze blowing off the river. In the dim light of dusk, her silhouette shadowed the waterway below. A lone shadow. A shiver crept down Sarah's arms, and her heart ached. The breeze picked up, and the wind tickled her bare arms, prickling her flesh with goosepimples.

If Meredith were here, they'd have seen half the city by now. Back home, Meredith was probably busy shuttling Amber and Steven to the pool, preparing them lunches, and making pretend forts with sheets and chairs—although undoubtedly, Meredith would rather be in Rome. *But where would I rather be?*

Again, Sarah stared up at the castle, and Meredith's voice echoed in her mind—not her recent voice, but the bell-like soprano tone that had brought audiences to their feet at Meredith's senior recital.

"Vissi d'arte. Vissi d'amore."

The opening lines to *Tosca's* aria were forever imprinted in Sarah's mind. *I lived for art. I lived for love.* How fitting that Sarah now stood where Puccini's heroine met her tragic end, taking her life after losing her love. Tosca's lover had been ripped from her, just like Philip had been torn from Sarah.

Sarah dropped her gaze to the Tiber, Tosca's tomb. In a way, she had lost more than Tosca—not just a husband, but her family and her baby. But if she was honest with herself, that life had been taken from her long before Philip. Her own biology was set against her. Tears dampened her eyes, and Sarah lowered her head. She wrapped her arms around herself and rubbed her exposed arms.

But deep within warmth bloomed, over her chest and through her belly. The sensation pulsed to a familiar song. *Tosca's* melody. Meredith's voice vibrated through her. Sarah lifted her gaze toward the castle. "*Vissi d'arte.*" She stepped away from the edge of the bridge, closer to the castle.

When was the last time she'd sat at an easel or drawn on a sketchpad? Wasn't art what she had lived for—to mix colors on her palette or bring a scene to life with gentle brushstrokes? "*Vissi d'arte,*" she repeated. Warmth replaced the chill on her arms and smoothed her prickled flesh. Sarah picked up her smartphone. "Where's the nearest art supplies store?" she said into the mic.

Ditta G. Poggi, her search engine informed her, was half a mile away and closed in an hour. Sarah stepped off the bridge onto the street and paused. She stared at the directions on her phone, her hands shaking.

Could she focus on art instead of her past? Could she push away the memories and create new ones—with her hands?

Chapter 6

SUBJECT: Booked my plane tix!

As she opened the email from Mom, Sarah's breath caught. Dear God, she really was coming. Sarah skimmed the email. Seven days. Not *too* long, but... wait.

All right if I stay with you?

She nearly fell off her wooden chair. In no way was Mom bunking with her in this tiny room. She sent a quick reply, snuffing the idea then snapping shut her laptop. She flipped the pages on the calendar and wrote "MOM" on the third week in December, then shuffled the pages back to August. She paused on October, where she had circled in bright red pen the sixth-month marker of her marriage separation—the date the divorce papers would most likely arrive.

A tightness grew in her chest again. The minute hand on the wall clock tripped over the six with a thunk, and Sarah let go of a breath. With a shaky hand, she returned the calendar to its current month. She had thirty minutes left of designated "work time"—thirty minutes before she could return to the city where she could bask in the mellow melody of splashing water from fountains and the tickling of the breeze off the Tiber. She had thirty minutes until she could drown out the looming divorce with the pleasures of Rome.

Her feet ached, and charcoal tinged her fingers, but

a broad smile spilled over her sunburned cheeks. The past few days touring the city and recording the sights in her sketchbook had left her invigorated. She strummed her fingers on the desk. Thirty minutes really wasn't enough time to get another project done—best end early. She packed her laptop in its case.

"*Buon pomeriggio.*"

Sarah jumped at the stern voice, banging her knee against the desk.

Sister Maria stood in the doorway.

"Sister...I mean, *Suor Maria, buon pomeriggio.*"

Hands clasped, Sister Maria stepped into the classroom. She rattled off words in Italian and glided to the bulletin boards on the far wall.

Scuola; *giorni*; *preparato*—the comprehensible words came infrequently. The final words left Sister Maria's mouth with the traditional inflection of a question. When she turned, she had one eyebrow raised so high it nearly touched her headdress. Sarah's jaw tightened. "*Mi dispiace,*" she stuttered. "I'm sorry. I don't understand."

Frowning, Sister Maria stepped toward the desk.

Did she expect Sarah to be fluent in Italian overnight? Sarah shifted her hands to behind her back. Hopefully, Sister Maria wasn't the type to rap knuckles.

"What are your plans for instruction?"

"Well, as I explained during our interview, the instruction will be done through immersion. This method is what we utilized in the US, and how we taught in my ESL classroom." Well, technically it hadn't been *her* ESL classroom. She'd only covered for the teacher while she was on maternity leave. Sister Maria looked unimpressed.

"And the parents?"

Sarah grasped the handout she'd printed that afternoon. "I've got them covered, too. I've prepared this handout." She handed Sister Maria the sheet. "It explains the benefits of immersion."

Scanning the paper, Sister Maria nodded. "And what about the open house?"

Stumbling back, Sarah gasped. "Open house?"

The head of school handed back the paper. "I'm sure Sister Angelica mentioned it. Monday night."

"Monday?" Her voice quavered.

"Anna didn't tell you either?"

Sarah shook her head. Her pulse quickened, and she dropped her hands to her side. If Anna could stop pestering her about Marco, perhaps the topic would have come up. *Monday. Parents. Oh, crud.* She'd need more materials to share—daily schedules, sample lessons—and she'd have to be ready to converse.

Oh no. She drummed her fingers against her thigh. What if they expected her to speak Italian fluently, too?

As Sister Maria stepped away from the desk, she ran a hand over a book jacket stapled to the bulletin board. "I'm sure they will appreciate the effort you've put into decorating the classroom."

"Thank you." She stared at the small Italian-English dictionary on her desk. Unless she grew a second brain overnight, she was screwed—absolutely screwed.

"Most of the parents do speak English, Ms. Miller."

Heart still racing, Sarah heaved a sigh and realized she'd been holding her breath.

Sister Maria raised her upper lip slightly.

Was she smiling?

"Most," she repeated. "Not all."

Sarah nodded. *Please let "most" be more like all but one—the one who happens to miss the open house.*

"But the whole school meeting will be in Italian. I expect you to introduce yourself accordingly."

"Yes, of course." She could manage…well, could with a lot of cramming.

Sister Maria clutched her rosary. "I also wanted to invite you to mass."

Sarah lifted a brow. "Oh. I…I'm not Catholic."

Softening her expression, Sister Maria fingered the red beads. "All are welcome."

Dropping her gaze, Sarah nodded. Even heathens who didn't know the difference between Saint Francis and Santa Claus? Not likely.

Sister Maria headed toward the door then stopped, wheeled around, and gave Sarah a once-over. "What size shoes do you wear?"

"I'm sorry?"

"Shoes." She pointed toward Sarah's feet.

"Oh—an eleven. I mean, a forty-two in European sizing."

"I figured as much. I have some old ones you can have." She motioned to Sarah's sneakers. "You won't want to wear *those* all the time."

Sarah looked down at her perfectly comfortable and presentable sneakers and slumped her shoulders. Couldn't she get anything right? She'd failed the Italian test, and now she couldn't dress to their standards either.

Once Sister Maria left, Sarah returned to her chair and plopped down. The hard wood smacked the back of her legs. So much for an easy year. She eyed the clock. Twenty minutes left. And so much for leaving early.

****

On Sunday, the dormitory students crowded the school's chapel, their chatter bouncing off the stone walls.

Sarah arched her back away from the stiff wooden pew. She'd spent two hours under Anna's tutelage the day before, and she still couldn't tell a rolled 'r' from a flipped one. Anna's translations of the mass would have been helpful. Unfortunately, Anna attending a sunrise service was as unlikely as Sarah understanding a complete sentence in Italian.

The priest chanted a foreign melody, and Sarah sighed. *Great—Latin now, too?* Resigning herself to her language ignorance, she relaxed into the back pew and wiggled her toes in Sister Maria's black leather flats. Sister Angelica delivered them to her the previous evening. They weren't all that different from a pair she'd brought from home, but the cork foot-bed offered more support for her high arches than the sneakers. Who knew?

As the priest continued the Latin incantation, the hypnotic rhythm softened Sarah's annoyance at her inability to comprehend it. No wonder so many people attended church—the service was quite therapeutic. Even if she had no idea what they were saying. When was the last time she'd been in church, anyway?

Sarah stiffened, the memory resurfacing of Philip's church—or rather, his mother's—for their wedding. They'd wanted to be married by a justice of the peace, but Philip's mom convinced them to use her church instead. Since she footed the bill for the reception, they'd felt obligated to accede to her request.

At the altar, the priest lit a candle.

This candle was a simple white taper, not like the braided unity one she and Philip chose. The blue and gold of the intertwined wax melded when they read their vows.

"Joined forever," the wedding official said.

"My soulmate," Philip called her.

His eyes alight with passion, he beckoned her with his husky voice. She'd never doubted his sentiment.

Perhaps, back then, he didn't either.

Bitterness clipped Sarah's tongue, and she gripped the edge of the pew, digging her fingernails into the wood. Sarah looked away from the candle.

Two men in ornate robes walked down the aisle with ornate metal containers steaming incense. A woodsy, balsam scent wafted in the air.

Sarah peered through the haze to the swooshing robes. The cream fabric of the robes was the same shade as her wedding dress—an off-white satin, empire-waist gown, specially made to fit her five-foot, ten-inch frame. Philip told her she'd never looked more beautiful than she did in that dress, and she'd felt good—elegant, graceful, confident in her appearance.

Sarah examined her current outfit—a washed-out shirt and black slacks. They were both a size larger than her wedding dress and both as simple as the tapered candle on the altar. She loosened her grip on the bench and slumped her shoulders. Kneeling boards opened with a thud, and Sarah sprang up in her seat.

Around her, men and women lowered to the padded planks and bowed their heads in prayer.

As the congregation prayed, Sarah hesitated, and

then joined them. She clasped her hands, closed her eyes, and attempted to empty her thoughts. But her mind was restless—a board squeaked, a person sneezed, a paper rustled. When she finally tuned out the surrounding noise, the result was worse. Memories streamed in like flowing water: her father walking her down the aisle, Mom dancing with Philip, and her carefully manicured bouquet of white and blue hydrangeas.

Sarah opened her eyes, and tears welled. A knot wedged in her throat, and her clasped hands shook.

At the front of the church, Sister Maria, eyes closed, mouthed a silent prayer.

All around were unfamiliar faces—calm faces, quiet faces, faces of people who knew nothing of her past. Steadying her hands, she dabbed at her eyes. This change was what she had wanted—a fresh start. This move was the best way to move on, to figure out what to do next…right?

Again, she lowered her eyelids and diverted her thoughts from the past and toward the future—*her* future. *God…Holy Mother…whoever it is up there. If anyone is listening, I just want to ask for some guidance. Where do I go from here?*

The priest chanted "amen," and the congregation echoed.

Sarah opened her eyes to the rustling sleeves of attendants crossing themselves. She started to stand but stopped. One request remained unasked. Dropping back to the kneeling board, she squeezed her eyes shut. *And if it's not too much to ask, please let me figure out this tongue-twister of a language…preferably before Monday.*

Chapter 7

The air was thick on Monday. In her pint-sized dorm-room, Sarah spent longer than usual in front of the mirror. She pulled on the hem of her gray skirt until it hit her legs mid-calf and retucked the navy blouse that hugged her waist slightly more than when she'd arrived in Rome—the effect of not only the daily Choctella but revisiting the gelato shop. She pulled back her bangs into a barrette, applied a thin coat of black mascara, and smeared a light pink gloss on her lips.

The parents of the local students would be convening in the auditorium in half an hour. As she walked into the bedroom, she rehearsed her introduction for the meeting. "*Mi chiamano Sarah Miller. Io sono insegnante di ingl—*" She stomped a foot and tensed her shoulders. Why did the Italian for "English teacher" have to be so complicated? And the stupid app wouldn't get to occupations for another four modules. "*Insegnante di inglese. Insegnante di inglese.*" She relaxed her shoulders then started again. "*Mi chiamano Sarah Miller. Io sono insegnante di inglese.*"

Yes! She slipped on Sister Maria's old shoes and repeated the sentence under her breath as she headed toward the main building.

A short while later, she sat with the dozen or so

other teachers in the chairs lining the small wooden stage. Sister Maria's podium stood front and center. A crowd of at least two hundred parents packed the auditorium.

With her chin up and shoulders squared, Sister Maria addressed the audience in Italian.

Sarah waited patiently as the indecipherable syllables echoed throughout the room. Then, at last, the moment arrived.

Extending her arm, Sister Maria turned toward the teachers. She gestured to the woman on the end of the row, three seats to Sarah's left.

The woman stood. "Adriana Pannetta," the *primo tre* teacher announced.

She continued beyond her name and title, saying something about tennis—no, or was it apples? What did it matter? All of the words were spoken in perfect Italian. *Perfect.* A tightness cinched Sarah's chest. *"Insegnante di inglese,"* Sarah mouthed to herself.

The man beside Adriana stood. "Roberto Errani."

He, too, stated his position and said something else Sarah didn't understand. The parents even laughed at what must have been a joke—hell, everyone laughed, except her. Sarah's heart pounded faster than the native speakers rattled their names.

"Flavia Vinci," the woman beside Sarah said.

The thumping in Sarah's chest drowned out the rest of Flavia Vinci's introduction. Then the teacher's muffled voice ceased, and only Sarah's heartbeat remained; all gazes in the audience were on her.

Clasping her hands, Sarah sprang to her feet and opened her mouth. She enunciated each vowel. She flipped her r's. She muted her t's. The pace at which she spoke would identify her as a non-native Italian, but hell, weren't her blonde hair and blue eyes already a dead giveaway? At least, she'd recited the words correctly.

Then her part was over. As she found the seat beneath her, she caught Sister Maria out of the corner of her eye. A light smile painted the sister's face. Sarah relaxed into her chair, her pulse simmering. By the time the remaining teachers finished their introductions, Sarah was busy doing a mental victory dance across the stage.

Sister Maria dismissed them, cutting Sarah's fantasized moonwalk short. Correctly saying *insegnante di inglese* was just the start. The harder test laid ahead—the parents. As she floundered to her classroom on the far side of the building, she tensed, the unease in her chest returning.

"Sarah!"

Anna's voice rang out as Sarah rounded the corner to the lower school classrooms. Sarah turned. "I thought you'd gone to your classroom."

"I'm going."

Anna pranced down the hall sporting cargo capris and a T-shirt that read *Math teachers have problems*. Sarah smiled. If Anna felt free to dress like this in front of the parents, perhaps she had been worrying for nothing.

"A plus on the intro." Anna gave a little wink.

"Thanks." Sarah remembered Sister Maria's pleased look. "Thanks to you."

"I'm good for more than just solving math problems." Anna stuck out her chest and continued briskly down the hall.

Sarah followed. "I hope the classroom visits go as well."

"I told you, just start all the conversations in English."

"You're sure they'll follow along?" Sarah gazed down the corridor. Italian words inscribed the signs. A small Italian flag waved above the entrance. Everything in the building screamed Italian except Sarah's classroom. She chewed her lip.

With Anna by her side, Sarah walked to the end of the hall to her classroom. Anna put a hand on Sarah's shoulder. "Relax. It'll be fine."

Sarah considered Anna. Wasn't this situation an odd reversal of how it should be? Anna was the novice teacher, the one who looked more like a student. Sarah was the one with years of classroom experience. She released her lip and shook her head, laughing under her breath. "Thanks, Anna. I owe you."

Anna headed for the stairwell and paused on the first step. "Drinks at *Al Forno's* after?"

"Sure." Sarah bit her tongue. She'd fill in Anna on her evening drink of choice, chamomile tea, later.

Smiling, Anna scampered up the stairs.

Her thoughts on a warm cup of a tea, Sarah reached for the door to her classroom and gave it a push. The door swung inward. She fell against the person on the other side, plowing into a broad chest. "Oh!" She jumped back.

Strong hands gripped her upper arms, steadying her.

She raised her gaze, and the apologetic gaze of a man stared down through black plastic glasses; he was the same man who had startled her at Sister Maria's office.

He stepped back, Italian pouring from his mouth.

Gasping, she squeezed past him and entered the classroom. His thick lips fluttered, the r's tumbling off his tongue like a purring cat. Sarah tried to slow down the words in her mind. *Signore Rossini* and *mi dispiace* emerged from the jumble.

He pointed to one of the bulletin boards.

All the while, he continued his foreign soliloquy. Sarah tensed her shoulders, and they crept higher with each word. Should she interrupt? Tell him she had no idea what he was saying?

He turned back. "*Staie bene?*"

A question. He was asking a question.

"*Signorina* Miller?" Mr. Rossini's eyebrows pressed together.

Silence hovered like the steam in Sarah's non-air-conditioned room after a shower.

He pushed up his glasses with an index finger.

Start with English. Always start with English. Sarah cleared her throat. "I'm sorry, Mr. Rossini, but I don't speak Italian."

Laughing, he sent his glasses down his nose again. "Of course, you don't," he replied in perfect English. "I'm sorry, I shouldn't have assumed. I was so startled, I forgot I was in the English teacher's room."

She relaxed her shoulders and smiled. "Please don't apologize. I'm doing my best to learn Italian—though I'm failing miserably so far."

"It just takes practice."

"So they say." She walked toward the front of the room, where she'd placed all the information packets for the parents.

Mr. Rossini followed. "I was just explaining I was running late from work. I didn't want to interrupt the meeting, so I came here instead."

Phew. At least she recognized his name from her combined class rosters of eighty students. She handed him a red folder. "You're Lucia's father, right?" she asked. "*Primo tre?*"

"Yes. How—?"

"Your last name, Rossini." She tipped her head to look him in the eyes. Even in heels, she wouldn't have matched his height. A cluster of butterflies rippled through her stomach, and she softened her voice. "Any relation to the composer?"

"Me? No, no relation. Rossini is a very common surname, you know?"

"Oh. I didn't realize." The fluttering in her belly vanished as fast as it appeared. He probably thought she was a complete moron. Rossini was likely as common as Baker or Miller. She always had to make a fool of herself in front of handsome men, didn't she? She dropped her gaze.

"But I do have a cousin in Seville that makes his living as a barber."

"Oh really?" She looked back at him. His lips ticked upward, and his round eyes fixed on hers. Sarah smiled back, and the fluttering in her stomach returned. "His name wouldn't happen to be Figaro?"

He widened his smile. "I do believe it is."

As he spoke, his baritone voice deepened. A multitude of questions swarmed Sarah's thoughts. Did Mr. Rossini really enjoy opera? Or was he just joking? Would he look more handsome with or without the clunky glasses? Either way, she wanted to keep the conversation going. Sarah opened her mouth.

But at the same moment the door swung open again, and the other parents streamed inside.

Mr. Rossini tipped his head and huddled in the back of the room.

Surely, he wanted to continue their conversation, too, because as she greeted the parents—each time careful to extend her hand first and introduce herself in English—she caught his gaze. He stayed in the back of the room, perhaps waiting for another chance to speak with her, for at least a dozen parent introductions. Not until Sarah explained to Mr. and Mrs. Giordano the importance of the assigned reading log did he slip out the door.

The next hour passed without incident. Had the evening ended there, Sarah would have clapped her hands and strutted back to her room. But at quarter 'til eight, she encountered an obstacle—Mr. Moretti.

A short, stout man with thinning brown hair, Mr. Moretti spoke as much English as Sarah did Italian. He pointed a pudgy index finger at the sheet in his hand and spoke.

As he jabbered in a terse tone, Sarah shifted on her feet and chewed her lip, searching her limited Italian vocabulary for words that matched his. She found none.

His hand gripping the paper, Mr. Moretti raised the *Learning Through Immersion* handout and repeated his question.

He practically shoved the handout in her face, and his words made as much sense as a pig's grunts. Sarah stepped back. She felt the gaze of several parents on them, but none came to her aid. They quietly exited the room as Sarah stood by helplessly. If only Anna were there to translate—or to shut him up with a sharp-witted comment. "*Mi dispiace.*" Sarah stumbled on the phrase.

Mr. Moretti lowered the paper just enough to reveal a glare.

Her heart raced. If she didn't calm him before another parent arrived—or worse, Sister Maria—she'd be out of a job faster than Anna could gel her hair. She took the paper from his hand. "*Signore Moretti.*" She summoned Italian words to her numb lips. "*Questo articolo—*" Her limited Italian vocabulary deserted her, and she switched to English. "The paper, it explains—"

His nasal voice squealed, and his face reddened. Sarah's stomach dropped.

"*Vito, come va?*" Mr. Rossini strode up to them, slapping a hand on Mr. Moretti's back.

Mr. Moretti turned to Mr. Rossini, and the two men exchanged a few words in Italian before Mr. Rossini gestured to the paper in Sarah's hand. "May I?"

Relief washed over her. "Please."

The two men conversed for no more than a minute before Mr. Moretti calmly extended a hand to Mr. Rossini as if a disagreement never occurred, "*Grazie, Eduardo.*" He turned to Sarah and nodded. "*Grazie, Signorina* Miller." Then he shuffled out the door.

Sarah stared in awe at Mr. Rossini's handsome face. Did he look like Henry Cavill? Antonio Banderas? She stifled an urge to hug him, because, of course, that response would have been entirely inappropriate. Instead, she beamed. "Thank you, Mr. Rossini. I wasn't—"

"Eduardo." He smiled.

"Oh…yes. Eduardo. I didn't think he would ever let up. What did he want?" Warmth crept up her neck, and she pulled at the collar of her blouse.

"He didn't understand the papers. They're in English."

Sarah frowned. *Of course.* Why hadn't she thought to have them translated?

"He doesn't grasp the immersion process either," Eduardo continued. "He's worried his daughter will fail to communicate with you."

Sarah bit her lip. "Oh, dear. I was hoping the handout would explain, but I guess he can't—"

"Read English?" Eduardo finished her sentence.

A dry laugh escaped her lips.

"Don't worry. I explained what the paper said. Vito is easily excitable."

She released her collar. "Well, I hope his daughter isn't."

He shrugged. "I'll let you be the judge. Just don't seat her next to Lucia, okay?"

"Sounds like she'll be spending most of her time in the corner," Sarah joked.

Eduardo laughed again.

His laugh wasn't loud or overbearing but a genuine expression of amusement. His eyes, so rich with warmth, smiled, too. For a moment, she lost herself gazing into them, even after his laughter subsided. She cleared her throat and stepped toward the table, where she pretended to busy herself with collecting the folders and handouts. "So, did you have a question?" She kept her gaze on the papers in front of her.

"Question?"

She stole a glance at him and nearly gasped. With his eyebrows pressed together and his glasses dipping to the edge of his nose, she knew where she had seen his face before. Michelangelo's *David*. His eyes, his nose, and his mouth were all strikingly similar to the image she'd studied in college. And she'd studied the *David* closely: the toned biceps, the chiseled abdomen, and the intricately carved genitals…

A deep blush rushed her face, and she shifted her gaze to the desk. Why was she so embarrassed? She wasn't undressing him with her eyes. Even if she *had* paid attention to the wide shoulders and narrow hips that now caught her eye, she needn't be ashamed.

How long had passed since she had felt the warmth of desire for a man? Sarah swallowed hard and fanned her face. Apparently, long enough that even an innocent attraction burned her cheeks bright.

He relaxed his brows. "Are you all right?"

Sarah froze her fanning hand in mid-flap. "Oh… yes. I'm still getting used to the temperature here." She pivoted to the table, careful to keep her back toward him as she moved papers back to her desk. "You never did explain why you returned. Did you have a question on the materials?"

"Oh, no. I found them quite thorough. Very well written. I…"

Sarah spun to find him staring at the floor as one hand massaged the back of his neck. Was he nervous, too? Eduardo looked back, a measure of doubt in his eyes.

"Actually, I was looking for Roberta. Did you meet her yet?"

"Roberta?" Sarah widened her eyes.

"Yes. She's my—"

The classroom door flung open, and a petite woman, wearing bright red lipstick and a dress that accentuated her tiny waist, entered the room.

"Roberta!" Eduardo took a step toward the woman. "We were just talking about you."

Roberta laid into Eduardo in an Italian rant, halting his introduction.

But she needed no introduction—her upticked eyebrow and fluttering lips spoke for themselves.

Sarah stumbled back and struggled against the flush creeping to her cheeks.

The woman was his wife.

****

Darkness had fallen by the time Sarah and Anna arrived at Al Forno's. Sarah sat beside Anna on the restaurant's patio, where draped strings of lights reflected off the damp cobblestones. Servers paraded by with trays full of steaming dishes. Locals lounged in metal chairs, a glass of wine or fork in one hand, leaving the other free for grandiose gestures.

"*Buonasera,*" a server greeted them.

Anna ordered a beer and a slice of pizza—the same thing she'd ordered the last time they'd dined there.

"Do you have any tea?" She handed the menu to the server, who stared at her like she'd grown a third eye. "*Té?*"

He nodded.

"Chamomile?"

Anna rolled her eyes.

The server scribbled on his pad and walked away.

"And some honey?" Sarah called after him.

He turned, scrunched his brow, and crinkled his nose.

"*Miele,*" Anna said. "It's called *miele.*"

"Oh." Sarah repeated the word to the server.

He scratched his head and shuffled inside.

"You don't want any lemon?" Anna cocked a brow.

Miss smarty-pants was also sassy. Sarah poked out her tongue.

"You really are hopeless."

Frowning, Sarah placed her napkin in her lap. "We have to work tomorrow."

"One drink won't do anything, except maybe relax you."

Sarah shrugged. "Usually does more than that for me."

"Then you need to drink more often."

Sarah arched her brow. *Right.* That suggestion would be as helpful as replacing peanut butter with Choctella—as her scale could attest.

The server returned with their drinks.

Sarah eyed the paper wrapper of the teabag. Chai. *Ah well.* Chamomile was too much to have hoped for.

"So, the parent visits went well?" Anna took a swig of her beer.

"As well as to be expected. One father gave me a hard time, but then Edua—"

The server returned with Anna's pizza.

Anna didn't dab at the cheese with a napkin. She just peeled off a slice of salami, gobbled it, and followed it with another throwback of the bottle.

Sarah's stomach growled. If only she could snack at night and not look like a beached whale the next day. She turned her attention to the table next to them. A petite woman with lustrous brunette waves leaned forward on an elbow. Across from the olive-skinned beauty, a man, casually dressed in an open-collared muslin shirt, reached for the woman's hand. "What were you saying?" Anna said through a mouthful of pizza.

"Me?"

Anna drained her beer. "Yeah, something about a parent."

"Oh, right." The couple beside them stared at each other with goo-goo eyes. Sarah choked on a laugh; an hour ago, she'd stared at Mr. Rossini that way. She shifted her gaze to Anna. "Nothing important."

Shrugging, Anna stood. "I'm gonna snag another beer. You want anything?"

"Milk." She tilted the coffee-colored tea toward Anna. "Not that milk will salvage this lackluster tea."

Anna rolled her eyes again and headed for the bar.

Alone at their table for two, Sarah replayed the night's events in her mind: Sister Maria's smile, Mr. Moretti's piggish interrogation, and the carefree banter—hell, maybe some would classify it as flirting—with Eduardo. Then the clickety-clack of Roberta's heels as she left on his arm.

As she let the memory fade, Sarah sighed and scanned the patio. The clientele were strictly couples. Some snuggled on one side of a table, and others ogled their partners, gazes fixated and mouths practically drooling. Rome was the city for lovers. Rome was the city Sarah found herself in when love was farthest from her reach.

Sarah winced. She threw down her napkin, stood, and walked to the edge of the patio. The shimmering lights of Rome sparkled behind the dim, rolling hills of Balduina. The basilica, the castle, and the Pantheon were all hidden in shadow.

A breeze rustled Sarah's hair. Her flesh prickled, and she wrapped her hands over her bare arms as she gazed toward the city. Light and dark. Shadow and luminance. She danced her fingers on her skin, and her right hand grasped an imaginary pencil. Could she capture it?

Her mind steadfast on the image, she hurried back to the table and withdrew a sketchpad and a stick of graphite from her purse. Flipping to the first empty page, which was close to the bottom of the pad, she sat, hunched over, and clutched the graphite in her fingers. She outlined the hills, and then the horizon. Then she shaded—shaded until her fingers ached and until a cool shade of gray tinted her hands.

"What are you doing?"

Sarah didn't look up at Anna. "Sketching."

"I didn't know you were an artist."

Sarah smudged the lines with her thumb then lifted her gaze. "I wouldn't call myself an artist." She stood, putting distance between herself and the sketch.

Anna walked around and joined her.

"Definitely not a masterpiece," Sarah said.

"Are you kidding? It's amazing." Anna returned to her seat and slid a small cup of milk across the table.

Retaking her seat, Sarah flipped the sketchpad closed and reached for her tea. She added a splash of milk before raising the cup to her lips.

"Wait a minute!" Anna snatched up the notebook.

Sarah jerked back her hand, and tea spilled over the tablecloth. "What?" She dabbed at the stain with her napkin.

"You're helping me with the school play."

"The what?" Sarah jerked upright. "No, no, no. I

83

don't do acting."

"You won't be on the stage, stupid." Anna opened the sketchpad to the most recent sketch and plopped it in the middle of the table. "You'll be designing the backdrops."

Sarah rolled her eyes.

But Anna just grinned and nodded.

Heaving a sigh, she agreed. Why shouldn't she add another impossible task to her list? She could design the backdrops...as well as she could speak Italian and control a gaggle of parents. She dropped her head in her hands. This year was panning out to be a walk in the park. Or perhaps, maybe this year would be the biggest mistake of her life.

Chapter 8

The following week, Sarah handed each of the *primo tre* students a copy of *Charlotte's Web*. "Girls, please turn your desks in a circle. Today, we'll begin reading our first chapter book." As the desks scraped against the floor, Sarah sandwiched her adult-sized chair between Siena and Cira as the clock on the wall ticked past twelve thirty. "Since we have a shortened class, we'll spend today reading aloud."

Thursdays were early dismissal, which should have meant an afternoon of grading vocabulary quizzes and drafting the weekly email to parents. But now, thanks to Anna, Sarah's Thursday afternoons between now and Christmas would be spent in play rehearsal. What exactly had she gotten herself roped into?

She flipped to the opening of the book. She'd worry about the play later; she had to get through the next half hour first. "We'll each read a paragraph. I'll start." Sarah switched to her storyteller voice and read. She paused at commas, animated the characters, and cadenced at periods. She read the words the same way she would have read them to her class back in Virginia, without slowing her pace. Over the last week and a half, she'd learned that even the youngest students spoke English far better than she did Italian. Not that she set a very high bar.

Having reached the end of a page, she stopped and

nodded to Cira to continue the reading.

The eight-year-old girl picked up where Sarah left off.

Sarah interjected every now and then to correct a pronunciation or explain the meaning of a word, but otherwise she simply listened. With each paragraph or two, she would ask a new girl to take over, until they approached the end of the first chapter. "Lucia, dear. It's your turn."

Lucia peeked over the top of her book and shook her head.

No? Why was Lucia refusing? The girl had already shown herself to be one of the smartest in the class; her essay on her summer vacation was written as well as the *primo cinque* students. Not surprising, given Eduardo's fluency. Sarah stood and crossed to Lucia. She crouched beside the girl. "Is something wrong?"

"*Signorina*, um, I mean, Ms. Miller," Lucia stammered, "I don't want to."

A snicker erupted from the circle.

Siena and Cira huddled together in laughter.

The girls shot ridiculing looks in Lucia's direction, and Sarah shushed them. Of course, Cira Moretti would be the bullish type. Maybe Sarah would have to put her in the corner after all.

Sarah turned back to Lucia, whose chocolate-colored eyes—a perfect match to Eduardo's—welled with tears. She placed a hand on Lucia's shoulder. "How about if I read with you?" she whispered.

With a half smile, Lucia nodded and eased her grip on the paperback.

Sarah returned to her seat and read the first sentence, switching between keep-your-lips-shut glares at Siena and Cira and you-can-do-this looks at Lucia. Her voice overpowered Lucia's, who spoke in a hush. When they reached the end of the paragraph, Sarah nodded for the next girl to begin, and the reading continued without further interruption.

The bell rang, and the girls rose to leave. Chairs squeaked, and chatter filled the room.

Sarah snagged Lucia, touching her arm. She waited until the room was clear before speaking. "I gather you aren't fond of reading to the class."

Lucia nodded, keeping her gaze fixed on her shoes.

"Has this nervousness always been a problem?"

"I don't know."

Sarah pursed her lips. If she were speaking to Cira, Sarah would have sharpened her tone. "Well, has it happened before?" She softened her tone.

Lucia shrugged. "Will you tell my mom?"

"She doesn't know?" Lucia looked up, her eyes pleading. Sarah winced, an ache growing in her chest

"Please don't tell her, Miss Miller." She clutched her backpack. "You can tell my dad, but not her. He's picking me up today."

"He is?" Sarah flushed, catching the enthusiasm in her response. She took a swift inhale before she corrected herself. "I mean, good, very good."

What is wrong with me? Being attracted to a student's father was bad enough. A married father was entirely inappropriate. Thank goodness, Roberta had been doing all the drop-offs and pick-ups so far; the last thing Sarah needed was to see Eduardo again. She fanned her face, blushing at the mere mention of him.

Sarah placed a hand on Lucia's shoulder. "I don't need to speak to him today. Let's see how you do with reading next week." She opened the classroom door. "Come on, I don't want him waiting."

Lucia didn't move. "Oh, he's not picking me up now."

"He's not?" Sarah slumped her shoulders.

"He's coming after rehearsal."

"Rehearsal?" Sarah lost her grip on the door, and it snapped shut. "You're in the play?"

Lucia nodded.

The girl's face was so ashen, Sarah might have thought she'd been assigned detention. Her thoughts in a jumble, Sarah again grabbed the doorknob and ushered Lucia into the hall, turning her toward the auditorium.

"Mama says she was *always* in the school play," Lucia said. "She says being on the stage makes you feel *splendido e famoso*."

If Lucia would finally string together sentences longer than four words, Sarah wouldn't be the one to interrupt.

"But it just makes *me* feel like throwing up."

A laugh rippled through Sarah. "Oh, Lucia," she said through a chuckle, "I'm sure you won't throw up." *Let's hope not.*

She and Lucia continued in silence. Once in the auditorium, Sarah left Lucia on the stage with a cluster of other girls and ducked into Sister Angelica's supply closet. She shoved a gallon-sized plastic bag in her pocket. Cleaning up her share of puke during her teaching days taught her one thing—preparation was key.

She returned to the stage, where Anna spoke to the gathered students in a mixture of English and Italian.

Sarah took a seat next to Lucia and dangled her long legs over the edge of the stage. She understood only the English portions of Anna's *Italinglish*: Christmas story, rehearsal schedules, and auditions for larger roles.

At the word "audition," Lucia stiffened.

Sarah leaned over. "I'll tell her to assign you a small role." *Maybe even a silent one.*

Lucia gave a pinched smile.

What kind of mother would make their child do something that evoked such fear? Sarah resisted a frown. Speaking in class was one thing, but participation in the school play was completely optional, and in Lucia's case, a cause for early-onset ulcers.

Shifting her weight, Sarah leaned back on her palms and let out a sigh. She was in no position to judge. She'd never parented a child—and she probably never would. A familiar pain grew in her chest, and tears threatened to unleash. But her students surrounded her. Anna, too. *Keep it together, Sarah.* She pinched the bridge of her nose and snuffed the thought. But the pain remained.

Tuning out Anna's voice, Sarah focused instead on the stage and auditorium. How large were the panels to be painted? Did they span the entire backdrop? What other scenery would be present? Of course, a manger and stable stood at the forefront, but Anna said they reused those pieces each year. Anna hadn't mentioned any substantial structures—no buildings, no cutout North Star.

North Star. That was it! Sarah bobbed on her toes. That was exactly what her panels should depict—the skyline of Bethlehem, the dunes of the Judean desert, and the North Star.

She closed her eyes. White from the city's lights highlighted a dark blue canvas. Waves of orange and yellow rolled across the bottom, picking up echoes of the same hues cascading from the focal point of the panels—the North Star. A tingle rushed her fingers, and she yearned for a brush. *Yes, that landscape just might work.* The ache in her chest subsided, and she opened her eyes.

In the back of the auditorium, Sister Maria and Eduardo entered through the double doors, engrossed in conversation.

Sarah narrowed her eyes. Was Sister Maria actually…laughing?

Without uttering a word, Lucia jumped to her feet, hopped off the stage, and ran toward them.

Sister Maria replaced the crinkled smile with her usual scowl. When Lucia reached them, she gave Lucia a perfunctory pat on the head then left her with Eduardo and strode toward Anna.

At the front of the stage, Anna hopped to the side, yielding the floor to Sister Maria, who addressed the students in Italian.

Sarah tried to pay attention, even translate the words, but her gaze drifted back to Lucia and Eduardo. Something about the two filled her heart with warmth. Could it be the way Eduardo lifted Lucia and swung her around? Or the playful defensive stance he assumed when he tousled Lucia's hair? Sarah rested her head on her hand, staring. Maybe the matching gleam in their eyes, apparent even from such a distance, captivated her.

A rumble of student voices and the scuffle of shoes

drew Sarah's attention back to the stage.

"*Buonasera.*" Sister Maria flicked her wrist, waving away the students.

"Auditions next time. Don't forget to study your lines." Anna cupped her hands around her mouth. "And your homework. Remember, B-squared minus four AC."

Some girls nodded, but most grumbled and scrambled away faster than Sister Maria could say *addio*. Sarah wandered backstage to look at the backdrops, but as soon as she walked past the curtain, she stopped. Her sight couldn't penetrate the darkness. Some light seeped beneath the curtain, but all it illuminated was piles upon piles of boxes. She'd need to ask Anna to turn on the lights.

She walked out front and scanned the conglomeration of backpacks, lunchboxes, students, and parents. Why did Anna have to blend in so well with the upper-school students? Hell, half the parents probably thought she *was* a student.

Then Sarah spotted Eduardo, and her heart skipped a beat.

From the back of the auditorium, he locked his gaze with her and smiled.

His smile lifted his glasses off his nose and was one Sarah couldn't help but return.

Bouncing on her toes, Lucia tugged on Eduardo's sleeve.

He ignored his daughter.

Maybe he didn't even notice she was there. At that moment, his gaze remained firmly on Sarah. She didn't move. She couldn't move. She couldn't even breathe.

Pouting, Lucia tugged harder on Eduardo's sleeve.

This time Eduardo's eyelashes fluttered, and he moved his gaze elsewhere.

Her chest burning, Sarah inhaled.

With heels dug in, Lucia pulled Eduardo toward the door.

As he struggled to maintain his balance, he shuffled his feet, his gaze flitting between his daughter and Sarah. He gave Sarah a brisk wave, and Lucia dragged him toward the exit.

Heat rushed her cheeks, and she raised a trembling hand and waved back.

Eduardo and Lucia disappeared through the door.

"Who are you gawking at?" asked a voice.

With a sigh, Sarah dropped her hand at the snarky tone.

Anna stood in front of the stage, chomping on her bubble gum.

"I'm not gawking." Sarah pressed her fingertips to her burning cheeks.

"Yeah, right." Anna ticked up a brow.

Sarah hoisted Anna up onto the stage. "Would you just show me the panels already?"

Anna exhaled heavily. "Fine." She ducked behind the curtain.

She walked straight into the darkness.

A series of thunks and swooshes echoed through the dark. The lights crackled on. Anna weaved through a maze of neglected props, pushing aside blocks of straw and reams of fabric, and stopped in front of three panels, each about ten feet high and eight feet wide, all of them painted black.

They looked more like the walls of a cell than the backdrops to a Christmas play. "These are what you used last year?" Sarah asked.

"Yep. Pathetic, right?" Anna stepped to the side.

A large, misshapen star came into view. She forced a smile, doing her best not to look like she'd just swallowed a lemon. "They just need a facelift." She ran a hand across the rough wood panel and gave it a slight nudge, but the panel didn't budge. "At least they're sturdy."

"The casters are to make them mobile, but"—Anna leaned a shoulder into the panel nearest her—"they're still too heavy."

"Well, I can't paint in this mess. We need to move them."

"Don't worry. Mr. Moretti will help us." Anna started back through the maze of props.

Sarah gasped. "Mr. Moretti?"

"Yeah," Anna called over her shoulder. "He made them."

Sarah tensed her shoulders. She looked from the kindergarten-level painted star, to Anna, and back. Mr. Moretti made these? Why hadn't Anna mentioned he was involved before? Why hadn't she—

The lights flipped off, one by one.

"Hey!" Sarah stepped over a trunk overflowing with costumes. "Wait." She reached Anna just as the last light shut off. "Mr. Moretti. Did you tell him I'm redoing the panels?"

"Don't worry." Anna flashed a smile. "I'm sure he won't mind."

Sarah couldn't tell if Anna's expression was legitimate or filled with sarcasm.

Chapter 9

Saturdays were reserved for touring the city, but Sarah skipped the journey to Pompeii in lieu of picking up supplies. With a can of basecoat purchased at a nearby hardware store in one hand and a bag of tubes and brushes in the other, she nudged her bedroom door open with her foot. She shoved the supplies under her bed—any other place would be a tripping hazard—and flopped on the bed. If only she could start on the backdrops today! But in no way could she start until they were out in the open. And that meant—her stomach knotted—enlisting the help of Mr. Moretti.

His beady eyes and nasal tone filled Sarah's mind. Maybe waiting a few days to get started wasn't such a bad thing.

A floorboard creaked above, and Sarah gazed at the ceiling. *Please let the little sprite be right about this one.* If she wasn't, and Mr. Moretti took offense to her covering his North Star, she might just need one of those plastic bags she'd stashed for Lucia.

Lucia! She sat upright. How could she have forgotten? She jumped up, aching feet and all, and headed upstairs. A flight of stairs later, a large wooden door, identical to her own, greeted her. Sarah had been here a month, and Anna's room remained one of the only unexplored places at the school. She knocked on the door and waited. What kind of blackhole lurked beyond? Half-eaten slices of pizza probably littered the floor, and dirty laundry likely hung from the rafters.

Sarah knocked again, harder. The door creaked then slipped open. "Anna?" She peeked in the opening.

Inside, a room identical to her own, only more lived in, stood. Stacks of textbooks teetered in a pile by Anna's bed. A collage of photographs pinned to one wall created a homey feel. Anna sat at her desk, with her back to the door, facing her laptop. Oversized headphones covered her ears like she'd just joined the Air Force, and the bass thumped to a steady beat. "Anna," Sarah said at a volume just below shouting.

Anna gave a little jump and pulled off her earphones. "Oh. Hey."

"I *did* knock." Sarah jerked a thumb in the direction of the door. "Door slid open."

Music still blaring from the earphones, Anna nodded and swiveled back around to her screen.

"I needed to ask you…" Anna was awfully quiet, especially for Miss Can't Keep Her Mouth Shut. And she leaned so close to the monitor she could practically kiss it. Sarah peered over Anna's shoulder but saw nothing—a security visor. *Go figure.* "What are you up to?"

"Just doing some research."

"Research?" *On a Saturday night? Fat chance.* She stepped closer. "On what?"

"Grad school."

Huh. Anna wasn't kidding. Sarah sat on the edge of Anna's bed. "Where at?"

"Oxford."

"Wow." Anna's choice of schools was more elite than Sarah's tea collection. "Think you've got a shot?"

Anna looked over her shoulder and smirked. "Of course. I graduated summa from MIT."

"Right." Sarah chewed her lip. Which was better summa or magna? Regardless, cum-anything from MIT was no small feat.

With a heavy sigh, Anna leaned on her elbow.

"What's the problem then?" Sarah asked.

"Eh." Anna lifted her eyebrows and rolled her eyes. "Not sure I'll apply."

Sarah stood. "What? Why not?"

"Why not?"—Anna snapped shut her laptop—"Applying is a pain in the ass is why not. Essays, transcripts, letters of recommendation…"

She couldn't let someone as bright as Anna throw away a dream because the application process took too long. "Right. Like you don't have a lot of time on your hands."

"Like *you* don't?" Anna glared.

Shifting on her feet, Sarah dropped her gaze to the floor. "I'm sorry, I didn't mean to—"

"No, you're right."

Anna spoke in a matter-of-fact tone. Sarah lifted her gaze.

From her desk, Anna gave a sideways glance. "In fact, we *both* have a lot of free time."

Her grin and dark eyes suggested she was up to something. "We do?"

"Yep." Anna jumped up from her chair and planted herself in front of Sarah. "Tonight, for instance. Bet you don't have any plans."

Sarah took a step back. Her calf hit the bed, and she steadied herself against the wall.

"Do you?" Anna cocked a brow.

"Well, I planned to do some sketching. Enjoy a cup of tea." Sarah rolled her lip. She sounded like a spinster.

"Ugh!" Anna dropped her smile. "You can't be serious. You're in Rome, Sarah. Why don't you come out with me?"

"Anna," Sarah said through a laugh. "My days of partying have come and gone."

"That's bull"—Anna slapped a hand on the chair—"and you know it. Come on—just this one time?"

Sarah sighed. Maybe she could make this arrangement work in her favor. "I'll consider it. On one condition."

"What's that?"

"I need your help with someone. Her name is Lucia."

****

At just past nine, Anna parked her red scooter in a dark alley.

Raucous young locals in tight clothes filled the street.

Sarah climbed off the back of the ride. Thank goodness the breakneck drive through narrow streets was over. How had she let Anna convinced her to jump on the back of that thing?

Well, maybe it had been a *little* fun—just a teensy bit. She ran her fingers through the knotted ends of her wind-blown hair and followed Anna into a stuffy, dark club. Music blared, and smoke hazed the air.

Anna headed straight for the bar. "Let's get a drink!" she called over her shoulder.

Behind a counter framed with neon-blue lights, a man in a metallic shirt greeted Anna.

She was clearly a regular. Sarah approached the bar.

He handed them two cups.

Sarah took a sip. A sweet syrup, followed by the bitter finish of vodka, hit her mouth. "I don't usually drink." The warmth of the liquor spilled down her throat.

"I figured." Anna sauntered over to the dance floor.

Bright lights flashed in a chaotic pattern, illuminating smooth-skinned faces and sweaty bodies. Girls with underdeveloped curves wearing short skirts gyrated to a techno beat. A wave of nausea hit Sarah's stomach, but the malaise wasn't just from the booze and strobe lights. Was everyone in this building at least five—hell, *ten* years—younger than her?

This outing was a bad idea. She turned to head back toward the entrance.

But Anna caught her arm and hauled her through the crowd.

A handsome young man held up a hand. "You made it!" He leaned in and kissed Anna briskly on the lips then extended a hand toward Sarah. "I'm Francisco."

"Sarah." She shook his hand.

"It's nice to finally meet you," he said. "Anna's told me so much about you."

"Oh, um…" She should have figured Anna would have an ulterior motive.

Anna stamped on her foot.

To avoid wincing, Sarah gritted her teeth. "Likewise," she lied.

Anna smiled and spoke something in Francisco's ear. They both shifted to the side.

A familiar face emerged.

"This is my friend, Marco." Francisco grinned. "I believe you've already met."

Sarah's heart leapt to her throat, and her stomach twisted. She turned to scowl at Anna, but all she caught was Anna's back.

Francisco pulled Anna into the jumble of bodies on the dance floor.

Damn it. She should have known Anna was up to something.

Marco stepped closer.

Sarah stumbled back and studied him. His light brown hair rested on gaunt shoulders. He nodded and took a swig from a beer bottle.

"Hi," Sarah said.

He whisked the empty cup from her hand. "Let me get you another."

"Oh, no." She waved her hand. "That's all right."

But he was already headed for the bar.

Sarah tilted back her head in a "why me?" gesture. She swallowed hard and followed him. Dressed in relaxed khaki pants, a striped *Ronaldo* jersey, and leather sandals, Marco looked ready to again pop his feet into the Neptune fountain.

He handed her another cup. "So, Anna tells me you're getting a divorce."

Sarah tensed her shoulders, and she squeezed the cup so tight the pink concoction inside splashed out the buckling sides. "That's right. But, still *technically* married."

"Ah." He sat on one of the barstools.

Sarah tapped a foot on the floor, glanced at the exit, and mentally retraced the route from the school.

But her memory was a blur of headlights and unfamiliar buildings. Could she even snag a cab around here? Damn it, Anna! Reluctantly, she hiked herself onto the seat next to Marco, and made zig-zags with her finger along the side of her cup—better than crushing it. "You study with Francisco?"

"*Ma va.* I'm taking a break from school. Working at a bar these days." Marco drummed his fingers on his glass bottle.

"And you don't work on Saturday nights?"

He gave a meek smile. "I called in sick when Francisco told me you'd be here."

Immediately, the tension in her neck subsided. The jitteriness in her fingers abated. Even the urge to claw Anna's eyes was gone. She smiled, placed her drink on the bar, and rested her elbows on the wood.

But she didn't respond. How could she? This situation was crazy. She didn't engage in flirtatious banter with men half her age. She didn't frequent bars. And she definitely didn't hook up with people she had just met.

Sarah stiffened in her seat. Philip frequented bars, even after they were married. The Thursday night meet-up on the corner of M and 2nd was his favorite. Those nights were his evenings shooting the breeze with his buds. Her stomach knotted. Had he met Amanda there? Were the buddies just a cover for meeting his mistress somewhere else?

"Are you all right?" Marco clutched his bottle.

"Huh?" Sarah shot a glance at him. His brows pressed together. "I'm fine." She pushed the memory—far away. "So, Marco, just how old are you?"

"Twenty-three."

Holy cow. He was even younger than she thought. She gulped her drink, the alcohol stinging the inside of her cheeks. Her eyes watered.

"Do you like it?" Marco asked. "I came up with it myself."

"It's good," she fibbed.

"Thanks." He widened his eyes.

The anticipation in his gaze grew, and Sarah fought against flinching. His efforts—skipping work and a made-to-order drink—at least warranted a response. What exactly should she say? *I'm too old for you? I'm not interested in dating?* She downed the rest of the drink. The features of Marco's face blurred. He might be young, but he was attractive, sweet, and he liked her. Warmth blossomed in her chest. Flirting just a little couldn't hurt, could it? After all, she was here to have fun—wasn't she? She leaned closer. "Don't you want to know how old *I* am?"

He gave a half grin. "You can tell me if you want, but"—he placed a hand over hers—"I don't really care."

Sarah smiled back. The only question remaining was whether she was drunk enough not to care either.

****

The warm yellow rays of the morning sun slanted through plastic mini-blinds. Sarah fluttered open her eyelids, letting them adjust to the light. Heaviness weighed her body, like she had molded into the firm mattress beneath her, and a steady beat pounded in her head. The residue of alcohol and bile in her mouth further soured her rolling stomach. Where was she? And what was that smell? A stuffy mixture of sweat, body odor…

Oh, damn. Sarah bolted upright. Sharp pains stabbed the back of her eyes, and she dropped her chin. She wore a maroon-and-gold-striped jersey—Marco's jersey.

Double damn. She hopped out of the bed, glancing only briefly at Marco's slumbering figure covered by a thin blue sheet. Searching through the clothes strewn on the floor, she found her own. Thank God for them. And thank God she hadn't brought Marco back to the school. She'd have been fired for sure. But where was she? She had no recollection of coming to his place, no memory of…of *anything* past chatting with Marco in a smoky bar.

With shaky hands, she grabbed her belongings and headed for a bathroom off the bedroom. She pulled on her clothes as she called. "Please answer, please answer," she whispered as the phone rang.

"Whaaaat?"

Sleepiness filled Anna's cranky voice. "Anna, please, I—I need help. I'm at Marco's. I…I didn't mean for this to happen. I need to get out of—"

"Sarah, calm down," Anna said through a yawn.

"Calm down? You drag me out and let me go home with a stranger, and you want me to calm down?" The throbbing in her head increased.

Silence reverberated on the line. "Give me fifteen minutes."

Sarah heaved a sigh. "Thank you, Anna." The line was already dead. She finished dressing and pulled her hair into a ponytail. As she turned to leave, something caught her eye. A used condom floated in the toilet. Bile climbed higher in her throat. She gagged then hurled—getting her head over the toilet just in time.

When her stomach was empty, she rinsed her mouth with water and examined her disheveled reflection in the mirror. She hadn't felt this horrible since…since the Ben Carter incident.

The night out had been just like this—a few drinks, and then…

Pushing away the thought, she flushed the toilet and watched the condom circle down the drain. How many years had transpired since she'd carried one of those around? Not since Philip. But she'd carried one in her purse in high school and college.

She shuddered. So much time had passed since she thought of her first GYN appointment—the first time she'd heard the term PCOS.

"Irregular cycle. Heavy periods. Oily skin." The doctor had tapped his clipboard. "All classic signs of polycystic ovarian syndrome. The condition is very common, Sarah. No need for concern."

Sarah turned to Mom, who sat beside her in the exam room. The expression on her mother's face confirmed Sarah's fears. The diagnosis was definitely something to worry about.

"I can give you some pills if you'd like to be more regular," the doctor continued, "but they're not necessary. When the time comes that you're ready to conceive, you might just need a little extra help."

She sneered, a jolt attacking her stomach. A little extra help. How many times had she repeated those words in her mind? How many times had she screamed them into her pillow at night? How many times had she proved the doctor wrong?

In the bathroom, Sarah stared down at the toilet where the condom floated before she flushed. But the doctor mentioned something else that day, just before leaving the room. Something she hadn't given much thought to in years. Of course, he spoke loud enough for Mom to hear as well, making Sarah's face color with embarrassment.

"Now, Sarah," the doctor had said, "don't let this diagnosis make you careless with contraception. You can get pregnant and contract STDs."

That statement was why, two days later, Sarah's mother handed her a shiny wrapper. "Just in case."

Sarah never thanked her mother for that advice. The sight of that same crumpled wrapper on the floor of Ben Carter's dorm room years later had brought her such relief. A knock on the bathroom door brought Sarah out of her daydream.

"Sarah?" Marco asked.

Great. He was awake. Could this morning get any worse? "Just a minute!" she called then opened the door.

"Sarah." He embraced her.

In his scrawny arms, Sarah stood rigid and resisted the urge to wriggle free.

With his hands still on her upper arms, he took a step back.

"Marco, um, I'm sorry about last night. I made a mist—"

"Why are you sorry?" He scrunched his brows. "Last night was amazing! You…you were amazing."

Okay, this day *could* get worse—definitely worse. "Marco, listen. I made a mistake. I had too much to drink."

He lowered his hands. "Are these feelings about your husband? Eduardo? Because I under—"

"What?" She went rigid. "Eduardo?"

"Yeah. You called me Eduardo last night—a couple of times, actually."

Way worse. Her cheeks burned. Eduardo? Why had she called him that name?

Her phone beeped in her purse just as a toot-toot from Anna's scooter whistled outside. She pushed past Marco and hurried to the front door, shouting over her shoulder, "I'm sorry, Marco...again."

"Wait," he called after her. "I don't even have your number."

Sarah hurled herself down the stairs and jumped onto the back of the scooter before he could catch up. Safe on the back of Anna's scooter, she reached the dorm twenty minutes later.

Students streamed from the chapel across the courtyard.

"I thought you were having a good time," Anna said.

"I honestly don't remember. Maybe I was."

"Sorry. I wouldn't have let you go with him if—"

"What happened last night isn't your fault." Sarah entered the dormitory. "Just don't give him or Francisco my number, okay?"

"Don't worry. I was getting bored with him anyway."

"Well, don't do anything rash on my account."

Anna gave a little snort. "We've been together six weeks. That's two weeks past my usual max."

A smile curving her lips, Sarah shook her head and turned toward her room. Then she froze.

Down the hall, Sister Maria stood at her door.

Sarah's heart skipped a beat. *Definitely worst day*

ever. Brushing her hands over her crumpled shirt, Sarah stepped toward her. But what was the point? She reeked of stale smoke and beer. The head of school would make her out. "*Buongiorno*," Sarah mustered a cheery tone.

Sister Maria wheeled around, revealing a smile. But it quickly faded. "*Buongiorno.*" Her voice was as cold as her expression. She scanned Sarah's outfit, and her scowl deepened.

"You weren't at mass. I came by to check on you."

"Oh, I'm fine, thanks. I—" Sarah broke off and folded her arms across her chest. What half-lie could she say that wouldn't send her straight to purgatory? "I wasn't feeling up to attending."

Scowling, Sister Maria arched an eyebrow above her wire-frame glasses.

Sarah shifted her gaze to the floor. Purgatory for sure.

"I'll leave you to rest." Sister Maria stepped to the side.

"Thank you." Sarah fumbled with her key.

"And, Miss Miller?"

Sarah caught the door before it closed but didn't meet Sister Maria's gaze.

"I don't usually interfere with my staff's personal affairs, but you've surprised me this morning. I hoped you would be a positive influence on Miss Franklin."

With a shoulder push, Sarah shut the door. She left her clothes in a heap on the bathroom floor. She brushed her teeth twice—once before the scalding hot shower and once after. After throwing on a nightshirt, she pulled on her fuzzy slippers and climbed into bed. The clean clothes and countless times she'd ran the bar of soap between her legs hadn't helped. She still felt dirty.

Curling up in the bed, she drew her knees to her chest. As she prepared to close her eyes, she caught sight of Sister Maria's hand-me-down flats. The black leather had faded to dark gray, and scuffs marked the toes. They were old and dirty. But they'd been tucked safely in her room last night, where Sarah should also have been.

Closing her eyes, she pictured the smoky bar and Anna's devilish grin, Marco's unkept apartment and his bare torso, and the hallway leading to her room and Sister Maria's disappointment. She pulled in her knees tighter and squeezed shut her eyes. But the tears fell anyway. This trip was supposed to rejuvenate her soul, not corrupt her morals. Would she ever stop screwing up royally?

Chapter 10

Midnight-blue latex paint flowed into a tin pan. As Sarah dipped in a foam roller, the strong scent permeated her nostrils. She applied bright white paint over the star and stepped back. The panel would need two coats for sure. She glanced around.

On the stage, Anna took command of the students.

Lucia sat among them, her legs crossed, clutching her script like a lifeline. With a creased forehead and a face tinged green, Lucia might need a barf bag.

Dropping the roller, Sarah hiked herself onto the stage, and tapped Lucia's shoulder. "Want to help me with the set?" she whispered in the girl's ear.

Lucia gave a pinched smile then looked to Anna.

With a nod, Anna waved them off.

Today's rehearsal would focus on auditioning the leads, so Director Superior Anna could survive without Lucia. Sarah wet a brush with paint and handed it to Lucia. "Why don't you work on the edges?"

Nodding, Lucia dabbed at the wooden canvas.

Large droplets of paint oozed down in streaks. "Like this." Sarah wrapped her hand around Lucia's and directed the brush in smooth, even strokes. After a few passes, Sarah stepped back. "Now you try."

Lucia smothered her brush in the jar of paint and extracted a blob.

Cringing, Sarah reached to correct her again—but

stopped herself.

Lucia smiled and the color returned to her cheeks.

Picking up the roller, Sarah knew she'd fix the streaks later. With Lucia by her side, Sarah fell into a rhythm. She painted the higher portions while Lucia sat on the floor, concentrating on the borders. Sarah finished her section first, and while she waited for Lucia to finish the bottom, she set down the roller and picked up Lucia's script. The word "*Oste*" was written on the front in Anna's boxy handwriting.

Sarah flipped through the pages until she found a single highlighted line, *Non sei il benvenuto.* Or in English, *You are not welcome. Oste.* That must mean the innkeeper. The innkeeper with only one line in the entire play. Well, Anna kept her end of the deal.

Memories of that botched night out flooded back: strong cocktails, Marco, Sister Maria. Details Meredith couldn't help but remind her of every time they spoke or texted. Why had she even told Meredith? If Meredith teased her about Ben Carter after all these years, when would she let up on Marco? She would need a severe case of dementia to ever let this one go.

"Are you happy with your part?" Sarah picked up the roller again.

Lucia shrugged. "That depends."

"On what?"

"Whether the innkeeper is a man or a woman."

Sarah laughed. "I suppose male roles are always an issue at an all-girls school."

Lucia's tan cheeks held steady in a frown and a dullness set into her brown eyes.

"Yeah."

"So, which do you prefer?"

"Mama doesn't like pants roles. She played Mary in her school play."

Of course, Roberta played Mary. Her classmates probably voted her prom queen, too, if such a thing existed in Italy. Sarah bit back her judgments. "Maybe next year you'll have a larger role."

"Maybe. I need to figure out how to get through one line first." Lucia frowned, and her brush rested on the panel.

Sarah cupped a hand around Lucia's shoulder and squeezed. "It just takes practice."

Lucia's expression didn't change.

"Like this." Sarah set the roller down again and reached beneath the drop cloths for her sketchpad. She flipped through a handful of pages—her early sketches of her backdrop plan. "I lost count how many times I sketched this scene. And I haven't even started painting yet."

"That's different. You're good at art. I'm not good at…at talking."

With a sigh, Sarah tossed aside the sketchpad and turned Lucia to face her. "Then we'll practice. Just us. As much as you need to. And when you're ready, you'll speak in front of them." She gestured at the stage. "Deal?"

Lucia gave a toothy smile. "Deal."

As she returned her smile, Sarah extended a hand and shook Lucia's.

Lucia's gaze lifted over Sarah, and her smile widened. "Papa!" She tossed her brush in the pan, splashing paint.

Sarah froze. Marco's words replayed in her head. *You called me Eduardo last night.* She knelt to wipe the splattered paint, keeping her back to Eduardo. Maybe he wouldn't notice her. Maybe he would just leave. Maybe—

"Good afternoon, Miss Miller."

Maybe she should learn to stop lusting after married men. Sarah turned. Eduardo stood right beside her, close enough for her to catch a whiff of his cologne and to see a hint of tanned skin beneath a loosened tie. *Definitely lusting.* "Good afternoon." She gave him a professional, polite smile.

Eduardo spoke to Lucia in Italian.

She scurried off in the direction of her backpack.

"I see you've enlisted Lucia as your assistant?" Eduardo pointed to a long drip of paint on the panel. "Not so sure that's a good idea."

"It's fine. The next coat will cover any imperfections."

"You're an artist then?"

Sarah shrugged. "I can't say I agree with that statement."

"Well, I'm sure your skills with a brush can't be worse than your Italian."

Sarah narrowed her eyes, only to catch his cheeky grin. She laughed. "I guess not."

"About that. I'd be happy to help you with your Italian." He drew a card from his pocket and extended it. "My mobile's on the back."

"Oh, thank you. That's awfully kind of you." *Kind of you to tempt me.*

"Great." He smiled. "*Addio.*" With a nod, he started in Lucia's direction.

Sarah examined the card. *Rossini and Associates, International Corporate Attorneys.* On the back, a number was scribbled in black ink.

Suddenly, the hairs on the back of her neck lifted. How had Philip and Amanda exchanged numbers? Had he given her a business card, too? She looked from the card, to Eduardo, and back again. Was Eduardo just being friendly—or something else? *Friendly. Definitely just friendly...right?*

"Did he just give you his number?"

"What?" Sarah jumped then shoved the card in her pocket. Anna stood by her side. "No. I mean, yes." Heat rushed her cheeks.

Anna's gaze tracked Eduardo and Lucia. "He's pretty hot."

"He wasn't asking me out." *I think.* "He offered to help with my Italian."

"*Sure.* Whatever you say." She elbowed Sarah in the side.

"Please. The gesture was friendly, I assure you." *Just friendly.*

"Riiight. Well, I've had one too many *gestures* from the dads around here."

"What?" Sarah's voice came out in a squeal. "You can't be serious."

Anna pulled a compact out of her pocket and applied bright red lipstick. "I'll tell you later. I've got to meet Juan." She spoke through puckered lips.

"Juan?" Sarah stood upright. "Who's Juan?"

"A doctor I met." She popped the makeup back in her pocket.

"Doctor?" Sarah took a step closer. "Spill it."

"Well for starters, if I don't leave now I might miss my 'check-up.'"

Sarah rolled her eyes.

Anna winked then dashed toward the exit.

Wait—Anna had a new boyfriend already? A father made unsolicited advances? And Eduardo…?

Sarah reached a hand into her pocket. The card remained safe inside. *Friendly. Definitely.*

The next morning, Eduardo's advance made Sarah contemplate attending student drop-off. But what if Eduardo brought Lucia? Sarah's stomach lurched. Or worse, what if Roberta did? She'd just stay in her classroom and get ready.

In her classroom, she finished sorting the black pieces of construction paper from the colored assortment—who could draw on black paper anyway?—and went to file the papers with her craft supplies. But as she opened the file cabinet, she had a thought—maybe they could use the black paper for a Halloween project. Bats, ghosts, witches' hats, and cauldrons—

Did they even celebrate Halloween in Italy? The minute hand on the clock gave a subtle click. Eight o'clock. *Stop thinking about future art projects, Sarah. The kids are here in ten minutes!* She shoved closed the file cabinet drawer and strode to her desk. Her calendar showed September. That month ended two days ago. How had she forgotten?

Right—head wrapped up with married men was how. She tore off the page then stopped. Red pen screamed at her. The circled date on the calendar meant the divorce papers.

She stepped back. They would arrive in less than a week. Only a week? In a few short days, she would be officially free of Philip Flynn. Her breath caught. She stepped back again, her back bumping the whiteboard.

Philip's bright green eyes and husky voice flooded her mind. "I love you," she heard him say.

Tears stung her eyes. When had Philip's affection begun to wane? When they took a break—as he called it—from conceiving? Or before that? Perhaps, when she'd stopped taking the pill?

She rubbed her hands over her arms, her arm hair thick under her palms—just one consequence of elevated PCOS hormones. Philip always said he didn't mind. Had he been telling the truth? She slid her hands down her sides, where her once sultry curves now resembled the outline of a roll of toilet paper. She drooped her shoulders—maybe more than her infertility sent him to another woman.

The door to the classroom opened.

"Good morning," students said in English as they entered.

Sarah turned her back, brushed away the tears, and regained her composure. *Shoot!* She'd been so wrapped up in her thoughts she'd forgotten to formalize her lesson plan for the class. She faced the *primo cinque* girls, who chatted quietly, and clapped her hands.

The conversation stopped, and they fixed their attention on her.

"Today, we will practice adjectives with a project." She held up a piece of paper. "I'd like each of you to draw..." She searched for something they could describe. "Draw a picture of me and write a description below, underlining the adjectives." She blurted the thought.

An hour later, as she paged through gross images of herself—towering, boxy figures with scrawled blonde hair, long necks, wide shoulders, and big feet—

Sarah regretted her hasty choice of subject. By the final period of the day, she was all but ready to set a match to the students' drawings.

She strode through the aisles of desks fighting back a cringe at the images. She stopped at Cira's desk and examined her crude drawing. *Ms. Miller is big*, read the caption.

Big? Big as in wide, or big as in tall? Judging by the stick-figure depiction, she guessed tall. Sarah tapped Cira's paper. "See if you can add another sentence."

From her seat, Cira mumbled something under her breath in Italian.

Sarah shot her a knowing eye. Best to keep Cira in line. The last thing Sarah needed was a parent conference with Mr. Moretti. She continued down the row. Drawings of matronly women in plain skirts and drab shirts decorated student desks. Sarah glanced down at her outfit and sighed. At least the girls omitted arm hair in their sketches.

She turned to the next row and approached Lucia's desk.

At her desk, Lucia hunkered down over her paper, working with a colored pencil.

"What's that you're drawing?" Sarah asked.

Lucia shifted her hands to reveal the writing beneath, *My papa says Ms. Miller is a beautiful swan.*

Sarah crept her hands to her neck. While not out of proportion to her long arms and legs, her neck was longer than most women's. "Lucia, your father said these words?"

Beaming, Lucia nodded. "He talks about you a lot. Says you're the prettiest teacher in school."

Sarah almost dropped her jaw, and she snapped it closed, her teeth clashing with the movement. "Lucia," she started but paused. What the hell could she say? Does he say these things in front of your mother? Does he have infatuations with other women? Sarah shook away the thoughts and glanced toward the paper. "Don't forget to underline your adjectives."

Beside her, Lucia responded, but Sarah didn't catch it. She was already walking toward the front of the class, her mind stuck on the idea of Eduardo cheating on Roberta. Heat tinted her chest and face. Anna was right. Eduardo's gesture wasn't innocent after all. Eduardo's actions matched Philip's. He sought only to satisfy his own needs, regardless of the consequences to his wife and—Sarah looked back at Lucia—and daughter.

Her throat tightened. No, Eduardo's choices made Philip's seem tame. Not only was Eduardo turning his back on his wife—but his entire family.

"Ms. Miller?"

Blinking, Sarah focused on the class.

Cira stood at her desk.

The rest of the students stared with questioning gazes.

"Ms. Miller," Cira repeated. "Can we go now?"

Sarah checked the clock—two minutes past dismissal. How had she not heard the bell? She cleared her tightened throat. "Class dismissed. And don't forget to turn in your papers."

The girls left promptly.

But this afternoon, Sarah didn't accompany them to the pick-up line. Clutching Lucia's paper, she headed straight for her dorm room, straight for her desk, and straight for Eduardo's business card. She balled it and tossed it in the trash. *Friendly, my ass!* Could she have been more naive? If her judgment of men were any worse, she'd have married an ex-con with a foot fetish and two mistresses on the side.

She dropped her gaze on the scrunched card, and her stomach twisted. Had she brought this attention on? If she hadn't fallen over him like a starry-eyed schoolgirl, she might not be in this mess. She sat at her desk and picked up Lucia's sketch—beautiful, sweet Lucia. If ever a reason existed to worry about Eduardo's behavior, Lucia was it. Sarah needed to fix this—for Roberta and, of course, for Lucia.

Heart pounding, she fished the balled-up card from the trashcan, flattened it on the desk, and rehearsed what to say. "Mr. Rossini, I must express my concern over our—" She bit her lip. "Mr. Rossini, I think it best we communicate only on a professional level, and…and did I tell you how much I admire your family? You really are blessed."

Maybe "blessed" was too much. "You must be proud," she said aloud. Yes! That excuse would work. The business card in one hand, Sarah picked up her phone and punched the digits. But as her thumb hovered over the call button, the phone buzzed with an incoming call. A US number, with no caller-ID. Sarah answered.

"Ms. Miller? This is Judy French, your attorney."

"Ms. French. Good after—" Sarah recalled the six-hour time difference. "I mean, good morning."

"I was just reviewing the documents from your husband's attorney."

"Oh." She shifted the papers on her desk, searching

for her planner. "So soon?"

"Ms. Miller, I'm calling because I have in my notes that you were to split the assets equally."

Sarah perked up. "Yes, that's correct."

"Well, I'm afraid he's changed the allocation."

"What?" The business card fell from Sarah's hand. She stepped back from the desk, her legs hitting the bedframe. "But we agreed on an even split."

"Did you have a mediator?"

Sarah's knees wobbled. "No."

"Did you sign any agreements?"

A shakiness struck her hands. "No."

"Then he has every right."

"But...I..." Ms. French was mistaken—*had* to be mistaken. Dropping to the bed, she pulled the phone from her ear and stared. Ms. French's muffled voice sounded in the room. Philip wouldn't have changed the terms? Would he have?

Chapter 11

How could Philip do this? *He* suggested the amicable split, *he* recommended dividing their assets fifty-fifty, and *he* advised not to waste money on mediators or litigation.

Sarah buried her head in her hands. *And I believed him.* "Stupid, stupid, stupid!" She slapped a hand on the desk.

Her phone dinged, and Sarah raised her heavy head. *New e-mail received. Sender: Judy French.* An angry pulse throbbed in her temple. She peeled her hand from the grainy hardwood and winced at the sting in her palm. She opened her laptop, pulled up the attachment, and scrolled. Near the bottom, bright yellow highlighted one sentence.

Proceeds of the sale of 850 Mt. Vernon St. shall be split as follows: 65% to Mr. Philip Flynn, 35% to Mrs. Sarah Flynn.

Sarah's stomach plummeted. "Sixty-five, thirty-five?" The words tore out of her mouth. "Damn it." She smacked the desk. "Damn it!" She whacked the desk again...and again. She hit the wood so hard her laptop shook—so hard her palm swelled.

With shaky hands, Sarah slammed shut the laptop. Ripe breaths came rapidly, and her pulse soared. *Effing Philip Flynn.* How had she been so naive to trust their verbal agreement? He'd probably always planned on this bait and switch. Or maybe Amanda suggested to squeeze her for another—

She punched several numbers into her phone's calculator—$8,540. $8,500! An angry growl ripped from her throat. Damn Philip Flynn and damn husband-stealing Amanda, too! Her phone still in her grasp, she pulled up Meredith's contact. But then she hesitated. Meredith had the brilliant idea for her to take this job. What had she said? "Everything will be fine." Meredith and her cheery attitude. She should have listened to—

As Sarah tightened her grip on the phone, she shifted her gaze to another contact—her mother's. The cross on the wall would have to burst into flames before Sarah called her. If she had to listen one more time to Mom's exasperated, "I told you not to leave D.C.," she might smash her phone into a thousand pieces—her laptop, too.

Her chest burning, Sarah exhaled and put down the phone. How had everything gone so horribly wrong? She toggled her phone between Meredith's and Mom's contacts, but she didn't call either. A new thought percolated, redirecting her anger from outward to inward; Meredith and Mom hadn't gotten her into this mess. *She* had. And she would have to get herself out.

****

Two hours and three cups of tea later, Sarah still sat in front of her laptop. Figures covered a sheet of paper. Each counter suit to Philip would cost eight hundred dollars. But how many counters would she need? One? Five? A dozen? And what if they couldn't reach an agreement? Litigation—costing at least ten grand—would be needed and flights to and from Rome. Another twelve hundred. And that scenario assumed

Sister Maria would even grant the time off.

Sarah snorted. Yeah, right. Sister Maria would more likely hand her a pink slip and march her straight to the confession booth. Sighing, she reopened her laptop and logged into her bank account—just over five thousand dollars left. Moving trucks, airfare, and the mind-boggling bill from the fertility center ate up the rest.

Hollowness grew inside her—a dark cloud replacing all rational thoughts. She scanned the desk—numerical figures, her silenced phone, a clutter of windows open on her laptop—and everything spun.

Cost aside, could she stand to prolong the divorce for one minute longer?

She finished the last drop of warm chamomile tea, pulled on her fuzzy, teddy-bear slippers, and buried herself under the covers. But a chill still rattled inside. Sarah hugged her knees to her chest. *Can I really make a counter suit?*

****

By Monday afternoon, Sarah still hadn't come to a decision. She only knew that the longer she waited, the more likely she'd need shock therapy—or at the very least, a prescription for strong anti-depressants.

"Are you listening?"

"Huh?" Sarah blinked. From her vantage point at the school's entrance, the daily pick-up line came into focus through the hazy eyes of a sleepless weekend.

"I was telling you Juan bought me these earrings." Anna cocked her head and pointed toward diamond stud earrings.

"Oh, right." Sarah studied the earrings, but like everything else in her view, they had no luster.

"They're very nice."

Anna squinted her eyes. "Are you sick or something? You don't look well."

"Me? No, no. I'm fine." Sarah yawned. If she took the deal, she could go back to the way things were. She could sleep and not worry about Philip Flynn ever again.

A horn beeped, and Anna's elbow jabbed her side. "He's waving at you."

"Huh?" Sarah scanned the staircase filled with departing students.

"Lucia's father." Anna pointed toward the line of cars.

At the front of a line, a blue Mercedes idled, and Eduardo stood next to the driver's side. He smiled and waved.

Sarah didn't raise her hand and didn't return his smile. She glanced from him to the back seat, where Lucia sat in a booster seat, and back to him. Where had her gumption to confront him gone? Where were the anger, the conviction, and the lust? None of the feelings remained. Her emotions shriveled like dry tea leaves.

Sarah dropped his gaze. How many more days could she go on like this? And to what end? Only one way remained to reconstitute herself—to live again. So what if Philip got the last victory? Her marriage had only been one long battle that slowly wore her down, anyway. She needed to be done with Philip Flynn. Turning on her heel, Sarah marched straight to her room, where she immediately sat at her computer, opened her email, and typed.

"Sarah?" Anna called through the closed door. "Can I come in?"

"Yeah." Sarah closed her laptop.

Across the room, Anna opened the door and entered. "What's going on? You haven't been yourself all day."

Sarah didn't look at her—she couldn't, for fear she might break down. "Nothing."

"What do you mean, nothing? You just ignored the hottest dad in school and left me standing there like an idiot."

Tears filled Sarah's eyes, but she blinked them away. Anna's tiny hand touched her shoulder.

"You can tell me."

"It's…it's…" Sarah's voice faltered as the tears fell. "It's my divorce settlement."

Anna rubbed her back. "Yes?"

"My husband… He…" Sarah wiped the tears with the back of her hand. "He's a complete a-hole." The story spilled out through a mixture of sniffles, sobs, and occasional profanity. She told Anna about everything: the affair, the failed fertility treatments, and the debacle of a divorce agreement. When the words finally stopped spewing from her mouth, she felt like she finished running a marathon. "Come on," she said to Anna, who made herself comfortable on her bed. "I'll buy you dinner." Sarah grabbed her purse.

"Wait." Anna caught Sarah's wrist. "What about the papers?"

"I don't know. I'll figure them out later."

Anna turned down her mouth. "I don't think so. Get on the phone." She stood. "Now."

Sarah stepped back. "I don't know, Anna."

"He's bluffing." Anna snatched Sarah's purse and rifled the contents. "He knows you're here, short on money, and desperate for this divorce to be over." She pulled out Sarah's phone.

Sarah took a long look at Anna. A nervous energy tingled in her fingers, and she seized the phone from Anna's outstretched hand.

"Call the bluff," Anna said. "Counter."

Inhaling deeply, Sarah pulled up her attorney's number. Was she really taking the advice of a twenty-three-year-old whose longest relationship lasted six weeks?

"What are you waiting for?" Anna scrunched her eyes and placed hands on her hips.

"Um, I…" Sarah's pulse quickened, but she pressed the green button. *Please go to voicemail.*

"Judy French."

"Oh, uh, hi, Judy. Sarah Miller. I've, um, I've decided I'd like to counter." Her heart thudded in her chest.

Anna flashed a reassuring smile.

"Great. What are the terms?"

"Terms? Oh, fifty-fifty."

"What?" Anna opened her eyes wide, and she grabbed Sarah's arm. "No! Sixty-five, thirty-five."

"Wait"—her voice quavered—"I mean sixty-five, thirty-five."

"And he pays lawyer fees," Anna said.

Sarah repeated the words to Judy.

"All right," Judy said. "I'll be in touch as soon as I hear."

"Thanks." Sarah hung up. Had she really one-upped Philip?

Anna grinned.

"I can't believe I just did that." Sarah released a

tight laugh.

"Feels good, doesn't it?"

With a smile, Sarah wrapped her arms around her waist, a glow blossoming inside. "Yeah. I guess it does."

"Al Forno's?" Anna lifted her chin.

The glow morphed into tiny bursts of energy pulsating through Sarah's chest, her arms, her fingers. She blinked and refocused on Anna, whose eyebrow was spiked up in question.

Sarah smiled. "Spaghetti alla carbonara?"

"You know it." Anna linked elbows with Sarah. "You going for the caprese salad?"

Sarah closed her eyes and imagined the scent of fresh mozzarella, thick slices of tomato with basil, and tangy balsamic vinegar. Her stomach rumbled. "As always," she replied. She followed Anna out the door. "And you know what? Tonight, I'm definitely saving room for dessert."

"Ooh. Are you thinking what I'm thinking?"

Sarah grinned and nodded.

"Gelato!" Anna said.

"Gelato!" Sarah said in unison. She grabbed Anna's elbow and dashed to the restaurant.

For the next few days, Sarah kept her phone with her at all times: on vibrate, shoved in her pocket during lessons or ringer on high, delicately placed on the edge of the sink during showers. But by Thursday's play rehearsal, she still hadn't heard from Judy.

Sarah finished sketching the forefront of the panels—an outline of the buildings. The scale seemed right, but something was off—the image didn't match the sketch in her book. She chewed the back of her pencil and stepped back. Why did the panels look so strange?

"*Signorina* Miller," said a voice behind her.

Spinning, Sarah found Mr. Moretti standing before her. He stared at the backdrop.

She dropped her sketchbook and stumbled back, nearly tumbling into the panels. She caught the edge of one with her hand and balanced herself. "*Buongiorno.*" She gave a tight smile.

With a curt nod, he approached the panels, rambling in his nasal Italian.

What was he saying? Order? Arrangement? She shook her head.

He frowned then continued with more grandiose gestures. He pointed first to the joint between the panels and then to her sketchbook on the floor.

"Oh, *capisco*!" She drew the blueprint for the right panel on the center one. How could she have been so distracted?

He squeezed out a wry smile, accentuating his pudgy cheeks. His eye twitched before a scowl settled on his face. In a swift motion, he bent down and unlocked the casters on the base and reversed the panels.

"*Grazie*," Sarah said.

He nodded then disappeared behind the curtain.

Sarah surveyed the three panels. The scene took shape. And Mr. Moretti wasn't upset. At least—no more than he usually was. She could cross out pissing off Mr. Moretti from her list of worries—well, for the time being. She made her way onto the stage.

Near the curtain, students rehearsed with Anna, Lucia among them.

Sarah planted herself behind Lucia.

Lucia flipped the page of her script, revealing the highlighted text.

Only a few lines remained before Lucia's. Sarah tensed. Would Lucia be okay? She'd only practiced with her once.

As she clutched the script, Lucia tapped her light-up sneakers.

Sarah took a step forward and patted Lucia's shoulder. "I'll read with you," she whispered in her ear. Lucia's shoulder relaxed under Sarah's hand.

"Thank you."

When the time arrived, Sarah read the line loud enough to cover Lucia's shaky voice.

Anna raised an eyebrow.

"Don't worry," Sarah mouthed silently.

As the words left her mouth, her phone buzzed in her pocket. Without bothering to excuse herself, she rushed off the stage, pressing the green icon as she barreled through the auditorium doors. "Hello?"

Silence.

"Judy? Is that you?" She wrung her skirt with her free hand.

"*Buonagiorno, Signorina Miller!*" a computer-generated voice said.

What? Telemarketers worked here, too? Sarah ended the call with an assertive thumb-click. She dropped her skirt from her hand and frowned. Would Judy ever call? Would this marriage ever be over?

Sarah returned to the auditorium, kicking open the door with her heel. Rehearsal had apparently wrapped up, as the children gathered their belongings and joined their waiting parents—all except for Lucia. She stood with someone Sarah had never seen before—a man about Eduardo's age, maybe slightly older, with slicked back hair and a goatee. Lucia cowered by the man's side. Sarah's senses rose to high-alert. As she started across to them, she narrowed her gaze, pursed her lips, and squared her shoulders. He'd need to show identification, hell maybe even provide fingerprints, before she'd let Lucia leave with him.

"I'd stay away from that one," Anna said.

"Why?" Sarah spun. "Who is he?"

"Remember our conversation about dads and their gestures? Lucia's dad likes to communicate with *his hands*."

His hands? Oh, hell no. Sarah took a step in Lucia's direction then stopped. "Wait—Lucia's dad? He's not Lucia's father." She searched Anna's face for an explanation.

Anna raised an eyebrow and cocked her head to the side.

Did she have to be such a know-it-all? Sarah peeked over her shoulder; Lucia reached the man. Sarah's pulse soared. She turned back to Anna and huffed.

"No," Anna said. "He's her stepfather."

Stepfather? Sarah gasped. Then Eduardo wasn't Roberta's husband. She slumped her shoulders. What had she done?

Chapter 12

Montgomery, Alabama. Juneau, Alaska. Phoenix, Arizona.

Sarah stared into the darkness. Was this the second or third time she'd recited the capitals? She pulled up the comforter, snuggled it under her chin, and forced herself not to check the clock.

Little Rock, Arkansas. Sacramento, California. Denver, Colorado.

She closed her eyes. Why wasn't Dad's trick working tonight? It always worked—except, apparently, when Eduardo's warm eyes, his mellow baritone, and his toned stature occupied her thoughts. She drove her foot into the mattress. God, she was stupid! How had she mistaken Eduardo and Roberta as a married couple? Judging by the way Roberta ranted at him, the pair wasn't likely to spend much time in the same room, let alone share a house together. She sighed. Perhaps if she worked more on her Italian, she wouldn't have been so confused.

From her bed, she eyed the wrinkled business card. Why had she ignored him at pick-up? Now, he probably thought she was moodier than a pubescent teen. She squeezed shut her eyes.

Hartford, Connecticut. Dover, Delaware. Tallahassee, Florida.

A girly giggle resonated through the walls. Sarah

129

checked the time, eleven thirty. With a groan, she crawled out of bed and grabbed her robe. Undoubtably, Flora was the offender; she was notorious for breaking curfew, especially on Sarah's watch. Probably did on Anna's watch, too, but Anna wasn't a stickler for rules. And Anna didn't have Sister Maria on her back.

Sarah dragged herself to the second floor and followed the laughter to the room of two upper-school students. She knocked lightly on the door then used her key to open it.

Inside, Flora twirled in a skin-tight dress.

On the bed, Natalia sat with knees tucked beneath her, her eyes bright.

"Girls, I called lights out at ten."

"*Bene*," Flora grumbled, coming to a stop. She hopped onto the bed and picked up two pairs of tights. "Which one do you think, Ms. Miller? Black or blue?"

Sarah frowned. "I said lights out."

"But Ms. Miller," Natalia chimed in, "Flora has a date."

Sarah folded her arms over her chest. "Not on my watch she doesn't."

"Not tonight." Flora laid the tights against her red dress. "Tomorrow."

Sarah raised an eyebrow then frowned. Even students at an all-girls school knew how to get a date. She backed out of the room, pulling the door closed. But just before it clicked shut, she poked her head back in and gave Flora a once-over. "The black." She smiled and closed the door. Flora had better hope Sister Maria didn't catch wind of—

At the end of the hall, Sister Maria stood. A glare etched into the nun's gray eyes.

Sarah froze. "Sister, I mean, *Suor Maria…Flora… sentire.*" She couldn't string together the words. She puffed her bangs from her eyes and stepped forward, starting again in English. "Flora and Natalia were, you know, being girls. But I took care of them."

With a straight face, Sister Maria nodded. "I saw the light from my room. Did you assign them detention?"

Sarah shook her head. "Just a warning." *Does that statement count as lying?*

Sister Maria turned toward the stairs.

With Sister Maria's back to her, Sarah silently crossed herself. Couldn't hurt. She scrambled to catch up.

"Quiet evening." Sister Maria fixed her gaze straight ahead. "Will you turn in soon?"

Faltering, she missed a step. She steadied herself with the banister. Was Sister Maria referring to her late-night—or rather, all-night-long—adventure with Anna? Sister Maria's words were burned into her memory. *I had hoped you would be a positive influence on Miss Franklin.* Sarah's cheeks burned. "Yes, I will," she answered.

"I don't mean to imply you shouldn't enjoy yourself," Sister Maria continued. "Perhaps just not to the extent Anna does."

Sarah let her gaze drift to the chandelier. Rows of crystals bounced light over the sweeping, spiral staircase. *I bet the theatres in Rome have even more grandiose décor.* "I would like to see the orchestra or opera or attend an evening art exhibit. I just…" She bit her lip as she let her voice trail off. Why was she telling this to her boss?

At bottom of the stairs Sister Maria placed a hand on her shoulder. "Time is needed to make friends in a new place."

"Yes, it is." Sarah started toward her room.

"I'd be happy to introduce you to some of the other teachers—or even some students' parents."

Sarah paused, her teeth finding the inside of her lip; she didn't turn back. Did Sister Maria know about Eduardo? Perhaps she'd caught Sarah staring like a schoolgirl? She didn't relish the thought. She also didn't relish Sister Maria's help in that area. If Eduardo already thought she was moody, how would enlisting the help of Sister Maria make her look? Like a nutjob? She released the grip on her lip and glanced over her shoulder. "Thank you, but I can manage."

After saying goodnight to Sister Maria, Sarah returned to her room. Her back pressed against the door, she stared at Eduardo's business card. A shiver tingled her spine. Sister Maria's assessment couldn't have been more dead-on. She should enjoy herself. She should make new friends. And...she should go out—maybe, even with Eduardo.

Sarah smiled and rushed to her bed, eager for sleep and eager for a new day. Because tomorrow, she planned for all of those things to happen.

****

The next morning, Sarah stood by the curb at drop-off, greeting the students as they exited their vehicles. Frowning, she picked a lint ball from her nicest twin-set; the pilling was compliments of the coin laundry on the corner. If only she owned a wardrobe like Anna's, or even Flora's—not that she could fit into either of their clothes. Well, maybe she could fit in Flora's clothes, but not Anna's toddler-sized get-ups. She sipped her third cup of Earl Grey tea. If she had many more nights like the previous one, she'd need to start taping up her eyelids.

She spotted a dark car with Lucia in the passenger seat. She pinched her cheeks and rubbed her lip-glossed lips. Her heart thudded in her chest. *Get a hold of yourself, Sarah. You're a grown—*

The approaching car wasn't a Mercedes, but an Alfa Romeo. And the driver wasn't Eduardo. He was Lucia's stepfather.

Sighing, Sarah took a step back.

Lucia rolled down her window. "Ms. Miller! Ms. Miller!"

So much for retreating.

The car stopped.

"Good morning, Ms. Miller." Lucia climbed out of the car.

"Good morning, Lucia." Sarah helped her from the car. She pressed a hand onto Lucia's backpack, slammed the car door, and started toward the building.

"*Buongiorno,*" a voice called out behind her.

Sarah stiffened but forced herself to turn.

Lucia's stepfather leaned across the passenger seat. "*Mi chiamo Leonardo de Luca.*" He drawled through the rolled-down window.

"Ms. Miller. Lucia's English teacher." *Please let him not understand English.*

"I'm Lucia's stepfather," he said in thickly accented English.

Today is not my day. "Nice to meet you." Sarah's phone vibrated, and she yanked it out as she backed away from the car. Who in the world called at this

133

hour? Mom. *Oh, hell.* She turned back to Mr. De Luca.

His gaze swept over her body.

A flush rushed her chest. Dear God, was he appraising her? She gave a curt nod, turned, and answered the phone. "Mom? What's wrong?" Behind Sarah, the Alfa Romeo revved.

"Sweetheart, I've got the best news!"

Sarah checked her watch and did the calculation. "At two in the morning?"

"I couldn't sleep. I was online, and guess what?"

"Make it quick, Mom. My class starts in five minutes."

"I just landed the most fabulous deal on a hotel, and it's only two blocks from your school."

Sarah's stomach dropped. "Mom, that place is a hostel. You have to share a bathroom."

"Oh, that's okay. I'll just use yours."

Mine? Did people in their thirties have strokes, because she felt like she was about to have one.

"And I've been meaning to ask," her mom continued, "did the divorce papers come?"

Definitely a candidate for a stroke. "Uh, no. Haven't heard anything." The crosses hanging at the entry of the school judged her. At least truthfulness wasn't a commandment. Respecting one's parents, on the other hand… Sarah swallowed hard. "I've got to go, Mom. Love you."

Yep, definitely not my day.

****

As the day wore on, Sarah's interest in seeing Eduardo waned again. How had she considered dating so soon? She hadn't even heard back from Judy—and if the news wasn't good, then she'd *really* be in for an awkward conversation with her mother…and Meredith. Neither knew of the divorce dispute yet.

As Sarah paced the rows in her classroom, she collected vocabulary quizzes from the *primo tres* students. At least she'd have something to keep her busy over the weekend. Would Philip's reply really drag on until next week? Could she survive two more days of waiting?

She scanned the papers as the students placed them on her desk. Lucia's was definitely a hundred. But Cira's? Sarah sighed. Did Mr. Moretti not encourage the child to study? She shoved the paper to the bottom of the stack—always best to grade the worst papers last. "Ten minutes left. Please take out your book and spend the rest of class reading."

The students pulled out their copies of *Charlotte's Web*. Most flipped to the middle of the book. Some, like Cira, were still on the third chapter. Only Lucia didn't read *Charlotte's Web* at all. Leaning forward on her elbows, Lucia was engrossed in *The Phantom Tollbooth*.

With a furrowed brow, Sarah walked over, knelt, and lowered her voice. "Lucia, where is your assigned book?"

Lucia scarcely pulled her gaze from the book. "I finished it. I asked my dad to get me this one." Her gaze locked on the page, she gave a head nod to the bulletin board. "I saw it on the board."

"Well, that book's for *primo quattro*, but I'm sure you can manage." Sarah smiled.

Lucia looked up at Sarah then, wearing a wide smile.

Sarah bent closer. "If you think it's okay, why

don't you stay after to practice your line? Will your ride mind?"

Lucia's smile broadened, and she shook her head. "That would be great." A few minutes later, when the students departed from the room, Lucia stayed back.

Sarah took a seat atop a student desk.

"You can put down the script, Lucia. I know you have it memorized."

Lucia lowered the script, which blocked her face. All trace of a smile was wiped from her face.

"Good." Sarah stared Lucia in the eye. "Now, I'll tell you a trick. Instead of looking me dead on, stare at my forehead." She pressed a finger to the center of her forehead.

At the front of the classroom, Lucia's gaze tracked upward.

"Excellent. To the audience, you appear to stare them in the eye, when you're not."

Lucia's brow line softened.

"Now, say your line."

Lucia's voice lowered to a whisper, her words indecipherable.

Sarah let a smile consume her face anyway. "Excellent!" She clapped. "Now say it loud—" Sarah's phone buzzed on her desk. She jumped up and grabbed it. Judy. Her breath caught, and she turned to Lucia. "I'm sorry, Lucia, but I have to take this call."

Her fingers shook—no, her whole body. She barely heard the faint thud of the door closing as Lucia left. She pressed the green button. "H-hi, Judy." The shakiness caused her to stutter.

"Good afternoon, Sarah. I've just heard from Philip's attorney."

"Yes?"

"The news isn't great, but he's reverted back to the original agreement, except…"

Jitteriness gave way to tightness. Sarah clenched her fists. *Except I have to pay his lawyer fees? Except now he's requesting alimony payments? Except Philip Flynn always has the last word?*

"…except he pays your lawyer fees."

Sarah nearly dropped the phone. "Come again?"

"I said, he agreed to pay my fees."

"Really?" She giggled the word.

"Yes, really."

After a celebratory dance around her classroom, Sarah rushed to the school entrance. Students gathered on the staircase and the sidewalk. Sarah elbowed past backpacks and pushed through a pair of giggling upper school girls until she found Anna.

"Anna! Anna!" She yanked on her friend's hand. "He took it. He took the deal! Well, not the whole deal, but almost." The story spilled out faster than Mr. Moretti could spew Italian. After she'd shared all details, Sarah sucked in the tepid autumn air, and her insides tingled with electricity. With a scrunched brow and open mouth, Anna looked like her head might start to spin. Then she broke into a smile—a genuine one. Not her usual smartass, I-told-you-so grin.

"That's so great!" Anna embraced her. "I knew it. We should celebrate, gelato, prosecco, the works. But—"A horn blared, and Anna glanced in the direction of the car. "But not tonight."

The jolt inside Sarah lost some of its energy. "That's right. Your weekend with Juan."

Anna picked up her duffel bag and slung it over her

shoulder. "I'm sorry. Bad timing. We'll celebrate Tuesday, when I'm back. I promise."

"Don't be sorry." Sarah gave Anna a send-off pat on the back. "I'll live vicariously through you."

Anna flashed a grin and hurried toward Juan's Ferrari.

Sarah gazed dreamily after them. Wouldn't a weekend in Florence be great? Not partying in the *Piazza della Signoria* like Anna but touring the halls of the *Uffizi*. She could walk the shores of the *Arno*; she could study the *David*.

"Ms. Miller," a low timbre resounded.

Sarah turned to see Eduardo approach. The sun glistened off his shiny curls, and his white shirt magnified his tanned skin. But something was different—a tightness set into his jaw and a stiffness consumed his usually relaxed shoulders. *Moody. He definitely thinks I'm moody.*

"Sister Maria tells me you're helping Lucia with her lines," he said.

"She does?"

Behind Eduardo, and across the schoolyard, Sister Maria stood with Lucia.

"Sister Maria doesn't miss anything." Eduardo ran his fingers through his hair. "I learned the hard way— more detentions than I can count."

Sarah gasped. "She was your teacher?"

"Principal. Six years."

"Is that why she's at a girls' school now?" She tipped up her lips in a smile.

Eduardo studied her for a moment, before he laughed.

His brown eyes gleamed, and his laugh was easy,

almost playful. The electricity in Sarah's veins recharged.

Eduardo's laughter subsided, and an uneasiness settled over him again. "I don't think she'd disagree. Anyway," his gaze shifted to his feet then Sarah's face, and back to his feet, "I just wanted to say thanks." He started toward Lucia and Sister Maria.

"Eduardo," Sarah called.

He stopped and wheeled around.

Sarah let the energy in her veins direct her. She swallowed hard, rolled her shoulders back, and smiled. "I wondered if you're still willing to help me with my Italian. I mean, if you're not too busy."

Eduardo's jaw softened, and his shoulders relaxed. His lips rounded into a smile. "Sure. When would you like to start?"

She relaxed her shoulders. "Whenever suits you."

"I've got Lucia this weekend. How about Monday? After school?"

"That would be great." Sarah's voice came out in an enthusiastic hurrah. She pulled it back, biting her lip. "I mean, I'd appreciate your help very much."

He smiled and held her gaze for a moment before turning to retrieve Lucia.

Sarah waited for them to depart—waited for one last infectious smile and carefree wave from Eduardo before they pulled away. A heady feeling swarmed her, threatening to make her sway. But beneath the dizziness, the electricity charged.

On the far side of the courtyard, Sister Maria stared at Eduardo's exiting car.

Was the stickler nun smiling? Sarah didn't step closer to see. Too many things raced through her mind:

the divorce, the deal, and a first date. She had to tell someone, and Sister Maria definitely wasn't that person. She raced back to her room, dialing Meredith on the way.

One ring.

Two rings. Shoot, was Meredith dropping Amber at the bus stop?

Three rings. Was Steven napping?

"Sarah? Is that you?"

Sarah reached her room, slipped inside, and slammed the door. "Meredith, I've got so much to tell you." The excitement in her voice returned, and she did nothing to mask it.

"What? What is—"

"I'm two signatures from divorce. Philip is paying my lawyer fees, and…" Sarah flounced on the bed, twirling her hair around one finger. "I've got a date." Hopefully, she didn't royally muck it up.

Chapter 13

The following Monday, Sarah sat in her classroom. She pulled her makeup from her desk drawer and applied a coat of mascara and a warm peach-colored lip gloss. With hardly a minute to spare between the children's departure and Eduardo's expected arrival, she settled on pulling her bangs into a clip. Why hadn't she thought to schedule their date for later in the day? Then she could have slipped into something more flattering than her frumpy work clothes. Not that the timing mattered much—she'd spent most of Saturday in search of a new outfit, but without Anna's help, finding a viable one was impossible. Did every boutique have to cater to five-foot-four-inch women who wore a size four, or whatever number that size translated to here?

She smoothed her skirt. At least she hadn't borrowed Sister Angelica's iron for nothing. Her work clothes would have to do.

A knock sounded on the classroom door.

"Come in!" Sarah shoved her makeup inside the desk.

Grinning, Eduardo entered. "Just making sure I don't plow into you again."

"How considerate," she teased, returning his smile.

He hesitated for a split-second as his gaze flitted from her eyes to lips then back. "You look different..."

Sarah held her breath. Was the makeup too much?

"…nice."

A smile curved Sarah's lips. "Thanks."

Eduardo took a step toward her. "Did you want to work here or somewhere else?"

"Oh, anywhere is fine." *Anywhere with some privacy.*

"It's a nice day. How about the park?"

What could be more perfect for a first date than a quiet bench secluded from passersby? "Sure." She forced any excitement from her voice. She walked a few blocks by Eduardo's side to one of the parks flanking *Balduina*. The lush green trees were a welcome change from the hustle and bustle of Rome. The scent of fresh grass and newly blossomed flowers filled the air.

Eduardo took a seat on a wooden bench shaded by evergreens. "So"—he crossed his long legs—"I haven't actually taught Italian to anyone before."

As Sarah joined him on the bench, she considered her response. "Why don't we talk about something else instead," or "Let's skip the lesson and move on to necking"—okay, maybe that idea was a little much. But the thought of making a move made her breath shake. "I appreciate your offer to help." She took care to make sure her voice came out steady.

"I thought maybe we could start with greetings then move on to typical phrases, questions."

"Sounds good." Sarah scooted a little closer.

He stared through his glasses then he cleared his throat, stiffened his posture, and delved into a lecture on formal and informal greetings: *ciao, buongiorno,* and *addio.*

His enthusiasm was cute, but Sarah inwardly

swooned. Why couldn't they pick up that conversation they'd started in her classroom a few weeks ago? *The Barber of Seville* was much more interesting than Italian greetings. Sarah suppressed a yawn, leaned on one elbow, and feigned as much interest as she could, but her gaze wandered to the sun dancing off the gray streaks in his hair.

Ten minutes into his lesson, Eduardo peered at her with a steady gaze. "Now," he said, "let's practice."

Sarah nodded. Was this a test? And more importantly, would he find her more attractive if she played the dumb blonde or the goody two-shoes student? Given her terrible Italian skills, hopefully he preferred the dumb blonde. Speaking only in Italian, she stumbled through a brutally slow exchange of vital information: names, where they lived, and jobs.

"*Insegnante*, teacher, has the same form for masculine and feminine," Eduardo explained. "The only difference is in the article. A man would say *io sono un insegnante*. A woman, *io sono un'insegnante*."

Uh…he said something different? She furrowed her brows. Yep, dumb blonde it would have to be.

"You try." Eduardo stared with raised eyebrows.

"Uh…" Sarah repeated what he'd said, but she sounded like a stuttering parakeet.

Eduardo laughed. "Well, that's a start." He scooted closer.

Yes! Hurray for dumb blondes.

"How old are you? *Quanti anni hai?*"

Sarah replied with what she thought was thirty-three.

He signaled the numbers three and three on his hands.

Sarah nodded. "*Quanti anni hai?*"

"*Trentasei.*"

After taking a moment to translate, Sarah held up her fingers—first three then six.

"*Brava.*" He smiled then looked away. "Are you married? *Sei sposata?*"

"*Si.*" The response spilled out before Sarah could stop it.

Eduardo jerked back, and his eyes shot wide.

"I mean," Sarah added in English, "I'm getting divorced. I just received the papers last week. That's why…why I've been a bit distracted."

"I understand," he responded in English. "I remember going through that process with Roberta. The negotiations, the custody battle." His eyes darkened. "Probably the hardest few months of my life."

"I can only imagine the difficulty when children are involved. Fortunately, Philip and I—" She stopped abruptly, shifted in her seat then started again. "Anyway, I'm sorry for the other day at school."

Eduardo waved a hand. "Eh, I chalked it up to unruly children." He inched a little closer. "So, *hai un ragazzo?*"

"A boyfriend?" Sarah raised an eyebrow playfully. "Is this part of the lesson or for your own interest?"

Laughing, Eduardo spread his left arm over the back of the bench. "Both."

Shaking her head, Sarah smiled—no, she beamed. Her smile lifted her cheeks so high, she swore they obscured her sight. "I want to jump."

"*Hai un…*" Should she begin with *una* or *un*? *Ragazzo* or *ragazza?* She hmphed. The words didn't matter. His answer would. She opened her mouth again, but his phone interrupted her sluggish response.

Eduardo sat back and pulled the phone from his breast pocket. His face soured. "Sorry. Work."

Sarah forced a smile, but the longer he talked, the more it slipped from her face.

When Eduardo clicked off the phone, he stood. "I have to get going." A sinking feeling seized her gut. She hadn't even found out if he had a girlfriend. She sighed, stood, and reluctantly followed him to his car.

"I'm sorry to cut our lesson short."

"It's no problem, really. You're busy."

Eduardo sighed. "Running a firm is hard. I have a secretary and an associate now, but work always creeps into my personal time."

Sarah lifted her chin. At least he categorized their meeting as "personal time."

"Perhaps we could continue later this week? Friday?"

"I'd love to." She smiled. "Same time?"

His phone rang again, and he groaned as he picked it up. "See you Friday," he whispered before hopping into his car.

Eduardo's car pulled away, and Juan's red sports car zoomed in.

Sarah waited by the curb. Anna would never believe her luck—not just one meeting, but a second one planned? Now they *really* had a reason to celebrate.

Juan strolled to the passenger side and opened the door, but Anna didn't get out. He leaned in, picked up a pair of bare legs by the knees, and twisted them out of the car.

Anna's clunky shoes hit the pavement with a thud, and her jelly-like body spilled out of the car.

"Anna, my God." Sarah brushed aside Juan and supported Anna. "Are you sick?"

Anna waved her off. "I'm fine."

Juan leaned into Sarah. "She refused to sleep, and…" He tipped back his head and mimicked drinking from an imaginary cup.

"I heard that." Anna shot a glare from dark-circled eyes. "I slept on the train."

"Six hours over three days isn't enough. Get some rest." Juan smacked Anna's ass. "Doctor's orders."

Sarah couldn't help but cringe. Was he really a doctor, or just some rich man with a fetish for roleplaying? Good looks and expensive car aside, if Sarah ever met him in a doctor's office, she'd declare herself healthy in a hurry. She grabbed Anna's elbow. "I'll take her inside."

He shrugged, muttered something under his breath, and slipped into his car.

Anna's knees gave out, and she started to fall. "Sorry."

Sarah clutched her waist, holding her upright. She slung Anna's duffel bag over her shoulder and started toward the dorm. "I figured the vampire lifestyle would catch up with you sooner or later. I thought you were the bunny who never stops."

Barely standing, Anna cocked an eyebrow.

Sarah rolled her eyes. "Advertising gimmick, my dear." With Anna attached, Sarah trudged into the dorm and up the stairs. For the first time since arriving, she wished for an elevator—Anna's bag weighed at least sixty pounds. Hell, carrying Anna might have been lighter.

Reaching Anna's room, Sarah flopped Anna into

her desk chair. She bent down to yank off Anna's boots. Only Anna could pull off green combat boots with a mini-skirt. "You heard your boyfriend." She hoisted Anna's arm over her shoulder. "Off to bed with you."

"Not yet." Anna's rag-doll body perked to life, and she pulled free her arm. "I've got to finish something first."

"Finish what?"

Anna flipped open her laptop.

A website was already up on the screen. *Oxford Graduate School Application.*

"It's due today."

"Anna, how could you have left it until the last minute? You're applying to Oxford, not a country club."

"I know, I know." Anna's hand fumbled with the mouse. "It's almost done. I...just need..." Her head sank into her elbow then plopped onto the desk. "...a little..." A steady whistle of breaths replaced her voice.

"Anna." Sarah planted her hands on her hips. "Anna!"

Anna didn't move; she didn't open her eyes.

"Well, if I ever," Sarah grumbled under her breath. She wheeled Anna's chair to the bed, tipped it, and dumped Anna in. Uncurling Anna's limbs, she covered her with a blanket. Sarah stepped to the desk. What was the harm in seeing how much she'd completed? If all Anna needed to do was click a couple bubbles, Sarah could do it for her.

She scrolled through the application: graduation with honors, scholarships, and publications. Anna hadn't fibbed—the application was nearly complete. Even the transcripts were uploaded. Only one question remained unanswered. *Why do you want to study at Oxford?* Anna typed in three words: *Enigma, cryptography, encryption.*

Enigma? Cryptography? Encryption?

Sarah nudged Anna's elbow. "Anna, what's the difference between cryptography and encryption?"

Anna muttered gibberish and raised an eyebrow but didn't open her eyes. She wriggled her nose, snorted, and then rolled to her side.

Great. Maybe if Sarah dated a computer engineer way back when, she'd have some idea what the hell Anna intended to write. What did codes have to do with Oxford? Sarah scowled in Anna's direction. But she owed Anna big time for the divorce settlement. She had to help her out, and if Sleeping Beauty wouldn't tell her, she'd have to figure it out herself—or at least, the Internet would.

Two hours, a slew of websites, and half a jar of Choctella later—thank goodness Anna had some food stashed in her desk—Sarah solved the puzzle. The Germans created the Enigma machine during World War I to encrypt messages; a British team later broke the code, greatly aiding the Allies in World War II. Oxford housed one of the world's most renowned cryptography research teams. Anna's motivation for studying at Oxford made perfect sense.

Sarah eased back in her seat and dipped her spoon into the Choctella. She licked off the sweet, gooey glob. And now, to concoct a response Anna might write. Sarah typed.

I was ten years old when I learned about the Enigma machine.

She stopped and highlighted the word "ten."

Giving her best true-to-Anna mischievous grin, she changed the "ten" to a "six." Anna wouldn't mind the embellishment...would she?

****

The following afternoon, Anna hadn't emerged from her room. Sarah covered for her by telling Sister Maria that Anna "wasn't feeling well." She didn't elaborate, and Sister Maria didn't probe, but her pursed lips and arched brow evidenced she wasn't buying the excuse.

Sarah planned on checking in on Anna after school, but an email from Judy changed her plans. The divorce papers were ready to be signed. So now she sat at her desk, and the electronic document displayed on her laptop. Philip's ornate signature decorated the top line. The second line, reserved for Sarah, was blank.

First, Sarah filled in the date—October thirteenth. They'd been married five years, six months, and eleven days—longer if she counted the two years they dated. And this electronic form was how it would end? No hug goodbye. No "we'll stay friends." No arrangements for their child.

Sarah lifted her hands from the keyboard and brushed away tears. The one thing she hoped to take from her marriage was a child. That precious miracle of life that she would have gladly given any percentage of the house for.

She reached for the touchscreen, to input her electronic signature, but stalled her hand midair. A shiver, emanating from her clenched gut, ran down her arms. Why? Shouldn't she be elated? Shouldn't she be glad to move on? To finally be done with Philip Flynn? She could have screamed "I'm free!" at the top of her lungs and at the same time also wanted to crawl into bed. She could have twirled, laughter seizing her gut but also could have cried.

She leaned back, and Philip's words echoed in her mind—the words he said the day they first met. *Sarah in 3B. How about that dinner?* He repeated those words, over and over. The exchange happened in the mail room of their apartment complex. As Sarah's first time living on her own after college, she'd been leery of talking to unfamiliar men. Even men as attractive as Philip. But he was persistent. Like a relentless melody, he wouldn't go away. Nearly every day she met him in the mail room.

"So, how about that date, Sarah in 3B?"

He asked the same question each time she ran into him. Eventually, Sarah succumbed. As an ache seeped into her chest, Sarah blinked away the memory. She wavered her hand and dropped it. How long would the memories of their marriage last? How long would Philip's song play in her mind?

Upstairs, the loose floorboard squeaked. Anna was up, and Whiz-kid wouldn't take long to figure out what Sarah did. Would she be upset? Grateful? Hopefully, she understood. A genius like Anna didn't belong at St. Theresa—at least, not in the long term. Anna needed to plan for her future. She needed a change. Oxford would be a change for the better.

Future. Sarah raised her hand again.

Change. She signed her name.

For the better. The cursor hovered over the Save button. Sarah closed her eyes and clicked. Her chest collapsed with a whoosh of breath. She'd done it. Her marriage was over. She'd freed herself from Philip.

Forever.

Upstairs, Anna's feet thumped lightly.

Before long, Anna would appear, and she'd demand answers. Sarah picked up her phone, which shook in her quivering hand. Taking a deep breath, she settled herself and sent a quick text to Mom and Meredith.

—*It's official. The papers are signed*—

Not a minute passed before her phone dinged. Meredith.

"I take it you got my message." No point bothering with hello.

"I hope you're pulling out the champagne."

"Not just yet."

"Well, that's not really why I'm calling. I want details, juicy description, on Eduarrrrdo?"

Sarah's heart fluttered, but...she refocused on the screen. Philip Flynn made her blush. Philip Flynn made her knees wobble. Philip Flynn stole her heart.

"Come on," Meredith urged. "You saw him, right? What happened?"

"I saw him. We had a nice time, but..." Sarah sighed. "But isn't a date too soon? I mean, I literally signed the papers five seconds ago."

"Pish. You're supposed to be having fun. You're not looking for a relationship."

Sarah chewed her lip. Flirting with Eduardo *was* fun. If they went out to dinner, or took in an opera, or toured an art exhibit, she'd have even more fun. "I guess so."

"And sex. When's the last time you had any? At least that you remember?"

"Meredith!" Heat burned Sarah's cheeks.

"Well? Am I right, or am I right?"

"I…" For a second, she lost herself in the possibility of waking up in Eduardo's strong arms, burying her head in his broad chest, and feeling the heat of his body pressed against hers. Warmth blossomed inside her, sending a rush to her chest and belly.

"Well?"

Sarah snapped back to the present. "Even if you're right, I wouldn't classify our meeting as a date but a lesson."

"Come on, Sarah! He's a man. He won't teach you Italian without an ulterior motive."

She grinned. "He did tell me I looked nice."

"See?"

"And we're going out—" Sarah bit her lip. "I mean, we're meeting again Friday."

"Like I said, he's into you."

"We'll see." But a smile planted itself firmly on Sarah's face.

"Be assertive, make sure you…"

A knock sounded on the door.

Anna entered. "You finished my application?"

Sarah froze. "Meredith," she spoke into the phone, "let me call you back."

Clicking off the call, Sarah stared at Anna. Her eyes, no longer shrouded in circles, were wide. Sarah took a deep, low breath. *Future. Change. For the better.* She only hoped Anna thought applying to Oxford was for the better.

Chapter 14

"Do I look okay?" Sarah stood beside Anna just inside the entrance of the school, watching the students hurry to their parents' cars on a rainy-day Friday pickup. Eduardo wouldn't be one of the dads in the cars today—at least, he'd better not. He'd bound up the stairs in a few minutes to meet Sarah. This lesson would be their second meeting—a meeting that would hopefully be more than just a lesson in Italian.

Anna scanned her up and down then unbuttoned the top three buttons on Sarah's blouse. "There. That's better."

Sarah frowned and re-buttoned one button. Was she really taking Anna's fashion advice? The girl who wore midriffs and combat boots with mini-skirts? The diamond studs in Anna's ears glinted. Well, Anna did know how to get a man. That expertise was what today was about.

Before she could overthink her choice, she undid the button again and stared into the washed-out afternoon. Students huddled under umbrellas, faces buried in ponchos, and made their way to idled cars.

Anna passed her a bottle of roll-on perfume. "Use this."

"This is ridiculous." Sarah dabbed the perfume on her wrists and neck, but she couldn't keep from smiling. She welcomed Anna's help, just as Anna appreciated her help on the Oxford application. In fact, Anna was so thrilled she suggested a visit to Al Forno's to celebrate.

"Six years old?" She'd thrown back a beer. "Sarah, you're such a terrible liar. You really should stick to the Miss By-The-Book act you've got going."

Sarah had laughed with Anna at that one.

"Do you want him to *want* you or not?"

Anna's voice brought Sarah back to the present. "Well, yes…and no." She handed back the perfume. "I don't want another Marco incident."

"Who's Marco?" Eduardo's rich voice boomed from the doorway.

Practically hopping out of her hand-me-down flats, Sarah spun. "Eduardo, where did you come from?"

"I stopped in to see Sister Maria first." He thumbed over his shoulder.

Beside her, Anna tapped a foot and cleared her throat.

Sarah shot her a wide-eyed glare that she hoped Anna read as "Don't embarrass me." "This is my friend, Anna. She teaches Upper Maths."

Eduardo nodded. "Pleasure to meet you."

Grimacing, Sarah held her breath.

"I'll let you two have some pri-vac-y." Anna flashed him a smile.

Sarah restrained herself from yanking Anna's spiky hair out by the roots. Her face felt like it would explode. From anger, or lack of air, she wasn't sure.

Grinning, Anna strutted down the hall.

"So…" Eduardo dropped his gaze to Sarah's exposed neck. "The weather's too wet to enjoy the park. Shall we grab drinks instead?"

154

"Drinks?" She released the stale air with the word. *Ben Carter. Marco... I don't even know his last name.* "No." The word tumbled out of her mouth. A furrowed brow replaced the playfulness in Eduardo's eyes. "I mean," Sarah started again, before he could reply, "I try not to drink." *Great. Now he probably thinks I'm a recovering alcoholic.*

Eduardo paused. "Do you want to stay here? Your classroom?"

If her mouth betrayed her, perhaps she better keep it shut. Sarah shook her head.

"Okay. How about my office?"

The offer wasn't as good as going for drinks, but it certainly beat the risk of having Sister Maria walk in on them unannounced. Sarah nodded.

As Sarah rode with Eduardo to his office, she regrouped by replaying the advice from Meredith and Anna. *Be assertive. Smile. Stick out your chest.* Well, maybe not that last part.

He made small talk with her along the way. How was Lucia doing in her studies? Had Mr. Moretti given her any more trouble? All through his conversation, his hands gripped the wheel so tightly his knuckles were white.

Eduardo wasn't his usual happy-go-lucky self. Maybe he was nervous, too? Or maybe he was offended she'd said no to drinks? Sarah sank back in her seat and spent the rest of the ride convincing herself that nerves caused his changed demeanor.

In the commercial part of town, Eduardo parked the car in front of a three-story building. He led Sarah to a glass door with "Rossini and Associates" etched in frosted letters. Inside, he gave a quick nod to a woman seated behind a reception desk then opened a set of double doors and led Sarah through. "So," he snapped shut the doors, "I was thinking we could work on verb tenses today."

Verb tenses? That certainly wasn't date-appropriate conversation. "Actually, I was hoping we might…" The words died in her mouth.

"Yes?" He thrust his left eyebrow above his glasses.

Sarah opened her mouth, but it felt like one of Anna's boots was lodged in her throat. So much for being assertive. She forced a smile instead.

Eduardo grinned.

But his cheeky smile and raised eyebrow told her he waited for her response. Sarah swallowed hard. "Verb tenses are fine." Then, as casually as she could, she pressed out her chest.

Eduardo's gaze drifted downward, but he quickly snapped it back. He pulled at his collar. "I'll get us some water."

His voice pitched more to a tenor, and he smirked. At least she could smile and push out her boobs. Sarah took the chance to examine the office. Spacious and uncluttered, the room was furnished with the executive desk, armchairs, and file cabinets one would expect in a lawyer's office. But her gaze was drawn to the Renaissance art that hung on the walls: Da Vinci's *Vitruvian Man*, Botticelli's *The Birth of Venus*, and Michelangelo's *The Creation of Adam.*

Sarah stepped to the far side of the room. A small metal frame encapsulated a paper CD insert featuring the faces of Luciano Pavarotti and Joan Sutherland— Verdi's *La Traviata*. The tattered edges of the insert weren't just a sign of its age, but of the owner's affection and respect for the music it contained. "You really *are* an opera fan." Sarah's words slipped out in a whisper.

"Yes."

His warm breath tickled her hair. She'd been so engrossed in the wall-hangings, she hadn't noticed him return. Sarah turned and was caught in his gaze. The room was so quiet Sarah could faintly hear the receptionist typing outside and could faintly hear Eduardo's quickened breath. Lost in his deep, steady stare, she knew their meeting was so much more than just an Italian lesson.

Eduardo cleared his throat. "Who doesn't love Verdi?" He handed her a glass of water.

Sarah cocked an eyebrow. "I'm partial to Puccini myself."

He narrowed his eyes. "Let me guess. Your favorite is *Bohème?* That's everyone's favorite."

Ha! But she wasn't everyone, was she? Sarah shook her head.

"No? *Butterfly* then?"

Shaking her head, Sarah stood tall, and a small smile crept to her lips.

He rubbed his chin. "Aha! *Tosca*. It must be *Tosca."*

Her smile widening, Sarah nodded.

He studied her. "So, you really are an artist, aren't you?"

"I would say that's a subjective term."

Laughing, Eduardo led her to the armchairs.

The chairs were positioned close together so that her knee brushed his, but Sarah made no attempt reposition herself—and neither did he. She smiled and delved into conversation that would be far too frou-frou for most. But for Sarah, their exchange was like enjoying a warm cookie and a cup of hot tea. She debated over the contributions of Verdi and Puccini. She bragged she saw the most Vermeers. Sarah joked Anna could tell them all the mathematical principles in Da Vinci's artwork. And not a single word was exchanged in Italian.

Two hours later, the clock on the desk chimed six times, and Sarah was eager to talk more. She cupped her face in her hands and leaned forward until her elbows touched her knees. "Why opera?"

"My mother." Eduardo set his cup on the desk, leaned back, and stretched out his arms and legs. "She was an aspiring opera singer. Probably would have been more successful if she didn't smoke. She introduced me…"

Sarah's phone dinged three times in her pocket, and she missed the rest of Eduardo's sentence. *Oh no.* Her alarm for hall duty. How had she forgotten? How had Anna forgotten? Her stomach clenched. If she didn't get back soon, Sister Maria would be looking for her. And who knew what punishment might be in store if she couldn't be found. She placed a hand on his sleeve. "Eduardo?"

"Hmm?" He put his hand on top of hers.

His touch was warm and soft, covering her fingers like a blanket. His thumb stroked the back of her hand.

On the desk, his empty glass blurred the hands of the clock. Sarah didn't move—couldn't move. Every muscle in her body clamped down like a fist. Was she nervous? Was she excited? Or was she afraid she'd rip off his super-hero glasses and throw herself on top of him?

Eduardo dropped her hand. "I'm sorry." He shifted his knees from hers, striking his right on the edge of the desk. He rubbed it as he stood. "I didn't mean to—"

"No." Sarah jumped to her feet. "Please don't be sorry. I...I..." She scrambled for an explanation. "I forgot I have to work tonight."

Eduardo retreated behind his desk. His gaze flitted from his feet to the clock, from the files on his desk to the *Traviata* jacket on the wall—anywhere but to her. "It's okay." He shoved files into a briefcase. "I have a lot of work to do myself."

The car ride back was quiet—too quiet. The wiper swooshed across the windshield like a whipping flag. The heater hummed. The tires splashed. Silence stifled the air like the thick mist outside. Sarah slumped in her seat. If only she had a few more minutes with him in his office. Not even flashing her boobs could save this date.

As the car pulled up to the school, the tires sloshed in puddled water. The gate, courtyard, and dorm blurred and melded into one.

Eduardo turned off the ignition, and rain drizzled on the windshield. "I'll walk you in." He didn't offer his hand.

Fog lingered at Sarah's feet and climbed the fountain at the center of the courtyard. Specks of stone façade peeked through the mist, but the buildings were otherwise hidden. Chatter echoed in the mist; dinner was over. The girls would come back any minute.

Moisture covered Eduardo's glasses and masked his eyes.

What emotion was hidden behind? Frustration?

Embarrassment? Disappointment? She stepped toward him. "Thank you so much for this afternoon. I really enjoyed our talk."

"Yes." Eduardo shifted on his feet. "You should get inside before you catch cold." He removed his glasses and brought them to his sleeve.

Sarah grabbed his hand. His skin was cool and slick. She took his glasses from him and cleaned them on the edge of her blouse. When she placed them back in his hand, she let her fingers rest on his—white on tan on black.

"Thank you."

His husky voice sent a shiver down her spine. Sarah lifted her gaze. His eyes, unmasked by both moisture and lenses, were rich and chocolatey. She tightened her fingers around his. "You're welcome."

Voices erupted behind him, and Sarah peered through the fog. Flora, Natalia, and a handful of upper-school girls emerged from the mist. Behind them strode a towering figure in black, Sister Maria.

Sarah released Eduardo's hand. "I'm sorry, but I have to go."

"But—" He bobbled his glasses, nearly dropping them.

"I can't stay." She raced to the dorm. In her room, she stripped out of her wet clothes and squeezed into her favorite jeans. She groaned. God, she royally screwed up this date. What would she say to Meredith? To Anna? *He asked me out to drinks, but I acted like I was in rehab. We had a great conversation, even held hands but...* She wiggled her fingers in the light of the desk lamp. His touch was so warm, so gentle, and so sincere. And she...she responded like she'd been just offered a pap smear.

A knock sounded on the door, and Sarah dropped her hand. What did Sister Maria want now? Another lecture? Was Sarah spending too much time away from school? Or was she in trouble for missing dinner? Was there a rule about that now, too? "*Un momento.*" Sarah yanked a T-shirt out of her dresser and slipped it on. *If it weren't for Sister Maria and her stupid rules, I might be spooning with Eduardo right now.*

She opened the door and her heart pounded. She gasped...*Eduardo.*

Chapter 15

"Eduardo? What are you doing here?"

"I ran into Sister Maria—"

"Sister Maria?" She poked her head out the door. The front door slammed, and a rush of air drifted down the hall, delivering a cloud of student giggles. The shadows of feet darkened the floor. Sarah darted her gaze from Eduardo to the shadows then back to Eduardo. Then she grabbed his shirt and yanked him inside. She kicked shut the door, and it closed with a thud.

She was alone with him, and he was close...so close. An intoxicating smell—his spicy cologne mixed with the dewiness of rain—filled the air. She still gripped his damp shirt, drawing the thin white fabric tighter against his muscular arms and shoulders. Sarah relaxed her hands to rest her palms against his hard, taut chest.

Eduardo stared down at her, a grin spreading. "Well, if I had known I'd get a greeting like this, I'd have visited you a long time ago."

His words sent vibrations through Sarah's hands, and she stepped back. A hot blush seared her cheeks. "Does she know you're here?"

"Who?"

"Who? Sister Maria. Did she let you in?"

He shook his head. "I entered with a group of

students. I asked them where your room was."

"You what?" Her voice came out shrill, and she stiffened her posture. "My God, Eduardo. Are you trying to get me fired?"

"Fired?" He lowered his chin.

"Sister Maria doesn't allow male visitors. This is an all-girls school, you know."

Eduardo furrowed his brow. Then he doubled over with laughter.

His deep, wall-shaking laughter must have resonated through the entire dorm. "Eduardo, please," Sarah pleaded.

He laughed so hard his eyes welled with tears.

Sister Maria would burst through the door at any second. Sarah stepped forward and grabbed his hand. "Eduardo, I'm serious. If you keep this up, Sister Maria will probably have me deported."

He quieted. "Sister Maria's tongue is worse than her lashing. I know from experience. But she might have a point." He removed his thumb from her grasp and ran it from the base of her wrist to the tips of her fingers. "Putting a man in a room this small with a woman is dangerous. Especially a woman who looks as good as you do in a pair of jeans and a T-shirt."

This time, Sarah felt her legs and arms go so limp she worried she might melt into a puddle. Freeing herself from his grasp, she stepped back, steadied herself against her desk chair, and struggled to catch her breath. "What are you doing here anyway?" Her voice came out in a raspy whisper.

Eduardo smiled. "Sister Maria. She told me you were working."

Sarah sucked in a breath and looked away. He

talked to Sister Maria? She was done for.

"I thought you were just making excuses," he said.

"Excuses?" She looked up. "Why would I do that?"

"I don't know." He cast his gaze downward. "Maybe for the same reason you never called me. Or for the same reason you said no to drinks—because you're not interested in me as more than a tutor or a friend."

Her heart dropped. "Eduardo, no."

He shifted his gaze. "But then I realized, maybe you're just shy."

Sarah nodded.

"Maybe, you're just nervous."

If she were any more nervous, she'd keel over. Yet somehow, with shaky legs, she stepped toward him.

In a quick stride, he removed the space between them. "I see an obvious solution to our problem."

"You do?"

"We need time to get to know each other. Time without distractions from work." He scooped her right hand in his, raised it to his mouth, and brushed his lips against her knuckles. "We need to go out on a date."

Her pulse quickened, and her legs threatened to give way. She leaned her hip into the chair. "A real date?" she whispered.

He nodded, his eyes alight. "I propose dinner. Tomorrow, my place. Unless"—he kissed her hand again—"you can think of reason we should—"

"No reason I can think of." Sarah bit her lip. She shouldn't seem so eager, should she?

He tightened his fingers around her hand, widened his smile, and held her in his gaze.

Sarah's breath quickened, and the air between them

thickened with her hot exhalations. She could stay in this moment, in his grasp and his stare, for eternity.

"*Aspettare!*" A young voice echoed in the hall.

Eduardo pulled back and dropped her hand. "Tomorrow." He darted toward the door with an extra spring in his step. "Six okay?"

"Perfect."

Eduardo opened the door, poked out his head then looked back. "I think the coast is clear."

Sarah smiled.

"Until tomorrow."

"Tomorrow."

He closed the door quietly behind him.

Sarah leaned back on the desk, jitters pulsing through her body. She was going on a date—a real date.

****

A knock sounded on the door.

Sarah opened her eyes. She turned to the clock next to her bed—nine thirty. When was the last time she'd slept in so late? She yawned, a smile percolating on her lips. She hadn't wanted to use Dad's trick of reciting state capitals last night—instead she'd reveled in Eduardo's cheeky grin, his witty compliments, and his sensuous touch.

The knock—or was it a thud?—sounded again.

"Just a minute." Sarah crawled out of bed, pulled on her robe, and opened the door.

In the hallway Anna stood holding a cup in each hand, her lips smooshed around a croissant oozing with Choctella. "Hmm mmm hmmm?" she said around the croissant.

At the sight, Sarah practically crossed her eyes.

Thrusting one of the cups toward Sarah, Anna then

used her free hand to dislodge the pastry from her mouth. "Would've used my key if I could've gotten to it. Here." She reached into the collar of her shirt, dug into her bra, and pulled out a bag, which she tossed over.

Bobbling it, Sarah caught the bag.

Anna stepped into the room. "I figured you could use some caffeine."

Sarah lifted the lid on the cup. The aroma of strong black tea with a hint of bergamot wafted out. "Earl Grey, my favorite." She took a sip—Earl Grey, indeed. Peeking inside the bag, she crinkled her nose. "A bran muffin?"

"No sweets for you until tomorrow." Anna ripped off a hunk of croissant, cocked back her head, and tossed it in her mouth.

Watching the action, Sarah salivated.

"That is…" She swallowed the bite and gave Sarah a grin. "Unless Eduardo serves some tonight."

Sarah widened her eyes against Anna's mischievous grin and strained against the bulging in her eye sockets. "How do you—"

"I'll coach you on Italian meal courses later. First things first." She tossed the half-eaten croissant on the desk and rummaged through the clothes in Sarah's closet.

Sarah took another sip of divinity before setting her cup on the desk and planting her hands on her hips. "Anna Franklin, could you please enlighten me as to how you know all the details of my personal life?"

"You know I'm a genius." Anna continued her rummaging.

"That doesn't make you clairvoyant."

Anna turned to Sarah and rubbed the wall with her hand. "I told you the walls in this place are thin."

"You were here? I thought you'd be out with—" She pointed a finger. "Wait a minute...Anna! You eavesdropped."

Anna wagged a finger. "Hey, I'm not the one sneaking men into the dorm."

"I didn't sneak him in. He came in by himself."

"Technicality." Anna returned to the closet, whisking hangers left and right. "But, to the point— why didn't you tell me he asked you out?"

"It happened less than twelve hours—"

"Eleven." Anna flicked a brow.

"All right, math nerd, *eleven* hours ago." She tapped a toe. "As I said, I assumed you'd be out with Juan."

"Eh, the doctor thing is losing its appeal."

"So soon? You haven't even been with him a month."

Anna shrugged. "I said six weeks was my max, not my min. But that's not important. What *is* important is you don't have a single outfit here that's respectable for a date."

"What about my black skirt and—"

"Nope." Anna grabbed her croissant and coffee on her way to the door. "Get dressed." She popped another bite. "We're going shopping."

After a forty-five-minute metro ride to northeast Rome, Anna led her into a six-story, New York Macy's-style, eat-your-heart-out department store, *La Rinascente,* Rome's one-stop shop for high-end fashion, décor, and accessories extraordinaire. Gleaming white travertine tile graced the floors. Bright lights streamed from cosmetic counters. If Sarah couldn't find something that fit her here, she really was a lost cause.

Grinning, Anna hopped on an escalator. "Shall we hit lingerie first?"

Sarah pinched a corner of her mouth. "That's not what I had in mind for a *first* date."

Anna shrugged. "I'm sure Marco's not complaining."

Gasping, Sarah scanned the store for any eavesdroppers. "Could everyone please stop bringing him up?" she whispered.

"Fine. We'll save lingerie for later."

At the top of the escalator, row upon row of racks boasted an assortment of dresses so diverse, both Anna and Sister Maria could find something here.

From the racks of dresses, Anna selected a chiffon gown and held it up.

Sarah frowned and picked up a black cocktail dress. "Too dressy."

"At least it'll be long enough." Anna shimmied down the rack.

"Very funny." Sarah examined the shimmery dress in her hand and winced. She'd be lucky if hit her mid-thigh. Groaning, she replaced it on the rack.

Lackluster, if not outright frustrating, shopping trips weren't unusual for Sarah because nothing ever fit. That's probably why she owned her button-up blouse in five colors and her A-line skirt in three. If she found something cut to fit her gangly limbs, she'd scoop up several pieces.

Sarah ran a hand over the chiffon gown—flowing green fabric, light and soft, with a sparkling crystal-embellished neckline. Philip's voice echoed in her mind. *You're looking lovelier than lovely.* She imagined his hand clutching her waist and parading her through crowds like she was his prize. The dress in front of her transformed from green to pink. The crystals shifted from the neck to the bust.

Sarah blinked, and the dress returned to the green one—not a dress never worn to a senator's inaugural gala nor a dress shipped off to a consignment shop because the owner's husband stopped inviting her to his events.

"What about this one?" Anna brought over a dark blue, cotton-knit dress and held it against Sarah. "Looks long enough. Try it on."

Sarah shrugged and took the dress into a changing room. The dress draped around the neck, leaving her shoulders and back exposed. The soft hemline hit just above the knee—a few inches above the intended mid-calf. The Empire waist hid her imperfect waistline then hung loosely. What bothered Philip more, her thickened waistline or the fact that her widening stomach held no child?

"If I had my master key, I'd be using it right now," Anna called through the dressing room door.

Sarah heaved a sigh and opened the door.

"Ooh la la." Anna gave a catcall whistle.

Scrunching her brow, she tugged at the fabric of the plunging neckline. "You don't think the cut is too revealing?"

"Of course not. It's perfect."

Sarah twirled. The dress stretched easily under her movement. "It feels comfortable." She checked the price tag. "And not too pricy."

"It also makes your boobs look bigger," Anna

added.

"Anna!" Sarah gasped.

"What? You know he'll be looking."

Straightening, she examined her profile in the mirror. Huh, maybe she could pass for a C-cup. "Okay. I'll get it." Now, if only she could guarantee Eduardo thought she looked half as good as Anna claimed she did.

Chapter 16

A knock sounded on her door at five minutes before six. Sarah covered her bare shoulders in the matching shrug she'd purchased that morning and sent a quick text to Meredith.

—*Wish me luck. And hugs and kisses to Amber & Steven*—

She turned off the volume and stashed the phone in her purse. *Shoulders back, chest out.* Wasn't that what Mom always told her? Or had Anna said it? She opened the door. There he stood, her Italian *pièce de résistance*, her perfectly steeped cup of tea. Eduardo wore a forest-green shirt that accentuated his olive-toned skin, and his cheeks had a freshly shaved glow.

He leaned in, kissing her on each cheek. He paused by her right ear. "You're radiant," he whispered.

His closeness revealed his cheek was as smooth as it appeared, and warmth bubbled inside her. The greeting was an Italian tradition, but one she had yet to experience—so much the better, to experience it first with him.

He pulled back, his gaze dropping. "The slippers are a nice touch, too."

Heat crept into her cheeks. Thank God she was wearing enough foundation to cover a zebra's stripes. "I can't believe I forgot..." She stepped back into her room. "Let me change them."

"You have any in a size forty-six? I could use a pair of those slippers at home."

Sarah slipped on Sister Maria's flats and returned Eduardo's banter with a playful flick of her brow.

"What? I always wanted a pair of…" He squinted and pushed up his glasses. "Porcupines?"

Sarah laughed. "They're teddy bears, Eduardo. Hasn't Lucia indoctrinated you in the species of stuffed animals yet?"

"I guess not." He extended an arm. "Now, if you don't mind, I've got a roast in the oven."

"God help us if it's a degree over medium-rare." She looped an arm through his.

"My thoughts exactly." He squeezed her arm and led her to his car.

After a quick ride, Sarah arrived at a high-rise apartment complex where a bellboy with a funny little red hat greeted her. As an elevator carried them up twelve stories, Sarah's stomach stayed on the bottom floor. Did Eduardo have to be good looking *and* rich? One would have been quite enough. She could think of plenty of things wrong with herself but none with him. She wrapped the shawl tighter around her shoulders.

The elevator stopped at the top floor.

"The penthouse?" Sarah swooned.

"I'm a sucker for the finer things in life."

Finer things. Sarah definitely wasn't in that category. She hugged the wrap closer. His flat was dark except for a lone desk lamp illuminating a stack of files, several briefcases, and a laptop. *A workaholic—that's his vice.* She knew a thing or two about men who valued jobs over relationships. Sarah shuddered.

"Are you cold?"

"Cold?" The temperature in the room was quite mild—probably from the heat of the oven. "No, I'm fine."

He extended a hand.

She gave him her shrug, and the coolness of her skin prickled in the warmth of the room.

Eduardo's gaze flitted over her neck, arms, and chest.

Sarah resisted the urge to snatch the shrug back. She took a deep breath, instead.

With his gaze steady on her chest, he widened his eyes as her breasts gently rose with her inhalation. He shifted his gaze back to hers. "I'd better check on dinner." He disappeared into the darkness.

Was she imagining it, or had his lower lip quivered? Sarah curled her own lips. Standing straight didn't feel like such an effort anymore. Maybe she really did pass for a C-cup. She walked over to the desk and its mess of papers. "You certainly aren't hurting for clients."

"I meant to clean that up."

"I make a habit of not bringing my work home, but I suppose that's easier when my home—if you can call it that—is fifty feet from my office."

"That certainly helps. I don't do work when Lucia's here. Or..." He rejoined her, holding a small remote in his hand. "...when I have guests." He pressed a button.

Somewhere a motor purred to life and all around the room, shades lifted from windows. Sarah immediately understood why Eduardo splurged on the penthouse. Tinted glass windows provided a panoramic view of the city—the twisting Tiber, the obelisk in St.

Peter's Square, and the *Castel Sant'Angelo*. But one building dominated the skyline—St. Peter's *Basilica*. The dome's golden orb and Gothic cross floated in the sky. The statues of the twelve Apostles hovered so close Sarah imagined she could reach through the glass and touch them.

"I've heard it said they're closer to heaven," Eduardo said.

Sarah shifted her head. "Who?"

"The statues."

"Then we must be, too."

Eduardo shifted his gaze to her, blinking his eyes rapidly. "That's funny. That's exactly what Sister Maria said."

"Sister Maria? She was in your place?"

"Once. When I was investigating my options."

"Wait—are you telling me you took Sister Maria apartment shopping with you?"

He gestured toward the room. "You can't deny the woman has good taste. Besides, I didn't have anyone else to go with." He turned back to the view.

Sarah kept her gaze on his face. Faint lines framed his mouth, and beneath his glasses, darkness tinted his usually mellow eyes. How did a man as friendly and charming as Eduardo not have anyone to go home shopping with? And Sister Maria? That outing sounded almost as bad as sharing a bathroom with her mother for a week.

The oven buzzed, and Eduardo stepped back. "I hope you're hungry."

His smiling eyes returned, and he led her to the dining table. Hungry she was, thanks to Anna's pre-date diet. But Sarah didn't regret it, because Anna's description of an Italian dinner was spot on—she practically needed to be a mathematician to keep track of the courses. *Apertivo, antipasti, primi.* By the time she reached the *secondi* and *contorni* courses, Sarah was sure she'd gained five pounds. But that didn't stop her from devouring the juicy *osso bucco* and buttery-soft risotto. Thank goodness she'd gone for the stretchy fabric dress.

After dinner, she helped Eduardo clean up. "You know, we were so busy stuffing our faces, I forgot to ask where you learned to cook like that." She wiped some crumbs into her hand. "Don't tell me Sister Maria helped you with your cooking skills, too."

Eduardo's laugh erupted from the kitchen, where he was busy packing up leftovers. He poked his head through the pass-through. "Thanks go to my Tuscan grandmother." He brought clutched fingers to his mouth and kissed them in a flamboyant gesture.

Sarah smiled back and returned the dishrag to the sink. "It's a miracle Lucia is so skinny."

"I don't think staying here two weekends a month is enough to fatten her up." The lines around his face returned as his eyes darkened.

Sarah touched his sleeve. "She's a wonderful child, Eduardo. You're so lucky to have her."

"Yes." He turned. "She's great. Kids are great."

Sarah stiffened. Was he looking for a woman who can give him more children? She gave a slow nod.

Eduardo placed his hands on her arms. "Why don't you make yourself comfortable while I fix some dessert?"

"Okay." As Sarah walked to the couch, she forced the exchange from her mind. *Fun. Not a relationship.*

Wasn't that what Meredith had said? She fished through her purse for her compact. She wouldn't let her past spoil her fun now—especially when that fun might include a kiss. She touched up her lipstick and popped in a breath mint, rushing so he wouldn't see.

Eduardo approached with a tray.

A touch of jitters hit her, and she clasped her hands in her lap to keep them from fidgeting. "Thank you again for dinner. I can't believe you went to such trouble."

"I enjoy cooking much more for others than I do for just myself." He set the tray on the coffee table. "Besides, I skimped on dessert."

The tray held two cups of coffee and a dish filled with blue, foil-wrapped candies.

He picked up a cup and offered it.

"Um, Eduardo...I don't actually drink coffee."

"Oh." He pursed his lips. "No coffee. No wine. What exactly do you drink? You only took water at dinner." He took a sip of the coffee.

Sarah gave a weak smile. "Tea. Usually tea."

"Ah." He placed the cup on the coffee table. "Well, I hope you have no objections to chocolate?"

"None whatsoever."

He picked up a candy from the dish and unwrapped it. "This candy is Italian. *Bacio.* One of my favorites." He lifted the candy to her mouth, and his fingers brushed her lips as he placed it inside.

Her lips tingled at his touch. Sweet milk chocolate melted in her mouth.

"And now I'd like to give you one myself," Eduardo said.

Chewing the candy, Sarah covered her mouth with

a hand. "One what?"

"*Un bacio*," he said in a whispered tone. "A kiss." He leaned in, but stopped, his lips inches from hers, his smile crinkling his eyes. "We really need to work on your Italian."

Sarah smiled back and closed the distance between them, pressing her mouth against his. His lips were soft and warm, and a hint of coffee remained on his breath. She lost herself in the rhythm of their mouths moving together. When she released him, the only sound in the room was his breath, heavy against hers. Sarah wiped smeared lipstick from his lips. "That was your best lesson yet."

"I'd be happy to teach you some other words." He bent toward her.

As he did, she caught a glimpse of the changing sky. She placed a hand on his chest, lightly resisting him. "Wait," she said in a whisper. She took in the warm halo of amber hues chasing the sun. "The sunset is so beautiful."

Eduardo shifted on the couch, his back settling into the corner. He extended his left arm. "Watch with me."

His embrace was as inviting as the picturesque scene, which begged to be painted. She scooted toward him and tentatively reclined.

He wrapped his arms around her, pulling her against his chest. "Mmm. This feeling is good." He squeezed her tighter.

She relaxed into him and gazed out at the slowly fading mixture of violet and ochre. The sun dipped out of sight, leaving a blanket of clouds, alight from dissipating rays. Yes, good indeed.

Finding the remote, Eduardo pressed a button.

Voices sang from some hidden source, as light as the clouds outside, blending in a familiar harmony. The *Lakmé* "Flower Duet." Sarah tucked her head beneath Eduardo's chin, letting the warmth of his body soothe her. She closed her eyes—just for a second—just long enough to bask in his tender embrace, to bottle it, and store it inside. In the same place where she held the memories of her father, of Steven and Amber, she now encapsulated this memory with Eduardo.

When Sarah opened her eyes, darkness surrounded her. The only light, a desk lamp, produced a steady flicker. A different song played now—a Verdi love duet. Pavarotti and Horne crooned. In the distance, the lights of the city illuminated the night like a swarm of fireflies. "Verdi. Your favorite," Sarah murmured.

Eduardo's chest rose with the quick inhalation of awakening before he exhaled.

A rush of air whisked her hair. Sitting up, Sarah scooted toward the middle of the couch. "I didn't mean to wake you."

He pulled back his legs with a mild grimace. "Another reason to conclude a meal with coffee." His gaze flicked to the two full cups on the coffee table.

Sarah stretched her arms above her head and smiled over her shoulder. "Tea does have caffeine," she teased. "But I'm sorry. I didn't mean to fall asleep."

"Don't be." He sat up. "I enjoyed being close to you."

Sarah studied him for a second. Was that a line, or was he being sincere? But out of the corner of her eye, a digital clock blared bright red digits. Ten thirty. She jumped to her feet. "My God, how many songs did I sleep through?"

"I don't know, but that's not the first time…"

Eduardo finished his thought, but Sarah didn't hear over her racing pulse. She was too busy envisioning Sister Maria peering out her window, catching Sarah entering the dorm after curfew. She picked up her purse and started toward the door. "I really need to get back."

"No, please." He stood, grabbed her wrist lightly, and pulled her back. "Stay with me." He closed his mouth around hers, letting his tongue brush against hers.

The kiss was deeper than before, and it sent a shiver up her spine. Sarah dropped her purse and slid her hands up Eduardo's back, pressing fingers into his muscular flesh.

He pulled away and murmured a hungry moan. Then he lowered his head and kissed the base of her ear, her chin, and her neck.

Sarah's breath quickened, and she combed her fingers through his hair—silky and smooth, like his lips.

His mouth followed the line of her dress to the valley between her breasts.

An inkling of doubt pulled her back. This date was, technically, their first. What kind of impression would it leave if she slept with him? She loosened her grip on his curls. "Should we be doing this?"

He pulled away briefly. "I don't see why not." His mouth found hers again while his hands reached for the zipper. He started to pull it down.

She couldn't stay the night…not tonight. Sarah stepped back from him.

"What's wrong?" He dropped his hands back to her waist.

She stroked his hair. "We barely know each other."

He pulled her left arm from his neck and kissed her wrist. "I feel like I know you better than most women in my life."

The statement was so unexpected, so heartfelt, it couldn't be true. Could it? "I guess I forgot to mention I have an eleven o'clock curfew."

Furrowing his brows, Eduardo released her arm. "What? Another one of Sister Maria's rules?"

Sarah dropped her gaze and gave a clumsy nod.

"Her age hasn't softened her one bit." He checked his watch. "What happens if I don't get you home in the next twenty-five minutes? Will you be forced to stay the night somewhere else? Here, perhaps?" He grinned.

"She doesn't like that either."

He cocked his head. "You speak as if from experience."

"I—" *Damn.* Had she said too much? She bit her lower lip. "I mean, she would rather me come home late than the next morning…I think."

He narrowed his eyes.

Would he probe further? Hell, if he ever acted as guilty as she, she'd have questioned *him*.

"I see." He whisked up her purse and extended it. "All right, I suppose I can't keep you here any longer."

On the walk from the car to the dormitory, Sarah rested her hand in Eduardo's, and his sports jacket hung over her shoulders. The cool, crisp air stung Sarah's cheeks.

"Feeling less nervous now?" he asked.

"A little." Hopefully, the rosiness on her cheeks didn't grow with the confession.

He squeezed her hand. "Nothing another date

won't take care of, I'm sure. How about Tuesday? I know you work the next day, but—"

"Sure." She flushed and suppressed a giggle. He wanted to see her again…in three days!

He grinned.

As Sarah climbed the stairs to the building's front door, Eduardo stayed by her side.

A chapel bell tolled in the distance. With each step, the bell tolled again.

Sarah's heart thumped louder, excitement brewing at the thought of another kiss.

"I had a wonderful time tonight, Sarah."

"Me, too." She reached for the doorknob, and the warmth of the building breathed into the night. "Goodnight." She stepped over the threshold.

Eduardo placed a hand on her hip and pulled her back. "Goodnight," he whispered before kissing her softly on the lips. He drew back and smiled.

Sarah didn't hide her smile, either. And surely her flushed cheeks were apparent. "Goodnight."

Still beaming, Eduardo turned and hopped down the steps two at a time.

With the bounce in his step, he looked more like a sixteen-year-old than a thirty-six-year-old. Sarah stepped back into the building and closed the door. She started toward her room but stopped.

Outside, Eduardo whistled the *brindisi*, the waltz from *La Traviata*.

She listened to Eduardo's whistle until the melody was too soft to make out. She resisted the urge to grip the sides of her skirt and dance off to her room. One date was too soon to feel so giddy. Something would go wrong…it had to.

Chapter 17

The next morning, Sarah bit into a dry piece of whole wheat toast. *Ugh*—bland would be an understatement. But if she wanted to shed the extra fat on her midsection before Eduardo's next invitation to stay the night—which hopefully would be soon—Choctella sobriety was a must. She chased the grainy bread with a sip of black tea—well, with a tiny splash of cream. A girl couldn't give up everything. As long as she didn't need to wriggle into blubber-busting, granny panties, she'd be content. Was that item even sold in Italy? If it was, she seriously doubted Eduardo had ever been with a woman who'd worn them.

Okay. Stop thinking about sex. She glanced at her phone. Nine a.m. was too early—too early to text Anna, too early to call Meredith, and *certainly* much too early to thank Eduardo for the date.

Two missed calls from Mom, both received during the date. If Mom wasn't the last person Sarah wanted to know about her date, she might call her; she was the one most likely to be up in the middle of the night. Meredith would certainly be sleeping, and she had a long time to wait until their usual Sunday afternoon catch-up. As for Anna…had she even come home yet?

Sarah washed down the cardboard bread and pulled up Anna's contact. She texted,

—*You up?*—

She paced the room but received no response. She sat back and drummed her fingers on the desk. How long should she wait to call Eduardo? Or did she just wait until he visited on Tuesday? Had they even discussed what time?

Opening her desk drawer, Sarah pulled out Eduardo's business card. She hadn't even given him her number. She typed in his digits, saved him as a contact, and chose an appropriate ringtone—the *brindisi* from *La Traviata*.

At nine forty-five, with no response from Anna, she twitched her fingers, letting her gaze stray back to the phone. She hovered her thumbs over the keyboard. How many years passed since she'd played this cat-and-mouse game? Too many. And she was too old to be playing games now. Besides, a simple thank you wouldn't come across as desperate. She entered Eduardo's contact into the sender's box of a text message.

—Thanks for last night—

She pressed Send then stared at her phone. Her chest tightened. The five flipped to a six. Nine forty-six. Maybe he was at church. The six flipped to a seven. Nothing. Maybe she should have gone to church. The seven flipped to an eight. Nothing. What the hell was she doing?

Ten minutes later, Sarah stared at her phone. When it dinged, she jumped. But the sound was only a notification of a new email—Mom. A wry laugh forced through Sarah's lips. This behavior was ridiculous—she was an adult. She lifted her chin. *Why is my mother up at four in the morning?* She opened the e-mail.

Subject: Don't be upset

Great. Don't be upset? What had her mother done now? Canceled her hostel in lieu of bunking at the dorm? She chomped down on her toast and read on.

Dear Sarah,

I called. I know you must be upset, but don't think about them. Your turn will come. I know it.

Call when you can.

Love,

Mom

The words blinded her. *My turn will come?* Those words were the ones her mother used when she talked about... Sarah gripped the arms of the chair. Who was having a baby? Meredith? No. She would have said something. Sarah's cousin, Nancy? Well, who cared? That girl had babies faster than Sarah could finish a container of Choctella.

Sarah chewed on her toast. Geez, Mom was prone to overreactions. Not like Amanda and Phillip were expecting. Sarah choked on the toast, the rough edges scraping her throat. Amanda, pregnant? She couldn't be. Sarah stared at the laptop screen. Did she dare look?

Trembling rushed her fingers, but she forced them on the keyboard. As she trudged her fingers over the keys, her pulse raced. She opened Philip's social media page. *Why, Mom, did you never unfriend him?* She scrolled down the page, straining her eyes to simultaneously look but not look. Then she found it. *So happy to announce that Amanda and I are expecting!*

Her stomach twisted. *No.* Sarah shook her head. *No.* The cardboard bread sat like a rock in her stomach—a rock she wanted to spit out and hurl against the screen. How could this pregnancy have happened? How could Amanda have *her baby*? She slammed shut the laptop and stood from her chair so fast it whipped back and hit the floor. She stumbled backward. Two years of demoralizing prodding, extracting, and injections, and not even one "yes," one pink line—not a single one. And this girl, this temptress, opened her legs and, voilà, she's—

Her phone beeped. Finally, someone texted her back. Meredith or Anna? Either one would know what to say to make her feel better. She grabbed her phone. *Eduardo*. Her breath caught.

—Sorry for delay.
Was in shower.
Can't wait to see you again, Bella Cigna—

Bella, beautiful. A smile played on her lips, and her heart melted. And *Cigna?* What did that word mean? She commanded her phone to translate. Swan. *Cigna* meant swan. "Beautiful Swan," she whispered. Closing her eyes, she felt his strong hands on her arms, and his soft lips on her neck. Her smile widening, Sarah opened her eyes and dropped her gaze to her laptop.

A coolness crept into her chest, and her smile faded. The phone slipped from her hand and dropped to the floor. She didn't retrieve it. "Beautiful swan," she whispered again, maliciousness in her voice.

Shaking her head, she stepped away from the desk, from the phone, and from Eduardo's sentiments. She bumped the edge of the bed, and she lowered herself to it and buried her face in her hands. Tears dripped down her face. *Not beautiful. Damaged. Broken.* She curled up on the bed, closed her eyes, and pushed away thoughts of Philip and Amanda, of her mother, and of Eduardo.

****

"I know you're in there," Anna called.

Out of the corner of her eye, Sarah glanced at the clock. 8:30 p.m, but she didn't budge. If Anna thought she was asleep, she might go away.

Anna entered anyway. "Are you sick?"

Sarah didn't answer. Sick was one word for how she felt—sick of her shortcoming or sick of having her past thrown in her face.

Anna touched a hand to Sarah's shoulder, shaking her. "Come on, Sarah. I'm getting worried. You've been sleeping all day."

Sighing, Sarah rolled over, and opened her eyes. "Fine." She sat up and stretched her arms in the air. "How'd you know I've been in bed all day?"

"I dropped by earlier. You were passed out." Anna snapped her gum. "Late night?"

Sarah shook her head. "Just tired."

Anna cocked her head in question but continued, "Well? How was the date?"

"How was what?" She rubbed her eyes.

"Your date, stupid!"

"Oh." She paused. Eduardo's words repeated in her mind. *Kids are great.* Sure, they were great if your body can carry them. With her lower lip quivering, she kept her gaze on the floor. "My date was fine."

"Fine?" Anna planted her hands on her hips. "Just fine?"

Sarah shrugged.

Anna was quiet then stood. "Well, if you're not interested, mind if I ask him out?"

"What?" Her pulse racing, Sarah leapt to her feet.

Anna pressed her pointer finger into Sarah's chest. "Aha! I knew it." She pushed Sarah back to the mattress. "You're a terrible liar."

Lips shaking again, she bit down—hard. The metallic taste of blood seeped into her mouth.

Her expression softening, Anna sat beside her. "Sarah. What's going on?"

For a moment, Sarah didn't speak. Her emotions—anger, sorrow, lust—were too varied and deep to understand. She took a deep breath. "It's my ex. Well, soon-to-be ex."

"I thought that was all settled."

"It is. It's…" Should she really confide in Anna? Children were bound to be the last thing from Anna's mind. Then again, how long could she hide this predicament from the know-it-all anyway? A day? A week? "It's something else," she said. "Amanda…the woman he left me for. She's…" She choked on the words. "She's pregnant."

"Oh, Sarah." Anna wrapped her arms around Sarah.

Tears streamed down Sarah's hot cheeks, and she buried her head in Anna's scrawny shoulder. For a few minutes, she wept openly into Anna's tight embrace. Finally, Sarah sniffed back her tears and wiped her nose.

"Genes." Anna handed Sarah a tissue. "They're not fair, right? She's probably got big tits, too."

Sarah didn't know whether to start crying again or to laugh. She hadn't given Amanda's cup size much thought.

"Maybe she's got fat genes," Anna continued. "Those are the worst."

Anna spoke in a snarky tone. The corner of Sarah's lip twitched, but she held back her laughter.

"Hey, I'm serious. She can't have *all* the good genes. DNA perfection is mathematically almost impossible."

A single laugh escaped Sarah. Anna always knew what to say.

"So, you gonna go out with him again?"

Sarah returned her lips to a hard line. "Eduardo?"

Anna nodded.

"I don't know. I need time to get over this loss first."

"Fine." Anna pursed her lips. "But don't forget, he's hot."

Yeah, he is. Sarah smiled.

Anna crossed to the door then pivoted on her heel. "And Sarah, just remember, for what it's worth, your friends, your family, hell, even Sister Maria—we're here for you."

"Thanks."

"Yeah, well, if I ever stay with someone long enough to get dumped, I expect the same from you." Anna left the room.

Sarah couldn't help but muster a shallow laugh.

Over the next few days, Sarah intended to heed Anna's advice, to call Meredith—heck, maybe even her mother—to discuss recent events. Instead, she wandered the streets of Rome. Strangely enough, on Monday evening she stood in a church of all places, among a crowd of tourists marveling at the chiseled dome of St. Peter's Basilica.

She'd been there before, many times, and even climbed to the top of the dome along the narrow, winding spiral staircase. But tonight, as she entered the cathedral, she thought perhaps she was drawn by its reverence. Perhaps she hoped to absorb some serenity from one of the numerous cloaked men of God circulating the nave.

She didn't head to one of the priests, however. She made her way to the stoic face of the Virgin Mary, holding the limp corpse of her son in her arms. Michelangelo's *Pietà*. She placed a palm on the translucent, protective case but immediately withdrew it. The coolness of the glass was like the frost on a December morning—a stark contrast to the stifling, stale air of the cathedral. Goose pimples marked her flesh, and she was unsure whether they were her body's response to the icy partition or the cold, chiseled stone it enclosed.

As she stared through the glass at Mary's somber expression, she realized the statue was more than just an exquisitely carved marble. The *Pietà* depicted a mother who'd suffered, who'd lost, and who'd sacrificed. Yet, not one tear showed on Mary's shiny, polished cheek—not a trace of agony emanated from her downcast gaze. No, Michelangelo's greatest work captured the silent grief of a woman, hidden deep beneath a sculpted, serene expression.

A camera snapped behind Sarah, and the flash illuminated her reflection in the glass—her own serene expression. She thought back to the day she too had begun to wear the mask of indifference. She recalled the coolness of the vinyl on the exam table and the medicinal scent of cleaning products and rubbing alcohol. But most of all, she recalled the doctor's sympathetic expression as he'd delivered the news she'd been expecting.

"I'm sorry," the doctor said. "None of the eggs

implanted."

Sarah winced. Three negative pregnancy tests should have been all the confirmation Sarah needed. But she came in anyway, clinging to desperate hope.

"These were the last eggs we fertilized. We'll need to determine the next course of action. Is your husband here?"

Feeling numb, she shook her head. That expression appeared again on the doctor's face—pinched, glassy eyes that could only be read as *I'm sorry*.

"Take some time to discuss it with him then." He squeezed her hand and had gotten up. "Call me once you've reached a decision."

Sarah stared at the statue. She'd had as much choice in the matter as Mary had in losing her son. Sacrifice was the only option.

The door to the nave opened behind her, and a chill rushed inside.

She turned and caught sight of the towering buildings in the distance. One of them was Eduardo's. Heaviness weighed on her chest. What choice would he make when he found out about her infertility? She picked up her phone and checked Eduardo's text from that morning.

—*Buongiorno, beautiful.*
Hope you have a good day—

How was she supposed to "just have fun" with Eduardo? How was this flirtation not the beginning of a relationship—a relationship destined to end just like her last one had? Tears blurred her eyes, and she gazed a final time through the glass. This time, she didn't see Mary and Jesus. She saw herself, holding an empty blanket.

Chapter 18

—Meet you at the fountain—

Sarah pecked back a text to Eduardo.

—Be right there—

She examined her outfit in the mirror: black shirt, black pants, and a black sweater. She looked ready for a funeral. At the thought, she sagged her shoulders; she *felt* ready for a funeral. Smoothing her shirt over the slacks that gapped at her waist, she turned to the side. She'd hardly eaten since learning of Amanda's pregnancy.

She placed a hand on her stomach. How far along was Amanda? Did her belly already swell? Tears brimmed Sarah's eyes, and she shifted her gaze from the mirror to the window.

A tall figure in a black leather jacket stood by the fountain.

Eduardo. She wiped away the tears, tucked her long bangs behind her ears, and plodded out of her room.

Rays of sun glimmered off the splashing water. The air was crisp and clean.

Eduardo lifted his gaze as she approached, a broad smile brightening his dark skin.

Sarah struggled to return the smile. A shadow crept over her mind.

"It's so good to see you." Eduardo wrapped his

arms around her.

"I'm happy to see you, too." She inhaled, smelling the leather and coffee mixed with his usual fresh scent.

He stepped back and took her hand. "You up for a trip into the city? I thought we'd check out an exhibit or two and grab dinner."

Every ounce of her wanted to go, to explore the city with Eduardo by her side and to just *have fun*. If only she knew how without becoming emotionally attached. If only she could stop falling in love with people who broke her heart. "That sounds lovely, but"—she drew her hand from his grasp—"I need to tell you something first."

"Okay." Eduardo shifted on his feet.

The descending sun shined into Sarah's eyes. "Eduardo"—his name came out in a sigh—"I think I've made a mistake. I'm not ready for a relationship yet."

Eduardo stared at her.

A silence fell between them, and the only noise was the spattering of the cascading water. Blinded by the sun, Sarah could only make out the tightness in his jaw and the stiffness in his shoulders. She reached for him, a part of her wanting to hold him and to forget what she'd just said.

He stepped back. "I should go."

The coolness in his tone stung almost as much as his refusal to be touched, but it also sparked something inside Sarah. "Eduardo, wait." She grabbed his hand, drew him close, and pressed her lips against his. For a split second, she again lost herself in him, savoring the suppleness of his lips and the smoothness of his chin.

He pulled back and stared down at her.

The sun at his back, she could see his eyes clearly

now. They were wide, dark, and moist with tears. Sarah's heart pounded and, at the same time, felt like it might stop beating altogether. "I...I..." She struggled to find the words. What could she say? *I'm too scared? Too confused? Too broken?* She dropped his hand. "I'm sorry, Eduardo. I truly wish you the best." His face was as stony as his sculpted counterpart—so lifeless and devoid of emotion.

"I'm sorry, too," he said in a tone as listless as his expression. Then he turned and walked away.

The sun dipped behind a cloud, and Sarah stumbled back to the bench. The water sprayed her back, and she shivered. Would she ever feel the warmth of a man again? Would she ever know love again?

****

The next few days were harder than Sarah expected. Wasn't freeing herself from Eduardo supposed to help her avoid pain, not incite it? If the longing inside after just one date was this visceral, she couldn't imagine how unbearable it would have been after weeks—months. Her body was sapped of energy and her mind stripped of ambition. Instead of planning what to do with her portion of the divorce settlement, she spent hours staring at the ceiling. Instead of perusing real estate listings, she passed the time sketching.

Another day of classes behind her, Sarah slumped, exhausted, in her chair at the front of her classroom. Maybe she could skip play rehearsal and go back to her dorm room. Maybe she could curl up in her too-short bed and wait for darkness.

The classroom door flew open, and Anna popped in her head. "See you in five."

"But—"

"No buts. Those backdrops won't paint themselves, will they?"

Before Sarah could say more, the door slammed shut. So much for feeling sorry for herself. Genius firecracker wouldn't give her an hour's reprieve.

The door snapped open again. "I almost forgot. Sister Maria said she wants to see you first."

Sarah sprang to her feet. "Sister Maria? Did you tell her?" But Anna's footsteps were already retreating down the hall. Sarah flopped back her head *Great. Just great.* She dragged herself to Sister Maria's office, suddenly understanding how the students felt when sent for detention. Would Sister Maria make her copy sentences from the Bible? Would she pull out a paddle?

Sister Maria's door was closed, and Sarah raised her fist to knock.

"*Entra!*"

Sister Maria's voice bellowed. Sarah hadn't even struck the door. She creaked open the door and stepped inside. "Good afternoon, Sister."

Sister Maria frowned. "I see we're still using English."

Giving a sheepish smile, Sarah shrugged. "Anna said you wished to see me."

Sister Maria motioned with an outstretched palm.

Rubbing her palms, Sarah eased into a seat.

"I received a call today from your mother."

Sarah reared back, nearly tumbling off the seat. "My mother?"

"Yes," Sister Maria answered. "She said she's been trying to reach you. She sounded quite concerned."

Pressing her fingertips to her temple, she gently

massaged the vein that throbbed there. If she'd known Mom would stoop to calling her boss, she would have returned her calls. Why couldn't her mom just drop the Philip and Amanda pregnancy? Why couldn't she just move on? "I'm sorry she bothered you."

"Her call was not a bother. I assured her you are well, just busy."

"Thank you." The relief in her voice was apparent.

"You *are* well, aren't you?"

"I'm sorry?" Sarah looked up into gray eyes.

Sister Maria's gaze searched Sarah. "You seem to not be yourself lately—taking to your room early and skipping meals."

How much does she know? Sarah chose her words carefully. "Oh, I just needed some time to myself."

"Would your behavior have anything to do with Mr. Rossini?"

How on Earth did she know? Sarah widened her eyes.

"Eduardo," Sister Maria clarified.

Hearing his name jabbed at Sarah's festering wound, tugged at the fragile strings of her composure. She dropped her gaze. "He told you?"

"Sometimes what's not said speaks more than what is." Sister Maria stood and crossed to the window. "He mentioned you, yes."

Sarah shifted in her seat. "How, um…how is he?"

Across from her, Sister Maria stared out the window. "He is…disappointed. Very disappointed."

The strings began to snap. One by one, until her heart felt as if it dangled from a lone thread. "I'm sorry to hear that." She forced out the words.

Sister Maria turned. "I know you are, Sarah."

Sarah? She perked up. Had Sister Maria ever called her by her first name before?

"I talked a bit to your mother today," Sister Maria continued. "About you."

Sarah leaned forward. "You didn't tell her about Eduardo, did you?"

"Of course not. I didn't tell her about anything. I only listened."

"And what did she say?"

"Just that something happened with your ex-husband that might have upset you. Is that true?"

Ex-husband. Sarah winced and nodded.

"You know, Sarah, I wasn't always a nun."

Sarah darted her gaze to Sister Maria, so devout in her white habit and black robe.

"I don't know much about this husband of yours, but I gathered he was no better than the few men I knew in my youth." She swatted the air. "Good riddance."

With a shallow laugh, Sarah squeezed out a smile.

Sister Maria mirrored it. "Unfortunately, Sarah, sometimes goodbyes are easier said than done. That is the phrase, yes?"

Sister Maria knew more about the secular world than she let on. Sarah nodded.

"Sometimes it takes a while for the scars to fade." Sister Maria placed a hand on Sarah's shoulder. "That's how I ended up in the convent, to heal myself."

"Did it work?" Sarah asked.

Squeezing her shoulder, Sister Maria paused. "Sometimes, Sarah, in order to let go of the past, you have to confront it."

Confront it? The ache in Sarah's chest deepened. What did that mean? Would Sister Maria answer the question or not?

"Now…" Sister Maria patted Sarah's back and returned to her chair. "I believe Ms. Franklin awaits your expertise with the scenery."

As she walked down the halls, Sarah tugged on the hem of her dress, her mind riddled with thoughts. Eduardo told Sister Maria about them? And her mother told Sister Maria about Philip? She shook her head. In less than two months, her new boss learned more about her than Mr. Rosen had in two years—so much for a fresh start. She opened the door to the auditorium, and laughter and a chorus of *ew*s spilled out.

On the stage, students pointed their fingers and covered their noses, and a crowd of raucous girls surrounded Anna. Their squeals made Anna's shushing and threats of detention barely audible.

Sarah flared her nostrils. "Anna!"

Anna looked over at Sarah, and the darkness in her eyes softened.

Chunks of partially digested food splattered on the floor. Sarah's stomach turned upside down and not because of the gruesome sight or the acidic stench. *Lucia.*

Huddled behind the left curtain, Lucia stood. Vomit covered the front of her outfit.

Sarah turned to the girls. "*Ascolta!*" Her voice sounded so loud and so callous, she could have been mistaken for Sister Maria in a rage.

With widened eyes, the girls froze.

"You should all be ashamed of yourselves. Mocking someone half your age." With narrowed eyes, she scanned the girls' faces. "How would you feel if someone laughed at you? Belittled you when you were already so scared?" She paused, letting the deafening silence knock some sense into them.

The girls dropped their gazes to the floor.

"Now, help Ms. Franklin clean up this mess. And if I ever catch any of you teasing a lower school student again, Sister Maria will be the *least* of your worries."

The girls gave curt nods.

Anna stood.

The girls scampered off like wounded puppies and Anna looked at Sarah as if she'd just rattled off the solution to a complicated equation. But Sarah ignored them all—except Lucia. She wrapped an arm around the girl's shoulder and ushered her to the bathroom. She helped her clean up, washed her face with a damp paper towel, and fetched a spare set of clothes from Sister Angelica's lost and found.

Lucia cried throughout.

"You're okay, Lucia," Sarah said in a calming voice. "No one will think any less of you if you don't want to do the play."

Still whimpering, Lucia wiped her swollen cheeks. "I can't do that, Ms. Miller."

"I'm sure your mother will understand."

"I know." Lucia nodded. "But everyone will call me *una bambina*."

Sarah offered her a tissue. "I don't think they'll call you *anything* after my threats today."

Taking the tissue, Lucia sniffled and frowned. "I have to do this."

"I understand, but..." Lucia performing in front of an audience seemed as likely as Sarah understanding Mr. Moretti's Italian. Sarah furrowed her brow. Maybe they could help each other? She lifted Lucia's chin. "Do

198

you think I can ever learn Italian?"

"If you practice enough."

"Could you help me?"

Lucia cocked her head to the side. "Of course."

"Let's make a deal. You help me with my Italian, and I'll help you with your stage fright." Sarah extended her pinky finger.

Chewing her lip, Lucia shifted her gaze to the ceiling.

Sarah kept her hand extended and her smile steady.

Finally, Lucia gave a swift exhale, lifted her hand, and looped her pinky around Sarah's.

"We'll do this. Together." Sarah pulled Lucia into her chest and stroked her hair—thick, brunette waves not so different than Eduardo's curls. The sensation brought back all the feelings she'd harbored when she'd left Sister Maria's office: longing, loss, and maybe even regret.

She passed a hand over the smooth strands one last time before letting go. That's what she needed to do—*let go*. And not just let go of Lucia but also the feelings trapped inside her. She needed to let go of her past, not confront it.

She patted Lucia's back. "You'd better go. I expect your mom's waiting."

Lucia nodded. "Yes, Ms. Miller."

"We'll start practicing tomorrow. Lunch."

Lucia exited the bathroom.

Sarah pulled out her phone. One person did need to be confronted—Mom.

"Sarah, my God! I've been so worried. How are you?"

Her mom's voice was dramatic enough for the

stage, shrill and shaky. "I'm…" Sarah paused. *The truth. Nothing more, nothing less.* "I'm good, Mom. Not great, but much better than I was when I heard the news."

Chapter 19

As October turned to November, Sarah met Lucia for lunch three times a week. Sarah spoke entirely in Italian—except for those times when she became so frustrated that she could feel heat rushing her cheeks. Then Lucia switched to English to explain. Sarah also helped Lucia make progress with her own struggles. After weeks of Sarah reading aloud with her in class, Lucia managed that on her own. Speaking her lines in the play was a more difficult challenge, but—well, she hadn't thrown up again.

The final Thursday in November was Lucia's next big test. Her scene would run during rehearsal, and Sarah decided a little extra practice beforehand wouldn't hurt. "Come on! We only have a few minutes." Sarah rushed down the hall, weaving through the oncoming students heading for dismissal.

"Slow down! My legs aren't as long as yours."

Sarah stopped and turned back to Lucia, who bobbed through the hall in her light-up shoes. If Lucia took after her father, in a short time her legs would be the same length as Sarah's. Sarah winced at the thought of Eduardo, as she always did, ever since ending things with him a month ago. She hadn't seen him since, except during drop-off and pick-up, and even then he always stared straight ahead through his windshield, never her way. But her thoughts of him hadn't lessened.

How could they? His face haunted her sketchpad. She saw his eyes in Lucia's. And Sarah certainly would never put on her fuzzy, teddy bear slippers again without thinking of him.

Lucia caught up.

Sarah snuffed the thoughts as best she could, a temporary dulling of the longing that never subsided. She grabbed Lucia's hand and guided her into the auditorium.

Mr. Moretti stood on a ladder on the stage.

Sarah ushered Lucia up.

He started down, calling something in his hasty, squeaky Italian.

"I'm sorry, Mr. Moretti," Sarah said automatically, in Italian. "Speak slower so I can understand you."

On the third rung from the bottom Mr. Moretti paused, staring with his beady eyes. "I said," he began, "rehearsal doesn't start for fifteen minutes. I'm changing the lights."

He looked at her as if she'd uttered a prophecy. "We won't bother you," Sarah answered back in Italian so clear she surprised herself. "Lucia needs to practice her lines."

"Ah." He climbed back up the ladder.

"*Splendido!*" Lucia pulled at Sarah's hand. "That was great!"

Sarah rubbed Lucia's dark hair. "Thanks. As they say, 'practice makes perfect.'" She stepped to the edge of the stage. "Now, for *your* practice."

"But..." Lucia motioned toward Mr. Moretti with her gaze. "Not with him here."

"He'll be here during rehearsal, along with fifteen others."

"I don't know, Ms. Miller." Lucia tugged a pigtail.

"You just read out loud in class. The stage is the same. Just a bigger room."

Lucia kicked at an imaginary object. "All right."

The girl spoke in the labored tone Sarah was accustomed to hearing from the girls whenever they lost an argument. She jumped down from the stage. "Okay. Whenever you're ready."

As she spoke, Lucia stared at the floor.

Her voice was so soft Sarah couldn't make out a single word. "Louder!" she called.

"I'm not sure I can."

"What?" Sarah scooped her hand around her ear, pantomiming she couldn't hear.

"I said, I'm not sure I can," Lucia answered in a clear voice.

Sarah flashed a thumbs-up. "Great! Just like that."

"There's no room for you here," Lucia said in Italian.

Sarah could actually hear her. "Yes! Now say it like you *mean* it."

"There's no room for you here," Lucia said again.

She spoke the phrase exactly as before. Sarah frowned. "Why don't you pretend I'm someone you don't like? Anyone you can think of?"

"Maybe my stepdad."

Go figure. "Excellent. I mean, fine. Pretend he's asking to stay with you and Eduar—" She caught herself. "I mean, your father."

Mr. Moretti raised a fuzzy brow. Sarah flushed.

"Okay." Lucia stepped forward and placed a hand on her hip. "There's no room for you here!"

Her voice was loud and confident. She actually

projected. Sarah gave a little hop and clapped. "Perfect, Lucia!"

"*Magnifico.*" Mr. Moretti called from the ladder.

Lucia jumped down from the stage, a smile on her face. "I don't think I can do it with everyone else here."

"Of course, you can." Sarah squeezed Lucia's shoulders. "You'll do great." While the children rehearsed, Sarah brushed stars of varying sizes, leaving room for the North Star in the center. But she kept an eye on the rehearsal as she worked, and as they neared the scene with Lucia's line, she put down her brush and parked herself at the back of the auditorium.

"Excuse me, do you have a room to spare?" said the upper school female who would play the role of Joseph.

"Come on, Lucia," Sarah said under her breath.

But from the stage came only silence. Lucia stared out at the auditorium, and her gaze found Sarah.

A paleness painted Lucia's face, and she stared out with widened eyes. Sneering whispers cut the dead air.

Sarah felt Anna's gaze on her, but she didn't let go of Lucia's gaze. In a split-second decision, she stepped forward and made her best Mr. De Luca impersonation. She rubbed her chin and gave a flagrant wink.

Lucia squeezed a smile. Then she narrowed her eyes, cleared her throat, and said her line.

No, she *performed* her line. Sarah broke into applause.

Anna flashed a glare.

Sarah silenced her clapping and straightened her smile. But as she returned to the backdrops, the memory of Lucia's cheeky grin fueled her enthusiasm. That grin stayed with her all through dinner, and even warmed her as she trotted across the courtyard from the dining hall, the fierce autumn wind whipping her hair.

****

Thanksgiving was unusual for Sarah. The Italians acknowledged the uniquely American holiday but didn't celebrate it. So, Sarah didn't enjoy traditional cranberry sauce or sage-spiced stuffing, but the school kitchen did make an effort, serving sliced turkey with roasted potatoes. Although Sarah didn't spend the morning watching the parades on TV with her mom, she did speak to her on the phone. Sarah even discussed with her mom the sites they'd visit when she arrived in a few short weeks.

But Sarah gave thanks. What she was most thankful for, as she huddled under a blanket in her room, preparing for another evening filled with sketching and reading a good book, was her friends: for Anna's constant friendship, even though she'd abandoned Sarah for a proper Thanksgiving dinner with some ex-pats in downtown Rome, for Lucia, as young as she was, who always brightened her day with her unending persistence and smiling eyes, and for Meredith—

I haven't called Meredith. Sarah sat up in her bed and checked the time—seven p.m. One p.m. back home. Steven should be going down for his afternoon nap. Sarah picked up the phone and found Meredith's contact.

"Happy Thanksgiving!" Meredith exclaimed.

"How are things? Your in-laws there?"

"Yeah. Helen's scrutinizing my pie crust as we speak."

Remembering Meredith's failed attempt at apple

pie a few summers ago, Sarah chuckled. Pies never were her strong suit. "Sorry I'm not there to help."

Since Sarah's father passed away, she, Philip, and Mom spent their recent Thanksgivings at Meredith's. Dessert was always Sarah's responsibility.

"I know. You usually do the pies!"

Sarah bit her lip at Meredith's frazzled tone. "You know I never made my own crust, right?"

"What? Those were store-bought?"

"Yup."

"Ugh! And I'll be picking crust from under my nails for a week. Thanksgiving isn't the same without you, Sarah."

A lump formed in Sarah's throat. "It's not the same here, either."

"Oh, Sarah. I really can't even imagine. Don't you have anyone to celebrate with? Anna?"

Meredith must have heard the loneliness in Sarah's voice; hers was filled with pity. Sarah crumpled her posture.

"Or what about Eduardo? Have you thought about calling him?"

Sarah swallowed hard. Meredith hadn't mentioned him in weeks. Was the fact she hadn't stopped thinking about him that obvious? "Um, no."

"Don't lie."

"All right." Sarah fingered the edge of the blanket. "I've thought about it."

"So why don't you?"

"I...I don't know. What if he finds out about my... problem?" Her heart sank.

"So? Who cares if he finds out? You're not marrying him. You're coming home in six months."

"Yeah." *Like I have hopes of ever getting married again anyway.*

"Speaking of which, did I tell you my neighbor's house is for sale?"

Sarah threw off her covers. "No. Which one?"

"The little blue house on the corner. Perfect size for you."

A painted, cedar-sided house with a red front door and black shutters. How wonderful would it be to live just a few steps from Meredith? She could help with the kids, go over any time for tea, and…

Who was she kidding? She couldn't get a loan without a proper job—one that paid far more than the measly twenty grand she would pull in this year. She'd need to secure a position back home first, and the posts for the next academic year wouldn't be up for at least a month. She frowned. "Maybe if it's still on the market in the summer."

"You know how fast things move here."

"I know, I know." She slumped into the pillow.

Shouting erupted in the background, followed by Meredith's muffled yell. "I'm sorry to cut our conversation short, Sarah, but apparently, my sweet potato casserole is burning."

"Of course." Sarah didn't bother to stifle her giggle. "Good luck with the pies." She paced around her room. Should she really reach out to Eduardo after all this time? What had Sister Maria said? He was disappointed.

This rumination is stupid. She paused in front of her desk and opened the drawer with Lucia's drawing. *Bella Cigna.* Her heart fluttered. She could get used to that kind of flattery. But could she give it up in six months? Worse—could she bear it if he stopped offering endearments?

She shoved back the paper and slammed shut the drawer. *I'm not thirteen.* So, why couldn't she subdue her restlessness? Why couldn't she stop thinking about him?

Sarah jammed her feet into her slippers, and his words ran through her mind. *The slippers are a nice touch.* She growled—*again,* she'd thought of him! She needed something to keep her hands and mind occupied; she needed to paint. After wrapping herself in a thick sweater and switching her shoes, Sarah ventured across the courtyard to the dark auditorium. The hard soles of Sister Maria's hand-me-down shoes clicked on the wooden floor, the sound reverberating through the halls.

The overhead lights switched on in the auditorium, and she studied the backdrops. Shades of blue blended delicately in the background. A pale-yellow hue brought the city of Bethlehem to life through stenciled windowpanes and shadowed chimneys. And in the center, the North Star glowed. The piece was technically sound...yet, something wasn't right. Why didn't it speak to her—breathe life into her like the ceiling in the Sistine Chapel? Or make her spine tingle like when she listened to *Vissi D'arte*?

She stepped toward the backdrops. What were they missing? She studied the piece, but no solution came. Sighing, she sat on the drop cloth and called Anna. "Having fun?"

"Don't I always?"

"How was dinner?"

"Same as last year. Puts my mother's Thanksgiving

roast to shame, but I'm not complaining."

"I would kill for some pumpkin pie right now." Sarah cocked her head at the painting. Was the star off center?

"I'm celebrating with a piece right now."

"Ugh. Not fair. Whipped cream, too?" Sarah tucked the phone against her shoulder, put out her hands so her thumbs met at the star, and measured to the edges of the backdrops with her hands. The star was centered for sure.

Anna's gulp muffled the line. "Mm-hmm."

"What's so spectacular that you're celebrating with pie…without me?"

"I did invite you."

Right. Like Sarah would fall for that one again. Getting inebriated with kids half her age made her list of never-agains.

"I got in," Anna added.

Sarah jumped to her feet. "Got in? You mean to Oxford?"

"Yep."

"Holy hell." Sarah slapped a hand over her mouth and scanned the room for any students. The auditorium was empty. *Whew*! She dropped her hand. "I mean, that's great."

"Thanks to one completely fictionalized essay."

Sarah smiled. "I should've been a used car salesman."

"Right."

Again, Sarah considered the painting. Were too many buildings in the forefront? No. Any fewer and it wouldn't be a town. "When will you tell Sister Maria?"

"Not anytime soon. They want me to visit in

February, and then I'll make my decision."

"That'll be fun. They pay for the trip?"

"Yeah. But I'm not sure I'll go."

"What?" Sarah flinched. "No sirree. I didn't spend two hours educating myself on some coding mumbo-jumbo for you not to even consider it."

Silence hung on the line. "What if grad school's not right for me?" She huffed. "And cryptography isn't mumbo-jumbo. The stuff is legit."

"Well, I think that's your answer right there." Sarah waited for an answer.

"Come on, Anna, isn't that what the visit's about? To help you figure out if Oxford's a good fit?"

Anna released a sigh. "I guess so."

"Then why pass up a free trip? You're not obligated to attend the school afterward."

Anna laughed. "Since when did you get so smart?"

A smile eased onto Sarah's face. "Since I started passing myself off as a genius."

"Ha! I think you might be one, too."

"Fat chance."

"Well, you at least deserve a piece of pumpkin pie. I'll bring you a doggy bag."

A rumble attacked Sarah's stomach at the thought. "I won't say no to that." She ended the call and returned to her dilemma. Why couldn't she find that spark in her piece? Anna had her love of math to drive her. Michelangelo had his faith. But what did she have? If only she could draw on something in her life—not just fuzzy memories of childhood nativity scenes.

Sarah stood. That was the problem. Not the number of buildings or the placement of the star, but what inspired them. Her lip firmly between her teeth, she shifted her attention from the glowing city to the left and right of the North Star, the space without light. Goose pimples prickled her flesh.

The sky.

She stepped closer, an image emerging in her mind. The blue sky, while more vibrant than Mr. Moretti's dim black, was too dark. It needed color. She knelt and rummaged through her tubes and cans. She dug out blue and red and squirted some into an empty drip pan, stirring until a deep violet emerged.

Yes. The picture in her mind clarified. She returned to the pile of paints, this time finding red and orange—the colors to paint a sunset. And not just any sunset, but the one from her date with Eduardo.

She squeezed them onto a piece of cardboard. The palette lay ready to be used. Sarah dipped her brush into the violet and reached for the backdrop. She hesitated, her hand quivering as she extended the soaked bristles. Did she really have time to transform it? The performance was only ten days away.

The sunset consuming her thoughts, she closed her eyes. "*Vissi d'arte, I lived for art.*" Opening her eyes, Sarah let her brush collide with the canvas. She allowed the motion wash the darkness and breathe life into the piece—and herself.

Chapter 20

Purples and oranges swirled behind a twinkling North Star; the streaks of light and dark blended together like the cream in one of Anna's lattes. The pigments electrified the canvas and recharged Sarah. The last nine days of laboring were about more than just revitalizing the painting; Sarah hadn't felt so rejuvenated, so light on her feet, since her date with Eduardo.

She stepped back from the artwork in place on the stage. A tingle rushed her spine, as the memory of Eduardo holding her on the couch flooded back—the warmth of his arms wrapped around her and his clean, intoxicating scent. This time, Sarah didn't snuff the memory. Working on the painting awakened an awareness; on some level, the painting was as much for him as for her. She hugged herself. Was that such a bad thing?

She replayed her conversations with Meredith and Anna. *You're not marrying him*, Meredith said. And her own advice to Anna, *Isn't that what the trip's about? To help you figure out if Oxford's a good fit?*

Maybe she should think of dating Eduardo as something like a free trip to England. Who wouldn't pass up that?

"*Splendido!*" Lucia said.

Sarah turned. Lucia was dressed in a burlap dress

tied at the waist with rope. A brown shawl covered her thick brunette waves. A cheap, but accurate, costume. "Thank you." She placed a hand on Lucia's shoulder. "Are you ready?"

"I guess."

"You guess? You'll do great! You've been so animated these last few days on stage. I can't believe how far you've come."

A small smile lit up Lucia's face. "Maybe next year I'll try for a wise man."

"Absolutely! Your mother will be so proud." She squeezed Lucia's shoulders. "*I'm* so proud of you."

"And my dad. He knows how much I hate to talk in front of people."

"So, he's coming to the performance?" Sarah said as casually as she could.

"Of course. He says he wants to talk to you."

"He does?" A blush heated Sarah's cheeks.

"He says he wants to thank you for helping me."

Sarah smiled. Perhaps she wouldn't need to call him after all. Perhaps the play would offer the perfect opportunity to gauge his interest.

She examined the scene she'd painted. Would he guess her inspiration? Did that night together mean as much to him as it did to her? Her heart thudded in her chest. The only way to know was to ask him.

****

Students, parents, and teachers packed into the auditorium, many seated in folding chairs that covered every spare inch of floor from stage to exit. Sarah stood in the back and scanned the room. Roberta and Mr. De Luca sat in the front row, on the far left. Eduardo was on the right, a few rows from the stage.

As the lights went down, Sarah thought about taking a seat. But she couldn't—she could barely keep herself from pacing the aisles.

Sister Maria took the stage first, and then Anna.

But Sarah didn't hear what they said. She was too focused on sending positive thoughts to Lucia. The curtain opened, and she glued her gaze to the stage. She memorized Lucia's entrance, and the closer the performers got to it, the more she scrunched her toes in her shoes.

Lucia bounded out.

She was so cute in her frumpy costume and overly rouged cheeks. The arch in Sarah's foot ached then she was still. Holding her breath, she crossed her fingers.

Lucia looked straight out over the auditorium.

Was Sarah imagining things, or was Lucia staring at the front row? At Mr. De Luca?

"There's no room for you here," Lucia said.

She recited her line as loud and as clear as the upper-school girl who played Mary, and her face was as fierce as Sarah had ever seen. Unable to help herself, she bounced on her sore feet and broke into applause.

A mother shushed her.

No doubt the woman was eager to hear her own child's line. Sarah quieted, her body relaxing, and took an empty seat. At the end of the performance, she joined the parents in hollering *Brava* as the students took their bows. Sarah gave them a standing ovation, warmth bubbling in her chest. She wondered, did Roberta feel the same way watching her daughter? Had Eduardo been one of the voices shouting *Brava?* She hoped so.

The auditorium lights flickered on, and Sarah

steadied herself for the encounter she hadn't stopped thinking about for a week. The quiver in her knees had nothing to do with Lucia's success.

"Miss Miller," a squealy voice said from beside her.

Sarah turned. "Mr. Moretti," she replied in surprise. Had he just addressed her in English?

"Your art. It's beautiful." He continued in thickly-accented English.

Sarah stared, her mouth hanging open. *He really is speaking English. Holy hell.*

"*Buonasera.*" Mr. Moretti gave a curt nod then the crowd swallowed him up.

"*Grazie!*" Sarah found her voice.

Mr. Moretti almost disappeared into the mass of people; he didn't turn.

The volume of the crowd steadily increased, yet the noise didn't mask the thudding of Sarah's heart in her chest. She searched the room and spotted Eduardo near the stage, Lucia at his side.

His gaze settled on her.

Those warm, chocolate eyes could melt her even from fifty feet away. Sarah clutched her chest.

"Miss Miller! Miss Miller!" Lucia shouted, breaking from her father's side. She weaved through the crowd, running straight past Sister Maria, straight past her mom, and straight into Sarah's side. "I did it, Miss Miller! I did it!"

As Lucia plowed into her, Sarah stumbled backward. She sensed Roberta's gaze—a glare, most likely—on her, but didn't care. She crouched and flung her arms around Lucia. "I knew you would."

Lucia's small hands pressed into Sarah's back.

For a moment, Sarah was lost in the warmth that passed between them, in the feeling that they were somehow connected, and in the knowledge that she'd made a change in Lucia's life. She closed her eyes. Was this the feeling of motherhood?

She clung to Lucia and gently stroked the soft waves of her hair. She imagined wiping the rouge from her round cheeks and brushing her hair before tucking her into bed at night.

Lucia pulled back. "Papa, Papa!"

Sarah slowly rose to meet him, her body reluctant, and her breath caught in her throat.

"Did you see Miss Miller's painting?" Lucia asked.

Eduardo smiled, first at Lucia, and then at Sarah. "After you, the backdrop was the star of the show. Pun intended."

Sarah opened her mouth to laugh, but the stiffness in her muscles refused to allow it. She smiled back instead.

Lifting an eyebrow, Eduardo gestured in Roberta's direction. "Your mother is waiting for you, Lucia."

Still beaming, Lucia bounced on her toes then raced across the room to Roberta.

Across the room, Roberta stared at Sarah and Eduardo with a narrowed gaze.

Eduardo stepped toward Sarah. "I'm sure you know how grateful Lucia is."

Sarah nodded. *And you?*

"And me," he said.

Sarah's heart skipped a beat. He could read her mind, too.

He reached for her hand but stopped. He shifted his gaze from hers, folded his hand, and placed it in his pocket. "And Roberta."

Her heart still fluttering, Sarah shuffled her feet and inched forward. "Working with Lucia was just as rewarding for me. Lucia is so full of life. And"—she arched her brow playfully—"she's a much better Italian tutor than you ever were."

Eduardo pushed up his glasses and smiled. "Oh really?"

"Yes." Sarah paused to listen to the conversations around them. "For instance..." She zeroed in on a voice. "The woman behind you is nagging someone about being late for dinner reservations."

Eduardo dropped his smile.

His frown was so pronounced Sarah thought his glasses might slide right off his nose.

A woman, with a petite build and tanned skin, slid next to Eduardo. "*Siamo in ritardo per la cena.*" She typed on her phone as she spoke.

A bead of sweat appeared on Eduardo's brow, and he tugged at his collar.

No. Sarah froze, a lump bigger than this woman's thick hoop earrings forming in her throat. *Please don't let her be with him.*

"Sarah, let me introduce Antoinette."

Antoinette peeked over her phone just long enough to flash a full-lipped smile and bat thick lashes. "*Ciao. Sono la ragazza di Eduardo.*"

Ragazza. Girlfriend. Sarah did her best to maintain a pleasantly neutral expression to cover the blow that knocked the wind out of her. She shifted her gaze from Antoinette, to Eduardo, and then to the crowd. Her chest burned, and the room spun.

"Sarah?" Eduardo gripped her arm.

At his touch, Sarah jerked back and inhaled sharply.

Eduardo furrowed his eyebrows.

Squaring her shoulders, she addressed Antoinette. "*Mi chiamo Sarah. Io sono un'insegnante di inglese di Lucia.*"

Eduardo widened his eyes.

Beside him, Antoinette snapped her gaze from her phone.

Sarah struggled to breathe. Had either of them noted the shakiness in her voice? Or that all the blood drained from her face? If they hadn't yet, they would soon. She shifted her attention back to Eduardo. "*Buona sera.*" She turned to go.

Eduardo caught her shoulder. "Sarah, wait. Can we talk?" He lowered his voice. "In private?"

"I can't. I…" Sarah searched for an excuse while trying not to focus on his hand resting on her shoulder—the same hands that had caressed her arms and had pulled her close while watching the sunset. Those hands now held another woman. "I have to go." She wriggled from his grasp and started for the door.

"Sarah, please?"

The words were more than a question—they were a plea. Sarah stopped but kept her back to him.

"Your painting," he said. "Was the scene…?" His voice faltered, and he cleared his throat. "Was the scene from that night?"

A mixture of joy and misery rushed through Sarah. She wanted to pull him close but also push him away, to kiss him but also slap him, and to cherish him but also despise him. Tears stung her eyes then burned her cheeks. How could she answer him, knowing he'd already moved on? She brushed the tears from her face, kept her head high, and rushed toward the exit.

By the time she reached her room, Sarah dabbed at her puffy eyes. She wiped her brow with a wet cloth and stared at her reflection: blotchy red cheeks, messy blonde bangs, and smudged eyeliner. She gripped the edge of the sink and the cool porcelain unyielded. How could he have found someone else and brought her to the play, when he knew Sarah would be present? He was the one who made their few dates feel like they'd been together for months. He was the one who'd told her he felt close to her—who called her his beautiful swan. Maybe all his heartfelt comments were lines after all. Except, he remembered the night together—the sunset.

Sarah loosened her grip on the sink and peered into the mirror—into her glassy blue eyes. How could she be angry? She was the one who called it off. She was the one who wasn't ready for a relationship. How could she blame Eduardo for this when she had no one to blame but herself?

Well, maybe Antoinette was *partly* to blame, or Antoinette's type, anyway. Eduardo would have left her for a smaller-bodied, prettier-faced woman eventually. How could a man resist the tight curves and tanned skin Antoinette offered?

Sighing, she picked up the washcloth again. She removed the mascara streaks from her cheeks and what was left of the shimmery gloss from her lips. Things were probably better this way. She should be concentrating on plans for next year, not opening herself for inevitable heartbreak.

When she'd finished cleaning up, Sarah slumped to

her desk, opened the listing Meredith sent her, and clicked on the specs. The quaint, blue-shingled rancher contained three bedrooms and two baths. The house had just enough room for a small art studio, and maybe, one day—too long, if her ovaries said anything about it—a child. Except, the likelihood of the house being on the market when she was ready was about as unlikely as Anna joining the convent.

A knock rattled the door.

"Yes?" Sarah called.

"*Signorina Miller. Sua Suor Maria.*"

Sarah smoothed her hair as she walked to the door then opened it. "*Buonasera.*"

"*Buonasera.*" Sister Maria gave a curt nod and rested her gaze on Sarah. "Are you all right?"

"Of course." Struggling to avert the stare of Sister Maria's murky gray eyes, Sarah forced a smile. "Why wouldn't I be?"

Sister Maria narrowed her eyes. "You seemed upset when you left the performance. In a hurry, at least."

Sarah kept a straight face. "Well, I…I have a lot to get done before my mother arrives."

"That's right. She arrives soon?"

Whew. She bought it. "In another week."

As the lines around her eyes softened, Sister Maria stepped back from the door. "Well, I look forward to meeting her. I'm sure we'll have a lot to talk about."

Sarah tried not to let her smile turn into a wince. "I'm sure she'd like that." Closing the door, she pressed her back into it. *Great.* Her mom and her boss cavorting—as if tonight's debacle with Eduardo wasn't bad enough.

Chapter 21

Anna left for Boston three days later. Sarah didn't bother to tell her about Eduardo. What would be the point? Anna would either tell her the whole situation was her own damn fault—how could she argue with that reasoning?—or worse, would suggest she call Marco. So, Sarah traded her fuzzy slippers for wool socks, barricaded herself in her room, and spent the first few days of break sifting through her sketchbooks and polishing off a brand-new jar of Choctella.

If not for Mom's impending visit, she might have spent her entire break that way. But only one thing could make things worse—Mom's condemning glare. She pulled herself together and did what any woman in her situation would do; she scrubbed the hell out of her bathroom.

"This is where you live?" Mom said when she arrived.

Apparently, the sparkling tiles did nothing to ease Mom's disapproval. "I told you my accommodations were nothing fancy."

"Fancy? I'd be better off sharing a shower in the hostel!" Mom poked her head in the bathroom and wrinkled her nose.

"The room is fine, Mom," Sarah said. "It's only temporary."

Mom raised an eyebrow and turned her attention to

Sarah's bed. "What exactly are your plans for next year?"

Sarah harrumphed before answering. "I don't know yet."

"You don't know *yet*?" Mom opened her eyes wide. "But it's nearly January."

"Can we have this conversation later? I want to hit the Vatican before it gets too crowded." Sarah grabbed her purse and started for the door.

Mom didn't move. "How much longer will you put this off, Sarah? You can't hide forever."

"I'm not hiding." *Am I?* And what did it matter if she was? Sarah dug in her purse for her keys. Finding them, she squeezed them so hard she was sure the metal would leave a mark. "Let's just go."

"Sarah, please. I know this divorce isn't easy for you." Mom placed a hand on Sarah's shoulder and squeezed. "I don't want you to throw away your life."

Why can't she leave this issue alone? Sarah pulled back, flailing her hands in the air. The keys flew out and clanked against the desk chair before coming to rest on the floor. "I'm not throwing away my life. I'm just figuring out what the hell to do with it."

With a frown, Mom dropped her gaze.

Sarah struggled to control her breathing, which suddenly became ragged. She didn't move to pick up the keys.

Mom didn't either.

A knock sounded on the door, breaking the silence. Sarah rushed to open it.

"I'm sorry to interrupt," Sister Maria announced. She took a step inside and extended a hand to Sarah's mother. "You must be Sarah's mother. So nice to finally meet you in person, Mrs. Miller."

Great. If Sarah thought her mother's prying was intrusive, just wait until the two of them combined forces.

"So, will you come?" Sister Maria asked Sarah.

"I'm sorry?"

Sister Maria gave an amused smile. "I asked whether you and your mother would attend Christmas Eve mass."

Christmas Eve mass? As if she'd thought past the next two days. They had to visit the *Trevi* Fountain and the *Colosseum*.

"Of course!" Mom said.

Sarah shot Mom a glance. "Mom, you're Methodist. You won't even underst—"

"Well, you know what they say, Sarah?" Mom clasped her hands. "When in Rome…"

Sarah rolled her eyes.

"*Magnifico*," Sister Maria said with a smile. "Friday. Eleven o'clock."

****

Four days later, Sarah and Mom headed to the chapel. Stars shone in the dark sky, and a gentle winter's wind brushed her cheeks.

Mom bounced through the courtyard, bubbling with excitement. "I can't wait! I hope the service is by candlelight."

Sarah stifled a yawn. The last few days with Mom exhausted her. If she had to pose for one more picture or browse one more souvenir shop, she might just go mental. And don't even bring up the stairs: the Spanish steps, the stadium seating in the *Colosseum*, and the trek up the winding staircase of the basilica. Of course,

Sarah climbed them all before, but she'd done so over months, not in the span of four days. Sarah's feet ached, and she slumped her shoulders. Would anyone notice if she nodded off?

Inside the chapel, Sister Maria, dressed in her traditional robes and habit, stood out in the tiny but crowded sanctuary. Sarah guided Mom through the dimly lit nave toward her.

"I saved you seats." Sister Maria gestured toward the second pew from the front.

The pew was empty, save for a lone man on the far side. His head was buried in a hymnal.

"The chapel's beautiful." Mom gazed around the room.

Sarah paused to take in the chapel's transformation. On the altar, a pair of candles adorned a table dressed in red velvet. Feathery evergreen branches draped down the sides. The organist played cheery Christmas tunes instead of the usual somber dirges. Beautiful, indeed.

"After you." Sister Maria motioned to Sarah to go in first. "I'll sit by your mother and explain the service."

"Thanks." At least she could enjoy the service—or sleep through it. But could she trust their conversation wouldn't veer from Catholic rituals? Sarah shrugged. Tame conversation was about as likely as the priest singing a gospel. Sarah led the way and shuffled into the narrow pew.

The man at the end glanced up from his book. He did a double take then stood.

Sarah stopped, and her heart quickened. *Not him. Anyone but him.*

"Sarah," Eduardo said. The hymnal slipped from his grasp and clattered to the floor. "I didn't expect to see you here."

Sarah was too shocked to move. "Yes." Her voice shook.

Eduardo knelt to pick up the book.

Swallowing hard, Sarah firmed her tone. "I mean, likewise."

As Eduardo returned to standing, his gaze flitted between Sarah and the hymnal. He rubbed the spine of the book and chewed his lip.

Mom nudged Sarah's side and mumbled.

But Sarah didn't catch what she said. She didn't turn to ask, either. She could only focus on the questions racing through her mind: *Is he alone? Where is Antoinette? And Lucia?* She glanced back over her shoulder.

With a wave her hands, Mom motioned to Sarah to scoot down the aisle.

Sarah looked past Mom to the stoic face of Sister Maria, who conveniently avoided meeting Sarah's gaze. She clenched her teeth. *Does hell have a special place for people who strangle meddling nuns?* She inched down the pew, making room for Mom and Sister Maria—and bringing her closer to Eduardo.

His gaze flicked from Sarah's face to the two women behind her.

Did he suspect Sister Maria's meddling as well? Sarah attempted a smile.

Returning an equally strained smile, Eduardo leaned over and kissed Sarah briefly on each cheek.

As she caught a whiff of his intoxicating scent, she sucked in her breath, her knees threatening to give way.

She steadied herself on the adjacent pew.

Eduardo pulled back. "I…" He rubbed the back of his neck. "I've been thinking about calling you."

Sarah tightened her grip on the pew.

"I wanted to apologize for the other night." He shuffled his feet. "At the play. I didn't mean for you to meet—"

He stopped before saying *her* name—the name that made Sarah want to chuck the hymnal at him.

"I can't believe your Italian," he said. "And your painting."

Sarah flinched. *Please don't ask again about the sunset.*

"You never did tell me your inspiration."

Sarah froze again, her body felt so stiff she might as well have been pinned next to the crucifix hanging in front of them. "Well, I…"

With a smile, Mom stretched around her and extended a hand. "Hello. I'm Rose, Sarah's mom."

Wow. Sarah never thought she'd see the day when imposing moms came in handy.

Eduardo extended his long torso through the cramped space, his chest briefly touching Sarah's, as he took Mom's hand. He spoke briefly with her.

The words were muffled by the pounding of Sarah's heart. The warmth of his body breathed through her, and his fresh scent filled her nose.

"How nice of your mom to visit." He pulled back.

"Yes," Sarah said. "Very nice." She kept her gaze straight ahead, but out of the corner of her eye, she could see Eduardo studying her. Why hadn't she bothered to put on any mascara? Lip gloss? Anything? Antoinette probably never left the house without looking perfect.

The organ's melody slowed, and the priest glided toward the podium. Before more awkward conversation could ensue, Sarah plopped onto the wooden seat.

Eduardo sat as well, his knee lightly colliding with hers. "Sorry." He attempted to reposition himself.

Sarah shifted closer to Mom, but the row was full, and the seating was cramped. "It's okay."

As he adjusted his position, he banged his shoulder and hip into hers. "Sorry." He crossed one leg over the other and pulled his knee to his chest.

Sarah sighed. Who thought to cram the two long-legs together? She cast an eye at Sister Maria, who was in deep conversation with Mom. *No strangling*, she told herself. *At least, not in church.* "It's fine, really," she said to Eduardo. "Please, I'm uncomfortable just looking at you."

With a warm smile, he settled back to resting his knee gently against hers.

Now at the pulpit, the priest began his Latin chant.

Sarah tried to pay attention to the service, but she kept focusing on the small spot where her knee touched Eduardo's. Her heart raced. *I just have to make it through the next hour*, she reminded herself. *Then the torture will end.*

At least, until school resumes.

The priest switched to Italian.

From the pew, Sarah concentrated on translating the words. Her pulse finally returned to normal.

Mom leaned in. "Your friend's very handsome," she whispered.

The whisper wasn't quiet enough. Sarah opened her eyes wide, and heat rushed her face. She might really strangle someone yet and glanced at Eduardo.

Grinning widely, he flicked up his left eyebrow. "I like your mother."

Sarah's face burned even hotter. She sank down in her seat and closed her eyes. *Can everyone please keep their noses out of my business?*

For the next half hour, her prayer was answered. Then the congregation joined in song—the "Ave Maria."

Eduardo sang along.

His mellow baritone voice sent chills down her spine. Sarah found herself not watching the cantor at the pulpit, but Eduardo. His lips rounded for *hora mortis nostrae*. His Adam's apple lifted for high notes and dropped for lows. When the song ended, she still stared, even as he retook his seat. "Your voice—" her breath caught—"is breathtaking."

Smiling so broad his glasses lifted, Eduardo tugged her hand. "Thank you."

Sarah drifted back to the pew.

He cocked his head to the side. "Yours, on the other hand... You'd best keep to painting."

Drawing a hand to her neck, Sarah was unsure if she should burst with anger or amusement.

Eduardo burst with laughter.

Nearby attendants shushed.

Mom bent forward for a closer look.

As Eduardo regained his composure, he placed a hand on her knee. "Sorry." He rubbed her leg. "I'm only teasing."

Sarah shifted her attention between his hand, his face, and back. His hand remained firmly on her thigh.

"Sorry." He pulled back his hand.

Her breath quickened, and Sarah struggled to find a response. *You don't need to be sorry—please, put back your hand.* Or, *please, I made a mistake.* She *wanted* to say so many things, not the least of which was that she wanted him back. But all she could do was lower her head and say a prayer that Antoinette might somehow vanish.

As the mass adjourned, Sarah filed out to the foyer, Mom on one side and Eduardo on the other. If she spent one more second next to Eduardo, the priest would be reading her last rites, for sure.

Sister Maria stayed behind to speak to the parents of a student.

Sarah walked with them to the front of the church.

"Do you have plans for Christmas?" Eduardo asked.

"We'll try to catch the service at St. Peter's," Mom answered.

"Better get there early," he said.

"I've heard." Sarah counted the steps to the church exit. Only six—no five—and she'd be free of this miserable night.

"Why don't you come by after?" Eduardo asked. "My place is so close to the cathedral."

What?! Sarah stopped short in her tracks. "Oh, I don't think so."

"I'm preparing a traditional meal for me and Lucia."

And Antoinette?

"Do you like fish?" he asked Mom. "Seafood?"

"Oh, I adore it!" She smiled at Sarah. "I'm sure we can come by."

Eduardo smiled broadly and rambled on about the

menu.

Sarah grimaced. *No, no, no! God in heaven, why are you torturing me so?* Which would be worse—another evening in his company or four days of never hearing the end of her refusal from Mom? She pressed her fingers to her temple, where her pulse throbbed. "All right," she said through clenched teeth. "What can we bring?"

Chapter 22

After escorting Mom to the hostel, Sarah returned to her room. The hour was late, technically the early hours of Christmas. She sat on the edge of her flimsy bed, wringing her hands. She had to find some way to back out of dinner at Eduardo's. Maybe she could pretend to be sick? Or maybe they could conveniently get hung up at St. Peter's?

She flopped back on the bed, flailing her arms to the side. This situation was hopeless. Mom would never allow her to back out. She'd gone on and on about Eduardo during the walk to her hostel. Sarah kept her lips zipped. What was she supposed to say? He called me *bella cigna,* and then I blew him off?

Bella cigna. His smooth, mellow voice played in her mind. *I can't believe your Italian and your painting.*

Warmth simmered in her chest. If he'd recognized the sunset in the mural, did he still have feelings for her? Sarah bit her lower lip. Maybe things weren't that serious with Antoinette? Maybe she could just…

She puffed her bangs with a "humph." Just what? Ask him to end things with Antoinette? Ask him to overlook her own fickleness? Why would a handsome, wealthy bachelor do such a thing? He probably had a black book thicker than Mr. Rosen's listings.

A light tap sounded on the door, and Sarah bolted upright. Who would be calling at this hour? Her mother? Sister Maria? Or maybe...Eduardo? "Just a minute!" Sarah threw a robe over her pajamas and hastily ran her hands through her hair. She rushed to the door and flung it open. "Sister Maria?" The disappointment in her voice was evident. She drew the robe closer to her chest and tightened the belt.

"I saw your light," Sister Maria said.

Sarah glanced over her shoulder. Light streamed out the window, dipping into the courtyard. Across the way, a soft lamp glowed in Sister Maria's office.

Sister Maria stepped past her into the room. "I hope you didn't mind me seating you next to Eduardo this evening. I could only hold the one row, you see."

With a lifted brow, Sarah pinched the corner of her mouth. If Sister Maria noticed, she didn't let on.

"I just came from speaking with him."

"You did?" Sarah's pulse quickened. "What did he say? Did he mention Antoinette? Did he mention—" She caught herself and broke off.

Sister Maria smiled, her stance—hands clasped at her waist—unwavering.

"I mean," Sarah continued, "I hope he enjoyed the service."

"Oh, yes. He said your singing brought him joy."

Cheeks burning, she dropped her gaze. "Of course, he did."

"I never did get to commend you on your accomplishments with the play," Sister Maria said. "The scenery and your work with Lucia. They were both marvelous feats."

"Thank you."

"Ones which didn't go unnoticed by the parents, including Eduardo."

Uncertain if she wanted to hear more or not, she lifted her gaze anyway.

Sister Maria stepped over to the desk and turned back the cover of a sketchpad. "You know, Sarah, sometimes we have to take risks to achieve our dreams."

Oh, no. What had Mom told her during the service? About Philip? The infertility? Finding the belt of her robe, Sarah threaded it through her hands. With each pass, the rope strung tighter.

"I've told you I joined the convent to escape my past. I stayed there, at a small monastery in rural Tuscany, for fifteen years." Sister Maria flipped through the pages.

A gentle calm settled into Sister Maria's voice, and the rustle of paper cut through the stiff silence.

She turned another page and paused to study it. "Giving up that place was hard—the monastery was my solace."

Sarah paused her weaving. "Why did you?"

"I was offered a job at a school here in the city. Eduardo and Leonardo—they were some of my first students."

"Leonardo De Luca?"

Sister Maria nodded. "I was scared to take the job, Sarah. I was scared to be around children."

"Scared?" Sarah dropped the belt. Of what could this iron fist of a woman be afraid?

"I love children but being around them was painful." An edge entered Sister Maria's voice.

Why would it be painful? Unless…Could she not conceive either?

"But coming here was the best decision I ever

233

made."

Sister Maria let go of the sketchpad and turned to face Sarah. She placed a hand on her shoulder. "What I'm saying is, sometimes we have to put ourselves in uncomfortable situations to get what we want—what we need."

Tears brimmed Sarah's eyes, and she again picked up the belt, pulling it taut. What was the sister saying? She should go back to fertility treatments? She should consider adoption?

Sister Maria squeezed Sarah's shoulder then backed away. "*Buon Natale*, Sarah."

Frozen in place, Sarah yanked tighter on the belt—so tight, she thought the fabric might fray. "Merry Christmas." Sarah's voice cracked.

Sister Maria turned to go.

Sarah let the tears drip down her cheeks. Soft sniffles muffled the gentle snap of the door closing. Why did Sister Maria have to give such vague advice? And why did her advice always incite sobbing?

Releasing the belt, she reached for the box of tissues on her desk. She froze her hand in mid-air, and she gasped. The sketchbook that Sister Maria studied lay open. The man in the picture stared with charcoal eyes—Eduardo's eyes.

For a moment, Sarah was suspended in time. She didn't blink. She didn't swallow. She didn't breathe. Sister Maria's words rushed her mind, and her chest burned. She drew a deep breath and lowered herself to the chair. Sister Maria was right. Sarah didn't know what she wanted to do next year. She didn't even know if she wanted to stay in Italy or go back to the States. But as she traced the outline of Eduardo's face, she understood one thing she knew she wanted for sure—one person. Eduardo.

****

The stairs creaked under Sarah's footsteps, fuzzy teddy-bear slippers and all. The hall and stairwell were dark—had been ever since the students left over a week ago. She strode along the dim passage, clutching her master key in her hand.

I shouldn't be doing this.

But what other choice did she have? The shops wouldn't be open on Christmas Day, and she sure as hell wouldn't win back Eduardo with an A-line skirt and button-up blouse.

Still, as she reached Flora's room, she hesitated, the key hovering in front of the lock.

Why couldn't Anna be her size? Then she wouldn't have to go stealing from the only student who was as tall as she was.

Borrowing, she reminded herself. *Just borrowing.*

She slipped the key in the lock and turned it. The snap echoed through the hall. Sarah's heart pounded. Could she really do this? Could she really win him back?

She flipped on the light and stepped inside. As she opened the closet, she bowed her head. "Please, God, let Flora have left something halfway decent."

****

After a cab-ride through winter's waning sun, Sarah and Mom arrived at Eduardo's just before four.

Lucia greeted them at the door. "Miss Miller!" She lunged out of the apartment and hugged Sarah.

Sarah tousled Lucia's hair, the softness tickling her fingers. As she pulled away, Sarah introduced her mother.

Sarah's mom knelt. "You can call me Mrs. Miller."

Lucia pressed her brows together.

"Tell you what," Sarah said. "To avoid confusion, why don't you call me Miss Sarah? Just for tonight."

Her mother by her side, Sarah joined Lucia in the foyer. Warmth and the aroma of garlic and herbs greeted her.

Eduardo approached from the kitchen. "Sarah! Mrs. Miller! What a pleasure to see you again." He motioned for them to come inside.

He wore the same apron Sarah remembered from her only other visit here. Her breath caught. She closed her eyes partly to relive the memory and partly to settle her nerves.

Eduardo helped Sarah's mother with her coat then turned to Sarah.

Sarah hesitated before removing hers. Was a skimpy dress really the right move? She clutched the zipper of her coat. *Too late to change my mind now.* She yanked the zipper.

"Wow! Miss Mill—I mean, Miss Sarah, where'd you get that outfit?" Lucia stared at her with widened eyes.

As Sarah drew a hand to the plunging neckline of the skintight sweater dress, heat rushed to the same spot. "I—"

Eduardo cleared his throat. "Lucia, didn't you have something to show Mrs. Miller?"

Lucia stared blankly.

Widening his eyes, Eduardo flicked his gaze in the direction of the window.

"Oh, yeah. Papa says I should show you the view."

Lucia grabbed Sarah's mother's hand.

"That sounds lovely!" Mom stepped toward the window but paused. "You look great," she whispered in Sarah's ear.

Sarah dropped her hand from her chest and forced herself not to tug at the hemline, which suddenly seemed shorter.

Eduardo stepped closer. As he took her coat, his gaze drifted from Sarah's face to her body. "Your mom's right. You look great."

"Thank you." *And thank you, Flora.*

Eduardo placed their coats on a rack and returned. "Now, I thought you might help me in the kitchen."

"Sure." *Sure?* Sarah shut her eyes. This evening was operation Win Back Eduardo, not a parent-teacher conference. She snapped open her eyes and rested a hand on the edge of her collar.

Eduardo's gaze followed her hands.

"I mean, I'd love to." Sarah spoke in a voice as gravelly and soft as she could muster. She danced her fingers around her bare neck. Eduardo tracked them like a dangled carrot.

He didn't head toward the kitchen.

"You said something about the kitchen?" Sarah prompted.

"Kitchen?"

Sarah stifled a giggle and nodded.

"Kitchen." Eduardo jerked back. "Right." He pulled at his collar, his Adam's apple exposing a deep swallow. "Shall we?"

She nodded and followed him.

"I thought you might help me with dessert," he called over his shoulder.

Sarah held her chin high. Perfect, this privacy was just the opportunity she'd hoped for to remind him of their date. "What was wrong with dessert last time?"

"Hmm?"

"The dessert you served last time. I enjoyed it immensely. Didn't you?"

He turned at the far side of the kitchen. "Last time?" He furrowed his eyebrows.

Sarah sauntered up, batted her lashes, and placed her hands on his chest. The warmth and firmness of his body threatened to unravel her, but she steadied her voice. "I suppose that would only be appropriate if we were alone."

He softened his brow line. "Oh…no…I enjoyed it."

Smiling, she plucked back her hands. The operation was going better than she'd expected. But now, for the hardest part—extracting details on his current relationship. On—she secretly cringed—Antoinette. "But what am I thinking? Of course, Antoinette wouldn't approve. Will she be joining us as well?" She turned her attention to a tray of empty cannoli shells and a bowl of a white fluffy substance she presumed to be the filling.

"Oh, no. She's out of town."

"Visiting family, I suppose?"

"No. Work."

"Work?" Sarah spun on her heel. "Who works on Christmas?"

He shrugged. "Financial advisers trying to secure a Chinese firm."

"Ah. Well, so long as she makes you happy. She does make you happy?" Sarah stared up at him. His honest eyes would reveal the truth.

But he shifted his gaze, casting his attention in the direction of the cannoli. "I don't know. I guess so." He picked up an empty shell.

Sarah tried to measure his feelings by the expression on his face, but it matched his response—indifference.

"How about we concentrate on dessert? That's a less loaded topic. Plus"—he dipped his finger in the white substance—"we'd better get these done before I eat all the filling." He brought his finger to his mouth.

Impulsively, Sarah grabbed his hand. Was the sultry outfit to blame? Or that she was alone with him? She didn't know. For whatever reason, she couldn't hold herself back. She wrapped her mouth around his finger and licked off the sweetened mascarpone.

With each stroke of her tongue, Eduardo widened his eyes.

"Mm." She closed her eyes as she lapped.

A cannoli shell snapped with a crack, and Sarah opened her eyes. A crumbled cannoli lay in Eduardo's other hand, its shattered pieces falling to the floor.

Sarah released his finger. Tongue explorations *were* definitely not part of the plan. "I'm sorry." She bent to clean up the broken shell.

"No, it's okay." He knelt beside her. "I just wasn't expecting that."

"Neither was I."

He laughed lightly. "I think I need a glass of wine. Can I get you one?"

Maybe some alcohol would help her relax? No, she needed to focus, not indulge in her desires. She smiled. "Maybe just some water."

He nodded and opened the refrigerator.

As he prepared drinks, Sarah reminded herself of her plan. Antoinette. Right. Focus! "So, does Antoinette like wine?"

Sighing, Eduardo dropped his shoulders and handed her the water. "Don't all Italians?"

Sarah frowned, picked up a cannoli shell, and spooned in some of the filling.

"Let me help you with that." Eduardo spooned the filling into a plastic bag.

Sarah sipped her drink. He sure liked skirting the Antoinette issue. Was that because their relationship wasn't serious? Or because their relationship was?

He handed her the bag.

With a steady hand, Sarah squeezed the mixture into the cannoli.

Eduardo wagged a finger and took the bag. "You have to squeeze firmly and consistently." He filled the cannoli like an expert pastry chef, placing a rosette dollop on the top. He cocked a brow and gave a devilish grin.

As she rolled her eyes, Sarah snatched back the bag. She did her best to emulate his process, forgoing the flourish on the top.

Eduardo gave a nod of approval.

As the stack of unfilled cannoli dwindled, uneasiness crept into Sarah's chest. She had no idea how he felt about Antoinette. "So…. have you been together long—you and Antoinette?"

Eduardo laughed. "You sure are asking a lot about her." He wiped his hands on his apron, placed his hand on Sarah's waist, and spun her. "Are you bothered that I'm seeing someone?"

"Why should I be bothered?" Sarah delivered her

well-rehearsed response. She let the silence hang for a second. "Would you be bothered if *I* was dating someone?"

"You mean other than me?"

She smiled—now, they were getting somewhere—and nodded.

He pulled her closer, locking his gaze with hers. "Yes, Sarah. It would bother me very much."

A wide smile spread across Sarah's face. This revelation was more than she could have hoped for. She reached up to embrace him.

"Papa! Papa!" Lucia called as she pranced into the kitchen.

Eduardo dropped his hand from Sarah's waist. "Yes, Lucia?"

"Have you finished your alone time with Miss Mill—I mean Miss Sarah yet?"

Sarah couldn't help but laugh.

"I suppose, Lucia." He turned to Sarah. "Let's finish our conversation later."

With a nod, Sarah exited the kitchen, wondering if she might have some more *alone time* later that evening.

Chapter 23

All through dinner, Sarah pined for a few moments alone with Eduardo. Not even Eduardo's flaky, baked cod or spice-coated shrimp could draw her mind from the question yet to be answered. Would he give up Antoinette to be with her? Mom made several futile attempts to give them some privacy.

"Lucia, dear, won't you help me get the coffee for dessert?" she offered.

"Papa always makes the coffee." Lucia stood tall and smiled.

And later, after everyone licked their plates clean of cannoli filling, Mom turned toward the child. "Lucia, would you mind showing me to the bathroom?"

Lucia reached for another cannoli. "Second door on the right."

Sarah's mother gave a feeble smile.

Of all the times for a mother's meddling not to work. Sarah gripped her knees under the table to keep her heels from jittering.

"Papa, can I watch TV?"

"Yes," answered Eduardo, Sarah, and Mom, in unison.

"I'll join you." Mom rose from the table.

Sarah took a casual sip of her water.

Eduardo cupped his coffee. "So"—he leaned forward on one elbow—"we've talked a lot about me tonight. What have you been up to these past few months?" He tipped back his cup.

"Well, I would like to say I've visited all of Rome by now, but I'm not even close."

"No?" He tilted his head to the side, narrowing his eyes. "No long walks along the Tiber? No candlelight dinners on *Via dei Coronari*?"

"Long walks alone, yes." Sarah set down her glass. "But I've never heard of the *Via dei Coronari*. And candlelight dinners? Please." She swatted the air. "The closest I've come is tea at *Al Forno's* with Anna. And the tea was total crap, by the way."

"Tea!" He smacked the table and stood. "I almost forgot." He cut the space to the kitchen in two long strides.

Sarah took advantage of his momentary absence to shift her legs from under the table, crossing them so her lean calves dangled in his direction.

Eduardo returned with a wooden box. He set it on the table and lifted the lid.

Inside was an assortment of teas: reds, blacks, greens, and even herbals, all neatly arranged in their paper parcels. "Eduardo! I can't believe you went to such trouble."

Smiling, he shrugged.

"Really." Sarah placed a hand on his. "Dinner itself was enough. But the tea, too?"

He cupped his other hand over hers. "Eh. The octopus was chewy."

"When isn't octopus chewy?" Sarah laughed.

He didn't reply; he only smiled and gently stroked the back of her hand.

Adrenaline coursed through Sarah's veins. Why

couldn't Lucia and Mom disappear for a while? Why couldn't Antoinette disappear indefinitely?

Focus.

She plucked her hand from his grasp and leafed through the teas. "When does Antoinette get back?"

Eduardo leaned back in his chair and folded his arms. He let out a sigh through pursed lips. "A couple of days." He flicked his gaze in the direction of Sarah's mother. "And how long is your mother visiting?"

"The same."

An uncomfortable silence stretched between them. Muffled Italian cartoons whined in the background. Sarah's heart pounded. If she was waiting for a better opportunity to tell him she wanted him back, she wouldn't find one. "Eduar—" she started.

"Does she need any souvenirs?" Eduardo said at the same time.

"Souvenirs?"

"Mrs. Miller," he called over to Sarah's mother, "might you be interested in a shopping outing with Lucia and me tomorrow?" He placed a hand on Sarah's shoulder. "And your daughter, as well?"

"Why, that sounds lovely, Eduardo. What did you have in mind?"

Sarah relaxed her shoulder under Eduardo's grasp. Tomorrow she would tell him, for sure.

****

Just after ten the next morning, Sarah and her mother arrived at the *Piazza Navona*. The hallmark of central Rome was covered with vendors selling marionettes, rosaries, and glass ornaments blown in Venetian factories.

Eduardo clutched Lucia's hand and guided her

through the crowd.

With her mother by her side, Sarah walked just behind. The air sent a chill over her face but hopefully a few moments alone with Eduardo would warm her cheeks.

Eduardo pointed out a food stall selling roasted chestnuts and pressed a coin into Lucia's hand. "Mrs. Miller, would you mind taking Lucia?"

Sarah's mom beamed. "Only if I can get some, too."

"My treat." Eduardo dropped another coin in Lucia's hand.

Lucia dragged Sarah's mother down the crowded promenade.

When they were out of earshot, Eduardo turned to Sarah and grabbed her hand. "Are you warm enough?" He rubbed her hand between his.

"Yes." She smiled. "I am now."

He smiled back, his breath fogging in the air. He strolled with her in silence, hand in hand.

Words didn't come as easily as the previous evening. Sarah knew the words that needed to be said, and perhaps Eduardo did as well. Was his silence also from nerves? Or was he waiting for her to speak first? Waiting for her to tell him she was ready for a relationship. Ready for him.

She cleared her throat. "I hear *Traviata* is opening soon."

"Is it? I hadn't heard."

"So, you won't be taking Antoinette then?"

He grimaced. "Sarah, things with Antoinette, they're…"

Eduardo continued, but Sarah didn't hear him. She

only heard someone shouting her name—and the voice wasn't her mother's. "No," she whispered.

"Sarah!" Marco's voice rang clear again.

Sarah froze. Her stomach clenched.

From within the crowd, Marco emerged, pushing past Eduardo and embracing her.

Eduardo recoiled, his chocolate eyes pinching under his glasses.

Marco hugged her like she was his long-lost love. Sarah broke free from his scrawny arms. "Excuse us," she said to Eduardo, grabbing Marco's shirt and tugging him to the side. "What are you doing?" Her voice was as cool as the air around them.

"Sarah. Is it really you?" He reached for her again.

"Stop!" Sarah stepped back.

With a tightened jaw, Eduardo flashed a stern gaze.

Sarah returned a strained smile, raised a hand, and mouthed, "Just a minute," then turned back to Marco with narrowed eyes. "What do you want?"

"Want?" He ran a hand through his long, flowing hair. "I don't know. I thought we could go out again. Last time was so great."

He stared with his puppy-dog eyes. *Great?* Of course, he thought last time was great. He'd gotten laid. Stepping back again, she glanced in Eduardo's direction. Lucia and Mom were beside him now. Furrowed brows marked their faces. Heat flushed her cheeks. If she didn't get rid of Marco fast, Mom might start an inquisition. She squared her shoulders. "Listen, Marco, I'm sorry, but…" She needed an excuse.

Across the way, Eduardo marched toward them.

Think of something…anything! Sarah's heart pounded.

Eduardo neared.

Sarah could scarcely breathe. The only thing worse than Sister Maria knowing about her one-night stand would be Eduardo knowing.

Aha—Eduardo! He was just the excuse she needed, especially since Marco thought Eduardo was her husband's name. She refocused on Marco. "I've gotten back together with my husband." A gritty edge entered her voice. "And he's here." She flicked a brow in Eduardo's direction. "So please, if I mean anything at all to you, please go. Now."

Marco appraised Eduardo. His easygoing, youthful face scrunched.

"Eduardo," Sarah called, "I'll be right there." She flashed Eduardo a smile then motioned to Marco with stern eyes for him to walk in the opposite direction.

With slumped shoulders, Marco stalked away.

Perhaps Marco recalled the name. Perhaps he finally realized Sarah wasn't interested. Sarah didn't know, and she didn't care. All she cared was Marco was gone. She let go of the cold air caught in her chest and crept back to Eduardo. "So, what were you saying?" She placed a hand on his sleeve.

Eduardo's gaze followed Marco into the crowd. He stiffened his shoulders and rubbed the back of his neck. Peering down through his glasses, his steady gaze questioning, he sighed.

Sarah's cheek twitched, her smile faltering. If a candlelight dinner on *Via dei Coronari* made Eduardo jealous, how would he react to her having spent the night with Marco?

"It's not important," he said in a whispered growl. He turned on his heel, brushing off her hand.

Sarah stood as still as the statue of Neptune, as cold as the frozen puddle surrounding him in the fountain.

For the rest of the outing, no one spoke about Antoinette, no one spoke about the upcoming opera production, and, certainly, no one spoke about resuming their relationship.

Chapter 24

The cacophony of horns, squealing tires, and rolling suitcases was deafening. Cars cut off buses, which pulled in front of double-parked taxis. Sarah hugged her mother goodbye, the hollowness inside her a stark contrast to this city full of life. Hollowness not because Mom was leaving, but because Eduardo had barely spoken to her since Marco's appearance.

Sarah gave Mom a send-off wave then wrapped her coat tighter around herself. She waded through idling cars, their exhaust hovering in the frigid air, back to Eduardo's black Mercedes.

When she tugged the car door shut, silence greeted her.

Eduardo looked over his left shoulder and pulled into the zooming traffic.

"Thanks again for driving my mom," Sarah said.

"Driving was the least I could do." He kept his gaze fixed on the road.

Sarah pondered another conversation starter. Where was the easy banter between them? The casual touches?

Damn Marco! If not for him, Eduardo would probably be calling Antoinette right now, apologizing for ending things over the phone. But no. Now, an offer to drive her mother to the airport was just a gesture of politeness rather than an excuse to spend time with

Sarah.

Finally, she was alone with him. No children pestered. No mothers hovered. Just she and Eduardo sat in the tight confines of a car for a thirty-minute ride. Sarah couldn't ask for a better opportunity to set things straight. So, why did she feel like she'd swallowed a baguette whole?

She gripped her knees, rubbing the denim fabric under her palms. These were the jeans she'd worn the day he'd officially asked her out—the jeans had drawn his gaze to her hips and thighs. He gazed with eyes so hungry his eyes could have jumped through his glasses that day. And now? He certainly wasn't appraising her today.

With a sigh, she slumped in the seat and shifted her gaze back to the window. Outside, scooters weaved through traffic. Stacks of signs, their names and symbols unfamiliar, lined the road. To the east, St. Peter's Basilica arched in the skyline.

Sister Maria's words suddenly flooded Sarah's mind. *We have to put ourselves in uncomfortable situations to get what we want.*

From the passenger seat, she stole another glimpse at Eduardo. Was he driving faster than usual? Was he that anxious to get rid of her?

Uncomfortable, indeed. Sarah took a deep breath and plunged in. "I'm sorry about yesterday. About the little interruption."

"Interruption." Eduardo gripped the wheel tighter and accelerated.

"Yes. I honestly had no idea Mar—" She bit her lip.

Eduardo gave a quick glance out of the corner of

his eye.

"Had no idea my *friend* would be there."

"Neither did I." His voice, devoid of its mellow tone, sounded flat and cold.

"Again, I'm sorry. Really." She placed a hand on his sleeve. He didn't pull back. That small glimmer of hope encouraged her to continue. "I was hoping that we could have talked more..." She hesitated, swallowed hard, and tapped her toes. "About us."

Eduardo snapped his head in her direction. At the same time, his foot caught the brake, and the car jerked. Horns blared. "Sorry," Eduardo returned his attention to the road.

Sarah pulled back her hand and clasped it with the other in her lap. "If you don't want to talk about it—"

"No,"—he cleared his throat—"I do."

She loosened her clenched hands. "Well, I just wanted you to know that I've decided I'm ready. Ready to date again."

He flicked his gaze toward her then back to the road.

"And," she continued, her voice shaking, "I know that you're with Antoinette now, but I wanted to tell you that if things should change, I—" Her voice broke, but she forced herself to finish. "I'd like to date you again. If you're interested, that is."

Her heart pounded. Her breath caught in her throat.

Slowing the car, Eduardo pulled into a parking lot. He shifted the car into Park and turned to face her. "Sarah, this thing with Antoinette is nothing. Nothing compared to how I feel about..." The sentence died in his mouth. He shifted his gaze back to the windshield.

"Yes?"

"I wanted to tell you yesterday, but then…" He tightened his hold on the steering wheel. "Then I see you with this guy—this kid. And I know it's probably nothing, but I can't help thinking." He ran his hands through his hair. "Listen, you broke off things because you said you weren't ready to date, but then here comes this guy. And let me tell you, if he hasn't dated you, he's sure as hell dreamt about it."

"Eduardo, wait. Marco is ju—"

"Marco?" He threw his head against the head rest. "Great. He even has a name."

"He's a friend of Anna's. He has a thing for me."

"I could tell that much."

Wriggling her hands, she cursed Marco. If only she could explain to Eduardo that Marco meant as much to her as Antoinette meant to him. Leaning over, Sarah pried his right hand from the steering wheel. "Eduardo, I promise I haven't dated anyone since you. I haven't even thought about it."

He relaxed his hand in hers.

"To be honest," she continued, "I haven't *thought* about anyone but you."

"Are you sure? Sure you're ready to date again?" His voice was light with shallow breaths.

Eduardo softened his dark eyes to a milk-chocolate brown. Sarah nodded and squeezed his hand.

As he smiled, he pressed his fingers into her palm. "Because if I have to go through the agony of letting you go again—and that was just after one date—I might just join the priesthood."

No sooner did the words leave his mouth than she lunged across the seat and kissed him.

****

252

Time suspended over the next few days. Afternoons were spent strolling through the park, with Sarah's head nuzzled in the breast of Eduardo's leather jacket. Conversations lingered over dinner in quiet restaurants, well past Sarah's bedtime. But the goodnight kisses, the gentle tug of Eduardo's teeth on her lip, with no worries of a student wandering past in the hall, were what Sarah wanted to bottle up.

Thoughts of his touches stayed long past recitations of the state capitals and well into the night. They remained when she woke and lasted until she received his "good morning, *bella cigna*" text. When would his eager hands unsnap that first button? When would his tender kisses drift below her chin? When would he not take her back to her dorm, but instead ask her to stay the night?

Their first date, so many months ago, was too soon for him to ask. But now, a handful of dates later, Sarah wondered when he might ask again. She lounged with Eduardo on the floor in front of his fireplace. "I can't believe break is almost over," Sarah said. "Anna comes back tomorrow."

"Another week"—he frowned—"until you're back at work."

Sarah nodded.

"Two until I have Lucia again."

"Two weeks?" Sarah sat up. "But I thought you had her every other weekend?"

"As part of the custody agreement, Roberta has her through the week ending with Epiphany."

"So long?"

"The gaps are always this long around the holidays." Eduardo placed a hand on her knee. "Having you to spend time with has really helped. Otherwise, I'd just be working."

"Working?" Sarah gave a light laugh. "Who works through the holidays?"

Eduardo gave her a sideways glance.

Right. Antoinette. Neither of them said her name—hadn't said her name since Eduardo ended things with her. Probably not the nicest Christmas present in the world, but from what Eduardo relayed, Antoinette was content to call it quits as well.

"Can't you renegotiate the terms of the custody agreement? You are a lawyer, right?"

Laughing lightly, Eduardo squeezed her knee. "International corporate law isn't quite the same. Besides, I can't really blame Roberta."

Sarah tilted her head.

Eduardo sighed, his gaze resting on the fire. The flames reflected off his glasses. "I wasn't always such a devoted father."

Stiffness crawled up Sarah's spine. Devoted father, or devoted husband?

He glanced over at her. "I wasn't unfaithful—nothing like that. Just..." He stopped, sighed, and then started again. "I met Roberta after returning from law school in New York. She was young and beautiful, and her father was a partner in the firm where I worked. I thought I loved her."

His voice was distant and cool, and his eyes an icy contrast to the warmth of the flames. Releasing a tight exhalation, Sarah felt the tension in her muscles ease.

"I didn't realize until later that she was just another challenge—I wanted to prove that I could give her things like her father did. I worked tirelessly to gain new clients and establish myself as the go-to man in the firm, only to spend my money frivolously on Roberta. And after we married, her father made me junior partner at the firm, and I worked even more than ever, feverishly establishing a strong clientele so I could open my own firm."

Sarah shifted closer, taking his hand in hers. His past, as painful as it was, made him the man he was today.

"That was about the time Lucia was born. I was determined to provide her the best. I...I'm sorry to admit that I worked even more after Lucia was born. I thought money would be a better gift than my time."

Aching to remove his guilt, Sarah nuzzled into his chest and squeezed his hand.

"I wasn't surprised when she left me." He rested his chin on her hair. "Lucia was only three. I was hardly home, and I was neither a good father nor a good husband. Not until they were gone did I realize what I'd lost. But my realization was too late."

He paused. "I never mourned losing Roberta. I'd known for some years we weren't in love. But I will never forgive myself for losing Lucia."

Sarah let his confession breathe. The crackle of the fire was the only sound in the room. How was he so brave to bear his secrets—his flaws? Did he expect her to share hers, too?

Blinking, she pushed away the thought. No. Tonight was about him, not her. "You're a wonderful father, Eduardo. Lucia lights up when you're around."

"When?" Eduardo snorted. "The all of four days a month I spend with her?"

At the bitterness in his voice, Sarah jerked back.

Eduardo turned, and tears glistened on his cheeks. He caught her hand. "I don't blame Roberta, Sarah. I can only blame myself."

"No one's perfect, Eduardo." *I'm certainly not.*

Sapped of his bravado, Eduardo sat lifeless.

Sarah pulled her knees up under her and lifted his chin so he was forced to look at her. "Eduardo, if my husband had half the heart you do, I would forgive him for what he's done. And if I were Roberta, or Lucia, I would forgive you, too." For a moment, he didn't speak—but his demeanor changed. His eyes filled with warmth, and his shoulders lifted.

He sat forward, placing a hand on Sarah's waist. "You have no idea how relieved I am to hear you say that." He wrapped an arm around her hips and pulled her close, leaning into her as he lowered her to the floor. His lips danced on her skin, skimming her neck, then her chin, and stopped behind her ear. "Sarah?" he whispered.

"Yes?" She shivered at his touch.

"I want to make love to you."

Sarah couldn't help but smile. She grasped his collar and eased him closer.

He returned his mouth to hers, kissing her deeply, his hands wandering over her body. When they found her breasts, he threw his head back with a groan.

A warmth spilled down her body, and she moaned.

"Bella Cigna, tu sei perfetto."

Perfect? Sarah stiffened. He wouldn't think as much once he knew of her secret—her flaws. What *would* he think? Would he want to be with her? Would he still be attracted?

Eduardo pushed himself up. "You, um, don't want

to?"

Oh no. How long was she lost in thought? "No," Sarah blurted. She sat up, shaking her head. "I mean yes. Of course, I want to. I...I'm just nervous."

"Nervous? Why would you be nervous?"

"I don't know. I haven't been intimate in so long." She fought against wincing. Why had she drunk so much with Marco?

"Too long." He ran a finger up the outside of her thigh.

Sarah shuddered at his touch. "Yes. Too long. I haven't been with someone since, since..." She swallowed the words.

"Your husband?"

Sarah didn't answer, but the guilt flamed in her cheeks.

With narrowed eyes and pinched brows, Eduardo pulled back. He rose to his feet. "You said he was one of Anna's friends?"

Sarah bolted to her feet. "I did. He is. I mean, he was just—"

"Just what, Sarah?"

"A mistake." She reached for him.

He jerked away his hand. "Mistake? Mistake?" he repeated louder. He stomped toward the far side of the room. "Like the mistake you made when you ended things with us? Or was that all the same mistake?"

She couldn't lose him now—not after everything she'd gone through to win him back. Sarah chased after him. "Marco had nothing to do with you—us, I promise." She clasped his shoulder. "This mistake happened before you and I ever went out." Under her hand, a muscle in Eduardo's shoulder contracted then softened.

He tipped his head to the side, raising an eyebrow. "Before?"

Sarah sighed. "It happened in the summer. I had too much to drink."

Eduardo turned, a crease marking his forehead. "But you don't drink."

"Exactly." Sarah released him and wrung her hands.

He shook his head and furrowed his brows.

"I don't remember, Eduardo. I had a few drinks, and the next thing I remember is waking up in his bed." Sarah forced herself to hold his gaze. The color in his eyes shifted from dark to light.

For a moment, he stared, and then his laugh cut the silence. "Well, maybe I should get you a glass of wine." He grabbed her hands and tugged her close.

Sarah released a heavy breath. "Very funny." She bent her head into his chest, inhaling his scent. "No wine. With you, I want to remember every second."

Chapter 25

"What do you mean you didn't sleep with him?" Anna shrieked.

Sarah settled onto Anna's bed, the rumpled comforter pushing into her thighs. The afternoon sun illuminated dust motes puffing from the bed. Sarah swatted them away. "I don't know. I got nervous."

"Well, will you sleep with him?" Anna yanked clothes from her bag and shoved them into her dresser.

Sarah twirled her hair. Bringing Anna up to speed on her relationship sent her back to her college days.

"Well?" Anna slammed the drawer; a bra strap caught in the closure.

"When the time's right." College reminded her of Meredith. She hadn't even told Meredith about Eduardo yet. They hadn't talked recently because Meredith was busy with the holidays: entertaining guests, putting away Christmas ornaments, and pleading with Amber and Steven that New Year's Day was officially the time to take the artificial tree down.

"Enough about me." Sarah examined her friend. With dark circles under her eyes, Anna looked like she hadn't slept in a week. "How was home?"

"Home? Boston doesn't feel like home anymore." Anna plodded back to her half-emptied suitcase. "Nowhere does."

Sarah took a moment to respond. "Maybe Oxford

will."

Anna heaved another pile of clothes out of her bag. "Maybe."

Where was her home now? Not D.C. Not Rome. Perhaps she and whiz kid had more in common than was apparent. Sarah shifted on the bed.

Anna sniffed a tattered sweater, shrugged, and hung it up.

Well, maybe not that much in common. Sarah's phone hummed in her pocket, and she yanked it free; the tune of Verdi's "Amami Alfredo" filled the air.

Anna raised an eyebrow. "Amami Alfredo or Amami Eduardo?"

Sarah stuck out her tongue and answered the phone. "Hi, sweetie."

Sweetie? Anna mouthed.

"*Bella cigna*, I missed you today."

His baritone voice warmed her. "I missed you, too."

"That's sickening," Anna said.

Sarah covered the receiver with her hand. "Would you stop?" she said, half-teasing, half-serious.

"I was wondering if I might steal you away tonight," Eduardo continued. "I got us tickets to *Traviata*."

"Really?" She sprang forward on the bed and widened her eyes.

"Box seats."

Anna let out a long yawn.

Jetlag. Even Anna couldn't beat it. "I can't pass that up," Sarah said into the phone. "I don't think Anna's up to hanging out tonight, anyway."

"Pick you up at six?"

"Sure." Tapping her feet on the floor—she could already hear the *brindisi* playing—Sarah ended the call. A smile tickled her lips. Who knew giddy felt so good? "He's taking me to the opera tonight."

"Oh yeah? Ends late, I bet." Anna flopped in her desk chair, resting her head on a hand.

"I guess."

"You gonna stay the night?" Anna eased her lips into a grin.

"Maybe?" A flurry of nerves seized her stomach. Excitement? Trepidation? Maybe a touch of both?

Anna rolled her eyes. "Tell me you have a gown to wear."

"Damn. I didn't think of that." She checked the time on her phone—one pm. She'd have to hurry.

Anna dragged herself out of her chair and snatched Sarah by the elbow. "Well, come on then. We'll have to go back to *La Rinascente*."

"Right." Sarah got to her feet.

"We can stop by the lingerie department, too, for when you come to your senses."

Sarah smiled. What would she do without Anna?

"You know sex with Italians is way better than with Americans."

Sarah gasped. "Really?"

"Oh, yeah. It's like their dinners—deliciously drawn out."

"Oh," was all Sarah could manage. A sudden heat rushed her belly. Maybe a detour to the lingerie department wasn't a bad idea after all.

****

Sarah contemplated the contents of her overnight bag. A change of clothes. Check. One brand new pair of black, silky underwear. Check. She reconsidered her mental list. Better make that two pair—just in case. She threw in a lacy red pair. Fuzzy teddy bear slippers? Why not? She tossed in those too.

Now for toiletries: toothbrush, makeup remover, floss. She picked up a strip of condoms—another gift from Anna—and hesitated. What if Eduardo questioned her choice in contraception? What if he asked why she wasn't on the pill? She dropped the condoms on her lap. Maybe she should tell him. He'd laid his baggage on the table. Shouldn't she, too?

She sighed, surveying the emerald green gown that hung over the door. Did she really want to spoil tonight's fun? If she didn't stay the night, she could steer clear of any talk of contraception or that might hint at her flaws—her secrets.

Her phone dinged, and she picked it up. Her mom. She hesitated then swiped the phone to accept the call. "Mom, I've been meaning to call," Sarah fibbed. She drummed her fingers on the back of the chair. She hadn't spoken to her mother since her departure. How many days ago was that? Five? Six?

Mom gave a light laugh. "I know you've been busy."

"A little."

Wait. She stopped her fingers from dancing. How did her mom *know* she'd been busy?

"I saw Amber and Steven the other day to drop off the gifts I bought in Rome. Meredith says to call when you get a chance."

"That's nice."

"So…you've been seeing a lot of Eduardo? He really is such a dear. And Lucia…"

Mom kept talking, but Sarah tuned her out. *Seeing a lot of Eduardo? How did she—?*

Oh no. Sister Maria. They couldn't have. But how else would she have known?

"He really is just perfect for you, dear," Mom said.

"Uh-huh." Sarah rushed to the curtains and peeked out. Across the courtyard, Sister Maria's light glowed.

"He's handsome, charming…"

Had Eduardo *told* Sister Maria? Or had she seen? Sarah cradled the phone on her shoulder, closed the curtains, and snatched up the strip of condoms.

"Did I mention he's handsome?"

"Yes, Mother." Sarah stuffed the condoms in a drawer.

"But the best part is he already has kids. Well, *a* kid."

"Mm-hmm." Sarah collapsed into her desk chair.

"And Lucia is absolutely darling, isn't she? You two are already practically like family."

Sarah sat up straight. Could she poke her nose any deeper? "Family?"

"The way you two dote on each other, you'd think she was your daughter."

Sarah's mouth rounded into a smile. "Lucia would be a perfect daughter."

"Of course, she would, dear. And don't think Eduardo hasn't noticed how close the two of you are."

"You think?"

"I know."

Sarah shot a glare toward the window. *Of course, you know.*

"Trust me, Sarah. This one's a keeper."

Silence hung on the line, and her mom's statement

echoed in Sarah's mind. *The best part is, he already has kids.* She tugged open the desk drawer and pulled out the sheet of condoms. If Eduardo wasn't interested in having more children, then perhaps she could put off the infertility conversation until later. Taking a deep breath, she let the air expand her belly, and calmness washed over her. "Mom, I'm sorry to cut our conversation short, but I've got some things to do."

She hung up, walked over to her bag, and placed the condoms inside. Would they open the door to more questions? Would she even have need for one?

Chapter 26

Eduardo eased the car to the front of the theatre. As the valet approached, he leaned toward Sarah. "You sure you don't want to catch tomorrow's show?" He motioned with his eyes toward her bag in the back seat.

"Very funny," she said.

"Leave at intermission?"

The valet opened the passenger door and extended his hand.

"Not a chance." She exited the car, and the cool air nipped her cheeks.

Eduardo trotted around the car, passing the keys to the valet.

"Besides," Sarah continued, "*Traviata* was written by *your* favorite composer, remember?"

Eduardo slid an arm around her waist and pulled her to his side. He gave a sigh. "Be thankful tonight's performance is a Verdi masterpiece and not a Puccini melodrama, or I'd never let you through the door."

Smiling, Sarah tucked closer and followed him through the column-lined entrance. Crystal sconces illuminated their private box, and soft red fabric covered the seats and lined the walls. Before taking her seat, Sarah leaned against the balcony and scanned the domed auditorium. Hundreds of boxes circled the room, each identical to theirs. On the floor, at least as many chairs separated the box seats from the stage. Above, sparkling chandeliers illuminated a fresco-embellished ceiling.

Sarah's spine tingled. Meredith would never believe this grandeur. She snapped a picture on her phone then took a seat next to Eduardo.

He thumbed his phone as well. "Just reminding Matteo I'll be in late tomorrow."

Sarah frowned. "I didn't realize you'd gone back to work."

"The place won't run itself. I've been out a week already."

"Oh." Sarah turned her attention to the program. When was the last time she'd thought of work? One—no, two weeks ago. She sank farther into the plush cushion. When school started again next week—was that only four days away?—she'd mostly see Eduardo on the weekends.

She tightened her hands on the program and snapped her head toward Eduardo. "You don't work on weekends, do you?"

"Weekends?" He didn't look up from his phone.

Sarah stared. This conversation was reminiscent to one she'd had with Philip.

In his seat, Eduardo flicked his gaze from his phone, to Sarah then back to his phone.

The orchestra warmed up, dissonant chords resonating through the hall. Sarah kept her gaze on Eduardo.

He tapped the screen one last time then slipped the phone into his breast pocket. He shifted his hand to her knee. "What were you saying?"

Applause rumbled through the room. Sarah drifted her gaze to the stage.

The maestro, who wore a tuxedo and held a baton, took the podium.

Her fingers tingled with anticipation of the overture. She inched forward in her chair. "Nothing."

For the next three hours, the stage consumed Sarah. She bobbed up and down to the *brindisi*. When Violetta abandoned Alfredo, she clutched the edge of her seat. During the death scene, she choked back tears. And when the curtains were drawn, Sarah wept openly. Clapping between sniffles, she turned to Eduardo to ask for a tissue.

His seat was empty.

Sarah scanned the box.

In the shadow of the entrance, Eduardo stood scowling, his phone pressed against his ear.

Concerned, Sarah grabbed her purse and joined him. Applause sounded behind her, and the audience rose to their feet.

Eduardo returned his phone to his pocket and said something to Sarah.

Under the noise of the applause, all she caught was the name Matteo.

He tugged her hand and pulled her into the foyer. "Matteo's mother," he said. "She passed unexpectedly."

His eyes were dark. Sarah squeezed his hand. "Oh, no. That's awful."

"Tomorrow." Eduardo hung his head. "I'll have to go in tomorrow to cover Matteo's meeting."

"Of course. Don't worry about me. I can take the bus back from your place."

Eduardo jerked up his head. His eyebrows met, and his gaze drifted from her to the entrance behind her. "I meant, we should postpone tonight. I need to prepare.

The Giuseppe case is one of our biggest clients."

Heat brushed Sarah's cheeks. "Oh." The expression popped out, and she forced a smile, but inside her heart ached. "It's fine, really."

"Are you sure?"

His muted eyes told her the question was asked out of politeness, not sincerity. He was probably already mentally scanning the files on his desk.

The doors behind them opened, and patrons rushed the foyer.

Sarah stepped back from Eduardo, letting bystanders brush between her and Eduardo.

"Of course," she said. But with the clatter of shoes and the swooshing of dresses, she was sure he didn't hear. How could he so easily be swept away with work?

****

Montgomery, Alabama. Juneau, Alaska. Phoenix, Arizona.

Sarah tossed over in her bed, the coils creaking. How idiotic was she to invest so much energy into their first night together? She'd purchased two negligées and three pairs of panties. She sighed. Stupid. Eduardo couldn't spare an hour of his night to be with her? How much preparing was necessary?

She glanced at the alarm clock. Three a.m. She jammed the pillow over her face.

Little Rock, Arkansas. Sacramento, California. Denver, Colorado.

Sighing, she loosened her grip on the pillow. Could she really be mad with Eduardo? She'd been the one to spring the idea of staying the night. The meeting was with one of his biggest clients. He wasn't brushing her off...was he?

268

No, no, no. They'd make up for it tomorrow. Sarah pulled the pillow from her face and considered her packed bag. As soon as he got off work, he'd call. She'd grab the bag, and voilà. No big deal.

She kneaded her fingers into the pillow. He *would* call, wouldn't he? Certainly, he wouldn't have brought any work home. Tomorrow was the weekend. Wait— had he ever answered the question about the weekend? Sarah groaned and flopped onto her stomach.

Hartford, Connecticut. Dover, Delaware. Tallahassee, Florida.

A floorboard creaked above her. What would she say to Anna? If she could fall asleep sometime before sunrise, she might wake before Anna. And then what? Avoid her forever? Ignore her texts?

Sarah rolled to her side. This reaction was too much—especially for a conversation about sex. She rounded her mouth into a smile.

Tomorrow she'd find out what sex with an Italian was like. She closed her eyes, hugged the pillow tighter, and imagined Eduardo's warm arms around her.

Atlanta, Georgia. Honolulu, Hawaii. Boise, Idaho.

****

Sarah sipped her second cup of tea, this one with two bags of her strongest black tea. What a shame she didn't like coffee—waking up would certainly be easier. Light streamed through her classroom window, dappling her lesson plans with winter's strong, morning light.

Today was a perfect day to take in a museum or wrap herself in a scarf and frolic through the city. Who wouldn't want to explore beautiful Rome on their last day of vacation? But the weeks of touring with her mother and Eduardo spoiled her; now she'd rather wait to have him by her side, his hand enveloping hers. She'd received no messages. That meeting must be damned important. Why else would he skip his usual morning text?

Yawning, she pushed the phone to the side. The students would be back on Monday; spending the day planning was a more practical choice, anyway. She flipped open her lesson plan book and penciled inside.

Several hours later, with a few days of lessons completed, Sarah received no message from Eduardo. She fidgeted with her phone instead of preparing for class. Should she text him? Ask him again if he worked on the weekends?

No. He was busy with his top client, remember? And what about poor Matteo? Maybe Eduardo needed to attend the funeral this weekend, not spend time with her. If that was the case, she couldn't avoid Anna that long. Sarah was surprised not to have gotten any scandalous texts. Then again, the time was only two p.m. Wonder Girl didn't get up until at least half past three.

One p.m. Nine in the morning back home. Amber should be off to school by now and Meredith free to chat. Tapping her phone's screen, Sarah pulled up her picture from the opera house, sent it to Meredith, and waited. Two minutes later, her phone rang.

"Tell me that's not what I think it is," Meredith said without a greeting.

She heard the envy in her friend's voice. "Yep."

"And that's all you send? No sound bites, no video? Just a still image?"

Sarah smiled. "I had to sneak even that."

270

"I suppose that will have to scratch my itch then."

"But the show was wonderful. No, spectacular. Their voices soared, and I swear I've never seen an orchestra that talented. Verdi. Did I mention the performance was Verdi?"

Meredith huffed. "Are you trying to make me jealous? I'm here cleaning up kid puke, and you're delighting in Rome's opera. How's that for fair?"

"Kid puke?" She straightened in her chair. "Really? Who's sick?"

"They both are. Today's main event is tag-team barfing, and I'm the referee."

"Oh, no," Sarah said through a laugh. "At least you don't have it."

"*Yet.* At least I don't have it yet." Meredith sighed. "But I can't complain. We got through the holidays without a sneeze, so this calamity is what I get, right?"

"That is always how life works, isn't it?"

"Yep. But enough about me. Tell me, who took you to the opera? I can't imagine you went by yourself."

"Well, since you asked," Sarah strung out the word and widened her smile, "I did have a companion."

"A *companion*. Now that is interesting. Please tell me more—" A muffled call sounded in the background, and Meredith cut off. "Crap." She sighed. "Or should I say puke? Either way, Mommy duties beckon. But please, I want a full rundown tomorrow, okay?"

"Tomorrow, sure thing." If she was lucky, tomorrow she'd have a lot more to tell.

"Oh, and before I forget," Meredith said, "Amber's teacher just announced her retirement. So, a position will be free for first grade."

"First grade, huh? Well, I'll have to give applying some thought." *After tonight, that is.*

****

Eduardo didn't call until close to nine o'clock. Back in her room, Sarah was so tired she strongly considered taking a shot of espresso.

"What a day," Eduardo said.

What a day, indeed. A boring morning followed by an equally mundane afternoon and evening. Hell, the highlight of Sarah's day was an afternoon nap strategically scheduled to avoid Anna. "That bad?" she asked.

"Well, getting two hours' sleep is never a good start."

"Tell me about it." Sarah yawned. But Eduardo— only two hours? Was he doing work that whole time, or thinking about her?

"But I was prepared, hell, over-prepared for the Giuseppe meeting."

So, his night was filled with work. Sarah pictured the desk in his living room—the stacks of files and papers. How often did he use that desk?

"The meeting finished early, and I had a late lunch then got back at it."

Late lunch? And he didn't bother to call or text? Or had he worked through lunch, fork in one hand, a report in the other?

"I just got back. Do you want to have dinner?"

"Dinner?" The question came out in a half-screech. "At half past nine?"

"Oh, right. I guess I worked through dinner. Well, do you want to come over? I could swing by and get you."

Sarah perked up. She reached for her overnight bag but froze, clutching the straps. "You don't have plans for the morning? Work?"

"Nope."

"Or the funeral?"

"Funeral?"

Sarah dropped the handles. "Matteo's mother?"

"Oh, yeah. I forgot."

"Forgot? Aren't you supposed to send flowers or something?" Hell, even Mr. Rosen sent flowers when Sarah's father passed. A long silence reverberated on the line. Heat rushed Sarah's face. So not only was he blowing her off, but Matteo, too? "Actually, Eduardo, I'm exhausted. Can we reschedule?"

"Reschedule?"

Sarah collapsed into her chair. "Yes. Maybe tomorrow."

"Maybe?"

"Why don't we touch base in the morning?" Sarah brushed a hand over the laptop keyboard, jostling it from sleep.

"Okay. What time?"

"Time? I don't..." A pop-up window announced a new e-mail from Meredith. *Subject: FWD: Ms. Greiger's retirement.*

Sarah clicked on the email and scanned through the paragraph. With thirty-five years teaching, Ms. Greiger would be missed, et cetera. Arduous search ahead to find a replacement.

"Sarah?"

"Yes?"

"Tomorrow," Eduardo said. "What time did you want to get together?"

"Um…" Sarah pulsed her finger on the touchpad. "I'm not sure, Eduardo. I'll text you in the morning. G'night."

If Eduardo said something more, Sarah didn't catch it. Her heart thudded as she opened another window, pulling up her resume. She hung up the phone. Could this job be any more perfect?

Chapter 27

A knock sounded on the door. Sarah opened one eye, and the blurry numbers of her alarm clock came into focus. Seven a.m. She threw the covers over her head and let out a humph. Anna really was taking retaliation to a whole new level. So what if Sarah ignored her repeated texts? Since when was she a pillow-talker anyway?

The knock sounded again. Since when did Anna knock? Sarah flung the covers off her face.

"Sarah? You up?" Eduardo's voice floated through the door.

She bolted upright. "Just a minute!" She slipped on a robe and stumbled to the door. "Eduardo, what are you doing here? How did you get—" She paused, her gaze down the hall. "Sister Maria?"

Eduardo shook his head. "Anna. Does that girl ever sleep?"

Sighing, Sarah opened the door a couple more inches. "She's pretty much a vampire. A genius, but a vampire." She motioned to enter.

Eduardo edged inside and shoved his hands into his pockets. His gaze shifted from his shoes to Sarah's face. "Sister Maria isn't here, anyway," he said in a somber tone. "She's gone with Matteo to the funeral."

Sarah softened her stance. Eduardo's eyes were apologetic.

"I called him last night. You were right, Sarah. Poor guy, he's a wreck. Sending flowers was the least I could do." He removed a hand from his pocket and took Sarah's in his own. "I should have sent you some, too."

Sarah's grogginess abated. "You don't need to do that."

He squeezed her hand. "Yes, I do. I was an ass. Here I was, a few days earlier, lamenting my wrongs with Lucia and Roberta, and then I do the same thing with you." He stepped closer and placed his other hand on her cheek.

His palm was warm and smooth, like the sensation coursing through her.

"I wanted to make it up to you. Make it up to *us*." He kissed her quickly on the mouth.

"Right now?" The steeliness in her voice was cut by a mild quiver.

"In *that* bed?" Shaking his head, Eduardo gestured to the bed and smirked. "Is your bag still packed?"

Sarah followed his gaze to her bag, which sat next to the door and gave a weak nod.

He dropped her hand. "Good. Because the train leaves at the top of the hour."

"Train? Where are we—"

"Florence." He shrugged. "I figured you'd like that more than flowers."

Florence! A shiver prickled her spine, and Sarah stopped herself from clapping her hands. The Uffizi? The *David*? The Arno? She planted a kiss on Eduardo's cheek, smacking her lips for emphasis.

He grinned and picked up her bag. "Shall we?"

Sarah gazed at the bag, and she bit her lip. "Just give me a few minutes." She ushered him out the door, ran to the bathroom, and brushed her teeth. She snatched her matching set of undergarments from the shower rod. Thank God she'd had sense enough to wash them. She threw them on, along with her favorite pair of jeans and a top, and rushed out the door.

****

The train eased out of the station, picking up speed, and Rome's buildings faded in the distance. Suburbia slipped into rolling countryside, and Sarah relaxed in her seat. "This trip won't put you behind on work?"

"Would it matter if it did?"

Sarah frowned.

"Relax." Eduardo patted her knee. "I told you I worked late yesterday. I have the weekend free."

Sarah fingered the soft fabric covering the seat. "So, if you don't work late, does that mean you work on the weekends?"

With a sigh, Eduardo pulled back his hand and rubbed at a crease in his forehead. "Running a business requires a lot of work. It takes more than just managing the cases. I monitor cash flow and market for new clients. Hell, I even have to make sure the office gets cleaned."

"Don't you have an office manager who can take care of that?"

Eduardo lowered his hand. "I have a secretary, but she can't handle those sorts of things."

I'm pretty sure every secretary in America performs those tasks. "Can't, or won't?"

"Both."

"Then hire someone who can."

Eduardo pinched the corner of his mouth. "You sound like Sister Maria."

"Come on, Eduardo, you're talking about cleaning your office and getting receipts to an accountant, not adding spices to your *bolognese* sauce."

"What's wrong with my *bolognese*? That's a family recipe."

Sarah snapped down her tray table and extracted a paper and pen from her purse. "Payroll, marketing, cleaning." She scribbled the words.

Cocking his chin, he lifted a brow. "What are you doing?"

"Writing a job posting. So, what else does this person need to do?"

Eduardo paused, leaning his head against the glass. He tapped a foot against the floor.

"Well?" Sarah prodded.

He shifted, squaring his shoulders so he faced her. "Well, the person would oversee the secretary and help with billing."

Secretary. Help with billing. Sarah added the tasks to her list.

Eduardo picked up the disposable cup of coffee and raised it to his mouth. He stopped, the paper cup just shy of his lips. "And coffee," he said. "The person would need to make a proper cup of coffee, because I'm spending half the day picking grounds out of my teeth."

"Excellent! These are all good!" Sarah smiled. "Keep going."

"Well, all right." Sighing, he pinched his lips with his fingers and scrunched his brow.

But then he relented, and for the remainder of the short trip, he spilled out the requirements until Sarah had no more room on her sheet of paper. With a new employee, he could focus more on his personal life—spend more quality time with Lucia…with her. Was it too much to hope for?

****

One hundred and fifty miles later, Sarah arrived with Eduardo at the Uffizi just as the gallery was opening. The city was asleep, and the winter sun peeked through the arched stone entrance. The waters of the adjacent Arno trickled in the background. Inside, shoe heels clicked on checkered marbled floors, and busts and full-size statues decorated the halls leading to the galleries.

Sarah didn't know what to look at first. She scanned the handheld map, her fingers trembling. She yearned to see everything at once. Botticelli? Da Vinci? Eduardo's finger appeared on the edge of the map.

He lowered the map. "We have all day, Sarah. Take your time."

All day? But she could spend an entire week and still want more. So much of the city was yet to be seen.

Behind Eduardo, the vibrant red of Raphael's *Madonna* drew her, and she raced off to study it. The hours passed quickly; she was so preoccupied with the art works.

In the early afternoon, Eduardo went off to pick up a gift for Lucia in the museum shop.

Sarah circled back to the Botticelli exhibit. She wanted to take another moment with one of the museum's most famous works, *The Birth of Venus.*

Bright reds and blues, vivid after some five hundred years, filled the canvas. The pale-skinned, blonde-haired goddess of love stood at its center, demurely covering her private regions as angels floated beside her. Sarah admired the delicate brushstrokes, the sharp contours of faces, and the shadows capturing the details of the human body. A blush crept to her cheeks. Did Eduardo find Venus's curves attractive, or would he rather cover them up, like the nymph in the painting?

She dropped her gaze to the floor. Was that why she revisited the painting? To examine Botticelli's capturing of human anatomy? To question what beauty really was?

Again, Sarah lifted her gaze. Even without the summary in the brochure, the title alone was enough to explain the painting's meaning. *The Birth of Venus.* Love. Temptation. Choice. She studied Cupid, his dropped jaw and widened eyes as he took in Venus's naked body. Two lovers whose course was meant to collide.

Sarah stiffened her shoulders. Was she ready to fall in love again? Or should she be focusing on her future, following up on the job application she'd submitted with a letter to the principal?

"Ready to go?" Eduardo asked.

Sarah turned to stare into Eduardo's gentle eyes. Could people *stop* themselves from falling in love?

Eduardo cleared his throat. "Unless, of course, you need more time."

"No. I'm ready. We've got to leave time for the *Accademia.*"

"And lunch." He looped an arm in hers.

"Aww," she teased, "you're putting off visiting your twin?"

Eduardo scrunched together his brows.

"The *David.*" Sarah started toward the doorway. "Please tell me someone has commented on your resemblance. The dark, curly hair. The Greek nose. You even have a voice like an angel!"

Eduardo threw his head back with a laugh. "I don't play the harp."

"Well, there is that."

He stopped at the doorway, unlinked his arm, and drew it to his shoulder, an imaginary slingshot at the ready. Puffing out his chest, he assumed the *David*'s stance. "But I do have his physique, don't you think?"

Admiring his square shoulders and playful grin, Sarah smirked. She could get used to this carefree side of Eduardo. "Oh, really?"

"Maybe not *exactly*."

Sarah laughed.

Eduardo peered over Sarah's shoulder at the painting of Venus. "She really is beautiful, isn't she?"

"Yes, she is." She gulped and ran a hand over her waist and down her hip. Very soon, he'd study Sarah's body—each curve and crevice. Would he find her as beautiful as Venus? Or would she turn him off?

Chapter 28

By the time Eduardo brought her to the hotel room, Sarah was tired, her feet ached, and a tightness pinched her back. She made a beeline for the king-sized bed and flopped onto a cloud of blankets. The mattress nestled her sore body and down pillows cradled her head. How had she survived four months in a lumpy, misfit bed?

She kicked off her shoes and stretched out her legs. Ha! Her feet didn't even hang off the end. Sarah closed her eyes and relaxed. The dreamy pillow-top supported every square inch of her back, arms, and legs.

"Comfortable?" Eduardo asked.

A moan escaped Sarah's lips, and she opened her eyes.

Eduardo stood above her, his chest raising and lowering with shallow breaths.

His gaze filled with the duskiness of desire, and a tension crept into Sarah's muscles that not even the luxurious bed could relax. Was the tightness from her nerves? Excitement? Both?

With his gaze still fastened on hers, Eduardo reached for something next to the bed.

A wine chiller. Was that bottle of champagne there all along? Sarah narrowed her eyes. "You're quite determined," she teased.

"Nothing wrong with loosening you up a bit." He grabbed the neck of the bottle, easing it from the ice.

"I think this bed is doing a fine job of that."

"That good, eh?" In a swift motion, Eduardo slipped off his shoes, firmed his grip on the champagne bottle, and hopped over her. He landed beside her with a thump. "Ah"—he fell back onto the pillows—"you're quite right. But who can resist a glass of champagne?"

"On an empty stomach?"

"Why don't we order in?"

Sarah swallowed hard, unsure if she was ready for their alone time to start so soon. She nodded.

Grinning, Eduardo uncorked the bottle.

Sarah studied his hands as he worked—his strong grasp of the slick base and his gentle nudge of the cork. She shivered, her insides tingling like the champagne, ready to bubble over.

Eduardo freed the cork with a pop, and frothy foam spilled out, dripping over his hand and onto the bed.

Without saying a word, Sarah grabbed the fluted glasses from the nightstand.

Eduardo filled them.

Trading him a glass for the bottle, she returned the champagne to ice.

"To no interruptions." Eduardo raised his glass.

"No interruptions." She clinked his glass. She took a sip—enough to get a taste of its sweetness and to calm the uneasiness that grew in her belly, but not so much that she might forget everything the next morning. The longing in his gaze returned.

"So, any requests for dinner?" Eduardo sank into his elbow.

"Whatever you suggest." Easing onto her side, she mirrored Eduardo's position.

Eduardo lifted a brow, downed the rest of his drink,

and tossed the empty glass on the far side of the bed. "How about an appetizer?" He danced fingers on her knee.

Lowering her gaze to the glass, she searched for a response. But chatter filled her head. *Which pair of underwear am I wearing again? I did remember to put on the black, right? My bra—is the push-up feature obvious?* And if the bra wasn't right, would she be discarded as quickly as the glass?

Eduardo tapped fingers up her thigh and over her hip.

Sarah squirmed away. As she jumped to her feet, she spilled her champagne.

Eduardo stiffened. "I'm sorry. I didn't mean to make you uncomfortable."

The lust in his eyes dimmed. "No…I…" Why couldn't she push aside her insecurities? Why couldn't she just enjoy herself? With a shaky hand, Sarah placed her glass on the nightstand and chewed her lower lip. *Don't screw up.* She forced a smile. "I just need a second." Then she dug inside her bag for the condom, placed it on the nightstand, and made her retreat to the bathroom.

"What's this?" Eduardo asked.

Sarah stopped mid-step, and her stomach turned. Please, God, not the contraception conversation. She slowly turned back to face him.

Between two fingers, Eduardo held the shiny packet, staring at it with crinkled brows. "You only brought one?" He tossed the condom on the floor.

The queasiness in her stomach was replaced by a knot the size of Mount Vesuvius.

Eduardo stood, strode to the closet, and yanked out

his suitcase.

Something rustled as he hunched over the bag.

He returned to the bed and set a bulk-sized box of condoms on the nightstand. "For you, I come prepared."

Sarah erupted in laughter.

"What?" Eduardo shrugged. "As if one would be enough." He trotted over. "You're beautiful." He grasped her hands and pulled her closer to the desk light. Extending his distance, he looked her up and down. His gaze lingered on certain spots: her neck, her breasts, and her hips.

With each pause of his gaze, the brown of his eyes grew richer, and the space between his breaths shortened. Sarah removed his glasses and lowered them to the floor.

Eduardo grabbed her by the waist and pulled her close, covering her mouth with his.

His body warmed her flesh, and she went limp in his arms. Sometime later, she awoke to the sound of the shower, but she didn't open her eyes. She nuzzled into the sheets, and the lingering warmth of their entangled bodies encompassed her. Eduardo's scent—so clean, so fresh—mixed with the sticky sweetness of their coupling greeted her like the aroma of a freshly steeped cup of tea. The muffled tune of the *brindisi* from *La traviata* sounded through the rush of water.

"*Libiamo! Libiamo!*" Eduardo sang.

Sarah pushed herself up on her elbow. Dusky streaks of light dipped in through the window. Puffs of steam escaped under the bathroom door. Eduardo's melody continued.

Eduardo. Her smile deepened.

Eduardo. She reclined back on the bed.

Eduardo. She closed her eyes.

"Oh, Eduardo," a husky voice whispered. Heat rushed to Sarah's cheeks, and she tightened her jaw—the voice was hers. The hands that clawed Eduardo's back, and drew him closer as he rocked gently back and forth, were hers, too.

She snapped open her eyes. Was she too passionate? Too reckless? She was the one who'd suggested they forgo the condoms after they'd blown through three. The barrier seemed unnecessary—she wasn't worried about getting pregnant, and they'd discussed the disease issue before. She'd longed to be closer—to feel him in every possible way.

From the bathroom, Eduardo's voice drifted to a whistle, also *Traviata*, but not the *brindisi.* He whistled the love duet.

Sarah relaxed the muscles in her face. No, she wasn't overzealous—at least not by Eduardo's standards. What was wrong with enjoying sex, anyway? Anna certainly did. Meredith, too.

So much time had passed—too much time—since she'd been intimate with a man. How many years had passed since she and Philip made love—since sex was more than a hasty chafing that coincided with Sarah's ovulation?

A knock sounded at the hotel room door.

"*Servicio!*" a man shouted.

"*Un momento!*" She draped the comforter over herself and opened the door.

"*Tu colazione.*" The man pushed a cart into the room.

Order in. Sarah stifled a laugh, noticing for the first

time a rumble in her stomach. They'd forgotten dinner completely.

As soon as she closed the door, she turned her attention to the food. Sliced meats and cheeses, crusty breads, and gooey pastries filled half of the cart. The other half contained steaming coffee, a pot of tea, and a carafe of milk. What should she try first? A meat and cheese sandwich? A pastry? Wait—was that a crock of Choctella? The growl grew even louder, and she smothered a croissant with chocolate spread.

Italians. Sarah took a bite and sweetness nipped her tongue. *They love their food.* What had Anna said about Italians? About sex and their food? She shoved another bite in her mouth and retrieved her phone. She pulled up Anna's string of texts—all unanswered.

—*How was it?*—

—*Wellllll?*—

—*Sarah?*—

—*Are you ignoring me?*—

Sarah opened the messenger to reply. At the same moment, the shower stopped, leaving only Eduardo's whistle echoing off the bathroom walls. Did she have time send a quick message?

The bathroom door creaked open.

I guess not. Sarah jumped back in bed, discarding the phone and croissant on the nightstand.

Eduardo emerged through the steamy vapor. "You're up."

Sarah nodded, her gaze hanging on him. With a towel wrapped around his waist, Eduardo emerged with beads of water sprinkled on his bare shoulders. His peppered hair was tightly coiled from washing. Her insides tingled, the feeling of bubbling over returning.

"I see breakfast arrived." He grabbed a slice of cheese and a piece of bread and tore off a hunk of each with his teeth. "I told you we'd order in," he said with his mouth full.

"Better late than never."

"I think that can be said about more than just the food." He winked, set down the bread and cheese, and settled on the edge of the bed. "Think you'll be ready to catch the early train?"

She stretched her arms above before smoothing her hands over the comforter. "That would mean saying goodbye to this bed."

Eduardo rested a hand on hers and drew his fingers over the back. "You know, *my* bed isn't much different. Why don't you stay with me?"

"Tonight?" She stared up at him.

"Whenever you want." He lifted her hand to his mouth and brushed her knuckles with his lips.

"What about my work?"

He shrugged. "I'll drop you off."

Sarah hesitated. What if someone saw her with him? Like the girls. Or Sister Maria.

"Don't worry about Sister Maria." Eduardo searched her expression. "Leave that to me."

"Well, in that case…" Was she dreaming? How could things get any better?

Eduardo leaned in. "*Mia bella cigna*, what would I do without you?"

Sarah didn't respond. His lips tickled her neck, and the essence of spice and freshness wafted from his hair. But in that moment, she knew exactly what she would text to Anna.

You were wrong. Sex is way better than the food.

Chapter 29

For the next few weeks, the days passed slowly. The hands of the classroom clock refused to find the twelve and the three, and the afternoons—in the hours between when the children left, and Eduardo picked up Sarah—were even worse. Not even Sarah's sketchpad could distract her. And hall duty? Interminable. How could a night away from Eduardo feel so long? Especially when the nights spent with him, which were more a regularity than not, slipped into morning faster than Eduardo rolled his 'r's.

Time was fickle, especially when measured by Eduardo's presence.

So, when Eduardo's weekend with Lucia neared, Sarah didn't want to let him go. Of course, she wanted him to spend time with his daughter—for both their sakes—but she didn't want to miss a minute of his time. Then she felt guilty for feeling anything but happiness.

"I can't believe a month has passed," she said one evening as she dined with him. "What do you two have planned?" She hoped her carefully crafted smile masked the heaviness in her chest.

"Two?" Eduardo lifted his brows. "Well, naturally you'll be joining us."

He wants me to join them? The weight in her chest lifted then bored down again. "Are you sure?"

"Of course, I'm sure." He squeezed her hand.

"Actually, I insist."

"Well, okay. If you insist." She relaxed her smile and squeezed his hand. She wouldn't be spending the weekend alone after all.

****

"Cheese?" Eduardo brought a block of Parmesan to the table.

In Eduardo's flat, Sarah sat beside Lucia, observing the interactions of the father-daughter weekend.

"Me! Me!" Lucia squealed, uncurling a forkful of spaghetti.

Eduardo paused, shaver in hand. "Is that how we ask?" His gaze drifted to Sarah. "Especially in front of a guest."

"Please!" She bounced on her chair.

Eduardo's admonishment apparently did nothing to dampen her energy.

He gave Lucia a generous helping then turned to Sarah. "Let me guess." He exchanged the shaver for a grater. "Just a dusting?"

Sarah smiled. "Don't you know me well?"

Eduardo shrugged and applied a scant layer to her plate.

"That's all you want?" Lucia asked.

Red sauce outlined Lucia's mouth. Sarah placed the napkin on her lap. "Someday you'll understand. Well"—she swept her gaze over Eduardo's elephant-sized portion—"maybe."

Lucia knitted her brows.

"Nonsense!" Eduardo twirled a heap of pasta on his fork. "Who doesn't love a woman with curves? Take Miss Sarah's curves. I never knew a woman could have such perfect curves. Maybe it's an American thing."

Sarah paused. Heat prickled her cheeks. Under the table, she slammed a foot on Eduardo's.

"Ow!" Eduardo hollered through cheeks stuffed with spaghetti. "What was that for?"

With lips pursed, Sarah motioned with her eyes toward Lucia.

Eduardo leaned in toward Sarah. "What? You don't want her to know?" He spoke in a hushed tone.

"Know what?" Lucia glanced between the adults. "You mean about you two?"

Sarah froze and looked at Eduardo. "You told her?"

"Me?" Eduardo rubbed the back of his neck. "I wouldn't tell her without asking you first."

"No one told me," Lucia said. "I overheard Mama talking to Leonardo."

Eduardo gave a thick sigh.

"Leonardo De Luca?" Sarah gasped.

Without taking his attention from Lucia, Eduardo nodded. "What exactly did your mother say?"

Lucia shrugged. "She said something about your relationship being inappropriate."

Sarah cringed. *Oh. My. God.* Roberta must have seen them together somewhere—or maybe she spotted Eduardo dropping her off at the dorm in the morning. Of all the people to find out about their relationship, Roberta would be the one. They should have been more careful!

"Inappropriate?" Eduardo bolted to his feet. "*Inappropriate?* As if she has any reason to say such a thing."

"Papa, what does in-ap-pro-pri-ate mean?"

Eduardo rubbed his forehead. "Why don't you ask your mother?"

Sarah frowned. This situation wasn't good—not good at all. Not only had she pissed off Roberta and Mr. De Luca, but now she'd upset Eduardo, too. She swallowed hard and cleared her throat. "Lucia, 'inappropriate' means to do something that's not...not..." She searched for a word. "Not proper."

"Like not closing the bathroom door?"

Sarah laughed. "Yes, Lucia. Something like that."

Eduardo clenched his fists and scowled.

Clearly, he wasn't amused; he looked ready to explode. Sarah stifled her laughter.

Lucia pressed her brows together. "But what are you and Papa doing that's inappropriate?"

"We're not doing *anything* inappropriate, Lucia." Eduardo spoke in a raised voice. "Sarah is my girlfriend. And if your mother has something to say about it, she can say it to my face." He collapsed into his chair.

Sarah snatched his hand and ran her thumb over his palm. She attempted to catch his gaze.

But he only glared at a spot on the table.

First Lucia looked at Eduardo, then Sarah, and finally at their hands. Her lips rounded into a smile. "Really?" She bounced on her chair.

Lucia's voice dinged with excitement. Sarah exchanged a look with Eduardo. Smiling, she looked back at Lucia and nodded.

"Well, that doesn't sound inappropriate to me."

A smile replaced Eduardo's scowl, and he gazed at Lucia then Sarah. He squeezed Sarah's hand. "No, Lucia, it doesn't."

The warmth spread from her hand to her chest. If only she could make it last forever.

****

Sarah placed a kettle on Eduardo's stove and plucked two bags of chamomile tea from the stash in the cupboard. She dropped one in each mug. Eduardo already adopted her nightly tea habit.

Down the hall, Eduardo busied with putting Lucia to bed.

When the kettle whined, Sarah removed it from the burner, not wanting the whistle to interrupt Lucia. She poured the water over the bags, wondering how Eduardo put Lucia to bed. Did they read stories? Did they sing songs?

Cupping the mug in her hands, she stepped into the hall and listened. Eduardo's warm baritone drifted from behind Lucia's bedroom door. He read a book—something about a witch and fairies. Warmth infused her chest. Could he be a more doting father?

She returned to the kitchen, picked up Eduardo's mug, and carried it to the couch. She placed their drinks on the ottoman and curled her legs beneath her.

Across from her, stacks of files teetered on Eduardo's desk. Had he touched them since they'd returned from Florence? He hadn't while she'd been there. Maybe that was because the new office manager, Carina, was working out so well. Sarah eyed the stack again. Maybe Carina should start making house calls.

"*Dormi, dormi bel bambin.*" Eduardo's voice, singing a lullaby, echoed down the hall.

Sarah stood and approached Eduardo's desk. If Eduardo would give up his working at home habit—as he'd told her he would—then returning the files to his office would be the first step. She gave a quick glance over her shoulder to make sure Eduardo was still in Lucia's room then snatched a fistful of folders and tucked them in his briefcase.

In the hallway, Eduardo appeared.

What would he say if he saw her? Sarah scurried from the briefcase and hopped onto the couch.

Eduardo entered the living room, and he lifted a brow. "You look guilty."

Sarah inched up her shoulders. "I packed a few of your files for Carina."

"Ah." Eduardo picked up his tea. "I suppose I should take those back." He threw an arm over Sarah's shoulder and drew her close.

She relaxed into his embrace. "Sorry, I should have asked."

He rubbed her shoulder. "No need to apologize. Actually, I'm the one who should be apologizing. I'm sorry Lucia put you on the spot tonight."

She avoided his gaze. "Does her knowing about us bother you?"

Eduardo pulled back and studied her. "Why would it bother me?"

Sarah shrugged.

He tucked her under his arm and lightly kissed her head. "I've been waiting for this moment, Sarah— waiting to have a family again."

Family. A warmth filled her breast. Sarah nuzzled into Eduardo's chest. Was that really what they could be? She closed her eyes. Wasn't a family everything she'd ever wanted—everything she'd dreamt of?

Wait—what if Lucia wasn't enough family for Eduardo? What if he wanted…more children? She sat up and sipped the last of her tea, and bitterness nipped her tongue.

Eduardo took her empty cup and placed it on the ottoman. "Sound good to you?"

"I'm sorry?" Whatever Eduardo said, she'd completely missed.

"Ice skating tomorrow? You, me, and Lucia."

"Right." She relaxed back into his embrace. Ice skating sure sounded like a family activity. "Sounds good." If only they were a family.

****

The ice rink sprawled below the *Castel Sant'Angelo*. Children and adults alike covered the ice. Some kids knelt over buckets, struggling to stay upright, while experienced skaters glided along gracefully, weaving among moms holding tiny-gloved hands.

Sarah tied her men's-sized skates and inched onto the ice. Like an awkward giant whose laces were knotted together, she wobbled. Why hadn't ice skating been on her parents' radar? She clung to the wall. At least concentrating on staying upright took her mind off Eduardo's comments about family.

Lucia skated past and twirled to face Sarah, skating backward. "What's wrong, Miss Sarah? Don't you skate?"

Sarah gave a pinched smile. "Is my inferiority that obvious?"

Eduardo slid behind her and laced his fingers in Sarah's. He pulled her from the wall.

Lucia raced back to them and grabbed Eduardo's free hand. "*Andiamo!*" She dug in the heels of her blades and started off.

The left side of Eduardo's body jerked forward.

Sarah lurched with him, her skates slipped wide, and her breath became ragged. She released Eduardo's hand and lunged at the wooden supports enclosing the rink.

"Lucia," Eduardo cupped his hands around his mouth. "Slow down."

"No, please." Sarah caught her breath. Thank God she didn't face-plant. "You two go ahead."

Frowning, Eduardo flashed his gaze in Lucia's direction. "She can wait. We can race later, can't we, Lucia?"

Lucia shoved her hands in her pockets and responded with a humph.

"Ed!" called a voice.

Through the menagerie of wool coats, leather jackets, and cowl-neck sweaters, Mr. Moretti and Cira appeared just outside the rink.

"Cira!" Lucia raced over to her classmate.

Eduardo took Sarah on his elbow.

Sarah fumbled by his side. She clung to him all the way to Mr. Moretti.

"Vito, so good to see you," Eduardo said in Italian. He extended his hand over the wall.

Vito glanced toward Sarah and back to Eduardo. "I didn't realize you and *Signorina* Miller were acquainted."

Eduardo grinned. "Yes, Sarah and are I quite *well* acquainted."

Mr. Moretti's pudgy cheeks balled in a smile. He gave Eduardo a playful punch in the shoulder.

Sarah dropped her jaw. First, Eduardo told Lucia—now, Mr. Moretti? The whole school would soon know she was Eduardo Rossini's girlfriend. Which wouldn't be a bad thing, except—her feet slipped on the ice, and she struggled to stay upright—Eduardo didn't know exactly who his girlfriend was; he didn't know about her flaws.

"Well, *Signorina* Miller, seeing as you and Eduardo are *well* acquainted, perhaps you can recruit him to help next year. You will be joining *Signorina* Franklin and me in putting on the play again next year, won't you?"

"Well…I'm not sure."

"The stress of production too much for you?"

Sarah scowled. "No…I…." She held her chin high. "I meant I'm not sure if I will be here, at St. Theresa's, or even in Rome."

Eduardo jerked, spun toward her, and furrowed his brows.

The motion pulled her off her balance again. She shuffled her skates, her right foot slid wide, and she went down, taking Eduardo with her. "I'm sorry." She struggled to stand.

Eduardo helped her to her feet.

His expression was as cool as the ice. Sarah winced.

He turned to Mr. Moretti. "I promised Lucia a race. I suppose I should squeeze that in before too long." He extended a hand to Sarah. "Would you like to join me?"

Sarah paused. Was he asking her to skate or something more? And if she said yes to more, did that oblige her to tell him her secret? She struggled to stay upright on her knocking knees. "You go ahead." She dropped the connection with his gaze. "I think I'm safer on solid ground."

Chapter 30

"Why don't you get a shirt? Like one of those bracelets old people wear, except yours can say 'infertile.'" Anna smirked.

Sarah smacked Anna on the shoulder. "Would you stop?" She scanned the school entry to make sure no one heard. The last car in the pick-up line drove off, and the other teachers and Sister Maria were out of earshot. Afternoon sun dappled the sidewalk.

Anna opened the door to the school and entered.

"My situation isn't a joke. Eduardo's been hounding me all week about my plans for next year. How can I commit to staying here—for him, for Lucia—when he doesn't even know? What if the truth changes the way he feels?" Sarah followed.

The door snapped closed behind Sarah, cool air rushing the entry.

Anna stopped and turned to Sarah, the dark in her eyes softening. "Sarah, so many options exist to work around this problem. Adoption, surrogates—hell, you might not even need that. You two are so made for each other it'll probably happen without even trying. I'm sure you already know all these things, and I'm sure he does, too. And if he's that into you that he's asking you to stay here, he'd be willing to try those."

Maybe he would be willing? Or maybe he wouldn't... Sarah bit her lower lip and dropped her gaze.

Anna rubbed her arm. "Hey, if things don't work out, I'm sure Marco's available."

Again, Sarah smacked Anna's shoulder. "You're awful, Anna Franklin. You know that?"

Anna winked and started toward the staircase. "Have time for happy hour before you meet Prince Charming?"

"How about afternoon tea?"

Anna stuck out her tongue. "Ugh, fine. But only if you buy me a cannoli."

Sarah smiled. "Why not? A sugar rush might help me get up my nerve. Let me wrap up a few things, and I'll text you."

With a nod, Anna rushed up the stairs.

Sarah returned to her classroom. But when she opened her door, she nearly jumped out of her shoes.

Mr. De Luca stood just inside. "Ms. Miller," he said in a thick Italian accent, "so good to see you again."

"Mr. De Luca, you gave me quite a surprise."

"I tend to have that effect on women." He stepped forward and flicked his meticulously groomed goatee.

Sarah inched to her desk and tried to find her voice. "What can I help you with? Perhaps some explanation on Lucia's reading assignment?" She shuffled through a stack of papers.

Mr. De Luca smoothed a hand over his slick, black hair. "Actually, I need to speak to you about my wife." He took a seat on the edge of her desk.

His strong cologne wafted in the air. Sarah sucked in a breath, and her stomach turned. "What about Roberta?"

Mr. De Luca rubbed his beard. "She's quite upset about your involvement with Mr. Rossini."

Sarah dropped the paper she'd been holding, and it fluttered to the floor.

Grinning, Mr. De Luca picked up the paper and tossed it back on her desk. "Given the circumstances, she's decided to remove Lucia from the school."

"What?" Sarah's voice came out in a shriek. "Remove her from the school? But Lucia loves St. Theresa's."

"Unfortunately, Roberta doesn't agree."

Sarah's mind darted in a thousand directions. *Can she really do that? What will Sister Maria say? What will Eduardo—Oh, God. Eduardo.* She squared her shoulders and looked Mr. De Luca dead on. "Roberta can't do that without Eduardo's consent."

He picked up a pencil from her desk and twirled it between his fingers. "Perhaps. But you know how long and stressful these court battles are. Maybe you and I could help them avoid all that trouble."

Alarm bells went off inside, but she had to know how she—no, they—could help. "How do you propose we do that?"

He stood. "Let's just say I've been known to persuade my wife to do, or not do, most anything. If you are willing to do me a favor, then I will make sure Lucia remains at St. Theresa's."

Prickles raced along her skin, and she backed up against the chalkboard. "What did you have in mind?"

Leering, he stepped closer. "Oh, I think you know." He seized her breast.

Sarah froze. *This isn't happening.*

He squeezed, kneading her flesh with his hand.

Her breath caught. *This can't be happening.*

The alarm bell inside blared, and Sarah slapped away his hand. "I'm afraid that wouldn't be possible." She pointed toward the door, her unsteady hand matching the quaver in her voice. "I would like you to leave." She swallowed. "*Now.*"

He strode toward the door, reached for the handle, and paused. "Suit yourself."

Lumbering from the board, Sarah slumped into her chair. Sweat beaded her brow, and a tightness cinched her chest. Thank God he was gone. She exhaled a shaky breath. But would he be back?

****

That evening, Sarah sat across from Eduardo at his dining room table. The candle flickered on the table, casting a shadow on the tablecloth. Staring at the dancing flame, Sarah swirled her spoon in her soup.

"You don't like the *ribollita?*" Eduardo cocked his head to the side.

Sarah lifted her gaze. "Sorry, I had too much table bread with Anna."

"Bread?" He lifted a hearty spoonful of soup toward his mouth. "I thought you did the low-carb thing."

"I do. I mean…" She dropped her gaze. The vibrant greens, oranges, and reds of the vegetables turned her already upset stomach even sourer. "Bread helps settle my stomach." *And keeps my hands occupied when I'm fidgety.* She cut a wedge from the rosemary focaccia loaf set between them.

Eduardo gave her a questioning look. "Your stomach is upset? Are you mulling over your plans for next year?"

Shrugging, she dipped her bread in the soup, soaked up some tomato broth then took a generous bite. She chewed slowly—deliberately. The longer her mouth was full, the longer she could stall.

Rubbing his chin, Eduardo watched her.

His intense gaze measured her as she swallowed, reached for the bread, and started chomping again. Should she follow Anna's advice and tell him about Mr. De Luca? Should she tell him about Roberta's threat to remove Lucia from the school? But what would that admission accomplish? Eduardo would be mad—hell, probably downright insane if she mentioned Mr. De Luca—and the situation would only worsen. Endless court battles could ensue...and poor Lucia—she'd be caught in the middle.

No. Another way had to exist to smooth things over with Roberta without getting Eduardo involved.

Eduardo leaned back in his chair and swigged his wine. "I hope you don't mind, but I took the liberty of asking Sister Maria about your position next year."

Sarah froze then slackened her jaw which was in mid-wrestle with the forbidden carbs.

"She said she'd love to have you back. That she'd help in any way to keep you here."

Sister Maria. She was the solution. She taught Roberta and Mr. De Luca in their school years. She would know how to knock some sense into them. Sister Maria would help her and spare dragging Eduardo into things.

"I've been thinking how I could help, too." Eduardo put down his glass and ran his fingers through his hair. "Maybe you'd be happier if you didn't live in the dorm." He leaned across the table and placed a hand over hers. "Maybe you'd be happier if you lived with me."

Sarah stiffened, and numbness seeped into her lips. *He wants me to move in with him?* "I…" What could she say? That her head swirled with thoughts, none of which had anything to do with moving in with him. Thoughts of Mr. De Luca, Roberta, Lucia, and Sister Maria churned in her mind. She eased her hand out from his and stood. "I need to go."

Eduardo jerked back. "Go?"

"Yes. I need to talk to Sister Maria."

Eduardo stood. "I'll drive you."

But Sarah already grabbed her purse. She raced out the door and hailed a cab. Hopefully, Sister Maria would fix the De Luca situation.

****

In the dormitory kitchen, Sarah sat in silence with Sister Maria; two cups of tea sat in front of them. Sarah tapped a foot on the floor, the chamomile doing nothing for her nerves.

Sister Maria rested her gaze on her mug. "And you didn't tell Eduardo?"

The sister stared into her mug, as if she were reading the tea leaves. Sarah shook her head. "I didn't want to worry him." She bit her lip. Maybe she should have told him. Wouldn't she want him to tell her if he were in a similar situation?

Sister Maria stood, her spine straight as a rod. "You are quite right. No need to upset Eduardo." She placed a hand on Sarah's shoulder. "But De Luca…that boy always has been a bad seed."

Mr. De Luca isn't a boy. Sarah raised an eyebrow.

"I'll take care of De Luca," Sister Maria said.

"Thank you, Sister." The words came out in a sigh. "Thank you so much."

Sister Maria turned to go then stopped. "Sarah. Have you given any thought to returning next year?"

Sarah clutched her mug in her hands. First the stress of telling Eduardo, then De Luca's threat. How much more could Sarah take? She gave a tight response. "A little."

"Well, I'll hope you'll give it some more."

That night, Sarah lay on her bed and stared at the ceiling, her mind on Eduardo. What was he doing? Had he gone to bed already? Or was he up worrying about how quickly she'd fled his apartment?

She exhaled and covered herself with the comforter. Scratchy and thin, the blanket was far from comfortable—not like Eduardo's down-filled one. She rolled onto her side, and a spring jabbed her in the side. God, this bed was uncomfortable.

Eduardo's words repeated in her head. *Maybe you'd be happier if you lived with me.* Who wouldn't want to live at Eduardo's flat? Who wouldn't be proud to call Eduardo hers? Sarah sank deeper under the covers. Would his offer remain once he knew the truth?

Her phone dinged on the desk—a text. Sarah threw off the blanket and picked up the phone.

—*Miss you, mia bella cigna*—

The knot in Sarah's stomach swelled. She closed her eyes. *Enough!* She'd endure no more fretful worries—no more nights contemplating his possible response. Opening her eyes, she let her thumbs find the keypad and sent a quick message.

—*Miss you too. Can you pick me up after work tomorrow? We need to talk*—

304

Chapter 31

Sarah paced in her empty classroom, wringing her hands in her skirt. Would she really tell him? *Yes. I really will tell him.* She stopped pacing and planted herself in her desk chair. She shifted her gaze to the clock on the wall—three o'clock. Fifteen minutes until everything could change.

Ugh! With a huff, she heaved back in her chair. *How do I tell someone I'm infertile, anyway?* Maybe Anna's shirt idea wasn't half-bad.

Her phone dinged—another text from Eduardo.

—Got here a little early. Take your time. I'll wait out front—

A weight bore down her chest; her secret slowly suffocated her. She pushed away the feelings and retrieved her sketchbook from her desk. Turning to a recent drawing of Eduardo and Lucia, she traced the outline of their matching eyes with her fingertips. Diamond-shaped white specks, carefully placed, indicated the light bouncing off their fudge-like eyes. The exaggerated graphite strokes of their crinkled smiles captured the fondness between them. Sarah stroked Lucia's cheek, a dimple etched in her pudgy, velvet skin.

Sarah picked up her pencil and hastily sketched in a silhouette between them—hers. Eduardo already had a family, and if she wanted to be part of it, she would need to reveal the truth. Her figure took shape on the page, and Sarah smiled. With each stroke of the pencil, the weight in her chest lifted. When her face was sufficiently sketched in, she tore out the page and tucked it inside her purse. *For luck.* She took a deep breath and headed for the door. Before she reached it, the door swung open.

Mr. De Luca sauntered in.

Sarah froze. "Mr. De Luca, I didn't expect to see you again."

He shut the door behind him.

"Where's Lucia?" She looked past him to the door. Did any teachers remain in the building? If she screamed, could they hear her through the closed door?

"With her mother." He crossed the room. His gaze darted from her, to the window, and then back again.

Sarah backed up, and she searched in her purse for her phone. She grasped it—thank God—pulled it from her purse, and punched Eduardo's contact.

But Mr. De Luca lunged forward, snatched the phone from her hand, and placed it on a student desk. "Talking on the phone isn't nice when you have guests, Ms. Miller."

He scanned her body like a predator surveying his victim. What if he was a predator? Sarah retreated, creating distance between them. She fidgeted her shaky hands and realized she'd left the phone on the desk by De Luca. *Dammit!*

"You should have taken my offer." He stared. "You've only made the situation worse by talking to Sister Maria. Now, Roberta is even more determined to remove Lucia from this school."

Sarah surveyed the room for an escape. Apart from

the door, which Mr. De Luca blocked, the way out was through the tiny window above her desk. She'd never wished for a petite frame more than she did now.

Mr. De Luca flashed his black eyes. As he took a step toward her, the right side of his lip curled upward. "This is the last time I'll extend my offer."

Sarah halted. "I haven't changed my decision." She spoke in a firm voice.

His mouth shifted from a grin to a smirk. "That's all I needed to know." He turned on his heel and headed for the door.

Sarah relaxed her shoulders; his smirk may have been sour but the change in behavior was as if someone flicked a switch. She let go of the stagnant air burning her lungs.

On the desk, the phone dinged.

Mr. De Luca whipped around, lurched for the phone then raised his upper lip in a snarl.

"Your boyfriend. You want to talk to him?"

Nodding, Sarah approached and held out her hand.

Mr. De Luca deepened his sneer and smashed her phone on the floor. He grabbed her forearm and shoved her against the desk. "Who do you think you are?" he said through gritted teeth.

Pain shot through her hip. "Stop!" She pushed him with her free hand.

He grabbed that, too and slammed her down on the desk.

Sarah opened her mouth to scream.

"Shut up!" He smacked her face.

A sting rushed her cheek, and a metallic taste coated her tongue—blood. Sarah clawed at him with her free hand and lifted a leg to kick him.

Shifting his weight, he pinned her to the desk and pressed his scruffy face against hers.

How stupid of her to think she could match his strength. Again, she screamed, thrashing her head from side to side.

De Luca released her left arm to cover her mouth with his hand.

With her arm free, she found a resurgent strength. She pushed against his chest with all the energy she could muster.

He stumbled backward.

"Get off her!" Eduardo shouted in Italian.

A relief washed over her. Her body sagged. Thank God, Eduardo came.

De Luca screamed something back in Italian.

Sarah had neither the strength nor desire to translate. Her body drooped and shook, and she leaned against the desk for support.

Both men hurled obscenities at each other.

Eduardo, who stood several inches taller than his opponent, grabbed De Luca's shoulders and threw him against the wall. He gripped De Luca's shirt with one hand and pressed his other against De Luca's throat. Anger raged beneath Eduardo's Italian curses, and his skin turned a new shade of burnt orange.

"*Ascolta!*" shouted a shrill voice.

Exhaling a sigh, Sarah turned. Thank, God, she'd come.

Sister Maria stood in the doorway. "What is this?" She spoke in rapid Italian.

Eduardo loosened his grip. He and De Luca both spoke simultaneously, gesturing with their hands.

Sister Maria held up a palm and turned her gaze to

Sarah.

The line between Sister Maria's eyes read of concern. Sarah sat on the desk, wiping the blood from her lip with one hand. "Mr. De Luca." Her voice quavered. "He tried to…"

The words wouldn't come out—she didn't want them to. Judging by the expression on Sister Maria's face, they didn't need to.

****

For minutes—or was it hours?—everything was a blur. Faces blended with bodies. Black robes mixed with blue *polizia* jackets. They all huddled around Sarah: Sister Maria, Eduardo, Anna, and even Sister Angelica. Their voices were distant, as if she were submerged underwater, the sounds coming through in muddled bits and pieces.

"Are you hurt?"

"What happened?"

Sarah moved her lips, but no sound surfaced. Her lip stung, and she touched her fingers to the wound. A rough scab scratched her fingers. She shifted her fingers to her cheeks and winced. Her left cheek throbbed.

Sister Angelica brought her ice.

Anna wrapped her petite arms around Sarah. "I'll ruin him. I'll friggin' ruin him."

From her fetal position, Sarah didn't laugh nor did she say a word.

Eduardo enfolded her in his embrace.

Why did his gentle touch bring no comfort? Why couldn't she stop trembling?

"Sarah, I'm so sorry." He squeezed her tighter, nuzzling his face in her hair. "Leonardo," he growled and stomped his foot. "*Stronzo!* How could he do this?

How could he hurt *mia bella cigna?*" He shifted, moving his mouth close to Sarah's ear. "He'll pay for this, Sarah. I promise you, he'll pay."

A blue jacket pushed through. *"Ho bisogno di una dichiarazione."*

The words skidded off her brain, incomprehensible.

"A statement," Eduardo translated. "He needs a statement."

Sarah blindly stared at the police officer.

He spoke in too-fast Italian.

"He needs you to come to the station," Eduardo said.

She just stared at the man's uniform: the brass buttons, the shield patch on his sleeve, and a white belt—a floppy loop where the handcuffs should have been. Was Mr. De Luca in the handcuffs?

"Sarah," Eduardo said softly. "We have to go with him."

Sarah searched the room, but Mr. De Luca wasn't there. The cacophony of murmurs around her faded into background noise, and in its place sounded Mr. De Luca's voice, harsh and forceful. *"You whore!"*

She shook her head, freeing herself of the memories, but she couldn't. She relived the scene in her mind, as if she were in two places at once.

I must get away—must leave here. I must get away from him.

Eduardo rested hands on her shoulders. "Sarah, please say something. Please."

His voice was pinched. Sarah stared into his concerned gaze, hoping his care would take away her pain. But her hands shook and her wounds throbbed. "I want to go home." Her voice came out in a whisper.

He rubbed her shoulders. "Of course, I'll take you home."

Sarah dropped his gaze. "No, not your home—D.C. home."

Chapter 32

Sarah huddled in the corner of her childhood bedroom in the US—her soul, a cavernous pit. No light penetrated the damp, jagged walls of her mind. Nothing alleviated her torment: not chamomile tea, not Choctella, and not her fuzzy slippers.

She forced herself to her feet, her knees aching from her prolonged crouch, and crossed to her dresser. She turned off the whirling ballerina nightlight. Hollow blackness surrounded her.

"Sarah," her mom called from somewhere in the house. "Come down and eat something."

Foggy with jetlag, Sarah plodded down the stairs. She found an overcooked chicken breast and mushy peas set on the dining room table. When was the last time she'd eaten? Yesterday? The day before? Who knew?

She floated into a chair and poked at her food. At the best of times, Mom's cooking was about as enticing as a jar of baby food. With no appetite anyway, she didn't feel guilty pushing away the plate.

Mom sat at the table. "I told you this job was a bad idea." She jabbed a fork into her own food. "Look at you. Just look at you."

Sarah turned her attention to the window. A light snow fell, and the sun cast the last of its rays off speckles of silvery ice. She shivered.

"You should've stayed here with me," Mom continued. "Kept your old job and met someone else." She leaned a forearm on the table. "Maybe I was wrong about Eduardo. Maybe he isn't that great after all."

Shoving back from the table, she glared at her mother. "This isn't his fault." She stalked into the kitchen, yanked open the cupboard, and found a box of sugary cereal. She stuffed a handful into her mouth.

"You won't finish your dinner?" Mom called from the dining room.

"I'm going to bed." The box hugged to her chest, Sarah climbed the stairs.

Mom called her name.

Sarah drowned out her voice with crunches. She couldn't take this haranguing by Mom now—not while she kept thinking about…She blinked away the thought, entered her room, and stashed the box of cereal under her bed. Desperate for sleep, she slipped beneath the covers. But as soon as she closed her eyes all she saw was the image of the haunting scene. De Luca scratched her cheek with his scruffy chin, the acrid saliva of his kiss turned her stomach, and his fist struck her cheek.

Sarah whimpered and curled into a ball. What would have happened if Eduardo didn't come? A mixture of half-chewed, corn-puff squares and bile mounted in Sarah's throat. She knew exactly what would have happened.

Her phone dinged, and she stared blankly in the direction of the sound. Anna and Eduardo were kind enough to get her on the plane to D.C.—the least she could do was return their calls. She picked up her phone. Her texts were full of a days' worth of messages saying:

—How are you?—
*—I miss you—*and
—When are you coming back?—

She pictured Eduardo's sympathetic eyes and felt the warmth of his comforting embrace. She snuggled deeper into her fleece blanket. As she reread his messages, she felt a soft light glow inside her.

—Miss you too—

She hovered her thumb hovered the Send button, and a voice inside stopped her. When would she see him again? She erased the message and tossed her phone to the floor. She trudged to the bathroom, found a bottle of Sleepquil, and took a generous swig. *Would she see him again?*

****

The numbers on the alarm clock changed. Her phone rang. Sarah alternated between hot showers and stolen sips of sleep medicine from the medicine cabinet. After some time—hours? days? Did it really matter?—Meredith visited.

Sarah met her at the dining room table, where her mother left a steaming pot of Earl Grey.

Meredith greeted her with a bear hug. "How are you?"

"Hanging in there." Sarah reached for the tea. "Where are Steven and Amber?"

"With Brian." Meredith eased into her seat. "I can bring them by later. I wanted to see how you were doing first."

"That would be nice." Sarah poured milk in Mom's dainty teacup and raised it to her lips. The redness of her hands matched the flower embellishment on the cup. How many times did she scrub these hands? She traced her gaze along her arm. A faint bruise tarnished her left forearm. She set down the cup, tugged on her sleeves, and hid her hands under the table.

Meredith popped a mini-muffin in her mouth and washed it down with a gulp of tea. She held Sarah in a steady gaze. "Your mom thinks you're on drugs."

The words were as calm as if she remarked on the weather. Sarah pursed her lips. "I figured she'd say something to you. Just like her not to confront me herself."

Meredith widened her eyes. "So, it's true?"

"I don't think Sleepquil counts as drugs."

Meredith frowned.

Sarah rubbed her chafed hands then her forearms. She felt De Luca's hands on her and smelled his musky aftershave. Again, she lifted her cup. If only she could spike it with vodka or antihistamines—hell, anything to erase the memory. "I'll stop," she said. "I promise. As soon as I stop seeing him—stop feeling him—when I close my eyes."

"Oh, Sarah." Meredith smacked the table. "You've got to make that bastard pay."

Sarah's hands shook. Her teacup rattled on the saucer so she set it down.

"You will press charges, won't you?" Meredith asked.

How could she press charges? She'd have to give a statement—would have to give a detailed account of the scene she wanted so badly to forget.

Meredith exhaled audibly. "I know this is hard, but you can't run forever—can't keep downing sleeping pills."

Sarah winced. "Sleepquil, not sleeping pills. And

I've only taken it for a few days."

"Five. Five days. Five days that he's been out there—he could hurt someone else. What about his wife? What about Lucia?"

A prickle ran over her skin. "Lucia," she whispered.

"What did you say?"

Lucia was in the house with him. She might even be alone. De Luca could…could hurt her. Sarah jumped to her feet and clasped Meredith's shoulders. "Lucia. I've got to protect Lucia." She rushed to the hall closet and yanked it open.

Meredith followed. "Sarah! What are you doing?"

Sarah pulled out her suitcase, only just recently unpacked. "I need to get back to Rome. Now."

****

"We have everything we need," the detective said in Italian. He smiled at Sarah. "You did great."

Eduardo wrapped an arm around Sarah's shoulders, tucked her bangs behind her ears, and kissed her hair.

Sarah leaned into him. His warm chest was the only glimmer of comfort in the sterile police station.

"I'm so proud of you." He led her to the exit.

Sarah smiled but didn't reply. Going straight from the airport to give her statement seemed like the best idea, but now, her aching legs made her doubt her decision. If she didn't get into bed soon, she'd topple over.

Eduardo placed her in the passenger seat of his car with a gentle touch. He walked around and got into the driver's seat then paused with the key in the ignition. "I should tell you something." He turned the key, and the engine purred. "Roberta…she's decided to leave De

Luca."

The statement awakened Sarah more than three pots of black tea could. She gripped Eduardo's forearm. "Thank God." The color in Eduardo's hazy eyes melted back to their warm chocolate hue.

He cupped a hand over hers and cocked a brow. "I didn't realize you'd taken up the faith."

Sarah laughed. Her first laugh since... She pushed aside the thought and soaked in Eduardo's attention. Calmness settled over her, as if life breathed back into her soul.

Eduardo pulled out of the parking spot. "Lucia will spend more time with me now. If all goes according to plan, I can modify the custody agreement."

"Really? That's wonderful!" Sarah moved a hand to his thigh. "I'll help you."

"I hoped you'd say that." He flashed a smile and sped down the road.

Sarah took in his cheeky grin. Would she finally find happiness?

****

Sister Maria graciously gave Sarah the rest of the week off, and she spent the next three days with Eduardo, relaxing and redecorating Lucia's room. Or rather, Eduardo lounged on the couch or experimented in the kitchen while Sarah changed the paint in Lucia's bedroom from beige to pink and replaced her drab cream comforter with a frilly pink one instead. Eduardo's modern, minimalist decor had no place in a nine-year-old's bedroom.

Sarah returned to work on the same day Lucia was due to come for her first long stay. She escorted Lucia home from school so Eduardo could get in an extra hour at the office. The flat was quiet when Sarah arrived with Lucia.

"Papa told me." Lucia raced straight for her room.

Sarah followed, biting her lip. If only she knew Lucia would like the design.

"Miss Sarah!" Lucia ran to the mural of instruments and musical notes. "It's beautiful!" She ran her hands over the wall, prancing from violin to piano and quarter note to half rest. She turned to face Sarah. "Did you paint this, Miss Sarah? Did you? Did you paint it for me?"

Lucia smiled with eyes as full of life as the notes dancing on the wall. Warmth flooded her chest. She nodded.

Lucia ran toward her.

Kneeling, Sarah wrapped her arms around the girl. If a heart could melt, Sarah's would have done so at that moment.

Pulling back, Lucia ran her fingers over the pink ruffles of the new comforter.

"Do you like it?" Sarah studied the girl's face. "Your father was worried my choice was too frilly."

Lucia hopped on the bed, and the river of blankets swallowed her up. "It's perfect!" She reached across to her nightstand and strummed the pink crystals hanging from the lampshade. "I bet he just *loved* these."

"Actually…" Eduardo's voice boomed from the doorway. He strode across the room and fingered the pom-poms that decorated the curtains. "I think these are my favorite. They remind me of Sarah's cheeks."

A smile set on her face, Sarah snatched up a pillow from the bed and tossed it at Eduardo. He had to spoil this moment with Lucia, didn't he?

Lucia giggled.

Eduardo ducked, and the pillow flew over his head. "I was only kidding—" He began.

Another pillow, this one on target, cut him off.

"Lucia!" Sarah said.

Laughing, Lucia rolled on her bed.

Eduardo adjusted his glasses and wagged his finger. "Is this what you're teaching my daughter these days?"

"You started it," Lucia stomped a foot.

Eduardo crossed to the bed and ruffled Lucia's hair. "Have you said thank you to Miss Sarah? She was determined to make this your space."

"*Grazie*, Miss Sarah. Thank you."

"You're very lucky, Lucia." He scooped her off the bed, nestled her under one arm, and then looped his other arm around Sarah's waist and drew her in. "And so am I," he whispered.

Later that night, Sarah helped Eduardo tuck Lucia into her bed.

Eduardo sang her a lullaby and kissed her cheek.

As she exited the room, Sarah flipped off the light.

"Tonight was amazing." Eduardo leaned back onto the couch.

"Yes." Sarah fell into his chest.

He wrapped his arms around her, hugging her close as he rested his cheek on her hair. "You're like a mother to Lucia."

Sarah sank deeper into his embrace. His chest was warm, and his breath tickled her brow. *Mother.* Would she finally be a mother? *But...* She flicked her gaze upward. A deep smile lit Eduardo's face. But would Lucia be enough for Eduardo?

He ran his fingers down her spine, lowered his mouth, and skimmed his lips against hers.

Goose bumps erupted on her skin, but her mind wandered. Should she tell him now about her past? Should she reveal her infertility?

Eduardo lifted her chin. "Sarah," he said in a hushed voice. "I love you."

The words were as welcome as any she ever heard—three simple words. Could she put those words in jeopardy by revealing her truth?

She ran her fingers through his hair and decided to reveal a different secret instead. "I love you, too."

Chapter 33

Over the next month, Sarah fell into a routine of playing wife to Eduardo and mother to Lucia. She orchestrated evening board games, styled pigtails, and packed lunches. She fluffed pillows, organized weekend visits to museums, and reveled in Eduardo's lovemaking. Her relationship with him truly matured.

Her interactions with Anna matured, as well. Where their conversations used to be about romps in foreign beds, they now had serious talks about the upcoming visit to Oxford. If Anna accepted, when should she tell Sister Maria? Was grad school the best place?

And what of Sarah's mother? She was unusually subdued during their weekend chats. Instead of probing and pressing for Sarah's future plans, she merely asked after Eduardo and Lucia or shared information about Steven and Amber.

All these changes were for the better. Things were going so well, in fact, that she almost brushed off thoughts of telling Eduardo her secret—but just almost.

One Thursday morning, her body heavy from sleep, Sarah slogged through her usual morning routine. She washed her face in what was her side of the sink and applied her moisturizing cream.

Beside her, Eduardo showered in steam-choked glass. "*Cigna,*" he called out.

Eduardo's chipper, early-morning-person tone brought a smile to Sarah's face. "Yes?"

"Have you ever wondered what our kids would be like?"

The question shocked her more than the cold water she'd splashed on her face. Her empty stomach lurched.

"I mean, do you think they'd be fair or dark? Or maybe a mix of both?"

Sarah couldn't respond. All her words were lost in the steam-clogged trenches of her mind. She stared at her pale reflection.

"*Cigna*?" He poked out his head. "Are you all right?"

"Huh?"

He stepped out of the shower and pulled a towel around his waist. "You do want children, right?"

Sarah hesitated. "Yes, of course."

Eduardo grinned. "I figured." He ruffled his wet hair with a hand towel. "That look you just gave me made me second-guess myself."

Sarah forced a smile and picked up her hairbrush. Fumbling it, she dropped the brush to the floor. Heat rushed her chest. "S-s-orry. I'm not awake."

He stepped behind her, retrieved the brush, and set it on the ledge. "I know we haven't talked about it in a while, but my offer to move in together is still on the table." He kissed her cheek then held his mouth next to her ear. "Maybe we could get a head start on that baby-making."

As her stomach performed cartwheels, Sarah froze.

"I'll make you some tea." He gave her a playful pat on her butt. "Because you're definitely not awake."

Sarah stared into the mirror. He wasn't

serious…was he?

****

"Baby-making?"

Meredith's voice was so loud Sarah practically dropped the phone. "That's what he said." One of the coils on her dorm-room bed jabbed Sarah in the back. Her stomach was still unsettled, despite barely eating anything all day.

Sarah usually loathed these dorm-duty nights that took her from Eduardo's plush, pillow-top mattress, but not tonight. Tonight, she needed the privacy of her own room to discuss this recent dilemma.

"Well, that's great, right?" Meredith said. "Isn't this what you want? A relationship? A family?"

Sarah bit her lower lip. *Ouch.* Was that blood? She ran her tongue over her lip. Had she chewed on it that much over the last day?

"Sarah? Are you there?"

"I…I don't know."

"You don't want to start fertility treatments again?" Meredith asked.

Why hadn't she told him? How had she put off telling him for so long?

Meredith gave an exaggerated sigh. "You haven't told him, have you?"

"No." Sarah rolled onto her side.

"Sarah, I thought you'd told him ages ago!"

"I know, I know. I've been meaning to. I just got… I'm scared."

"This has gone on too long, Sarah. You need to tell him."

Meredith's tone was the same one she used when scolding Amber or Steven. "I will. I promise." Sarah's call waiting buzzed. "Meredith, I gotta go. That's probably him calling."

"Sarah, stop avoiding this."

"I will. Call you soon." She clicked over to the other line. "Eduardo?"

"Miss Miller?"

"Yes?" She pulled the phone from her ear and checked the unfamiliar number. "This is she. May I ask who's calling?"

"This is Rita, from Hyattsville Elementary."

"Oh, hi." *Isn't that where Amber goes to school?*

"We received your application."

Application? What application? Sarah bolted upright. *That* application—the one for the first-grade teaching position.

"We wanted to know if you could do an interview."

"Interview?"

"We know you're overseas but thought we could do the interview virtually."

"Virtually…right." Sarah chewed her lip. What did she have to lose? The interview required no obligation. Maybe she had something to gain—a fallback plan. Another job was exactly the security blanket she needed.

"Miss Miller?"

"I'm here. What day did you have in mind?" Sarah bit her lip and sent a sting of pain through her face. Should she really be doing this?

****

The timing was perfect. Lucia was with Roberta, and Eduardo would work until four. Hell, even Anna was preoccupied with packing for her trip to Oxford.

Instead of spending her Thursday afternoon developing lesson plans, Sarah positioned her webcam. When was the last time she'd interviewed for a job? The brief meeting at the placement agency in D.C. certainly didn't count. And the one with Mr. Rosen? Ugh—what an interview that was. The coffee-making question should have been a red flag. So much for cubicle work—she would never go back to that.

She scanned her classroom: the empty desks, the newly decorated bulletin boards, and the Italian flag. Hopefully, she wouldn't need this fallback plan. That was, of course, if Eduardo took her news of her infertility as she hoped. The uneasiness in her stomach, which grew ever since Eduardo's baby-making comment, intensified.

But just in case he didn't take the news well…

The laptop speaker dinged, and she clicked onto the call.

The school's principal and vice principal both launched into the interview. They asked her questions about pedagogy and curricular objectives. They probed her on her classroom management and engagement techniques.

Throughout, not once did Sarah knock her knees on the desk. Not once did her voice quaver. Aside from the constant queasiness, she was as calm as her mother on muscle relaxers and as at ease as Anna in a room full of coeds.

The principal smiled. "I expect you'll be hearing from us very soon."

"I look forward to it." She ended the conference call, snapped shut the laptop, and sank back in her seat, closing her eyes.

Please let the conversation with Eduardo go as smoothly.

She opened her eyes—and nearly fell off her chair. In the doorway stood Eduardo and Sister Maria.

"When did you plan to tell me?" Eduardo's bass timbre was nearly a growl.

Sister Maria gave a curt bow and backed out of the room.

"Eduardo..." Sarah rose to her feet in a daze. How long had he stood there? The sharp line of his clenched jaw told her he'd heard enough. She took a step toward him, her knees threatening to give way. "I can explain—"

"Explain?" He cut her off in a voice close to a shout. "Is this why you keep putting off talking about moving in?" He gestured wildly with his hands. "Because you have no intention of staying at *all*?"

Sarah flinched. "No, I..." Her shaky voice broke. Her whole body quivered—her hands, her legs, her squeamish stomach. "I do want to be with you. Please let me explain." She reached for him.

But he stepped back. He spun on his heel and strode out the door.

Sarah chased after him and down the hall. "Eduardo, wait!" She didn't care that other teachers poked their heads out of their classrooms to witness the scene. She followed him all the way to the school entrance.

Without turning back, he pushed open the door and rushed outside.

Panic driving her forward, Sarah was ready to follow.

"Let him go." Sister Maria's voice echoed in the

hallway.

A lump forming in her throat, Sarah eased her pace. He didn't stop. He didn't want to talk to her now.

Maintaining his stride, Eduardo stumbled down the stairs.

"He needs time to cool off," Sister Maria said. "Wait before you talk to him."

All hope of fixing this situation now ceased. Her eyes burning with tears, Sarah stopped short of the door.

Eduardo turned right at the fountain and headed toward the street.

Sarah watched him until the door slammed shut, a gust of chilly air whipping her face. As sobs overtook her, Sarah buckled, dropping to her knees.

Sister Maria took her elbow and guided her away.

Inside Sister Maria's office, Sarah sat in her usual seat. Tears burned her eyes, and hysteria shook her body.

As Sister Maria paced around the room, her robes swooshed with each stride.

The only stillness lay outside, where the branches of a fig tree peered through the window, stark in their winter slumber. Sarah focused on the tree; she imagined snow falling on her face, numbing her lips and cheeks. The tension in her chest subsided a bit, and her shuddering reduced to mild trembling, but her stomach was so turned, she thought she might hurl.

Sister Maria stopped in front of Sarah. "He's been this way for as long as I can remember. Even as a child I couldn't talk to him when he was upset." She offered Sarah a tissue.

Sarah blew her nose and nodded.

Sister Maria glided behind her desk and sat, waiting. Sister Maria's gaze, with its cloudy gray eyes—so gentle, so kind—asked the question. The woman behind the eyes would listen, and she wouldn't judge. Sarah gripped the tissue in her hand and let the words pour out: her infertility, her secrecy from Eduardo, and her selfish reasons for doing the interview. Once and for all, she laid out for Sister Maria her fears and insecurities. "I have to tell Eduardo. I have to tell him everything I've just told you." Sarah dabbed at her cheeks with the near-shredded tissue.

At first, Sister Maria remained silent, as she had during the whole of Sarah's confession. A tear trickled down her wrinkled cheek, following a crease before disappearing into the ridges of her aged skin. She made no attempt to wipe it away. "I never told you why I joined the convent."

Her voice sounded as old as the woman behind it.

She stood and walked over to the window, her back to Sarah. "I had a child once—a beautiful little girl."

The words *child* and *had* pierced Sarah's soul like daggers. Pain, she was sure, was only that much more visceral for Sister Maria. To stop the half-sob, half-gasp from escaping, Sarah clapped a hand over her mouth. She suddenly understood the unspoken bond between them.

Sister Maria turned and gazed at Sarah through foggy eyes. "I was but a child myself. Not yet seventeen. My parents forced me to give her up. Then they sent me away to think about my sins."

Sarah rose, crossed to Sister Maria, and hugged her. How could this woman's frail body carry the pain of losing a child? The silent anguish of Mary rushed to

Sarah's mind—the stoic face and the hand lifted in prayer. She shuddered and clutched Sister Maria tighter.

"The only thing that kept me going was knowing that my child, my flesh and blood, was with parents who loved her." Sister Maria pulled back from Sarah's grasp, her tired gaze locking on Sarah's. "A couple who couldn't have children themselves."

Sarah staggered back to her chair and lowered herself. "Thank you for telling me, Sister Maria. You are a strong woman"—*so much stronger than me*—"but..." She rubbed her hands down her thighs in a soothing movement. "Why are you telling me this now?"

"I've known Eduardo nearly as long as I've kept my secret. Of all the children who have passed through these doors, he's the one who felt most like my own." A smile crept over Sister Maria's hollowed cheeks. "I know he'll understand."

Sarah released a heavy breath. *Please, God, let her be right.*

Sister Maria approached and took hold of Sarah's shoulders. "He will understand, Sarah. Now,"—she squeezed Sarah's arms and raised her to her feet—"I expect he's had enough time to cool off."

Sarah stared back at Sister Maria—so strong and so calm. She imagined—hoped, wished—some of that energy transferred through Sister Maria's touch. Nodding, she turned then stopped. She rushed back to Sister Maria and embraced her again. "Thank you, Sister." She kissed her wrinkled cheeks. "Thank you for everything." Releasing her embrace, Sarah hurried to the door. As she passed through, a shiver rushed her spine. What if she couldn't be strong? What if Sister Maria wasn't right about Eduardo understanding?

****

"Eduardo?" Sarah opened the door to his flat. The room was dark—so dim she could barely make out the outline of his body on the couch.

He sat hunched over his knees, his hands clenching his hair.

"Eduardo," she said in an exasperated tone. She rushed to him and placed a hand on his shoulder. The light from the kitchen illuminated his tear-stained face.

He pulled back. "Leave me alone!"

The harshness of his tone forced away the words she hastily prepared in the cab ride over. She hesitated then took a seat next to him. "I don't want to take the job, Eduardo. I want to stay with you."

He flinched then gazed at her as he stood. "None of this makes any sense. I don't understand."

His eyes looked wounded; his tone sounded panicked. Sarah jumped to her feet. "The interview was a mistake." She positioned herself in front of him. "I was scared, and I...I panicked."

His expression softened. He let out a sigh as he placed a hand on her cheek. "I know you're hesitant to make a commitment."

"No, it's not that. It's—" As she wrung her hands, a twitch unsettled her cheek. "—it's...something else."

"What?" He dropped his hand and lowered his gaze. "What else are you keeping from me?"

Her heart pounded, and she struggled to steady her voice. "I—I..." She closed her eyes, and somewhere in her mind, she heard Tosca's aria, *Vissi d'arte, vissi d'amor*. Clinging to the second line, she let the aria sing through her. "I love you, Eduardo, and I hope you'll still love me after I tell—"

"Sarah," he interrupted. "I'll always love you." He reached for her.

No. She needed to tell him—now. No more delaying. Pressing a hand to his chest, Sarah held him back. She let the pounding of his heart beneath her fingers calm her. "I have a medical condition, Eduardo."

He furrowed his brows.

"Nothing life-threatening. It prevents me from…makes it difficult for me to…"

His gaze searched her.

She shifted her attention to the floor. "To conceive."

The muted hum of forced heat deafened Sarah's ears. Eduardo's chest tightened under her hand. The thumping of his heart marked the passing of each dreadful second. One beat, two beats…six beats.

"Are you sure?" he asked.

She nodded.

His face twisted, and he stepped back. "So, you're saying you can't have children?"

Sarah wrapped her arms around her stomach. "Not without assistance. Even then, I'm not sure."

His gaze flicked from her to the floor. He walked to the dining room table and sat facing her.

Sarah searched his face for a sign of the empathy Sister Maria promised but found none. Her legs wobbled, and she propped her knee on the couch for support. "Please," she pleaded. "Please say something. Anything."

"Why didn't you tell me this before?" He stared at

the table.

His tone was a mixture of condemnation and disappointment. Sarah struggled to stay upright. Would he ever forgive her?

Chapter 34

"Geeze, Sarah, don't look so green." Anna shoved a skimpy dress into her suitcase. "I haven't seen someone so upset since Veronica found out she was knocked up."

Sitting atop Anna's bed, Sarah dug her fingernails into the mattress and shot a glare at Anna.

"You know, the girl who eloped with the German?"

Sarah intensified her glower.

"What? She had morning sickness, so that, combined with the shock, hit her hard."

"Anna," Sarah nearly shouted, "that's hardly an appropriate example."

"Oh, right. Sorry." She stood on top of the suitcase, garments oozing out the seams, and crouched down to zip it. "Eduardo wants time to think, eh? About what?"

Sarah expelled an audible breath. "I suppose whether he wants to settle for someone like me." The truth weighed heavy on her chest.

Anna frowned. "Would you stop degrading yourself? More likely he's questioning your trust—why you kept so much from him."

"Well, the truth is all out now." She closed her eyes. Why hadn't she told him before? Why?

Anna hopped off the half-zipped suitcase and gave Sarah a sidelong glance. "You love him, don't you?"

Sarah nodded.

"I've never loved anyone before." The black in Anna's eyes frosted over, and silence ensued. Then Anna blinked, furrowed her brows, and pinched her lips. She wrapped her hands around Sarah. "Guess you're pretty upset, huh?"

Embraced in Anna's bear hug, Sarah's throat tightened, and she swallowed hard. How she'd managed not to cry since leaving Eduardo's the previous evening, she wasn't sure. She'd existed only in a daze. Her conversation with Meredith, her bedtime cup of tea, even her restless sleep felt surreal. Had she even eaten dinner? Breakfast?

Anna squeezed her tighter. Sarah gave in, and the tears flowed. The reality that her relationship with Eduardo might be over washed away the numbness, bringing only heartache. She rested her weight on Anna and unloaded her emotions. Her tears gave way to sobs. Her shudders intensified to waves of spasms, her stomach clenching, and the muscles in her arms contracting. Finally, exhausted, she settled into a gentle sway.

"Don't worry." Anna dabbed at Sarah's cheeks with a tissue and swept Sarah's bangs off her dampened brow. "He'll call soon."

Did she *want* him to call soon? Sarah sniffled. What if he said their relationship was over?

"I wish I didn't have to leave you like this," Anna said. "You shouldn't be alone while you wait."

Sarah shrugged. She could talk to Meredith if she needed to—even Sister Maria. But barricading herself in her room and wallowing in self-pity seemed the most likely choice. Because clearly being a crybaby was the mature way to handle this situation. She rolled her eyes.

"You know." Anna drew out the last word

A mischievous spark glinted in Anna's eyes. The uneasiness swelled in Sarah's gut.

"I bet some proper English tea would cheer you up."

Sarah stared at Anna. "You're not suggesting…"

"I most certainly am." She tugged on Sarah's sleeve. "Come on. We've got some packing to do."

Five hours later, against her better judgment, Sarah found herself passing through the familiar automatic glass doors of Rome's airport.

Anna dashed toward the nearest, electronic check-in kiosk.

At departures, Sarah paused to gaze at the cars zooming past the curb. The last time she'd been here, Eduardo drove one of those cars. She dropped her gaze to her shoes—Sister Maria's shoes. They were the same shoes she'd worn on her first date with Eduardo—the same shoes she'd worn when she'd chased him down the school's corridor.

"What are you doing?" Anna returned.

Sarah ran a toe in a line across the floor. "I'm not sure if this impromptu trip is such a good idea. Maybe I should stay here."

"So you can mope around all weekend?"

Sarah flinched, pulled her foot next to the other but couldn't think of a response.

Anna grabbed her elbow. "Come on, you've already bought your ticket, and Sister Maria gave you the time off."

Sister Maria had been generous to pay her during her absence so long as she'd prepared the lessons for the substitute. With dirt-cheap airfare in Europe and Anna covering all lodging expenses, why should she stay at home and sulk? Sarah lifted her gaze. "Yeah. I guess."

Anna led the way to the kiosk.

Sarah entered her information, took her documents from the dispenser, and placed them in her purse, brushing her phone. She gripped it. "Do you think I should let him know I'm going away?"

"You'll only be gone for a few days. Besides, his call will connect with your cell."

Sarah chewed on the alternatives—stiff conversations with Sister Maria and idle state capital recitations on her spring-jabbing mattress. At least in England, she'd have a host of tea shops to occupy her mind. She released her phone and darted a final glance at the cars streaming by. She sighed, grabbed the handle of her rolling suitcase, and followed Anna to security.

After a quick jaunt over the Channel and a stopover to drop off luggage at their hotel, Sarah stepped into the British Museum.

"Come on!" Anna marched through the crowd.

The echoes of tourists' voices bounced off the acoustically perfected dome. "Slow down!" She caught up with Anna in one of the exhibit halls. "Geez, Anna. This isn't a race."

Anna shot up a brow. "Of course not, this isn't a race. This tour is a meticulously planned route to cover all the top exhibitions in minimal time." She whipped out a folded piece of notebook paper from her pocket and snapped it open.

She held a diagram so intricate in its red-inked lattices it resembled the plans for the next nuclear bomb more than a route through the museum. "Obsess much?" Sarah lifted a brow.

Anna squinted her eyes. "This, my friend, hits all the contributions to science—with extra time built in for the mathematical ones—in just under two hours."

"Uhhh…nice, Anna, but if you don't mind, I'd rather wander around. I'd only slow you down, anyway."

Anna humphed. "Fine but take my picture first. My arms aren't long enough to get a good shot."

Sarah noticed the chiseled piece of stone behind Anna. *The Rosetta Stone,* the placard read. "What does the Rosetta Stone have to do with science and math?"

"Code breaking is just another form of translation. A very sophisticated one." Anna posed for the shot, pretending she held the massive rock on her shoulders.

Using Anna's phone, Sarah took the picture, wondering what Anna was talking about, but she wasn't about to let IQ-through-the-roof Anna keep her from exploring the museum—especially if she only had two hours.

She left Anna to wander through the galleries and let her hand frequently migrate to her cell phone. Mummies, Asian vases, and bronze filled the bountiful rooms. Masterpieces or not, the primitive works didn't intrigue Sarah. They couldn't compare to Michelangelos, Botticellis, or Vermeers.

When she roamed into a Roman art gallery, she was drawn to a languid figure captured in heavily cracked plaster. A stark-faced woman stood on a shoreline, reaching for a departing ship. A man stood on the ship's deck, his face turned to the horizon.

Sarah dialed up her audio-guide.

"*Ariadne Waking on the Shoreline*," said a British-accented voice. "While scholars disagree on the consequence of the abandonment of the Greek goddess by her lover, Theseus, they all agree she left her home and suffered terrible sorrow."

The blood drained from Sarah's face. What if Eduardo was on that boat? What if she was the one left behind? She pulled her phone from her purse—no missed calls, no voicemails, and no text messages.

"So, is that really his boat?"

Sarah turned and jumped.

Anna stared at the painting.

Sarah dropped her phone back in her purse. "What do you mean?" Sarah furrowed her brows.

"You know? The ship of Theseus? Theseus's paradox?"

Anna gave her that look again. That *I'm smart, you're not* look. Sarah exhaled against the tightening in her throat. Perhaps grad school would give Anna the intelligent company she needed for these conversations. "No, Anna, I don't know, but I'd love if you'd enlighten me." She looped an arm through Anna's. "How about over a nice cup of tea?"

"Fine," Anna said with a dramatic sigh.

Hopefully, a cup of tea would be the distraction she needed to forget about Eduardo. Sarah checked her phone again. Well….maybe?

****

With Anna, Sarah traversed streets more congested than Rome's and hopped on subways far cleaner and deeper. Along the way, she listened to Anna's explanation.

"You see, over time, every last board on Theseus's

338

boat was replaced, one at a time, as each one rotted or broke or whatever. So that at the end, no part of the original boat remained," Anna said. "So—is the boat still the same? Is it fundamentally the same object?"

What on earth is she talking about? Shrugging, Sarah followed Anna off the blue line train, and a recorded voice chimed, "mind the gap."

"It's a classic thought experiment!" Anna climbed aboard an escalator. "I can't believe you've never heard of it."

Sarah shook her head and boarded the moving stairs. Above, at street level, lights from the digital screens blared obnoxious ads—Piccadilly Circus. She placed a hand to a throbbing vein in her temple. The dreary London fog was doing wonders for her tanked mood. "Are we almost there?"

"Almost." A block later, Anna entered a glass door.

Sarah stepped into the warmth of the café. The noise and shoulder-rubbing with strangers ceased. The pendant lights streamed a warm glow, a welcome contrast to the somber sky. And the smell... Sarah inhaled. Bergamot, vanilla, and fine black tea wafted in the air. She relaxed and took a seat at a small table with Anna and ordered a pot of tea and a plate of scones.

Sarah sipped on tea better than any she'd ever drunk. The tea was strong; the bergamot was light and airy. She delved into an assortment of scones smothered in clotted cream. The new substance tasted like butter, only smoother and slightly sweeter. Sarah barely spoke to Anna during the tea; she was too preoccupied with heaping various jellies on flaky pastries.

When only crumbs and puddles of tea remained, she leaned back in her chair and considered loosening the button on her jeans.

"Told you." Anna smirked.

Sarah smiled back. "This does help keep my mind occupied...kind of."

"Don't worry. Just give him time. He'll call."

The ship of Theseus sailed in Sarah's mind—sailed farther. Was Eduardo on it? "I'm trying my best not to think about it."

Anna stood. "Good thing you've got tour-guide extraordinaire."

"Good thing." Sarah rolled her eyes.

In her mind, the boat crested the horizon. Choppy waves enveloped a frothy blue sea.

She downed the last drop of her tea, popped the button on her pants, and followed Anna out into the street. If only she knew whether Eduardo was sailing away.

****

Early the next morning, Sarah arrived in Oxford with Anna. While Anna explored the city with other prospective graduate students, Sarah stayed back in the hotel room. The cramped space had lead-paned windows overlooking medieval buildings, towering spires, sandwiched row houses, and manicured lawns. The town begged to be explored, but Sarah plopped on the full-size bed she would share that night—if Anna even went to bed, that was—and pulled out her phone. No word from Eduardo.

Anna's advice echoed in her mind. *Give him time.* Hadn't two days been enough time? She tapped her feet on the footboard. Maybe her phone wasn't working. Flipping to her text messenger, she found a slew of texts from her mother and Meredith—all unanswered.

Right. She'd seen them before—had forgotten about them when she hadn't found one from Eduardo. A ton of emails filled her inbox, too. She scanned through them; maybe she'd overlooked something.

An email from the principal of Hyattsville Elementary caught her attention. Subject: *Job offer enclosed*.

Sarah's heart went into a flutter, and a trembling spilled down her arms. Would she really have to use her fallback plan?

No, she couldn't think about returning to the States, not now. She needed to wait for Eduardo. With a shaky hand, she turned the ringer to high, placed the phone on the nightstand, and lay back on the bed. He would call soon…wouldn't he?

****

That evening, Sarah hiked herself onto a stool at an Old English pub, examining the fluctuating bars on her phone.

Anna sat beside her, leaned up to the lacquered bar, and rattled off an order.

Arching her back, Sarah adjusted herself on the stool. "How'd the visit go?"

Anna scooped a handful of pretzels from a bowl on the bar and shoved them in her mouth. "Stellar." She spoke through bites.

The bartender placed two froth-filled tankards in front of them.

"You ordered me a beer?"

"Looked like you could use one." Anna took a swig.

Sarah dipped a finger into the foam and licked off the froth—malty and yeasty. Her stomach soured; she swallowed hard. "So, have you made your decision? You will start in the fall?"

"Need to check out the nightlife first." Anna swept her gaze over the bar.

"Here"—Sarah slid the glass toward Anna—"offer them my drink."

Anna shrugged but didn't refuse, keeping the full brew next to hers on the counter.

Sarah ordered a ginger ale and sipped while she examined a crowd of young people gathered in the back of the pub. They weren't as rowdy as the bunch she'd met at the club in Rome, but they enjoyed themselves all the same. Darts whizzed to boards. Beer mugs clanked in the air. A *fútbol* match played on a big TV. Anna would get along just fine here.

As her stomach returned to normal—whatever normal was these days—she prepared to fill in Anna on her news. She took a slow inhalation before she spoke. "Heard from the school today; I got the job."

Anna opened her eyes wide. "So soon?"

Sarah nodded.

"When do they want an answer?"

"As soon as possible."

Anna chewed her lip and circled a finger on the rim of her glass. "Well, having options is nice."

Sarah slid open the menu and sucked on her straw. Yes, she had options—sausages and mash or shepherd's pie, Yorkshire pudding and roast or fish and chips, and…stay in Rome or move back to the States?

Was that decision even up to her? She glanced down at her phone, and her heart sank. Or did it rest in Eduardo's hands? She shoved the phone in her pocket and pushed the menu across the bar. "I'll have the fish and chips," she said to the bartender.

"Likewise." Anna peered over Sarah's shoulder at the young people in the back. "I think I recognize one of the other prospectives. Mind if I join him for a bit?"

Sarah tipped her soda in Anna's direction. "Enjoy yourself."

"You sure?" She tipped her head to the side and softened her brows. "Want to come with?"

"That's okay."

Anna shrugged and dashed from the bar, beers in hand.

Sarah sipped her drink, concentrating on the fuzzy bubbles dancing down her throat. The clamor of rowdy laughter diminished. Even the ass-numbing stool felt almost comfortable.

Just as Sarah finished the glass, her phone dinged in her pocket. She reached for it so quickly, she fumbled and dropped it. She lunged to the floor and snatched up the phone, whacking her head on the bar as she stood. Her head throbbed. She swiped the screen—a text from Eduardo.

—Can we talk?—

—*Yes. Call in a sec*—

Sarah typed back as fast as her shaking thumbs would allow. She pulled some money from her purse and threw it on the counter. Her phone dinged again.

—*I'll come by*—

Sarah quickly texted back.—*Not home. At Oxford. With Anna*—

The bartender slid a plate of greasy food in front of her. A sudden queasiness seized her gut, but she wasn't looking at the food. She stared at the phone.

—*Oxford? When are you back?*—

—Tomorrow—

The phone shook in her trembling hands. Maybe she should just call? To hell with waiting for his text or waiting to meet in person. Her phone dinged with a new text.

—Ok. Let's talk tomorrow—

The ginger ale in her stomach climbed to her throat. Tomorrow? Tomorrow?! She'd waited three days, and he couldn't tell her *now*?

Sarah pushed away the plate of food. The carbonated soda stung the back of her mouth. Only one reason existed why he wouldn't tell her over the phone. He wanted to end it.

She hovered her fingers over the phone keys. Should she tell him she missed him? Should she just pick up the phone and plead—tell him over and over again how sorry she was and how much she loved him? She moved her fingers but couldn't force them to type the words she longed to say.

—Ok—

Without waiting for his response, she eased her phone back in her purse, and the effervescent feeling from her soda drifted away. The crowd behind her roared. The TV blared. Her dinner reeked of overused oil and fish.

She ran to the bathroom and threw up.

Chapter 35

Sarah's breath was ragged. Her forehead beaded with sweat. But her stomach wasn't done with her. She wretched again and again, until ginger ale and remnants from lunch filled the pub's toilet.

She stood, wiped her bangs from her sticky brow, and flushed the toilet. She couldn't remember the last time she'd heaved so much. Yes, losing Eduardo was gut-wrenching, but she had no recollection of vomiting after Philip left. And they'd been together for years, not months.

Maybe she had a bug, something from school, or from Lucia. Pushing open the stall door, Sarah made her way to the sink. She splashed water on her cheeks. They were cool—no fever and no chills, either. She turned off the faucet. Maybe the queasiness was from nerves after all. She'd feel better tomorrow, after she talked to Eduardo—after she knew her future.

For now, her time was better spent resting. She would catch an early train back to London with Anna then travel onward to Rome via plane. Sarah yawned—the thought of travel exhausted her—and headed for the bathroom exit.

She paused with her hand on the door handle. Posters cluttered the door—one caught Sarah's eye. The flyer pictured a woman in distress speaking to a doctor. *British Pregnancy Advisory Service, BPAS—here if you need us,* the caption read. Sarah's skin prickled, and she dropped her hands to her stomach. Her mind replayed one of her many conversations with doctors—this one being a memory from her youth.

Now, Sarah, don't let this diagnosis make you think you can be careless with contraception. You can get pregnant.

Pushing away the words, Sarah blinked and yanked open the door. *No, that's not what this feeling is. You can't get pregnant, remember?* She rushed out. Anna was back at the bar, a guy seated beside her, eating fish and chips. Sarah made eye contact and waved.

Anna grinned and mouthed, "Don't wait up."

Sarah shook her head. At least she'd have the bed to herself for the next few hours.

A crowd of students burst through the door, and the chill of the night rushed Sarah's face. She turned her back to the blast, catching Anna again in her sight. She shivered as Anna's words echoed in her mind. *I haven't seen someone so upset since Veronica found out she was knocked up.*

These thoughts were ridiculous. Sarah stepped out into the night. Why was she even torturing herself with the notion? True, she'd been nauseous and teetering on a migraine for four days, but these were obviously from stress. And missed periods? Well, how could she even go by those? Her periods were as irregular as Anna's dating tendencies.

She knew the symptoms of pregnancy, she'd read about them for years: fatigue, nausea, and sore breasts. Sarah stole a glance around. The street was empty. In a swift motion, she lightly squeezed her left breast. Tenderness was evident. Her breath quickened, and she squeezed again, this time harder. "Ow!" she squeaked. The pain incited giddiness, but she lulled it. She had to be sure.

Scanning the street, she spotted a green cross flickering ahead—a pharmacy. Without even deciding the best course of action, she sprinted toward the store.

****

A five-minute wait for a cab was nothing. A five-minute wait for the cookies to cool was longer. But the five-minute wait for pregnancy test results? Eternal.

Sarah sat on the edge of the hotel tub and stared at the plastic stick in her hand. A fuzzy, blue mark emerged in the result-box. Her breath caught, and her hand started to shake. The sign couldn't be...a plus sign.

The test slipped from Sarah's grasp and clattered to the floor. She closed her eyes and rubbed her brow. *I must have imagined it. I can't be...*

She snapped open her eyes and stole a look at the test again, but the mark hadn't changed. *Oh my God, oh my God.* Dizziness swept over her, and Sarah placed a hand on the wall to steady herself.

But she had to be sure.

Fifteen minutes later, Sarah laid three sticks—one long and white and two with green tops—on the bed: a blue plus sign, two pink double lines, and a flat out "*sì*." Never in her life had she gotten a positive pregnancy test, let alone three. She pressed a palm to her stomach, closed her eyes, and let the child within her breathe life into her listless being. Warmth swelled in her chest, a smile spread across her face, and tears ran down her cheeks.

"My baby," she whispered. She shoved the tests

into her purse, curled up in bed, and stroked her stomach. "*Il mio bambino.*"

****

The plane ride back to Rome seemed longer than the outbound journey. Sarah could have attributed the time lapse to Anna's incessant chattering about Oxford being the best thing that had ever happened, but she knew that wasn't why. She cradled her belly, the miracle inside a bittersweet secret. Because she couldn't tell Anna or even Meredith. Only one person deserved to know first.

She wasn't even sure how far along she was. She tried to count the days. Weeks? Months? Too much had happened since the last time she'd been with Eduardo. But the date didn't matter. Eduardo's decision did.

What if Eduardo didn't want to be with her? What if he'd already made up his mind? How would the pregnancy affect his decision?

The plane dipped, and Sarah lurched forward. She clutched the armrests as the plane shook in turbulence. The "fasten seatbelts" sign flashed. Sarah closed her eyes. Why did everything she did, everywhere she went, have to be so out of balance?

The balanced scales of her favorite Vermeer rushed her mind: the light blooming from the window, the faint smile and perfectly pinked cheeks, and the woman's stomach, plump beneath a fur coat.

The turbulence passed, and Sarah opened her eyes. But she still felt like she swayed, drifting in an uncertain direction. Would her scales ever be balanced? She dropped her heavy head toward the window and let out a sigh.

"For God's sake, Sarah, you look like hell," Anna

said beside her.

Sarah turned, her lips pursed. "I don't exactly feel well."

"Relax. I told you everything will be fine."

Fine? Fine?! In what way would things be fine? Not only did she have to worry about her own future, but the future of her baby. Where would she raise him—in Italy or the States? Would Eduardo be part of his life or just provide financial support? The thought of not being with Eduardo, not hearing his lullaby for Lucia, and not seeing him hold their baby in his hands filled her eyes with tears, and the nausea rose to a new level.

Anna shook her head, dug in her pocket, and retrieved a tube of lipstick. "Here. Put on this."

Sarah pushed it and reached for the barf bag instead. "Not now, Anna."

"It's pink." Anna waved the lipstick in front of her. "Lipstick will brighten you right up."

"Fine." Sarah took the lipstick and smeared some on her lips without bothering to use a mirror. "Happy now?"

Anna smiled, curled her legs up under her, and pulled on her oversized headphones.

Sarah clung to her upchuck bag, hoping she wouldn't have to use it and turned her head back to the window. Soft clouds stippled the sky. Rays of sunlight streaked the horizon. For a moment, warmth shimmered inside her. What if Anna was right? What if she was worrying for nothing? Maybe Eduardo would forgive her. Maybe he could understand. Maybe they could be together—a family, a real family.

The plane dipped into the clouds, and soft cotton

clouds veiled the light. The cabin shuddered, and sweat prickled Sarah's brow. She closed the shade on the window.

No, Eduardo's forgiveness was too much to hope for. She needed to prepare for the worst—for taking care of herself and this baby without him. Because the road ahead might just be as rough as the turbulence.

Sarah thought of the *Woman Holding a Balance* again. No ring shimmered on the woman's hand, and one didn't rest among the jewelry on the table in front of her, either. Yet, her scales were balanced.

Sarah placed a palm on her belly and imagined the life within moving closer to her hand. With or without Eduardo she'd balance her scales—she had to. Because this decision wasn't about just her anymore. This decision was about her and their baby. Sarah held on to the thought, and the hope, and let it rock her to sleep.

When she awoke, the plane arrived in Rome. Groggy and nauseated, she mindlessly followed Anna through immigration.

The corridor opened to the arrival hall. Tourists and locals swarmed. Friends hugged. Children gripped hands. Lovers kissed.

Clutching her phone, Sarah shoved her hand in her pocket. How soon did she have to tell Eduardo she was back? She tensed her shoulders. A cup of tea, a slathering of Choctella—hell, maybe a swing by the chapel for a quick prayer—might be in store first. Because she needed to rehearse every word and every syllable.

"I'm making a pit stop." Anna retreated to the bathroom.

"I'll wait here." Sarah remained motionless, letting

the buzz of foreign languages numb her ears. Hello. *Buongiorno. Hallo.* Leonardo da Vinci airport was where her adventure first began. Would it also be the beginning of the end? The pinch in her shoulders increased, sending tightness down her arms. She lifted her gaze to the bodies pushing past, higher, to the signs above the shops, and higher still, to the metal rafters flanked with billboards—advertisements for stores, restaurants, museums.

Her mind flashed back to the art she explored that year: the *Pieta*, *The Birth of Venus*, the *Ariadne*. The weight on her shoulders eased. All were strong women. All faced their fears. All persevered. This time she needed to do the same. She loosened her grip on her phone and raised it to eye level. She started to type.

—Just arrived. When do you want to talk?—

She waited, her gaze locked on the phone and her breath caught in her throat. With each second the screen remained unchanged, the burning sensation in her chest grew stronger and deeper. Dizziness swept over her, and she leaned onto the handle of her suitcase.

Where was Anna? She could stand the wait with Anna as a distraction. Sweeping her gaze to the bathroom entrance, she saw no sign of her. She scanned the crowd whizzing past. Among them, a lone figure stood unmoving.

Sarah blinked. She must be lightheaded, because she could have sworn the person was—

No—it couldn't be.

Sarah inhaled deeply, the air clearing her foggy brain. She looked again, gasped, and stumbled back.

Across the crowd, the figure moved.

As he approached, she couldn't deny who he

was—Eduardo. Steadying herself, she fought against the tightening in her throat.

He buried his hands in the pockets of his black leather coat and weaved through the crowd.

Sarah clawed at her hair—had she even brushed it today?—and smoothed her wrinkled clothes.

Eduardo reached her and smiled. "How about we talk now?"

His easy smile turned her tense muscles into gelatin. With shaky hands, she returned the phone to her purse. "Eduardo, what…what are you doing here?"

He widened his smile and turned his head.

Sarah followed his gaze to the entrance to the bathroom.

Across the terminal, Anna leaned against the wall and winked.

"Anna and I exchanged numbers before you left for the States. After…you know…" He wrung his hands.

Sarah didn't care how he'd gotten the information. She threw her arms around his neck, pressed her cheek against his chest, and took in his familiar scent.

Eduardo pulled her in, enveloping her.

She clung, embracing the deep sense of comfort he always brought. "These have been the longest three days of my life."

"I'm sorry." He stroked his hands down her back. "I needed time to wrap my head around things."

"Please, don't be sorry." She pulled back. "This fiasco is my fault. I should have told you, told you everything, and told you sooner." She grabbed his hand. "I'm so sorry, Eduardo."

He stared down at her.

He tightened his face, as if resisting the urge to cry.

Oh, God. Had she misjudged why he was here? Was he here for something other than reconciliation? She loosened her grip on his hand. "I understand if you can't forgive me." She dropped her gaze, the words catching in her throat. "I understand if you want to end things. But I need to tell you someth—"

"Sarah," he drew out her name in his mellow baritone, "Of course, I don't want to end things."

She stared up at him. "You don't?" The passersby blurred, and the announcements on the loudspeaker muffled. She focused every morsel of attention on him.

"No."

He pulled her closer and put his hands on her waist. She couldn't breathe. His steady gaze reeled her in, stole her breath.

"I want you to tell me you're not taking that job," he said. "I want you to tell me you're staying here, with me."

A half laugh, half cry escaped Sarah's lips. She leaned into him, resting her cheek on his chest once more, his strength and firmness steadying her. Tears of happiness ran down her cheeks. "I won't take the job, Eduardo. I want to be with you, with Lucia."

"Well, thank God, because that proposition sure beats my fallback plan of joining the priesthood." A quiet laugh resonated through his chest. He placed a finger under her chin and lifted. "Always?"

Sarah's heart fluttered, and her mouth refused to move; her lips were as useless as her wobbly legs. She forced out a clumsy nod.

Eduardo broadened his smile, lifting his glasses off his slender nose. He removed them as he leaned in, his mouth finding hers.

Pulling back, Sarah absorbed his cheeky grin. "I just need to tell you one last thing. One tiny thing."

The smile on his face faded.

She leaned in to whisper in his ear, "I'm pregnant." She pulled back.

Eduardo furrowed his brows then widened his eyes. As he lifted Sarah off her feet, he grinned. He whooped something in Italian.

Sarah didn't catch what he said. She was too busy praying he didn't drop her as he swung her.

He lowered her to the ground and pressed his forehead against hers. His eyes were wet with tears. "*Mia bella cigna, ti amo.*"

"I love you, too." Heart warming, she closed her eyes and let the heat spread from her chest down her arms and into her fingertips—her whole body pulsated under his love. She leaned in and pressed her mouth against his.

In that instant, with the entire world encompassed in the microcosm of their embrace, Sarah knew one thing for sure—her scales were finally in balance.

Epilogue

Two Months Later

Sister Maria sifted papers at her desk and with an arched brow peered down at the one on top. "Your evaluation is quite good, Sarah."

Smiling, Sarah had no doubt her final evaluation would go any other way.

"I've started the process of renewing your paperwork with the agency." Sister Maria passed a sheet across the desk.

Sarah considered the contract. She didn't comment on the lack of a salary increase. What did she need the money for anyway? Eduardo insisted on paying for everything. And maternity leave? She'd discuss those details with her later, too.

"I gather you won't be keeping your room in the dormitory?" Sister Maria crossed her hands on the desk.

Sarah shook her head. "I'd like to move out as soon as the girls leave for summer. That is, if that timing is okay."

Sister Maria nodded. "This place won't be the same without you and Anna."

Without a word, Sarah held her gaze. She was right—it wouldn't. Anna heading off to Oxford would be a return to normalcy for Sister Maria but would leave a gaping hole in Sarah's life. Who would she dine with at Al Forno's? But who would keep Anna out of trouble? At least Anna would only be a short plane trip away.

Sister Maria's gaze fell to the ring on Sarah's hand. "I hope the engagement will be short."

Sarah gazed at the sparkling two-carat diamond. *Great.* Sarah could add Sister Maria to the growing list of people who wanted the wedding to happen as soon as possible—a list that included Eduardo, Mom, and Meredith. What was the rush? She placed a hand on her abdomen, on the bump that was easy to hide under loose garments—maybe a *tiny* rush. "We'll see." Sarah smiled.

Sister Maria raised an eyebrow, breaking her stoic expression.

That Sarah once thought this woman incapable of a smile was hard to believe. She knew better now.

"I wanted to ask you about one other matter," she said. "The Christmas play—any chance you'd be interested in assuming Anna's role as director?"

Sarah couldn't help but jerk back. Her? Director? She was about as good on stage as Lucia. Or rather, how Lucia *used* to be. "I…um…"

"Mr. Moretti has offered to help more as well."

Mr. Moretti? Sarah swallowed hard against a wave of nausea. Ah, hell. He was the last person she wanted to see more of. She opened her mouth to respond—with what, she didn't know.

"If you're not inclined, that's fine."

Thank God. Sarah exhaled. "Not really."

"But I have another idea for you, now that the backdrops are done."

Sarah shot up an eyebrow.

"I thought you might like to offer art classes. Give the students another option for after-school activities."

"Art?" Sarah shifted forward to the edge of her seat. "Really?"

Sister Maria nodded.

She could have the students make clay models of their favorite Roman busts—maybe even take a field trip to visit galleries. They could sit in the courtyard and sketch the fountain, or even walk to the nearby overlook of Rome and capture the view in acrylics...or watercolors.

"That...that would be wonderful." Sarah couldn't contain the enthusiasm in her voice.

"Good. I'm glad that's settled." Sister Maria stood and headed toward the door.

Sarah followed, noting Sister Maria's feet gliding under her black gown. Her dress, like her austere expressions, masked a compassionate woman beneath. Sarah's fingers tingled. Would she have ended up with Eduardo without Sister Maria's help? Would she even be in Rome? She paused at the door. "Sister?"

"Yes?"

"Thank you. Thank you for everything." She embraced Sister Maria, her friend and her confidante.

****

Later that week, Sarah sat beside Eduardo as he drove the car. With a phone to her ear, Sarah rolled her eyes and tipped her head side to side.

"Are you sure you two don't want to stay here?" Mom asked.

"I'm sure, Mom. Eduardo's already booked a hotel."

Eduardo silently mouthed something.

Sarah didn't catch his words. "He needs to be close to his business meetings," she fibbed.

Eduardo cleared his throat. "We can stay there," he said in a raised whisper.

Sarah widened her eyes, covered the receiver, and shot him a glare.

"What was that Eduardo said?" Mom asked.

"Nothing." Sarah furrowed her brows and flashed Eduardo a reprimanding stare.

"I could have sworn—"

"He was just reminding me we have to get to our appointment." Eduardo chuckled and rolled his eyes.

"All right, dear. I hope it's about the wedding."

"Uh…" Sarah stumbled on her words. She planned to tell Mom about the pregnancy during next month's visit. Hopefully, she'd have answers for the wedding interrogation then. "Something like that, yes."

"See you in a few weeks then. Love you."

"Yes. See you."

Eduardo twisted his smile into a frown.

Be nice to your mother was written all over his face. Sarah brought the phone back to her ear. In all her mother's prodding, all her snooping, had she ever had anything but Sarah's best interests in mind? Why did Eduardo always have to be right?

Well, he did err, gravely, she might add, in his preference of Verdi to Puccini.

"I love you, too, Mom," she said. "And I know I don't say it enough, but I hope you know I appreciate everything you do. I mean, who else can say her mom and her nun-boss united for a match-making feat?"

Mom laughed. "The same dynamic duo is ready to play wedding planner."

"Right, Mom." Exactly why she hadn't told her mother about the baby. "I'll let you know when we're ready."

Sarah ended the call and shook her head. Mom was sure to be dialing Sister Maria this very minute, initiating another meddlesome operation.

Eduardo parked the car in front of a small stone building.

Sarah couldn't quite translate the sign, but she didn't need to. She'd been there before. Her calmness quickly gave way to anxiousness, and her stomach—or was it the baby?—grumbled in protest.

Eduardo placed a hand on her knee. "I'm excited, aren't you?"

Sarah nodded and instinctively placed a hand on her swollen belly. Today was a big day. Not as nerve-wracking as their first visit, when the doctor confirmed the pregnancy, but one every parent anticipated.

Eduardo covered her hand with his. "I think the baby's a boy." He grinned and puffed his chest. "With Rossini good-looks, for sure."

Sarah rolled her eyes. "Let's just hope he, or *she*, doesn't have your appetite, else we'll have to buy a second refrigerator."

He winked. "Nothing wrong with that." Eduardo exited the car and trotted around to the passenger side.

He took her hand as he helped her out. "Eduardo"—Sarah grabbed his hand—"do you think Lucia will mind if the baby isn't a girl? I know how much she has her heart set on a sister."

Eduardo kissed her forehead. "I don't think she'll mind at all."

Sarah squeezed his hand and followed him inside.

Like every other obstetrician's office Sarah was in, fetal development charts and pictures of content mothers hung on the walls. The medicinal scent of rubbing alcohol and latex gloves lingered in the air. The vinyl fabric on the exam table was the same, too. Sarah eased onto it, the coolness of the table sending a shiver up her spine. She stiffened.

Eduardo grasped her hand. "Relax. Rossini good looks, remember?"

Sarah opened her mouth to laugh, but only a shaky exhalation came out. What if the baby's heart beat too slowly? What if he was too small? Too big?

Cold gel shocked her skin, followed by an uncomfortable pressure. A loud swooshing sound filled the room then went quiet. More swooshing, then—

Sarah gasped. The sound was more beautiful than Eduardo's tenor and more resonate than Meredith's vibrato.

A heartbeat.

The heartbeat was soft and fast, like a hummingbird's wings. Sarah waited years to hear that heartbeat and thought she might never hear it.

The technician pressed a button and images displayed on a screen. Sarah adjusted her gaze to the fuzzy outlines—the white dancing on black. The motion on the screen was so different from the photos Meredith showed her of Amber and Steven in utero. The life inside Sarah wriggled and squirmed, kicked and poked. All the while, the heartbeat pulsed— sometimes hurried, and other times slowed.

"*Staie bene*?" Sarah asked.

"*Sì.*" The technician smiled and shifted the device to a different position.

The baby settled, and the parts came into focus: curled-up legs, tiny fingers and toes, and a dew-drop nose. Sarah's lip quivered, and warmth filled her chest. A baby. Eduardo's baby. Her baby. She blinked, sending tears down her face.

Eduardo brushed them, kissing her cheek then nuzzling his chin into Sarah's hair. "*Lei è perfetta,*" he whispered.

Perfect. This time Sarah had no objections, no doubts in Eduardo's assessment. Perfect, indeed.

"*Perfetto,*" the technician corrected. "*Un ragazzino.*"

Eduardo drew back, his dark eyes wide. "A boy?" He grinned. "A boy." He flicked his eyebrows.

Warmth blossomed in her chest, as Sarah smiled, too—a broad smile that spread from ear to ear. Lucia would have a younger brother. Eduardo would have a son. Sarah didn't care whether the baby was a boy or a girl. Because she already had everything she needed, and everything she'd ever wanted: a child, a partner, but most of all, a family.

A word about the author...

Wendi Dass is a math professor and author from Charlottesville, Virginia. Her writing interests include literary short stories, flash fiction, and novel-length women's fiction and romance. Wendi's short stories have been published in several small journals, including *Black Fox Literary* and *Pilcrow & Dagger*, among others. When she's not devising deceptively delicious problems for her students she can be found drafting her latest story.

Thank you so much for reading *Bella Cigna*. If you loved this book, please take a moment to leave a review on Goodreads and Amazon. Positive reviews help me continue writing great stories.

For more information on her writing, visit her at:
https://wendidass.com